SUFFER THE INNOCENT:

they are expendable

By
C. Vaughn Mobley

Copyright

This book is dedicated to my husband, Ed, for his continuous support and encouragement.

Special thanks go to my granddaughter, Abby, for the wonderful cover art and design. I gave her a vague idea and she ran with it.

This work is the collaborative effort of friends, family members and others who read the book and gave much needed input, criticism and reinforcement. You know who you are.

CHAPTER ONE

The few sweaty customers who'd come in for lunch at Melba's Diner hadn't stayed long. July, August and September had melted together in a sticky welter of hot nights and hotter days, and the diner's ancient air conditioner had finally stopped wheezing out cold air two days ago.

Jessie DuBois paused to look at the clock and sighed. Thirty minutes more. Just thirty minutes more and she'd be out of there.

Earl Price, the only remaining customer, sat in a booth in Jessie's section. He slouched on his tailbone, arms stretched across the back, fingers tapping to the beat of the Merle Haggard song wafting across the diner.

He was mid-thirties maybe, with greasy dark hair hanging limply from a loose ponytail. The beginning of a beer gut hung above an oversized belt buckle that said "**RIDE IT HARD**."

His sly gaze found and locked on Jessie; followed her as she worked.

A clump of mud, straw and probably cow shit came off his boot, and like a big turd, lay on the grubby tile floor under his table.

Just another crude jerk with a crude mouth who'd been coming in the last four or five months to eat some pie, drink some coffee and try out a new pick up line. And he never left a tip, either.

Jessie hunched a shoulder and blotted a trickle of sweat as it ran down her temple. Making her way down the length of the front counter, she wiped it down, shoving condiments out of the way and scooping them back into semi-organized clumps as she went.

She tossed her towel onto the counter and shoved a stray curl of dark hair behind an ear. The sooner she waited on him, the sooner he'd stop staring at her ass and take himself off somewhere else.

CHAPTER TWO

Just above Patterson Road and on the north side of Coon Creek, the woods covering a vast limestone deposit known as Midnight Ridge begins.

Two men climbed the steep incline. One followed the other at a distance; wary of dry twigs hidden in the centuries old carpet of dead leaves. Both men were hunters, stalkers. Assassins when required. They had been recruited and trained by an anxious government in the aftermath of 911. Both had gone where assigned, doing the dirty jobs no one talked about.

At the top of the ridge, where it soared more than 200 feet above State Road 37, Jonas Aronson walked south along the fence at the edge of the ridge. Stan Chastain, at some distance behind, kept him in sight but angled his path up and sharply north to a thick mass of bushes and scrub trees. Aronson stopped where the ridge squared off and angled away from the highway. He slowly rotated his view as he sighted through a GPS rangefinder and recorded notes in a digital recorder. Chastain couldn't position himself close enough to see what the other man focused on or hear what he was saying, but he took video with his phone. The lab would use Aronson's body angle and a GPS map overlay to identify what he was focusing on.

Aronson finished his task, started his trek down, and disappeared into the trees. When he was well out of sight, Chastain kept low and moved to the edge of the ridge where Aronson had been standing. He looked into the hazy distance where the highway ran in a series of gentle curves through miles of patchwork farms and forest, and saw nothing obvious, nothing useful, nothing unexpected or suspicious. Nothing that hinted at what Aronson was planning.

That Aronson was planning something violent Chastain didn't doubt for an instant. He had smoldered for eleven long years in federal prison, and had promised to get even with anyone and everyone who had had a hand in putting him there.

The day of his release, he'd dropped off the grid. Disappeared. No one had known where he was or what he was doing, but two weeks later, the woman whose testimony had gotten him convicted had been tortured and beheaded. His attorney had been found hacked to death a few days later. They couldn't prove it was Aronson, but a note left with the woman's body said:

"THIS IS JUST THE BEGINNING"

Six months ago, almost two years after his release, he'd resurfaced in southern Indiana where he and about forty other men appeared to be working a once-abandoned limestone quarry. Many of the men were ex-cons or ex-military, which didn't mean they were planning some kind of terrorist attack in and of itself, but anything Aronson was involved in needed a closer look, especially when he'd popped up within miles of Crane Naval Weapons Support Center.

The Department of Defense had assigned an undercover operative to infiltrate the crew at the quarry. After a month, the only information of interest he'd reported was that some of the men had ties to TRV or The Righteous Voice, an ultra-right wing group.

A few days later, the agent had been found floating face down in Big Buck creek. Fishing tackle and an old lawn chair overturned and partially in the water, had been found on the creek bank a few miles upstream from the body. There had been no signs of violence except for a contusion to the back of the head. The autopsy confirmed that the man had drowned, and he had drowned in the water of the creek.

There had been nothing to tie the quarry operation to the man's death. It had looked like an accident.

Sanctioned kills that looked like accidents had been Aronson's specialty in covert ops, and the DOD was certain this was his work.

By killing the man, Aronson had made a mistake. He had proved that he and his crew had something to hide.

Analysts at the DOD had only suspected the possibility of some kind of extremist activity at the quarry before the operative's death. Now they were convinced.

The DOD believed TRV was behind whatever was happening at the quarry. TRV was suspected of bombing a gay rights rally, killing more than fifty people and injuring hundreds more. They wanted Aronson, but they wanted TRV more, and their ultimate goal was to use Aronson to get to TRV. They knew some destructive event was developing, they just didn't know what.

That was what Chastain was there to find out, and even though he knew in his gut that Aronson was planning something, he hadn't gotten jack shit to tell him what it was.

On the way down the ridge, Chastain let Aronson get a good distance ahead. Going down the steep ridge was noisier than going up, momentum making placing a cautious foot more difficult. He didn't necessarily need to keep eyes on Aronson now anyway. Chastain had hacked the GPS module in Aronson's truck so he would know when it moved and where it went.

CHAPTER THREE

"Damn it!" Jessie steered the battered old Chevy over Coon Creek Bridge to the side of the road where it lurched to a stop in the brittle grass and crumbled asphalt of the shoulder.

A pair of crows flapped away from a small, greasy carcass smashed flat in the middle of the narrow, pitted road, their raucous cries the only sound in the heavy air.

Her cell phone had no minutes left, but she looked at it anyway and then tossed it back in her purse.

The sun burned down on her through the cracked windshield. The late summer air was completely still. No hint of cooling breeze whispered its way through the skeletal corn stalks marching through the fields to the south.

To the west, a bank of thunder clouds darkened the distant sky. Maybe today was the day they'd gather strength, blow closer and drench the choked earth. Or maybe, as they had for the past ninety-three days, they would dissipate and blow away.

Somebody would come down this little spit of deserted county road eventually, but she wasn't going to sit around and wait. It wasn't like she'd never changed a tire before.

The spare, buried under a tangle of bailing wire, rags, rusty towing chains and frayed jumper cables, was nearly bald with a bulge on one side like a growth. At least it had air in it.

Half an hour later, filthy and soaking, Jessie hefted the flat up into the trunk, slammed the lid, and leaned against it to catch her breath.

Heat danced and simmered on the roof of the car and thinking about getting back inside made her head pound.

It was quiet out here, deserted, especially this time of year, when the corn had grown old; dry and frail, it stood in the heat, waiting for the harvest.

She wasn't afraid in the familiar isolation, any more than anyone out here would be afraid to sleep with windows open to the cool night air.

Jessie'd lived all her life here and the only place she'd ever been truly afraid was home.

She'd started working at Melba's Diner when she was fifteen, planning to save her money until she had enough to get out of Brewer, except her daddy'd always found it no matter where she hid it.

When Jessie was born, he'd been sitting in the smoky dark of Piney's bar out on State Road 144, losing all his money and her momma's wedding ring to Billy Bartley in a game of Texas hold 'em.

Her momma, her whole family stretching back into time without end, had lived out their days making do, having nothing, scrimping and scraping, the sweat of desperation a constant prickling on their skin.

It was a life that trapped you where you were and didn't allow for dreams and plans, that kept you too busy tryin' to scratch together that next tank of gas or shoes for your kids or last week's rent to think of a way out.

And once you believed it was impossible, it was easy to stop fightin' and tryin' to do right. When the despair and poverty got to be too much, it was easy to start spending what little you had on things that could make you feel better for a while, like whiskey or meth or crack. Then your life became a different hell altogether: one lie after another to the people who cared about you, each lie a razor that sliced a little chunk off your soul. The worst lies were the promises you made to yourself in the dark heart of your life. Those promises, never kept, were what killed your soul.

She'd watched as her older brother, Junior, had started down the same path her daddy'd followed. Jessie's path would not be her daddy's or her brother Junior's or her momma's. She had set her feet down a different path and promised herself she would keep on it until she got where she wanted to go. She would do whatever she had to do to get there.

Life was life and you had to live it. You couldn't ask God for a do-over and you couldn't just choose not to live. Day followed day. The sun rose and set. You opened your eyes in the mornin', and welcome or not, a new day was yours. You only had three choices: you trudged through life

12

where you were and wished for more, you put a gun in your mouth and pulled the trigger, or you figured it out.

Thirteen years later, she was still working at Melba's, and while those thirteen years had been going by, she'd been figuring it out. She'd figured out where to hide her money so her daddy couldn't find it, and she'd figured out that running, just getting away from Brewer, with nowhere and nothing to run to, wasn't the answer. She'd made a plan, a plan that would get her what she wanted. A way out. And she was almost there.

Paper-dry leaves on withered corn stalks rustled. Jessie lifted her face into a tiny sliver of breeze that kissed her cheek and was gone, dancing away across the field.

During childhood summers she'd raced down this road on her bike to spend whole afternoons in the cool, quiet safety of the library in town, stopping on the way back to splash bare feet in the icy water of Coon Creek.

She checked her watch: almost five. Her shift at Melba's Diner ended at two, but Mandy had called in sick – again - and Jessie'd stayed until Melba could get someone else to come in. She'd tried to talk Marybeth into staying, but since Marybeth had spent most of the day talking about her latest, greatest, cutest potential boyfriend and the shopping, manicure and pedicure she was planning for the big first date tonight, Jessie'd just wasted her breath and lost her temper besides.

The shade of the trees beside the creek looked cool and inviting. Memories of ice cold water pulled her. She pushed herself away from the car. What the hell. She was already too late to help Momma with supper. A few more minutes wouldn't matter.

≈≈≈

Chastain saw Aronson stop near the bank of Coon Creek and instead of ducking into the culvert below the road, he stood still, head cocked a little to one side.

Chastain slid behind a tree and waited. An instant later, the sound of a car reached him.

Back tire flat, a car limped across Coon Creek Bridge. After a minute or two, the waitress from Melba's, opened the car door and got out. She went around to the trunk and rooted around for a few minutes, threw the spare on the ground, pulled out the jack and began to change the tire.

Aronson ducked low and used protruding rocks to cross to the other side of the creek, where he squatted behind the biggest of the small trees near the culvert.

Chastain eased himself down onto one knee, watched Aronson watch the girl and hoped he'd leave her alone.

The girl finished changing the tire, leaned against the trunk, and wiped her hands down the front of her shorts. As he watched, the girl pushed herself away from the trunk of the car and walked toward the creek.

"Son of a bitch," Chastain whispered.

≈≈≈

The change from bright light to shade blinded Jessie for a few seconds and she paused to let her eyes adjust.

The creek wasn't as deep as she remembered, probably due to the lack of rain, but water still burbled over the limestone slabs that made up the creek bed. She held onto a thick sapling and half slid, half jumped down the bank and took off tennis shoes and socks. She stood in the creek for a minute or two and just let cold water run over bare feet. She stooped and splashed her hands in the flow, rubbing off as much of the dirt from changing the tire as she could, then patted a meager handful of icy water over her face and down the back of her neck.

The slight rattle of a pebble as it tumbled down the bank behind her made her turn.

He stood only feet away, crouched down slightly between her and the road. His eyes looked flat and cold in the filtered light. She sucked in a breath and froze.

14

Seconds that felt like hours passed. She stepped back and without consciously making the decision, turned to run.

He was quick, and the instant she started to turn away from him, his hand shot out and grabbed her wrist, yanking her back against him. His other hand came down hard on her mouth, cutting off her scream.

A backward kick with her bare foot connected with his shin and he grunted but didn't loosen his hold. With her free arm she elbowed him in the ribs as hard as she could, spun and aimed for his crotch with her knee. The blow was deflected when he turned, but caused him to lose his grip on her. She swung her fist, heard a satisfying "smack" when it made contact with his face, and while he was momentarily off balance, she lurched up the steep bank, wet feet slipping in the clay.

She tried to scream, but all that came out were raspy, gasping cries.

Using both hands and feet, she was scrabbling for purchase when his hand closed around her ankle. He yanked and she fell hard. As she slid down the bank toward him and into the creek, her shirt bunched up, leaving her stomach bare to be raked by rocks and twigs.

Her desperate hands found a tree root and she used the leverage it provided to flip herself onto her back. A wild kick with her free foot caught only a glancing blow across his hip and then he was on top of her, astride her, the weight of his body crushing the breath out of her.

He put his hands around her neck and squeezed. She bucked and writhed, clawing and scratching, leaving bloody welts on his arms and hands, until he grabbed a jagged rock from the creek and hit her.

Pain exploded inside her head, her vision blurred and she went limp without a sound.

From his position high up on the ravine, Chastain rubbed his tired eyes and sighed.

≈≈≈

Still astride the girl's limp body, Aronson struggled to slow his breathing and his whirling thoughts. Stupid! Stupid, stupid, stupid, he thought. He should've just ducked into the culvert under the road and kept going instead of stopping to watch some stupid bitch change a tire. He knew better than to let himself get distracted during a job. Shit! He couldn't just leave her here. She'd scratched him. The DNA under her fingernails would identify him. He didn't have a shovel, couldn't bury her, couldn't hide her body in the woods to be found by some 'coon dog.

The body of a dead girl would bring attention to the area. Cops would search the woods and ask questions; the media would come with their cameras and helicopters, and he couldn't afford a spotlight on the area right now.

Fucking bitch! Why couldn't she just get back in her car and go away? By the time he realized she was going to walk over to the creek, it was too late for him to move without her seeing him. Blinded by the transition from bright sun to shade, she'd walked right by him.

Rivulets of red ran from the girl's face into her dark hair and spread, soaking into the sandy mud of the bank.

He'd hit her hard, but not hard enough to kill her; she was still breathing. He raised the rock to finish her off, but stopped.

The girl moaned and moved her head slightly. A body wasn't easy to maneuver, even a fairly small one. He didn't see any reason he should drag her dead weight to his truck if she could walk.

He'd seen her in town, a poverty stricken little nobody making starvation wages working in the local greasy spoon. If she disappeared, people would think she'd just taken off.

He remembered how she'd looked, changing the tire, her ass in the air while she bent over the jack.

She moaned again.

He dropped the rock and touched her face, fingertips gently drifting over soft skin to her jaw, down to her neck where he circled it and squeezed. The sight of his own blood weeping from scratches she'd made enraged him. His other hand fisted in the V of her shirt and he pulled down, ripping it open.

Over the slight gurgle of the creek flow, he heard a car in the distance.

The creek bed was at least ten feet lower than the road, dark with shade and masked by brush and small trees, but he felt exposed and rolled off her into a crouch. Keeping low, he grabbed her roughly under the arms and dragged her backwards through the water, toward the road, seeking the dark shelter of the culvert that ran under the bridge.

≈≈≈

Pain. Jessie's mind was clouded with it. She was aware of movement, and there were sounds, but they were far away. She was floating, but at the same time heavy, too heavy to move.

Her thoughts were fragmented, bits and pieces coming together, then breaking apart again.

She felt him then, knew the weight of him, the feel of him as he forced himself inside. Recognized it for what it was and tried to fight, but she was too cloudy, too weak. Her mind retreated, seeking the darkness where pain and awareness could be kept at a distance. She sank back into oblivion.

≈≈≈

Aronson squatted with his back to the wall of the culvert and watched her, used his foot to prod her, but she was still out. He'd have to move her car. If she'd taken off on her own, as he wanted everyone to think, she'd hardly do it from out in the middle of nowhere and leave the car behind.

He found the keys to the car in the pocket of her shorts, gagged her with her bra and tied her wrists together with one of his bootlaces. He pulled her hands over her head and looped the other lace around a bolt in the seam of the culvert pipe.

Even if she came to, she couldn't get loose.

CHAPTER FOUR

Sheriff George Farber pulled up behind Tommy DuBois' light blue Chevy Cavalier. Piece of shit probably broke down. Didn't look like anybody was in it, but he got out of his cruiser to glance in the open windows.

No keys in the ignition. A small canvas purse was on the passenger side floorboard.

He shaded his eyes against the glare of the sun and looked slowly around.

The driver's license in the purse belonged to Jessica Marie Dubois. He looked at the date of birth and felt old. She'd be twenty-nine this year. The wallet had some twenties and several smaller bills, just under $150, a lot of money to somebody like Jessie DuBois.

The road ahead was empty, and on either side of it, there was nothing but corn. He looked at the tree line behind him, tucked the purse under his arm and walked that way.

The radio in the cruiser crackled and Sherry, daytime dispatcher for more than three decades, wheezed out, "Hey, Sheriff, this is dispatch, over."

"Well crap." He turned back toward the car.

"This is Farber."

"Hey, state's workin' a wreck out on 37, and they've got the northbound lanes closed about a half mile south of Bronson's south pit. They want to know could we send a couple of county units to re-route traffic onto 60. All I got free right now is Unit Twelve. Can you assist? Over."

"I'm out on Patterson Road. Tell State I'll be there in ten. Out."

Great. It was Friday afternoon, hotter than blue blazes, everybody would be on their way somewhere to start their weekend, 37 north was closed and a whole lot of people who didn't know where they were going would be driving the county roads.

He stowed Jessie's purse inside the trunk and headed for SR 37.

CHAPTER FIVE

"Chicken shit!" taunted Elvie. Even at the tender age of fourteen, a born manipulator like Elvie knew how to work a chump who had something he wanted.

"I ain't chicken shit," hissed John. "I'll go, just not 'fore Grandpa goes to bed."

"We gotta' go now, while we still got a couple hours of daylight. I done told you we can't do it in the dark, John."

"How you know it's weed, dude?" Lyle picked at a scabbed-over pimple. "You're the one got money from us to buy that prime weed a while ago that turned out to be parsley or some shit. Guy must've seen that "dumb-ass" you got tattooed on your forehead a mile away."

"It wasn't neither parsley. It was weed, just not very good weed." Elvie struggled to hold back the smirk trying to jump out of his face. What Elvie had given John and Lyle might've been a bag of stems, seeds, a handful of real smoke and something from his mom's spice rack thrown in, but what had been in Elvie's bag at home had been some really good shit.

Lyle scraped the scab off, looked at it and put it in his mouth. "And you ain't never seen it when it's growing. It ain't gonna look the same."

"I do too know what it looks like, ass wipe. I was with my brother when we went to one of his friends' house and he grows it in his basement with special lights. I'm tellin' ya, it's the same stuff. I cut through Anderson's back pasture last weekend and it was growing all over."

Lyle dabbed at a little bead of blood from the pimple. "How'd it get out there in old man Anderson's field?"

"How the hell should I know? Bobby Anderson prob'ly put it out there before he got sent to juvie." Elvie planted himself in front of John and leaned in. "Look, we gotta' do it now. We're gonna' have to have a truck, and I could get my dad's keys, but not 'til after he goes to bed and then it'll be too dark. We can't use the lights or Old Man Anderson might see 'em through the trees.

"Your Grandpa keeps the keys to that old truck on a hook in the kitchen. You go in and make sure he's watching his shows on TV, tell him you're going to Lyle's house for supper, then slide on in there and grab 'em. Piece-a-cake." He gave John a shove toward the porch and headed around the side of the house, Lyle right behind.

Elvie waited until he heard the front screen door slam and John's voice shouting over the news on TV, then eased up the back steps and onto the porch. Peeking through the screen into the kitchen, he saw John slip in and lift the keys off the hook next to the refrigerator.

As John came through the back door, Elvie plucked the keys out of his hand and jumped off the back stoop. He grinned at Lyle, then strolled over to the big barn until he was out of sight of the house.

The ancient farm truck would make some noise when John fired her up, but the old man couldn't hear shit. He'd never know.

CHAPTER SIX

State Detective Dan Carlisle's day had been in the toilet before it could even really be called a day.

His sleep had been disrupted when the air conditioning quit working sometime in the middle of the night. He woke drenched in sweat, with the foggy remnants of a bad dream hanging over him.

With windows and French doors open, he'd laid there in the dark listening to an owl hoot nearby, and the nocturnal rustling of raccoon and possum in the underbrush.

The phone woke him up again at four in the morning. A call before daylight was never a good thing since it meant death, and most of the time, grief for someone.

The homicide was a kid. Christ. Cases involving kids were the worst, especially the little ones, the three or four year olds who were still young and innocent enough to trust, but old enough to know fear and dread and betrayal. Those cases left him with a sick feeling in his gut, the images sporadically flashing in his head without warning for weeks afterward. And the dreams . . . Jesus.

This morning, he'd driven to the trailer park at the edge of Brewer with dread roiling in his gut and when he'd gotten there, he'd found a three year old boy: Nicholas Higgins, a little blonde guy who'd ended up the target of his mom's boyfriend's rage and frustration. Bloody and battered, there was little left of the boy he'd been, the boy Dan saw in the pictures liberally sprinkled around the tidy living room. They showed him from the beginning of his life: wrinkled, perplexed newborn, to the end: impish, grinning toddler, blue eyes sparkling with mischief.

It was the same story, or variations of it, over and over. A young woman, not much more than a kid herself, gets knocked up by some loser and ends up trying to support herself and a kid, alone, with no skills, little education and no real way to make a decent living. So she hooks up with some guy, another loser with a minimum wage job who starts to feel trapped and resentful after a while. He slaps the kid around, then the slaps get harder, and one day the open hand gets doubled into a fist.

Even then, most times, the kid gets bruised up and sometimes a broken bone or two, but he manages to survive. Sometimes Child Protective Services gets called in and sometimes they don't.

But then there's the poor little bastard who gets in the way the day the boyfriend has a run in with the boss, or maybe even gets fired for no damn reason except that the prick boss has it in for him. The boyfriend has a crappy day, a crappy life, he hates himself and the world, and on that night, the kid doesn't feel good, or he whines, or shits in his pants, or maybe he had a crappy day and doesn't know how to deal with it except to cry.

That's the night everything comes together to turn a loser with a chip on his shoulder into a murderer.

That's what Dan and his partner, Charlie Mayhew, had faced at the start of their day, with the boyfriend, Brad Loyal, crying in the back of one of the cruisers. Dan had wanted to rip the door open, haul the guy's ass out of there and beat him to a pulp, because he'd been at this long enough to know that the tears weren't for the kid, they were for himself.

Sometimes, he felt that same anger and contempt toward the mothers. Despite their sobbing and wailing, he knew, when their eyes wouldn't quite meet his and the child's skinny arms and legs were covered with old bruises and scars, that he'd pull the kid's records and find trips to the ER for stitches or broken bones or concussions from "falls."

Some women flat didn't care. Some had a need for love or money or security that was greater than their responsibility to their own flesh and blood. Some had an unlimited capacity for self-delusion and rationalization. Some were the victims of abuse at the hands of the boyfriend themselves. Whatever the reason, they knew and they didn't stop it.

In this case, Elise, the mom, didn't know. He was as certain as he could be about it and that made it worse. He'd carried the sounds of her grief with him all day.

The boy's folder was lying on his desk, the file tab, neatly labeled: "Higgins, Nicholas Adam," and he felt a surge of grief, fresh and sharp for young Nicholas, another life reduced to words and pictures in a file.

Cramped from sitting in one position, Dan leaned back, arms over his head in a bone cracking stretch. He ran spread fingers through thick, short waves of blonde hair and yawned. The desk chair squeaked as he came back upright and he propped his elbows on his desk, fingers rubbing tired, red eyes. It was just about five o'clock and it had been a really long day.

The cubicles of most of his co-workers were quiet, the lucky ones who weren't on duty or in the middle of an investigation. Charlie was already gone. He left a little early to spend some time with his kids. No one stayed here who didn't have to on a Friday night. Most preferred to take work home on the weekend, try to have a semblance of a home life if they could, knowing they might be up reading or writing reports into the night, while their families slept.

He stared at the chaos that was his life: at the multitude of notes, memos, phone numbers and reminders tacked to the walls of his cubicle, at the in-basket overflowing with paperwork, at the pile of fat folders taking up one corner of his desk.

He grabbed three of the folders and slid them into his briefcase. No reason he had to stay here to read them. He loosened his tie. It was Friday. It was time to go home, pop open a beer and sit on the deck.

CHAPTER SEVEN

Tommy Dubois walked into the kitchen, asking his wife for the third time where in hell Jessie could have got to. Glenna stood at the sink peeling potatoes, her back to him. She just shook her head.

He'd made damn good money today working with Harlan on a piece of heavy equipment at Bronson's Quarry, but Harlan hadn't let him have even a beer and he was dry as a damned bone.

He paced back and forth behind Glenna, his boots scuffing against the worn linoleum, antsy with the effects of a day of forced sobriety. "Where is that damned girl? I got some errands to run." He looked out the window over Glenna's shoulder. "I'm gonna' go on out and see if I can't get that truck runnin'. I know it's a short in the wirin'. I just can't find it."

The screen door slapped against the frame and seconds later, Glenna saw him walk to the shed where he'd been working on the old truck for a couple of days, off and on.

Friday was the one day this semester Jessie didn't have class. It was after five thirty and she should have been home by three to get supper started.

Glenna put the potatoes on the stove and took two tomatoes from the windowsill to slice.

She rolled her shoulders trying to work the kinks out. She was tired after a long day at the nursing home, changing soiled bed linens, fetching and carrying. The physically demanding routine of lifting and bathing patients whose minds or bodies had decayed and betrayed them got harder every year.

She'd just pulled the last splinter of meat from a chicken neck when she heard the old truck start up with a roar. It shot out of the narrow shed and into the driveway, then out onto the road.

Glenna turned the heat down under the pots and went outside, taking out her annoyance at Jessie and her anger at life in general on the weeds in the now depleted garden.

This late in the summer most of the plants were done for the year. She and Jessie had spent many scorching days canning green beans, corn and tomatoes. Tomorrow, they'd can spaghetti sauce made from the last of the tomatoes and put up a few jars of pickled watermelon rind. Jessie was the only one of her five kids left at home now, but Glenna still canned and stored food with a desperation left over from all those lean and hungry winters when she'd had so many mouths to feed.

It was still sunny, but shadows from the dense forest beyond the clearing crept toward the garden. Glenna rose to her feet and brushed the dirt off her knees. Damp tendrils of black hair lightly mixed with gray stuck to her flushed cheeks. Fine lines of worry and disappointment surrounded intense blue eyes. At fifty-four, she was still a slender, attractive woman, even after five kids.

It sure was hot; too hot to stay out here in the sun and too hot to go back into the kitchen where the stove had raised the temperature even higher. She rinsed her hands in water from the hose and walked around the house to the shady front porch. She sat on an old metal porch chair, rough and pitted with rust, but still cool against her skin.

She glanced at her watch. It was after six o'clock. The first flicker, a tiny spurt of worry, shot through her. Jess always told her when she wasn't coming right home and it wasn't like her to be so late.

She noticed a cloud of dust rising above the trees before she heard the sound of the car coming up the winding gravel road. She got slowly to her feet when she saw the two-tone brown car bristling with antennae.

It was George Farber, a man she'd known since high school. He got out of the car and placed his hat on his head as he closed the door. Aside from a few strands of grey in his rusty brown hair, he looked about like he had back then: tall and lean, with solemn brown eyes and an easy smile. He was holding Jessie's purse.

Glenna stood and put a hand on the porch rail, her mouth suddenly dry. "What're you doin' with Jess's purse, George?"

He rested one booted foot on the lowest wooden step. "Hey, Glenna. She home?"

She sighed with relief: he hadn't come to tell her Jessie was dead in an accident. "She hasn't made it home from work yet."

"How 'bout Tommy?"

"He's out runnin' an errand. He'll be back directly. Why?"

"Found that old blue Chevy out on Patterson Road."

He looked over his shoulder at the sound of Tommy's old truck wheezing up the road.

Tommy braked hard when he saw the sheriff's car, wheels locking up on loose gravel. He downshifted into first and shot into the slot beside the house. He shut the truck off, hopping down before it stopped its rattling and huffing. He slammed the door, hinges squawking, and hurried around to join his wife.

"George." Tommy nodded, a brief jerk of his head at the sheriff. "What you doin' out here?"

"I was just tellin' Glenna that Chevy of yours is sittin' out on Patterson Road." He removed his hat to scratch the top of his head. "I found Jessie's purse in it, but no one was around."

Tommy shrugged, clearly unconcerned, but Glenna was worried. "Even if she got broke down and had to walk, she'd be home by now. And she wouldn't walk off and leave her purse."

George resisted the urge to give her a comforting pat on the shoulder. "Well, maybe somebody came by, she got to talkin' and forgot about the purse. Probably a friend gave her a ride and they didn't come straight here."

He looked at Tommy again. "Need to move the car out of there, Tommy. Don't want somebody drivin' into it in the dark. I can call a tow truck or you can go get it. It's on Patterson just this side of the bridge over Coon Creek. It's not gone by dusk, I'll have it towed."

Tommy gave him an annoyed look. "I'll go after supper."

"Make sure you do." Farber looked at the darkening sky. "Might want to go before the storm hits 'less you want to get wet."

CHAPTER EIGHT

Jessie woke up slow. She felt pain first, and for a little while, that was all there was as she hung suspended between unconsciousness and awareness. Barely awake, she struggled sluggishly against the restraints that held her and groaned into the gag.

She was cold, so cold. Water was sliding around and under her making her shiver and her teeth chatter. She rolled slowly onto her side and curled into a ball, but the effort made everything spin and brought on a wave of nausea, so she concentrated on keeping completely still, as her senses slowly cleared.

Aronson knew she was awake. She'd been just beginning to stir when he got back. He'd been watching her little movements, saw her breathing change. Could tell when she remembered.

He'd never taken a woman like this before. He craved the building excitement of the chase, the sly pursuit of his prey. Watching them, their private places covered but not obscured by tight shorts, tight jeans, skimpy, low-cut tops; flaunting, teasing, luring, promising.

He went inside their homes when they weren't there, absorbing their smells, touching what they touched, caressing the scraps of nylon and lace that had been next to their skin. Invisible, undetected, but there. And somehow, as time passed and he got closer, they knew.

But he'd never before let a woman distract him while he was working. Both his work and his pleasure required complete concentration. The fact that he had her to deal with now was the very reason he never let one facet of his life spill over into the other.

She rolled over so her back was to him, knees pulled to her chest, as if she could hide herself from him. Stupid bitch.

He squatted next to her and released the bootlace tying her bound hands to the culvert. He ran a finger down her spine and chuckled when she flinched, then grabbed her hair and pulled her to her feet, her back to his front. With his other arm around her waist, he backed until he could slide down the corrugated wall of the culvert, pulling her down with him between his spread his legs, her bare bottom solidly against his crotch and her back against his chest. Before she could straighten her legs, he brought his knees up and crossed his ankles in front of her feet so that she was trapped there between his thighs with her arms pinned to her sides.

He put his cheek next to hers, then buried his face in her hair and breathed in, long and slow. She shuddered and tried to pull away, but he jerked her back, turned his head so his mouth was right next to her ear. "I saw you, little girl," he whispered. "All bent over with your sweet ass in the air, just begging for it."

When Jessie tried to turn her head away, he grabbed her jaw and roughly brought her ear back to his mouth. "I wouldn't have bothered you though. You shoulda' just got back in that car and gone on your way." He rubbed his chin on her shoulder. "But instead, you brought it to me. Like a gift. Now, it's rude to refuse a gift like that, so here we are."

In this position, his body surrounded hers, enclosed it, contained it. He'd never felt like this, as though he could absorb her very being into his, a strange, sharp, but not unwelcome sensation, intensifying the aching heat in his groin.

Sweat popped out of every pore and his heart started to pound as he worked his hand between his body and hers. She began to struggle, panting and crying as he opened his fly and freed himself. He tightened his grip around her waist, and then lifted her, maneuvering her body onto him. The gag muffled her screams as he thrust upward. He gripped her more tightly, inhaled deeply and drew in her smell: salty and sweet, sweat and fear and shampoo. He could feel every breath, every movement, every quiver and wave of fear. He wanted to feel this way forever and reduced his pace, each long, slow stroke excruciating, balancing on the sharp edge of orgasm for what seemed like an eternity. He sank his teeth into her shoulder, tasted blood, and allowed himself to slide over.

CHAPTER NINE

"Jesus Christ," Lyle stopped at the gate leading into Old Man Patterson's back pasture and waited for the other two to catch up. "It's the fuckin' pot mother lode."

Lyle released a twist of wire hooked over a bent nail and pushed on the gate.

Elvie held up a hand. "Who's that truck belong to?" The three boys gazed across the creek beyond the small pasture at the black Blazer parked in the shadow of the tree line. "It ain't the old man's. He don't drive a Chevy."

"Maybe it's somebody out huntin'," suggested John.

"Better not be on old man Patterson's land." Elvie shaded his eyes from the sun with one hand. "He ran them Durbin boys off with a butt full of rock salt when he caught them hunting in his woods."

"Well, he don't likely want no one in his field pickin' pot neither, Elvie." John nodded toward the Blazer. "And we don't want nobody see us pickin' it neither."

The three boys studied the Blazer in silence and longingly eyed the patchwork of hip-high marijuana plants.

"Maybe we should come back later," said John.

"No! Just wait a God damn second." Over the week since he'd first spied the plants, Elvie's avaricious brain had been busy considering possibilities. In his mind, the plants were now his and he wasn't about to leave them behind.

He'd spent a week thinking about little else besides getting out here and getting his hands on the pot. Way his luck ran, he figured he'd get out here and it wouldn't really be pot, or it would have been all trampled and killed, or hell, even eaten by the damn bulls.

It was real and it was still here. He wasn't gonna' walk away empty handed. No fuckin' way.

He handed the box of garbage bags he carried to John. "I'm gonna' go check out the truck."

"No! Are you crazy?" hissed Lyle. "What if somebody's in there?"

"Nobody's in there, Lyle. In this heat? Hell, nobody'd be in there with the windows all rolled up. I'll just check it out."

Elvie jumped the fence, slid down the creek bank then up the other side and approached the Blazer. A hand on the hood told him the truck had been there a while, it wasn't hot. He peered in the driver's side window to verify that the front was empty. Making a tent against the back door window with his hands, he rested his face on them and made out a cap and a jacket on the back seat and some tarps folded up in the back.

He pulled up on the handle of the locked back door and made his way around the vehicle trying them all.

"All the doors were locked," he reported when he got back to Lyle and John. He took the box of black plastic bags from John, tore it open, grabbed several and waded into the field.

"Think one of us better keep a lookout?" asked John. "What if the owner comes back?"

"Good idea." Elvie reached down and began tugging on the stem of a plant. "You go first."

Lyle shrugged, walked over to the edge of the field and started pulling up plants, but kept an eye on the truck.

The pile of black bags by the gate grew steadily, and soon there were twelve, stuffed tight. Thunder rumbled in the distance from the west and Elvie called across the pasture, "John! Go get the truck."

John nodded and set off at a trot. They'd parked the truck in the trees by the road, not wanting to risk someone seeing it out in the field. He was glad to call it quits. His back was killing him from standing half bent over, and he hadn't thought to bring gloves, so his palms were blistered.

He'd felt less and less sure about this plan of Elvie's and wished he hadn't let him talk him into borrowing the truck. Now that he thought about it, John was the one who'd get into trouble for taking the truck, not Elvie. And Elvie wanted to store the grass and let it dry in an old disused barn on his grandpa's farm. If somebody found it, it was John's ass, not Elvie's. Elvie thought just because John's grandpa was old and almost deaf, that he was stupid. But he wasn't.

Elvie threw his last bag on the pile, lit up a smoke and counted the bags, then sat and leaned against the fence post, his busy brain calculating how much he was likely to make. He'd toss a few bucks to John and Lyle, just to keep them quiet, but what were they gonna do if he kept the money anyway? It wasn't like they could go to the cops, and they were both pussies. They wouldn't do nothing and he'd have all that money for himself, not to mention enough pot to keep him high for a couple of years. He stretched and smiled a little to himself.

Lyle looked at the pile of bags and began pacing. He thought about how much time they'd get if they got caught and wondered what juvie was really like. It made him sweat more than he was already. He didn't understand how Elvie could just sit there, smiling, relaxed, head back against the post, blowing a cloud of smoke into the air.

The wind had kicked up with the coming storm, but it was still hotter than hell, so he walked back to the line of trees beside the creek. He felt like the whole world could see him, standing out in the middle of the field. He wished John would hurry up with the truck so they could get the hell out of there.

CHAPTER TEN

The murky light in the culvert had dimmed and Aronson thought it was dark enough in the shade of the trees to make a move. Be better to wait until dark, but he had to be in Bradley by 9:00 and he would be cutting it closer than he liked as it was.

He took a razor knife out of his back pocket, pulled Jessie into a sitting position, pushed the blade out of the handle and held it up where she could see it. Blood matted her hair and had dried around the gash at her hairline where a huge knot had formed. She swayed drunkenly and tried to focus on the knife. He put his face an inch from hers, "I can slit your throat with this faster than you can blink. You do anything - make a sound, try to get away, anything - and I'll use it."

He removed the restraints from her wrists and re-laced his boots while she put her clothes back on. Desperate to cover herself, she huddled away from him and hurried as much as she could. Only two buttons remained on her blouse and she buttoned those, but was still exposed.

When she was dressed, he used his belt to bind her wrists, pulled her to her feet and drug her behind him out the other side of the culvert.

It was still almost full daylight in the open fields, but the sun was low in the sky and in the streambed, between high banks and protected by densely growing trees, it was as if dusk had already fallen.

Jessie took a few lurching steps, reeled to the side, stumbled, fell to her knees and retched up the bile that was all she had in her stomach. The world was spinning and she couldn't keep her balance, like when she'd been a kid and had spun and spun and spun around and thought it was funny, how she couldn't stay upright. There was nothing funny about it now.

He turned, yanked her to her feet, got behind her and shoved. "Keep moving."

She was pushed along front of him, stumbling and tripping, stomach heaving, swarmed and bitten by mosquitoes. It seemed like they'd walked for miles when he stopped suddenly.

The air had turned greenish thundercloud dark. The wind came up suddenly, slashing through the canopy of leaves that arched over the creek, followed by the patter of rain. Aronson hustled the girl up the bank and over to the Blazer. He opened the door to the rear cargo area, unfolded a tarp for her to lie on and waved with the knife for her to get inside. When she hesitated, he nodded toward the floor of the cargo area and said, "Get in." He saw her focus on something behind him and turned.

Coming toward him from the other side of the creek was an old farm truck with a wood stake bed. It came through the gate and into the pasture, making a wide arc before it stopped, pointed back the direction from which it had come.

A boy jumped out of the cab of the truck and he and another boy started throwing black plastic bags into the bed. One of the boys called over his shoulder, "Lyle! Where you at, man? Get over here and help."

Aronson' focus shifted when he caught movement to his left and he locked eyes with Lyle, standing just across the creek, eyes round and staring, mouth open.

Aronson released his gun from the holster at his back and was about to squeeze the trigger when Jessie threw herself into him, nearly knocking him to the ground.

Then it started to rain in earnest, coming down in dense grey sheets, followed by the sound of hail ripping through the leaves above them.

The boy turned and ran toward the truck screaming, "Get in the truck! Get in the truck! He's got a gun!"

John paused in the act of throwing a bag in the truck. "Who? Who's got a gun?"

"The Blazer. The guy in the Blazer! Just go! Get in the truck," screamed Lyle again.

John focused on the Blazer for an instant and although he still didn't know what was going on, headed around and jumped in, grinding the old truck into gear.

Elvie tossed the last two bags into the bed, then ran for the cab and scrambled in just ahead of Lyle.

Aronson grabbed Jessie by the hair and pulled her to her feet, hit her once in the face and tossed her into the back of the Blazer. "Lay still and keep your mouth shut." He threw another tarp over her and slammed the door.

Jessie huddled under the tarp, dazed, unable to move, unable to think, shaking with fear and cold. She was still wet from lying in the creek and her teeth chattered so hard she thought they might crack. The temperature had dropped, the rain had soaked her again and the blustering wind had blown goosebumps on her wet skin. It was warm under the tarp with the heat of the day still trapped inside, and she gladly soaked up the small comfort he'd unwittingly provided.

The man started the engine and drove fast over rough terrain, the swaying of the vehicle tossing Jessie around the back of the Blazer, the movement of her body softly swishing under the tarp. Her last fuzzy thought as she drifted out of awareness was to wonder whether her momma had begun to worry about her.

≈≈≈

Aronson left his headlights off as he drove out of the field and onto the road. The track the boys were on would come out on the other side of the farm and he headed that way. Rain was making the field wet with soggy grass and patches of mud that made his tires spin. A big truck like those boys had would be even harder to maneuver in this mess and wouldn't pick up much speed in a hurry.

The storm howled around them, bending some of the smaller trees almost double, the tops of slender sycamores bowing down in the onslaught of wind and rain. The hail intensified, marble sized chunks of ice bouncing and rolling off the hood of his truck, dancing in the road. There! A streak of lightning lit the road ahead revealing the farm truck in the distance.

≈≈≈

John struggled to see through the rain and keep the truck in the narrow ruts of the rough track. "What the hell happened?" he shouted over the noise of the engine laboring in second gear and the storm outside.

"The guy with the Blazer!" Lyle shouted back, "He came back and he had a gun! He pointed it right at me! And he had Jessie! The waitress that works for my Aunt Melba. He had her!"

Both John and Elvie's heads snapped around to look at Lyle, "What do you mean?" Elvie asked, "What do you mean, he had her?"

"Her hands were tied up and her face was all bloody! We gotta' go into town," he said urgently, "tell the sheriff. Maybe they can stop him!"

"No fuckin' way!" shouted Elvie. "Are you crazy? You wanna' do time, Lyle? We got enough pot in the back of this truck to put us in juvie for a million years."

Lyle's face paled even further, then he offered, "We can dump it! Someplace where we can come back and get it later!"

"We go to the sheriff and we'll be there all fucking night! And then you think they're just going to let us leave, climb back in the truck and drive away? Do you have a license? I don't. John don't.

"They'll have our God damn parents down there. We'll be grounded for life for taking this truck and they'll want to know where we were when we saw the guy, and then they'll want to know why we were there."

Elvie spaced his words out, emphasizing each one. "We. Can't. Say. Nothin'. Lyle,"

"We can't just let the guy take her!"

"What do you mean we can't?" Elvie shouted back, "he already did! We don't even know who he is. John and me, we didn't even see him."

"If we don't do nothin', she don't have any chance at all! None! 'Cause nobody else knows but us. We give the sheriff a description of the Blazer, somebody might see it. If we don't say nothin' nobody'll even look!"

"He's long gone, Lyle. You think he's gonna' drive around the county with her in his truck all night? He's gonna' put her somewhere where no one can find her and there's nothin' you can do, there's nothin' John can do, and there's nothin' I can do."

John let the argument rage around him as he made the turn out of the farm and onto the back road, relieved to be on the relative stability of gravel instead of mud. He hit the gas, the tires spun, dug in and the truck began to pick up speed.

"I saw him, and we saw his truck." Lyle said, "You looked inside. What did he have in there? We could tell them that. They might pull him over and that'd be enough for them to arrest him, go to his house, look for her."

"He ain't from around here, you stupid shit! He didn't have a Brewer County tag on his truck. You know how many Black Blazers there must be in this state? They can't stop 'em all."

Knowing he'd already lost the argument, Lyle said stubbornly, "We can go to a phone booth. They still have one at the Citgo. We can at least tell them what happened."

Elvie said, "Yeah, and have everybody there see us. Somebody'd recognize us for sure."

Lyle turned to John, his look pleading for agreement. "John?"

John didn't respond for a minute, wishing he could come up with a way to counter Elvie's argument, but he couldn't. Jessie'd always been real nice to him when he'd gone into Melba's, but Elvie was right. His grandpa had already made one trip to the sheriff's office this summer because he and Elvie'd broken into the high school just for the hell of it and got caught. He'd expected anger and lecturing from his grandpa but he'd just looked at John like he'd stabbed him in the heart. As much as he hated that Jessie was in trouble, they'd be in deep shit if they went to the sheriff.

He stopped the truck at the stop sign at Patterson Road. To the right was town; to the left was the old barn where they were going to stash the pot while it dried. He turned left.

≈≈≈

Aronson caught glimpses of the truck in flashes of lightning. He was gaining on it. The truck stopped at the sign at Patterson Road and turned left instead of toward town.

Must be going home, Aronson thought. He'd have to make sure they didn't get there. If that stupid bitch hadn't ruined his aim, he'd have dragged all three of their carcasses into the creek until he could get them to a ravine to dump them. Would have been messy but he'd cleaned up bigger messes than that before. Stupid, God damn bitch. Because of her, this whole damned operation could go sideways.

He'd shut the boys' mouths and make it look like an accident. He was good at that. The roads in the area had lots of curves and drop offs. He'd force the truck off the road into a tree or into one of the ravines beside the road. If any of the kids survived, he'd make sure it wasn't for long. If the truck didn't catch fire on its own, he'd take care of it. Even in this downpour, gasoline would burn. There wouldn't be anything left but a burned up truck and three burned up kids. Too bad. They'd lost control in the storm.

≈≈≈

There'd been silence in the truck since John made the left turn. God damn Elvie, Lyle thought, looking out the window. Why'd he listen to him anyway? He stared into the side view mirror as a flash of lightning lit up the world, bright as day.

"Shit!" croaked Lyle. "I think he's behind us!"

"What?" said Elvie, "Where?"

"Couple of hundred yards back."

Elvie looked out the back window, craning his neck to see over the plastic bags in the bed. "I don't see nothin'." Another flash of lightning showed the Blazer coming up the road behind them. "I see him!"

"Hold on," John gritted out as he took a curve too fast. He'd driven the old truck dozens of times working on the farm with his grandpa, but he'd never had it up to more than twenty miles an hour. Probably hadn't been driven over forty for the last ten years, but he was about to see how fast it would go. He kept the gas pedal to the floor, the speedometer climbing slowly but steadily until, rattling and shaking, it hit sixty-five. At least the road was curvy which meant the guy in the SUV couldn't crank it up much more than John could. Not in this rain. Even so, he thought as he slowed slightly for a tight curve, the guy was bound to catch up with them. His SUV would handle better than this old truck.

"What you think he'll do if he catches us?" Lyle shouted.

"What do you think, shit for brains?" Elvie shouted back. "We just gotta' make sure he don't catch us. Don't this thing go any faster?"

"I got the pedal on the floor, Elvie," John responded.

"This shotgun loaded?" Elvie nodded toward the weapon in the gun rack mounted on the rear window.

"Hell no, Elvie. You think my Grandpa's crazy keepin' a loaded gun in this old truck.? Doors don't even lock." He thought for a moment, "Check the glove box. Maybe he put some shells in there."

Elvie pawed through the contents of the glove box, pulling out papers, wrinkled and yellow with age, registrations, napkins, some packets of ketchup and salt but no shells.

He slammed the door to the glove box closed and disgusted, said, "What kind of fuckin' dumb-ass keeps a shotgun with no shells. 'Bout as useful as tits on a bull." He looked nervously out the back window again.

Lyle was quiet. He couldn't quite take it all in. It seemed fantastic, like something in a movie.

"I can't believe that guy took Jessie," he blurted out, anxiously checking the mirror again. He couldn't make out the Blazer through the rain, but he could feel it creeping up on them.

"Yeah, and we saw him," Elvie said. "Son of a bitch catches us, we're dead." The boys all looked at each other and realized that what Elvie'd just said was the literal truth.

"I think I see him!" screamed Lyle, "He's catching us!" He gripped the edge of the door, knuckles white, eyes glued to the side view mirror, "Oh God, oh God, oh God, oh God...."

CHAPTER ELEVEN

Chastain pulled his truck to the edge of the road and tried to see through the pouring rain. The GPS told him Aronson was headed toward him and he expected to see the boys in the truck go by any second with Aronson right on their tail.

Shit! Damned kids.

He wasn't supposed to interfere with the target in anyway. He was supposed to follow, observe and report, period.

But he couldn't just stand by and watch Aronson murder three kids.

They'd been in the wrong place at the wrong time and Aronson wouldn't flinch at taking out a few kids if he felt threatened.

The little waitress at Melba's had been in the wrong place at the wrong time too, but there was nothing he could do about her. He'd watched Aronson take the girl and had followed protocol. He'd let Aronson have her and now she was on her own.

He didn't let his mind drift to the crime scene photos of the woman who had put Aronson in prison.

The farm truck appeared out of the rain, barreling toward him. He hoped Aronson wasn't too close as he gunned his engine and burst onto the road before the boys were completely past him.

≈≈≈

Aronson was maybe a hundred and fifty feet behind the boys when a dark blue pickup pulled out from a side road in front of him.

"Shit." He gritted his teeth, slammed on the brakes and veered left to go around, but the pickup hogged the center of the road, going about twenty miles an hour. He could see the farm truck fading in the distance as he swerved back and forth trying to find a way around.

The pickup slowed even more and the left turn signal came on. Good, Aronson thought, turn and get the hell out of my way. 200 feet, 400 feet, 500 feet and still the guy didn't turn. Then the turn signal went off and the pickup began to speed up, still straddling the center of the road.

"God damn it!" Aronson went left again trying unsuccessfully to get around the asshole.

The pickup slowly increased its speed until it topped out at forty-five miles an hour. After another minute or so when the pick-up didn't move any faster or get out of the way, Aronson said, "This is horseshit." He swerved sharply to the left, hitting the gas at the same time. There was just enough flat shoulder to allow the Blazer by.

≈≈≈

Lyle stuttered in his excitement. "A-a-a pickup! A pickup just pulled out in front of that Blazer. C'mon, John! Give it some gas! He's way back there, stuck behind that truck."

The dark blue pickup, with the Blazer behind it, disappeared in the rain and distance, and John kept the pedal to the floor.

After two or three minutes, the truck began to slow and the sound of the engine abated.

"John!" yelled Elvie in a panic, "What's wrong with the truck?"

"Ain't nothin' wrong with the truck. I'm slowin' down."

"Are you crazy? Go! Go! Oh, Jesus he's gonna' catch us!"

"Shut up, Elvie! There's a fire road up here on the left but I gotta' slow down to take it. I don't want to use the brakes 'cause the brake lights'll come on."

"We can't slow down! We can't slow down! We don't know how far back he is."

"You think we can outrun him? You think I should lead him back to Grandpa's? We keep goin' he's gonna' catch us for sure. We gotta' lose him."

"But he could be right behind us. We don't know how long he got stuck behind that pickup."

"You see him, Lyle?" asked John.

"Not yet."

"Me neither." John slowed even further, downshifting into second, anxiously scanning ahead for the road. He'd turned out the headlights when they'd first seen the Blazer behind them, and in the early dark and rain, it was hard to see. As far as he knew, the only time anybody used the road was during hunting season to get to their tree stands. It was grown over and hard to find, which was good for them, but John was terrified he'd miss it. "There!" he downshifted into first with a jerk. They seemed to be crawling, barely moving, until John started to turn, then it felt like the truck was flying. It tipped up on two wheels as John took the corner, then came back down so hard Lyle hit his head on the window and bit his tongue. The rear of the truck came around and missed a tree by inches, then straightened out and John hit the gas. If the guy hadn't seen them turn, they'd be alright. If he had, they were screwed, because the road ended about a half mile ahead.

≈≈≈

Aronson floored the Blazer, fishtailing around curves at sixty-five, hitting eighty on the straight patches, hoping to catch sight of the truck again. After about ten minutes, the road ended at a T and the boys could have gone either way. He'd lost them!

Damn it!!

They'd go to the cops, but what could they tell them after all? With the rain coming down like it was, the boys across the pasture couldn't have really seen him. And the boy down by the creek couldn't have gotten a good look at his face either, not really. He was wearing a hat pulled down low on his forehead. They could identify his truck, but there had to be a dozen trucks that looked like his in the area. He'd change out the plate just to be on the safe side.

The boys would tell the sheriff where the girl had been taken from, but this downpour would've washed away any lingering evidence. Of course, now they'd know she wasn't a run-away, but they wouldn't be searching the woods for her if they knew some guy had put her in a truck and driven away with her either. He could get pulled over, but once he'd stashed the girl and got rid of the tarps, what could they do? Without the girl actually in the SUV, or a positive ID from the boys, wasn't a damn thing any cop could do.

It would've been better, cleaner, if he'd managed to catch the boys and silence them, but he hadn't.

Move on, he told himself.

CHAPTER TWELVE

Jessie woke up as the Blazer slowed and made a right turn, bumped over a series of ruts for a minute or two, and stopped.

She heard the door of the SUV open, then a few seconds later, close again. The SUV pulled slowly forward.

She was groggy, but aware again of her surroundings. The engine stopped and Jessie's heart pounded. They were now at a place where he must feel safe. But safe to do what? Torture her? Rape her again? Kill her? What's he going to do to me?

He opened the rear door, pulled up the tarp and reached for her.

She recoiled, using her feet to push herself up against the back of the back seat, and when he reached in to pull her out by the binding on her wrists, she kicked out, grazing his jaw.

He stepped back, knocked her foot to the side and dragged her out by the hair. She was off balance, but tried to draw her bound hands far enough back to swing at him from the side. He raised a forearm and blocked the blow, knocking her sideways to the dirt floor with a backhanded slap. He rolled her on her back, put his knee in her chest and leaned in hard. "Don't fuck with me."

≈≈≈

Aronson locked the cellar door behind him and looked around, made himself stop and listen. He was rushed, thanks to the girl and chasing after the boys, but getting in a hurry and ignoring your surroundings was a good way to get yourself killed. Rain pounded the roof and leaked through in several spots. There was a persistent drip coming from the corner over the counter and another in the dining room beyond, but nothing unusual. The kitchen windows that were still intact were grimy with years of rain and dust outside, and greasy smoke inside. The old house was about to fall in, with sagging gutters, broken siding and several holes in the roof.

The house, surrounded as it was by vegetation run wild, was barely visible from any direction, but it was the cellar, not the house that had interested him. Eight transit containers with C-4 explosive and weapons couldn't be kept at the quarry. He'd needed secure storage for those, and a safe base of operations. It had required some work: reinforcement, sound proofing, a generator, surveillance cameras and a cell phone signal booster, but it was hidden, completely secure and perfect for his needs.

There was plenty of room for the transit containers and other, smaller, storage bins. Aronson's cot, few personal possessions and supplies in an aluminum locker occupied part of one wall near the back. In the back corner were two rough cubicles. One had shelves, floor to ceiling, with dusty jars of green beans, tomatoes, pickles and other unidentifiable substances. The other had a plank door and a hasp for a padlock. It contained a massive workbench against the back wall over which hung a pegboard suspended by chains from the joists overhead. Hammers, crowbars and other household tools had probably hung on it at one time. That was where he'd tied up the girl. She hadn't gone willingly into the cellar, putting up a surprising amount of resistance for someone as beat up as she was, but that suited Aronson just fine. The more they fought him, the better he liked it.

She'd gone still when he'd pulled out the razor knife. His gun would have worked as a deterrent, but a knife was better. Women really hated a knife.

CHAPTER THIRTEEN

John pulled the truck into the deserted barn and turned off the ignition. The three boys sat for just a few seconds without talking, listening to the engine tick as it cooled, watching dust motes float across the beam of the headlights until John turned them off.

Then Elvie said, "Okay, let's go," and nudged Lyle to open the door.

When John looked at Elvie, he saw anticipation and satisfaction in his eyes, but no guilt or remorse.

Finally, John opened his door, jumped down and went around to the back of the truck, but before Elvie could pull the first bag out, John hauled back and punched him in the face as hard as he could.

"What the fuck?" Elvie began as he scrambled to his feet, fists doubled, spitting blood.

"That's for calling my grandpa a fuckin' dumb ass," John said, his jaw thrust out pugnaciously.

"I never..."

"Yeah, you did. When you couldn't find any shells for the shotgun," John interrupted. "I wish I'd never have let you talk me into this. You coulda' got us killed. And if anybody finds out about what we got in these bags, we'll go to jail."

While they'd been sitting in the truck on the old fire road, with dark gathering around them and the rain beating down, he'd been thinking. Elvie'd fast-talked him again, had made it easy to tell himself they couldn't have done anything to help Jessie. To keep himself out of trouble, he'd probably let her die.

And the pot! He'd promised himself he'd stop smoking and he'd been doing okay. Then Elvie'd come along, convinced him again, to do somethin' he shouldn't. And he'd let him! Elvie used people. That's what Elvie did.

He took an aggressive step toward Elvie, "and how come we gotta' store the stuff here, in one of Grandpa's old barns? Why not in your barn?" He took another step. "I'll tell you why, 'cause if somebody finds it before it gets dried out enough to sell, I'll go to jail and you can say you didn't know nothin' about it. I ain't stupid, Elvie."

He looked down at the ground. "We shoulda' tried to help her." He held back the tears with an effort. "We shoulda' at least tried."

He pulled a bag off the truck and threw it on the ground. "You can just take it." Guilt laid heavily on his heart. "You and Lyle split up whatever you get for it. I don't want no part of it."

"I don't want it neither." Lyle's blue eyes were steady on Elvie.

Elvie hadn't planned on giving either Lyle or John a big piece of the take, but now it was his, all his. He shrugged. "Okay, fine." Elvie nodded like he was making a concession.

John pulled another bag off the truck. "You got 'til next weekend to get it out of here, then I'm gonna' burn it. We should probably just burn it anyway."

"John, you can't burn it, are you crazy?" When John didn't answer Elvie decided he was bluffing. "Well, let's unload it." He hauled a bag out of the truck. "We gotta' get it up in the loft, out of sight. It's gotta' be hung upside down while it dries."

"You want it hung upside down, you hang it upside down. Somewhere else. I get these bags out of Grandpa's truck and I'm done. I come back out here next weekend and this pot ain't gone, I'm burnin' it," he threatened again.

"But it'll rot," Elvie said, angrily, "we can't leave it in them bags, it'll rot!"

"That ain't my problem."

Elvie took a step toward John, but Lyle stepped in between them. "You wanna fight, Elvie?" He was shy and awkward, but he was big, a lot bigger than Elvie.

They unloaded the truck in silence, Elvie's rage and frustration radiating off him in waves.

When the truck was unloaded and the bags stashed in the hayloft, the three climbed into the cab and rode back to the house in silence. It was still raining, but not as hard, and when they reached the house, John was surprised to see lights still on in the living room. He felt like it was at least midnight, but it wasn't even nine.

He parked the truck back in its spot and without looking at Lyle or Elvie, went in the house and put the keys back on the hook. He trudged slowly up the stairs to use the bathroom. He stared at his reflection in the mirror. Funny, he didn't look any different.

He felt like a monster.

≈≈≈

Elvie rode his bike away from John's, working on a new plan for the marijuana.

He wasn't gonna' let John burn it, and he wasn't gonna' let it rot in the bags. The old barn at John's had been the easiest place to keep the stuff 'til it dried but he'd come up with another way. Had to be someplace dry. Had to be someplace deserted.

"Yes!" he said with satisfaction when he thought of the perfect place: the Riley's half-burned barn.

It was one of dozens of deserted farm buildings in the area, left to decay and fall down when the Riley farm had gone under and Dirk Benson had bought it up. All Benson had wanted was the land so the barn had sat there until one year during a bad storm, it'd got struck by lightning and one end of it had burned before the rain put the fire out.

Nobody ever went there and the roof was still mostly there over the rest of the barn.

Elvie tried to think of a reason not to use it and couldn't come up with one.

Now, he just had to think of a way to get the plants from John's over to Riley's barn.

CHAPTER FOURTEEN

By nine, Aronson was in Bradley, a small town about a dozen miles north of Brewer. He was walking to the end unit in a tiny strip mall that served as a kind of boundary between a run down, crime-laden part of town and an area that was being slowly restored by its residents into a community, with the renovation of many of the century-old houses in various stages of completion. It would be a while, years maybe, before the store attracted the interest of anyone besides the youth of the area who'd decorated the walls of the building with graffiti and gang symbols.

Amazing that there were gangs in a town this small, with a population no more than ten, twelve thousand, Aronson mused. Thirty years ago, gangs were something the folks in this town would've only heard about on TV, trouble far away in some big city-New York, LA or Chicago. Now it was right on their doorstep.

The commercial realty sign out front was surrounded by weeds and had been used for paint ball target practice. Behind the building, an eight foot chain link fence ran the length of the strip mall with a line of small trees and overgrown bushes blocking the view from the one story duplexes on the other side of a scrubby field. The security lights were burned out or had been shot out by neighborhood kids with pellet guns, and it was nice and dark back there.

Aronson parked his truck a few blocks from the store and walked back, his hooded jacket protecting him from the rain that had decreased to a drizzle. He didn't mind the rain; it kept foot traffic to a minimum, and those few who were out kept their heads down.

He could've driven the truck into the store, parked it in the truck bay, but he was more likely to slip in and out unnoticed on foot.

Aronson put on thin, tight, surgical gloves and checked the strip of tape he'd put across the top edge of the door and its frame. Satisfied that no one had opened the door since his last visit, he picked the lock and went inside. His rubber soled shoes made no sound on the concrete floor as he went about setting up the two portable lamps, two folding chairs and long table he'd stashed there after his first visit.

He turned one of the lamps on and did a slow scan of the narrow, empty storeroom. He was always there two hours early. It gave him plenty of time to do a thorough search of the place, look at the cameras that monitored the back and front entrances of the store, see if there had been any activity since he was last there.

Walters would bring the last payment tonight. Cold hard cash.

Walters always had Combs and Dietrich with him. Aronson didn't like either one, cocky bastards.

They strutted around, acted like they were the fucking Secret Service, making a big deal out of sweeping the place for microphones, walking the perimeter with their flashlights.

Dietrich was a stupid shit. So was Combs. They'd never done a close examination of any of the many metal shelving units still attached to the walls. Even if they had, they would have had to lie on the floor and shine a flashlight on the underside of the lowest shelves to see the cameras that were attached to three of them. Tiny, fiber-optic lenses were fed through and attached to the legs. The lenses were tightly focused on the two folding chairs he'd placed in the center of the floor. With three angles, he had no need to guide Walters into one chair or the other and at each meeting, he'd allowed Walters to seat himself first.

He turned the equipment off: He'd use the remote in his pocket to turn it back on once Walters' men had showed off for their boss.

≈≈≈

Walters watched Aronson count the money as he stowed it in a heavy, black nylon bag and wondered if he felt fear or doubt about the job he was about to do.

Walters was a righteous man, guided by the word of the Lord, the Supreme Being who had created them all. His notions of right and wrong were rigid and unshakeable. The will of God was crystal clear to him, leaving no room for interpretation, debate or argument. This operation was a calling for Walters, a mission in the name of God Almighty.

The government, the body that was created to represent the people of America had passed law after law, aided and abetted by the judiciary, rejecting God, destroying family life, paving the way for a crisis he was certain would eradicate life as they knew it.

The men who controlled this country had taken God away from the children, forcing schools to eliminate prayer, or any mention of the almighty, going so far as trying to have the word "God" removed from the Pledge of Allegiance.

Cities and towns across the country had been forced to deny the supremacy of the Lord, removing his word from their buildings, abolishing adornments celebrating the birth of the son of God.

Abortions, an abomination in the eyes of the Lord, were performed every day. A man and a woman could lie together, have relations and create a child together with no thought of marrying, of becoming a family. They escaped the consequences of their behavior by walking, unashamed, into a clinic where a doctor would murder their child for a fee. How could the body of men who would make such a thing possible be allowed to continue?

Bill Clinton, the former President, the leader of the country had committed adultery, fornicating with a woman not his wife, in the sanctity of the oval office. It had been a sad reflection of the lack of morals inherent in our lawmakers, when he was impeached but not convicted for lying about it under oath. It had been a sad reflection of the lack of morals of the American people when he'd been re-elected anyway.

Nothing that occurred during the subsequent administrations had given him any reason to think that the path of Godless destruction the country followed would be changed by its leaders.

The country's moral compass had been destroyed. Random shootings and stabbings, violence of one stranger against another was escalating, spreading into businesses, government centers, colleges, even grade schools. The stressed out, angry, anxious, emotionally battered members of the rat race were hanging onto sanity by a thread. They paid their bills - barely, they got to work on time - barely, they paid their taxes – barely, and made it through each day – barely.

Average Joe, the guy next door, to the shock and horror of those who knew him, killed his wife, his children, his parents. People driving their cars turned, in an instant, from law-abiding citizens into thugs wielding two ton weapons on four wheels. Workers came to jobs armed with automatic weapons and blew their co-workers away.

The country didn't need foreign terrorists to destroy it. It was destroying itself from the inside out.

Nearly twenty years before, Walters had formed an alliance with a man named Leroy Likens. They had made it their mission to draw the faithful together as a single, mighty force, and sixteen years ago, The Righteous Voice had been born.

During that time, The Righteous Voice had grown to more than thirty million followers and had made Walters and Likens obscenely rich.

While TRV rank and file fought against abortion mills, stem cell research and gays in the military, handpicked TRV followers had infiltrated every branch of the armed services, the FBI, the Secret Service and most urban police departments. Throughout the country, isolated TRV compounds had been established, complete with trained militia.

Walters and Likens were prepared to use their power and wealth for the salvation, not merely of men, but of the country itself.

CHAPTER FIFTEEN

John lay on his back and stared at the ceiling. He was exhausted, tired down to his soul, but he knew he wouldn't get any sleep that night. His thoughts whirled around in his head. He kept thinking about what they could've done to help Jessie. They could've made an anonymous phone call to the sheriff. They could've, like Lyle had suggested, stashed the pot and then gone into town in the truck. They'd have gotten in trouble, for sure, but at least he would know he'd done what he could, and if she never came home, it wouldn't be because of him.

He worried that the man who had chased them might have gotten the license plate number of the truck. That it would lead him here to the farm. To his grandpa. To him.

He put his earbuds in and cranked up the volume on his MP3 player, seeking oblivion in the music.

≈≈≈

Elvie stood outside the back stoop at John's and listened. He didn't hear nothing except the refrigerator humming in the kitchen.

He'd gone home as usual. He had a curfew because of breaking into the high school, and he tried to act like he gave a shit what his mom and dad thought by being home by ten. It was nine o'clock on school nights. They'd threatened him with juvie if he didn't, and by the look in his dad's eye, this time he could tell his mom wouldn't talk him out of it. At least being home by curfew kept them from yapping at him. He didn't know how his older brother had stood it long enough to get through high school and get out on his own.

He'd gone to bed, worrying about the pot and how he was going to get it to Riley's. After an hour or so, he'd hit on the solution, so simple, he couldn't believe it had taken him so long to think of it. Why not use John's grandpa's truck? The old man'd never hear it start up. John probably would, but what was he gonna' do? Tell his grandpa Elvie stole his truck to move the pot John had helped pick? Not a chance.

Elvie'd dressed again and stood with his ear to the door, listening for his parents up moving around. The TV in their bedroom had been on, but it was always on once his parents went to bed. They'd turn it on and then fall asleep, his father's snores competing with Jimmy Fallon.

He'd ridden his bike back to John's and hid it in a bunch of bushes next to the driveway. Silently, he'd moved around the outside of the house, looking in the screened windows, listening for movement inside. He'd looked upstairs at John's window. No lights were on.

The old man had probably been in bed by nine and was sound asleep by now. Folks in the country, at least the farmers, mostly kept early nights and early mornings.

Sure as he could be that John and his grandpa were asleep, he slipped across the porch to the screen door and pulled. It was hooked. Damn it, why wasn't nothing ever easy?

He went back down the steps and over to the barn, looking for a thin piece of cardboard. He didn't find that, but he did find a used plastic milk jug somebody'd cut up to make a grain scoop. He looked around and found the razor knife they used to open bags of feed and used it to slice off a square of plastic. The make-shift scoop he tossed in the trash and shoved some stuff over it.

Back on the porch, Elvie slid the thin edge of plastic between the screen door and the frame and worked it up until it lifted the hook out of the eye, unlocking the door.

Damn, I'm good, Elvie thought as he opened the door and tiptoed across the kitchen to the hook where the keys were. Just as he'd watched John do earlier that evening, he lifted the ring off the hook and headed back to the door. He heard a creak and froze, then darted quickly to the door, not daring to breathe until he was safely out of the house and going down the steps.

He stopped again, listening for more noise, but heard nothing. He got to the truck and slid inside, wondering if the creak of the door would wake John up, but not really caring if it did. In some perverse way, he hoped John would wake up and try to stop him. Elvie pictured John running behind the truck, shirtless, barefoot, trying to catch him, and chuckled. He could imagine him, furious as Elvie drove away, unable to stop him and unable to tell. It'd almost be worth taking the punch John had delivered earlier.

CHAPTER SIXTEEN

Aronson hefted the strap of the duffel over his shoulder and shrugged it into a more comfortable position. He'd waited nearly half an hour after Walters and his goons had gone.

Walters and Likens, the men who had hired him, had had a lot of ideas, a lot of plans they couldn't pull off because they didn't have the training or the experience.

Contact had been made with Aronson by an anonymous person who knew another anonymous person who knew what The Righteous Voice was looking for.

They were at a disadvantage. They only knew of Aronson what they had been told, augmented by rumor and some inferences of his own, but Aronson knew *everything* about *them*. He had done his homework, had made it his business to know, down to what grade schools they'd gone to.

Walters and Likens had been cagey, cautious in their initial dealings with him, their conversations vague, with a lot of innuendo and posturing.

It had finally come down to Aronson saying, "You want something blown up? You want somebody dead? Either tell me what you want me to do or find somebody else."

It turned out that what they wanted Aronson to do was kill the President of the United States, and the vice president, and as many senators, congressmen, judges, and innocent bystanders as possible.

Then, they had explained, while the country was in chaos and people believed they were under attack by ISIS or some other terrorist organization, new leaders, handpicked by Walters and Likens, would take over and guide the people back to the word of the Lord.

Aronson had doubted that the vast majority of Americans would stand still for having TRV's version of religion stuffed down their throats, chaos or not, but he hadn't hesitated. It was a perfect opportunity. He would have his revenge, and get paid for it. With the unlimited budget being offered, he would find a way.

His computer skills had been honed while he was in prison, and if someone knew how to negotiate the black market that thrived beneath the surface of the internet, they could obtain just about anything. He'd sniffed around, just to see what was out there, put out some feelers, and after six weeks, the mention of a small shipment of VX leaving Crane Naval Weapons Support Center had gotten his attention.

He knew that the single most important advantage in transporting deadly chemicals is keeping the transfer secret. Not only is the route, date and time restricted to a handful of personnel, the fact that the chemicals are even being moved is kept secret. The only personnel qualified to transport these chemicals are from the Technical Escort Unit, guys who are Staff Sergeant or higher and trained in everything there is to know about the chemicals they may have to deal with. Transports are in constant touch by radio until the cargo is handed off to the receiver, and if a radio check-in is missed, or if suspicious activity is reported, heavily armed troops are sent in immediately by helicopter.

The best and most devious minds in the world had tried to think of every scenario that would place hazardous cargo at risk, and then had come up with ways of keeping it from happening. Their record was sterling: Crane had never had any transport breached by a hostile force, ever.

According to the chat room post, a small quantity of VX was being used at Crane to test a new generation of chemical sensors. When the testing was done, the remainder would be transferred from Crane to Newport to be neutralized.

VX was perfect for Aronson's purpose. It wasn't a gas as some people thought. It was a liquid, the consistency of motor oil. A drop on the skin was enough to kill, but unless it was swallowed, symptoms could take up to eighteen hours to appear. This would allow the contaminated person to spread it to anyone or anything he touched.

The chat room posts hinted that information about the VX shipment might be for sale. That was enough for Aronson. Anyone could be bought. They just needed to hear the right number.

Aronson had studied satellite images, maps, geological charts and any other information he could find about the area between the two facilities. Late one night, he'd seen how he could get his hands on the VX. He'd made some calls, traveled to the area and had formulated a plan.

He'd laid out his two stage proposal to Walters and Likens. The first phase of the project, and the most time-consuming and expensive, would be not only to obtain the VX, but also to eliminate the possibility of capture once he had it.

The second stage would be easy in comparison. Aronson had asked himself, what gatherings, over the last twenty years, had had the largest number of politicians present? Aside from the Inauguration and the State of the Union Addresses, funerals brought out the biggest number of political fat cats.

Aronson had identified three men, two politicians and one Supreme Court Judge, who attended churches with huge congregations, and whose funerals, based on practice, would be conducted there.

During the funeral, after the sniffer dogs and chemical monitors had cleared the area of any possible threat, the sprinkler system of one of these three churches would deliver the VX. The mourners would be wet, but unaware of the contamination, and would go on their way, spreading the VX everywhere they went.

He had to make sure the VX couldn't be detected during the lengthy and intensive Secret Service scrutiny before the President's arrival. To do this, weeks ahead of time, Aronson would plant one or more small VX-filled floats in the sprinkler system water supply, and use remote waterproof detonators to time the release. Since the water supply for the sprinkler system in most large buildings is divided from the water for the rest of the building at the main line under the street, until the chemical was needed, it would be enclosed not only in its own protective containers, but in water pipes hundreds of feet from the building.

Unlike in the movies, not all sprinkler heads in a system open when only one is exposed to direct heat. Because of this, Aronson decided only one head, in the center of the sanctuary, should be fitted with a remote heat source.

Water from one sprinkler head would reach a wide area, and the contamination would spread as people touched the pews, other inanimate objects in the path of the spray, and each other. A malfunction of one sprinkler head was believable. More than that would be suspicious.

Since the church would have to be broken into for access to the sprinkler head, he'd decide which would be the easiest target after he had the VX. That decision would determine which man would die.

The plan was solid, doable, and incredibly expensive. The fee for the information about the VX alone was not unreasonable, but to ninety-nine percent of the population, it was an enormous sum of money.

Likens and Walters hadn't even blinked.

In addition to paying the informant, expensive equipment would have to be obtained, men with specialized skills, beyond the scope of the militia Likens was so proud of, would have to be hired. Explosives, weapons, computer equipment and specialized vehicles, the list seemed endless. The informant had demanded his fee up front, a demand that had been unacceptable. After some posturing and bluffing from both sides, Aronson had negotiated an agreement with the informant for ten cash installments of one million each; with the balance payable by wire transfer once the job was done.

Walters had coughed up the money like clockwork. Tonight, he brought the last advance payment. One million dollars. Ten thousand one hundred dollar bills. Ten thousand pieces of paper that would never make it to the informant, because he didn't know about it, hadn't asked for it. Ten thousand extra pieces of paper that would belong to Aronson, because the number the informant had quoted and the fee Aronson had quoted to Walters were just a little different, just ten thousand extra pieces of paper more. Aronson looked at it as his share for services above and beyond, a sort of finder's fee.

He locked up the warehouse and set out for the Blazer. Just in case, he pulled his gun of choice for concealed carry, a Glock 26, subcompact, semi-automatic, from the holster at the small of his back and put it in his jacket pocket.

He didn't want to have to fight the jacket if he needed to reach for it.

The neighborhood he walked through was a mixture of big old houses occupied by the very old or the very young. Three story brick buildings on corners here and there used to be the local drug store or a grocery; maybe a bakery or the neighborhood bar with rooms above for family or for rent. Many were still empty, the sweep of revitalization not yet drawing the kind of money it would take to restore them. Trees, a half a century old, lined the tree plot next to the street, their roots heaving concrete slabs of sidewalk out of line, the uneven surface creating a hazard for the unwary. Every time he'd made this trip, he'd imagined predators, who had somehow heard of the tightly packed wealth in the bag he carried, lurking in the doorway of every derelict building.

Tonight the predators weren't imagined. Tonight they were real. He was approaching the second corner and was a little more than a block away from the truck when they stepped boldly from a doorway and stood in his path; three smirking men with the bad-ass, menacing stance of three against one. Preoccupied, he hadn't seen them, hadn't sensed them, didn't know they were there until they stepped out. One, short and stocky, the glitter of a meth high and blood lust in his eye, let him see an evil looking knife as he circled around behind, cutting off his escape. Another, older and mostly gone to fat, had a pistol, nearly lost in his meaty fist, pointed at his chest. The third, tall and skinny with a shaved head, took a step toward the street, boxing him in between a parked car to his right and the wall of the building to his left.

They would rob him, take his bag and make him empty his pockets, but first they wanted some fun. Wanted to see some fear. Wanted to feel their power. Maybe slice him up a little, make him bleed. "Gimme' the bag, bitch." The one with the gun smiled and put out his hand to grab the strap.

Aronson had his own gun in his hand, still in his pocket but with the bag of money between it and Fat Boy with the gun. He half-crouched and spun, simultaneously working the Glock 26 out of his pocket and hitting Fat Boy's gun with the bag, knocking it out of his hand.

Aronson heard "Shee-it, mother fucker" from behind him and then an arm wrapped around his neck and he felt the burning pain of a knife thrust in his back, on the left side, just below his rib cage. Before his assailant could pull the knife free for another stab, Aronson threw his head back and broke his attacker's nose, spun away from the hand with the knife, brought the gun up, jammed it into the man's sternum and fired. The man's legs went out from under him and he dropped like a stone. Aronson stumbled, and fighting to stay on his feet, brought the gun across and fired two shots, hitting Fat Boy, who, with a roar of rage, had charged him. Fat Boy hit the ground and Aronson turned, prepared for another attack, but the third man had vaulted over the hood of the car and was on his way into the dark recess between two houses across the street.

All in all, it had taken about ten seconds.

He turned the corner and trotted to the end of the block, ignoring the pain in his side. He was bleeding, he wasn't sure how bad, but he could feel it running, warmly soaking into his shirt and his pants.

He slowed, not wanting to call attention to himself. He was memorable, just being there, a man alone, in this neighborhood, at this time of night.

He could see the truck just ahead; almost there, half a block to go. He keyed in the lock code from the passenger side, yanked the door open, threw the duffle on the floor and slid inside, pulling the door closed and laying down across the console in one motion.

It wasn't the most comfortable position with the console digging into his armpit and his side throbbing like a mother, but he forced himself to lay still and relax, letting his racing pulse slow and his ragged breathing settle into a more normal pattern.

In the distance, he heard a siren.

Shit! Cops already on the way meant someone called 911 at the first gunshot and that unknown someone might've looked out a window in time to see him pop Fat Boy. If so, they'd be able to give at least a rudimentary description: a lone man, blonde, tall, medium build, dressed in dark clothes, carrying a large bag. He'd stick out like a fucking sore thumb if the cops stopped him.

The sound of the siren would pull people out of their beds or away from their late night TV and bring them to the windows, to look out and wait for a glimpse of the cop car; see what was going on.

Aronson needed to get out of there now, before anyone else saw him and reported a strange truck parked on the street. People knew if there was a vehicle that didn't belong parked near their houses. They knew what kinds of vehicles their neighbors drove and if they'd lived there long, the vehicles their friends and families drove too.

He was going to have to take a minute or two to stow the bag and make a few changes to his appearance. Might keep him from being forced to shoot a cop tonight.

He reached between the bucket seats to the back seat, grabbed a grubby, turquoise Miami Dolphins baseball cap and slapped it over his blonde hair. Just removing his jacket wouldn't accomplish much, since his shirt was also dark and long sleeved, but he had a tan jacket he could put on over it. It would help, anyway.

He rolled onto his back, laid the Glock on the seat behind his head and unzipped the jacket, awkwardly working his arms out of the sleeves.

Teeth gritted, he grabbed the steering wheel for leverage and pushed himself into a half-sitting position. With most of his head still below the bottom edge of the window, he peered cautiously out to make sure no one was near. Slumped down on his tailbone, he pushed the seat all the way back, took a couple of deep breaths, and then hefted the duffle up between the seats and let it fall onto the back floorboard. After taking another quick look around, he crawled painfully between the seats and into the back where he squatted, panting, on the floorboard.

It felt like someone had stuck a hot poker in his side and left it there, twisting it every time he moved, but he had learned over the years, not so much to ignore pain as to disregard it, to work through it. He'd been in worse pain than this.

The front of the cushioned rear bench seat pulled up, revealing a hidden compartment beneath where he stashed the bag. He put the tan jacket on, pulled the black one off the front seat and slid his hand in the pocket for the truck keys.

They were gone.

He reached into the other jacket pocket, then checked each of his pants pockets and ran his hands over both front seats. He'd put them in his jacket pocket, he was certain of it.

Shit! They must've come out with the gun.

They were probably lying in the middle of a pool of blood about two blocks from here just waiting for a cop to pick them up and put them in an evidence bag.

God damn it!

He blew out a frustrated breath. He'd have to hot-wire the truck. Easy enough if you had the right tools, and fortunately, he did, in the toolbox in the back.

On his knees on the back seat, he had the toolbox out when he felt the truck move.

The tall skinny guy who had been with Fat Boy and Meth Head was standing in the street, face pressed against the back window glass. Two beefy young guys stood just behind him, long hair wet, hanging down, wearing leather vests with no shirts, their multiple piercings and dangling chains gleaming in the faint light of the street lamp down the block. One of the two held a sawed-off shotgun pointed at Aronson's head.

Skinny held up a cell phone so Aronson could see it, then let an evil grin, full of rotted teeth, spread over his face.

The slimy mother fucker had followed him, and then called his friends.

One of the two young thugs crossed around behind the Blazer as Skinny held up a buck knife and pressed it against the glass, then suddenly grabbed the handle in his fist and slashed down. Aronson felt a jerk as the knife penetrated the tire, which was repeated immediately when the kid slashed the rear tire on the other side.

Pain retreated as adrenalin surged and Aronson went cold with fury. These mother fuckers had just messed with the wrong guy, he thought as he remained completely still, except for the hand moving to the Glock on the seat beside him. He fired through the glass at the guy with the sawed off shotgun almost before the muzzle had cleared the seat back. The guy turned as he fell and his finger pulled the trigger as he went down. The blast of shot took most of Skinny's head off and splattered the Blazer with blood, brains and skull. Aronson cut the third punk down before he got ten feet.

That ought'a wake the neighborhood up, he thought grimly as he jumped out of the SUV.

God damn it! The cops would be all over the place in no time and the Blazer was covered with his prints. With two flat tires, it wasn't going anywhere, at least not quickly and not quietly.

More sirens had joined the first and were getting closer. Lights had gone on in some of the houses on the street.

He stuffed the Glock into a side pocket of the duffel and emptied the cavity beneath the seat, sliding a second Glock 26 with a full clip in the holster at his back, slinging the strap of a Glock 18 with a folding shoulder stock and a thirty-three shot clip over his shoulder. He clipped the belt of an equipment pouch containing burglary tools and some other odds and ends around his waist.

He needed to be gone, but couldn't leave the truck just sitting there. A few holes punched in the gas tank with a screw driver started the flow of fuel splashing onto the pavement and under the truck. Backing away, he opened a flare from the emergency road kit and struck the cap on the end to light it. The flare hissed bright hot flame, and already turning to run, he tossed it under the back of the Blazer. The gasoline lit with a whoosh just as a cop car, lights flashing and siren screaming, turned onto the street a few blocks down.

Aronson turned and ran between two houses, setting the dogs barking.

Across the street, in the darkness under a tree, Stan watched Aronson run between the houses and decided he couldn't follow. The cops were damn near on top of him.

He'd go back to the store, Aronson was sure to head there to hole up for a while.

CHAPTER SEVENTEEN

Jessie woke up confused. Her thoughts were jumbled, muddled, and she was surprised when she heard herself whimper. She hurt. Worse than she could ever remember and thought, for just a minute, before she came fully awake, she'd gotten in the way of her daddy's fists again. She wondered, vaguely, where her momma was and tried to roll over, but couldn't move her arms and started to panic.

Then she remembered.

She forced herself to slow her breathing and lie completely still. She listened closely: there was the steady, muffled throb of an engine and the regular, wet, plop of water dripping. Other than that, it was quiet. It meant, she hoped, that the bastard hadn't come back yet. He could've come in while she was unconscious and she might not have heard him, but she didn't think he was down here in the cellar with her now.

When they'd gotten to the house, he'd dragged her inside and down the steps into the cellar without a word, pulling the box knife out when she'd started to struggle. She hadn't been going to beg, to plead, but she'd found the words coming out of her mouth along with sobs she couldn't suppress. He'd tossed her inside a wooden enclosure all the way in the back and slammed the door. After a few minutes, he'd returned and released her bound wrists, only to tie her again, attaching her wrists with thin cord to opposite legs of an old wooden workbench, so that she was lying on her back with her arms spread, her ripped blouse offering no protection from his greedy eyes.

He'd knelt down beside her and pushed the blouse further open. When she'd tensed and flinched away, he'd laughed softly and stood up, "Relax, little girl. We've got plenty of time. Scream all you want. No one will hear you."

He'd moved around for a few moments, then left her alone, going quickly up the stairs he'd dragged her down not ten minutes before. Then the lights had gone out and she'd heard a door close.

The floor over the front part of the cellar had creaked as he'd moved across it, then she'd heard another door open and close.

After several minutes of silence, she'd released the breath she didn't know she'd been holding and had experienced a small amount of relief. She hadn't realized how hard she was concentrating on his movements, watching his eyes, looking for something, anything, that would allow her to brace herself for his next assault, defend herself somehow.

Once he'd gone, she'd pulled and tugged on the cord until her wrists were bloody, but she couldn't get free, and her struggles just seemed to pull the cords tighter.

Then she'd let the tears flow, playing and replaying what had happened at the creek, what she'd done or not done, what she might've or should've done to change what happened.

After a while, exhaustion and the effects of her injuries had taken over and she'd fallen into restless sleep.

Her shoulders ached from lying flat on her back with her arms extended and slightly above her head. In addition to the pain stabbing through her head, every cut, scrape and bruise throbbed and she felt a drop of blood run down her arm from the cuts she'd worn in her wrist.

She spread her unbound feet out as far as they would go, moving each in an arc. There was nothing to feel but dirt.

She thought about Momma and whether she was awake or asleep and if she was worrying about her. She wondered if anyone was looking for her.

Not likely.

Since she'd been working at Melba's, folks had gotten to where they were polite, even friendly, but she was just a waitress; someone to fetch and carry, fill their cups and clean up their mess.

When she was younger, she hadn't been shunned, exactly, but she knew how most folks felt. Thinking about what might be going on in that run-down house out on Ice House Hill had made them uncomfortable, still did, so they'd just looked the other way.

They hadn't helped her then and they wouldn't help her now.

If she was going to get out of here, she was going to have to do it herself.

Maybe she could get him to untie her for a while. Maybe she could find some way to hurt him, disable him, keep him from hurting her. Maybe, maybe, maybe.

She tried to keep from thinking about the possibility, probability of her own torture and death: how and when it would happen, what she would endure first, but the thoughts crept in around the edges, making her eyes well with tears and an ache spread across her chest. Too bad the ache wasn't a heart attack. If she had to die, she wouldn't mind it so much if it meant the man would come back wanting to make her scream and bleed and beg, but find instead of warm flesh and terror, a cold, silent corpse.

She tried to hold in the tears, but her thoughts turned to what he'd done to her in the darkness of the culvert; the first time, thankfully, vague and fuzzy, but the second clear and ugly and real. She clenched her jaw and made no sound, while tears streamed down the sides of her face and ran down her neck into her hair. She couldn't keep the images and sounds from re-playing in her head and kept hearing him panting and grunting in her ear, feeling his teeth on her flesh, biting down as he jerked and pulsed inside her.

CHAPTER EIGHTEEN

Aronson headed back to the store, but only long enough to check his wound, see if it was serious.

He was relieved to see that while painful and bloody, it looked like the knife had passed through his side above his waist, slicing through skin and muscle without hitting anything vital, going in about where a love handle would be, if he had one, and coming out just under the edge of his rib cage. A couple of inches and the ass-hole might've punctured a lung or sliced up a kidney. He thought about waiting for a while there at the store, where he knew he'd be safe, and waiting for the cops to clear the area, but he figured they'd be busy chasing their tails for a while, trying to figure out what had happened and who they were even looking for. It made more sense to go before the cops developed a description of him, even a poor one.

He left the store and went the opposite direction from where he'd been jumped. It didn't take him long to find an older, nondescript truck, which he got running in under twenty seconds. Once he'd put some distance between himself and the store, he wove in and out of dark residential streets, strictly following the speed limit, coming to a full stop at every stop sign, until he found another truck, a little newer, but same make and color, and traded license plates. Most people didn't notice their license plates, guy wouldn't notice his plate wasn't his plate for a while and now the truck Aronson was driving no longer had the plate from a stolen truck on it. Chances were no one would know the truck was gone before he made it back to the house, but better not to take any chances.

He headed back to the farmhouse and while he drove, thought about Skinny and how his buddy with the sawed off could've taken Aronson out before he even realized they were there. Instead, Skinny and his friends hadn't wanted him dead as much as they had wanted to show him how smart they were, torment and play with their prey a little, show who had the upper hand. The psychology of killing, he guessed. Instead of a cold kill, out of necessity, they'd needed something more from it and it had gotten them killed. It was a need he understood all too well.

Having absolute power over another human being made his heart pound and his blood heat. It wasn't the killing that he craved, it was what went before. The killing was an anti-climax, never bringing the relief he sought, never living up to his expectations.

He knew better than to divert any of his energy from the job; it jeopardized the operation, the men he worked with, and him. He thought about the girl. She was a distraction he didn't need. He'd lost focus on the job and it could have ended in disaster. There was only one way to get her out of his head and he would take care of it as soon as he got back to the house.

CHAPTER NINETEEN

Glenna stood at the window in the living room. It had been full dark for a long time now, and she'd turned the lights out in the house so she could see down the road with what little moonlight there was. The Big Buck River ran about a hundred yards behind the house and she could hear it running fast, swollen with the recent rain. An owl called and was answered by another. The wind rustled through the trees, making the leaves shudder and dance, shedding rain with a rapid tattoo on the ground below. It was all so normal and the thought had her blinking back sudden tears.

She had an unobstructed view of the narrow gravel road that passed in front of the house and it was a good vantage point to wait and worry; she'd be able to see headlights coming from a quarter mile away.

When they'd gone out to get the old Chevy it was gone. They would've passed it if Jess had driven it home. Glenna knew that, but had hoped anyway that they'd get home and find the car next to the house and Jess inside. But there was no car and no Jess.

Glenna was barefoot, but other than that hadn't undressed. The rain had cooled things down. The windows were open and the damp breeze blew goose bumps across her bare arms. The scarred linoleum was cool beneath her feet, but she didn't want to leave the window to put her shoes on or get a sweater to wrap up in. She knew it was illogical, but in some way, she felt that it would be bad luck for her to leave the window. If she just stayed right here, straining her eyes into the night, she'd see the lights of the old Chevy coming up the road with Jessie behind the wheel, full of a story about giving a ride to a friend and getting lost out on the backroads; or telling Glenna, "Don't you remember, Momma? I told you I was goin' to go over to school for a study group."

But she hadn't. Jessie wasn't in bed because something bad had happened to her. Glenna shook her head, trying to clear the thought away.

Tommy was asleep, or passed out, his loud snoring audible even at the other end of the house.

She'd spent many long, unhappy nights just here, looking into the dark, arms wrapped around herself, eyes dry and searching, trying not to imagine where Tommy was, waiting for him to come home. It'd been a long time since she'd bothered. Or cared.

The first time he'd been out all night had been right before they lost the garage. He'd been late before, but that morning, when she woke up at 3:30 she'd known he wasn't in the house. She'd gotten up and looked out the kitchen window toward the shed. The lights had been out. He hadn't been out there either, and she'd known, she'd just known he wasn't coming home that night.

Her imagination had had him, arrested, killed in a fistfight, murdered.

She was normally calm, difficult to rile, but once she lost her temper, she had a blazing tongue. She'd had her hands full with the kids and a part time job, and had been helpless to stop him from pissing everything they'd had away. That next morning, when he'd finally come home, still stinking drunk and reeking of whiskey, she'd let him know just what she thought about his drinking, his gambling and his friends.

After almost ten years of marriage, he'd hit her. He'd split her lip open for questioning him, interfering with him, he'd called it.

She'd known about the violent side of his nature. He'd been in countless fistfights and had even been arrested for assault and battery twice, but his violence had never been directed at her. In an odd way, early in their marriage, she'd felt secure, safe, having someone like Tommy, tough and mean, standing between her and the world.

Before that day, she'd thought her life couldn't get any worse, but she'd discovered that it could. He'd crossed a line that morning and she didn't know, at first, what that meant.

After he'd stumbled up the stairs and fallen into bed, she'd pulled herself together, got the kids up and ready for school, all the while pretending nothing had happened, ignoring her throbbing cheek and swollen lip. When Mason, only seven or eight at the time, had asked about her cut lip, the lie, that she had fallen, had slipped out without conscious thought.

She'd thought about little else that day at work. She'd told herself that she should've seen how upset Tommy was about the garage, she should've known better than to get in his face, it was her fault, she shouldn't have jumped in his shit as soon as he came through the door, she should learn to control her temper.

Later that day, when she got home from work, he'd had flowers in a vase on the kitchen table and he'd apologized and said how sorry he was. He'd repeated all the things she'd been thinking all day. It would never happen again.

But it had.

She'd learned to keep herself and the kids out of his way when he came home mean drunk. When she didn't move fast enough, she'd learned to camouflage the bruises with make-up and avoid her brother, Harlan, until they disappeared.

She'd left Tommy once, packed up the kids and rented a trailer with money she'd borrowed from Harlan. Tommy'd showed up at almost midnight the day after she'd moved in, and when she wouldn't let him in, had kicked down the door. He'd been drunk, armed with a hunting knife and angrier than she'd ever seen him. He'd shoved her against the wall, grabbed her by the throat and said very slowly, "You ever think about leavin' me again, I will find you and I will kill you. Last."

He'd jerked his head toward the back hallway where the kids were probably awake now. "After I kill them. I'll let you watch."

He'd given her fifteen minutes to get her shit together, sat down on the couch and took a slug out of the bottle he had in his back pocket, and left the hunting knife resting on his thigh. Glenna had believed him. Still did.

She'd hustled the kids out of bed and shushed Duane when he'd started to make a fuss. They must have sensed her fear, because they'd quieted down and quickly did what she told them. The twins still had been seven or eight, maybe, and Jessie'd been only four, but Junior, almost thirteen, and Mason at eleven had had such grave, somber looks on their faces. They'd been old enough to understand and it broke her heart to have her babies see her as a scared, helpless woman. She was their momma. They still needed her to be that all-knowing, brave and infallible fiction in their young eyes, and that night she believed it had been lost forever.

She'd herded them all into the living room and out the ruined front door. Pausing in the doorway, she'd looked back at her husband, passed out on the couch, head tilted back, snoring. Her eye had been drawn to the knife.

It'd be quick, she'd thought. Just a quick slice and the fighting and bruises would be over. Her kids would be safe.

She'd walked over to him and slowly reached for the knife. She'd looked at the blade. Tommy kept it sharp as a razor. She'd looked at his face, mouth slightly open, cheeks puffing with each exhale. When had he changed from the man she adored to one she wanted dead?

The thought had startled her. She'd never crystallized the feeling before, never brought it into focus. Did she want Tommy dead? She'd looked at the knife again, then his face.

Her life and her kids' lives would've probably been better without him, but she hadn't wanted to kill him.

She'd laid the knife on the couch next to him and gone out to her kids.

That had been more than twenty years ago.

Glenna shifted, easing an ache in her back and sighed.

Now she was standing here again, staring into the darkness, waiting for headlights to come up the road, racking her brain for some innocent, harmless reason for her one and only daughter to be still out there instead of home and in her bed. She'd thought about everything Jess had said over the last couple of days and whether she might've mentioned having a date or something tonight until her head ached.

But there was nothing, so Glenna continued her vigil alone, trying not to think about where Jessie might be, what might be happening to her.

CHAPTER TWENTY

Bradley's police department, like Brewer's was small and didn't have the equipment, personnel or manpower to investigate a crime like the one they found when they responded to several 911 calls, so Bradley, like Brewer, Brewer County and the other little towns in the area, contracted with the state police to investigate cases like this. Once the city police secured the scene their job was pretty much done and they passed the investigation on to Dan and Charlie.

"What a mess," Charlie grumbled, looking at the scene. "Four dead guys, one critical and a car fire all within two blocks of each other.

"All the stiffs are local, but haven't been in the area long. The two over on Ryerson are Ben Close and Johnnie Nielson. Close is the stiff, shot in the chest; Neilson's gut shot, might make it, might not. Over here, we got Billy Harvard with the sawed off, Lenny Dillard over there," he indicated with his head, "and Dan Hodges with most of his head missin'."

"You get a statement from the old guy that called Close and Nielson in?" Dan was shining a light on the front seat of the Blazer.

"Yeah, Fred Wilkins," Charlie replied. "Says good riddance to bad rubbish. Says he doesn't sleep too good and dogs barkin' woke him up. Got a lot of kids cuttin' between the houses last couple of months, dumpin' his garbage cans, breakin' into his garage; couple of weeks ago, painted gang graffiti on the side of his house. Tonight, he got up to see what was makin' the dogs bark and saw Hodges with two other guys he didn't recognize in the doorway of the empty building across the street. Says Hodges is from a house across the alley from him. Three guys livin' there, different women in and out and lots of foot traffic comin' to the back door; dealin' drugs and runnin' prostitutes outta' there for the last four, five months, according to old Fred. Said he's called and complained to the city cops a couple of times, but they come out, talk to him and that's where it ends. Said he even offered to let 'em set up surveillance from his attic window.

"With that tiny vice budget the city cops've got, the Lieutenant that heads up that department's got his hands full. Same unit's also got robbery and violent crimes. Says the house has been on their radar, probably cookin' meth, dealin, and doing everything else Fred thinks they were and then some, but couldn't get a warrant without more than what they had and they hadn't gotten around to doing any surveillance. These guys were fairly new to the area, according to him.

"Fred says this guy comes walkin' down the street, carryin' a big bag, and looked to him like Hodges and the other two were tryin' to hold him up. Probably were since he said the fat guy, Nielson, had a gun. Somebody dropped a knife too; could of been the guy, could of been Close. Forensics'll print everything, see who was packin' what.

"Anyway, Nielson's got a gun out, he reaches for the bag and all hell breaks loose. Before Fred knows it, Hodges is high-tailin' it out of there and Neilson and Close are on the ground. He heard three single shots, not automatic fire."

"Did Fred get a look at the shooter?" asked Dan.

"Yeah, sort of. Light hair and was a little shorter than Hodges. Hodges was pretty tall, hard to tell with most of his head gone, but I'd guess six foot two or three. So we're lookin' at six feet, anyway. Dark clothes, but couldn't really give us more than that."

"So basically, we've got shit." Dan shook his head.

Charlie continued, "There was blood on the knife got dropped over on Ryerson and didn't look like Close or Nielson had any stab wounds, so maybe one of 'em got the guy. Might get lucky and get some DNA off it that'll give us the shooter."

He rubbed the back of his neck. "Up to that point, he looked like a guy just tryin' to defend himself when he was gettin' held up. Maybe he's even got a license for the gun." He looked at Dan's raised eyebrows. "Yeah, and maybe he don't. But fact is, he had a gun, like a lot of folks do, whether they're supposed to or not, and it looked like self-defense all the way 'til we get over here."

"Over here," he looked slowly around at the havoc, "it's somebody real scary."

One of the uniforms had diligently placed numbered placards next to the shell casings in the street, the weapons, the burned flare, the broken glass and anything else he thought could be related to the incident. Nicki, the crime scene tech was snapping pictures. She'd started with the bodies first. The city cops had covered them and the brain matter on the truck with white plastic sheets, and the area was ringed with portable screens to keep onlookers who had gathered on the other side of the crime scene tape from viewing the blood and gore. But even with city cops on guard, some asshole with a cell phone might try to sneak a video and put it up on YouTube.

No one was going to be able to I.D. this guy by looking at his face, she thought as she snapped several pictures of brain and skull fragments where they had splashed onto the Blazer and the street.

"Both back tires flat," Charlie said. He shined his flashlight into the back of the Blazer, then the back seat, where broken glass glittered and shimmered. "Shell casings back here. Looks like our shooter shot from inside the truck. Nice little hidey-hole he's got under the seat, too.

"Wonder what he was doing in the back seat, though. Think there might have been two of 'em, one driving, one shooting out the back? Maybe Harvard, the guy with the sawed-off took out the back tires, got the fuel tank."

"Maybe, except Fred only saw one guy approach Hodges, Nielson and Close over on Ryerson. Over here, Harvard, Hodges and Dillard were on foot, too. Wasn't a car chase." Dan shone his flashlight on the rear tire next to the sidewalk. "Doesn't look like Harvard took out the tire, at least not with the shot gun. Big slice in the sidewall." He walked around to the other side. "This one too."

Dan bent over and looked under the rear bumper at the gas tank. "Couple of holes in the tank. There'd probably be more if Harvard hit it with the sawed-off.

"We run the prints, we'll find our guy's at least got a sheet, probably a warrant." He leaned down and looked at the fuel tank again. "I'm thinkin' he put some holes in the tank, the gas leaked out, and then he lit it up with the flare. Probably thought he'd get rid of any evidence in the truck by burning it, but because of this little incline," he nodded down toward the curb, "most of the gas ran downhill and pooled under that little Honda." They both surveyed what was left of the little red car about thirty feet ahead of the Blazer. "First units on the scene put the Blazer out with extinguishers, so damage is all on the outside. Honda wasn't so lucky."

One of the uniformed cops approached. "Talked to one of the 911 callers. Carol York lives two houses down." He nodded up at a second story window. "Said she was up with a sick kid and heard the first three shots over on Ryerson, but thought it was somebody setting off firecrackers. Says it happens all the time in this neighborhood.

"Said about five, maybe ten minutes later, she was getting back into bed when she looked out the window and saw the three guys standing in the street around the back of the Blazer. Didn't know there was a guy in the truck until she heard the shots and saw the muzzle flash. She's pretty shaken up. I told her you'd want to talk to her."

≈≈≈

"I'm an emergency room nurse; see a lot of pretty gruesome stuff, but you just don't expect to watch three guys get blown away, right in front of you, you know?" Carol York was sitting on a bar stool at the island in the kitchen, sipping a cup of herbal tea, cradling it with both chubby hands to keep it steady.

"My kids' rooms are in the back and they slept through the whole thing: gun shots, sirens, everything, thank God. I'd have hated for them to see that. Once a kid sees something like that, it sticks with them for a while, sometimes forever, you know?"

"Why don't you just tell us what you saw?" Dan asked.

Carol gave them a look over her teacup. "There isn't any way this guy is going to know I talked to you, is there?" She nervously licked her lips. "I wouldn't want him coming after me; I've got three kids and I'm all they've got, you know? My husband, Brad, their dad, died three years ago this November. He had a brain tumor."

"I'm sorry." Charlie leaned against the counter. "It's tough, losing someone like that. How old are your kids?"

"My oldest, Brad Junior, we call him Buddy, is eight. Becca's next, she's five, and Melissa, Missy, just turned three today. I think that's probably why she got sick - too much excitement on top of too much cake, too much ice cream and too much Kool-Aid."

"Could you pick this guy out of a line-up, you think?" asked Charlie.

"I doubt it. I've been trying to get the city to put up a street light, but so far, haven't had any luck. It was really dark and I was pretty much looking at the top of his head, you know? And he had on a cap, a baseball cap."

"If you can't I.D. the guy, he's not going to care about you," Charlie reassured her, "but anything you can tell us would help. What color was the hat?"

"Light blue, a pale color, anyway, but I don't think it was white. He had on something light colored, a long sleeved shirt or probably a jacket. Dark pants, jeans, maybe."

Dan looked up from his notepad. "He was wearing a light colored shirt? Not a dark colored shirt?"

"Yeah, but it was kind of bulky, like it could have been a jacket. I think it was a jacket."

"Could you tell how tall he was?"

She shook her head. "Not from the angle I was at."

"You saw him stand up when he got out of the Blazer, right? Did his head stick up above the roof of the Blazer?"

"Yeah, it did. His whole head would have been above the roof. Maybe even some of his shoulders. But he might have been standing on the curb."

"Was he white? Black? Hispanic?"

"He was a white guy, I think. His hands were pale, definitely not black."

"Build?"

"Not fat, not even chunky, but not skinny. Kind of medium, I guess." She shook her head. "Not much to go on. Sorry."

"Could you tell if he was hurt? Injured, I mean?" asked Charlie.

"He wasn't limping or holding himself or hunched over or anything?"

"He seemed to be fine, far as I could tell."

"Could you see his hair at all?" Dan asked. "Dark? Light? Any idea?"

She shook her head, looking apologetic. "I didn't see him all that long, either. It happened so fast, and I was watching the guys he'd shot to see if they were moving and I was trying to call 911 all at the same time."

"That's ok, you're doing fine." Dan flipped to a new page in his notebook. "Just tell us, in as much detail as possible, what happened. Whatever you can remember."

Carol nodded and told them what she'd seen: the three men in the street, the one with the shotgun getting shot, the shotgun blast, then the third guy getting shot.

"After the shooting stopped, the man got out of the SUV and took something out. Oh! He had a big black bag. Maybe a big gym bag." She screwed up her face, trying to remember. "Then he went behind the truck and did something back there. He started to run away, kind of trotting, you know, and then the truck started burning. Then he was gone."

"Where did he go, did you see?" Charlie asked.

"He went across the street and between the houses."

"Which houses?"

"The white one and the light blue one. The light blue one is the Murphy's. Their daughter goes to school with Buddy. I don't know the people in the white house. It's an older couple, no kids." She put her cup on the counter and ran one finger around the rim. "I was putting on my robe, going to go out and see if I could do anything for the guys in the street when the first cop car got here, so I decided to stay put, in case my kids woke up."

"And it was just the one guy, right?" asked Charlie. "You see anybody else?"

"No, just the guys that got shot and the one guy that came out of the SUV." She paused, then continued, "I just couldn't believe what I was seeing, you know?"

Charlie nodded and pocketed his notebook. "Have to say even in my line of work, I'd be pretty shocked if this kind of thing happened right in front of my house."

"You mind if we take a look out your window?" Dan asked. "Help put things in perspective, see what you saw."

Carol's face turned slightly pink. "Sure, if you won't mind the mess. Wasn't expecting company in my bedroom."

"No problem," said Charlie. "Couldn't be worse than mine."

CHAPTER TWENTY-ONE

Elvie pulled the truck up beside the barn, directly below the huge hayloft door. He'd done the same thing dozens of times at home, working around the farm with his dad, tossing hay bales out into the truck to be taken out to the cattle. He wanted to get the bags in the truck and get out of there as fast as he could, and flinging the bags from the upper floor down into the bed of the truck was the fastest way he could think of. A lot faster than they'd gone up, that was for sure. In less than ten minutes, the bags were loaded and he was back in the cab headed out toward the road.

≈≈≈

Aronson was getting sleepy in spite of the throbbing of the knife wound, a side effect when the adrenalin rush he'd experienced earlier wore off. He straightened in the seat and turned the air conditioning on full blast, turning the vent so that it blew directly on his face. Better, he thought, shaking his head to clear it.

He turned off the highway onto the county road that would lead, eventually, to the farmhouse. It was out of the way, but avoided going through Brewer. He'd gone into the little town several times, especially when he'd first gotten to the area, just to get the lay of the land, the attitude of the people. He'd even gone into Melba's a few times. No better place in the world to pick up information about the inhabitants of a place than the local diner, but no one who'd seen him on any of those visits would recognize him now.

He could've driven through town and saved himself about fifteen minutes, but at this time of night, he'd likely be the only one driving around Brewer. He knew how small town cops were. A strange truck driving through town late at night was a target and when he'd hot-wired the truck, he hadn't taken the time to make sure all the lights worked. Be just his luck to get pulled over for a broken taillight driving a truck with wires hanging out of the steering column. This wasn't the time to let his guard down, just because he was tired and hurt.

His thoughts strayed. He and his men were ready. They'd finished their final preparations today, which was how he and the girl had crossed paths. He'd been up on the ridge overlooking the highway, checking sightlines measuring distances so time calculations could be checked again, making sure the ground at the edge of the ravine looked undisturbed. Just a final check. His men were good and knew their jobs; it was just his habit to check and never take anything for granted. They'd spent just about every night for the last two months drilling a series of holes, big enough to sink pieces of two inch PVC pipe loaded with explosives. They'd filled the holes with dirt and small rocks. He knew the holes were there but couldn't see them.

He thought about the girl back at the farmhouse and rubbed the small bruise on his cheek. None of the others had ever managed to hurt him. Most women had no idea how to defend themselves against an attacker, but this one had been a hellcat. If she hadn't been scratching the shit out of him, leaving his DNA under her nails, he'd have enjoyed the fight, would have prolonged it.

He had some time to kill while he waited for the informant to provide the date and time of the shipment. He'd been told he'd have the information at least two days ahead. If he was going to have a couple of days with little to do, he didn't need to spend them alone, now did he? He remembered her taste, the way it had felt sinking his teeth into her soft flesh. He'd get some rest and then have some fun. He hoped she would stay asleep until he woke her. He wanted that instant when the sleepy, relaxed confusion in her eyes turned to terror.

He saw taillights ahead and slowed, realized he'd unconsciously sped up thinking about the girl. As he closed in on the vehicle ahead, his headlights reflected off black plastic.

He stopped thinking about the girl and zeroed in on the truck, an old farm truck with a wood stake bed, plastic bags piled in the bed.

"Well, what do you know?" He backed off, giving the truck a little room. He couldn't be positive it was the same truck, but with the bags in the bed, it was damn near a sure thing. He couldn't tell who was in it. Might be the boys, might not. Either way, the truck would lead him to them.

≈≈≈

Elvie pulled up to the cattle gate and got out to unlatch it. The headlights lit up the side of the barn, black at one end, weather-beaten gray at the other.

He didn't know what time it was, but thought it was around one. If he had to guess, he'd say John's grandpa probably got up around five or so and he wanted to have the truck back long before anybody was up and around. He'd already decided to leave the keys in the truck when he took it back. The old geezer would just think he or John had forgot and left them there. It'd be one less chance for him to get caught.

He should have time to get the plants up in the loft and out of the bags at least. He could ride his bike back out here tomorrow, tie the plants in bundles and suspend them from the rafters.

He stopped the truck next to the barn and turned the engine and headlights off. He wished he'd thought about bringing a flashlight. It was dark as hell with the moon behind the clouds. He thought about turning the headlights back on, but was afraid someone would see them from the road and come back there to investigate.

He climbed out of the cab, walked around to the back, got up into the bed and began throwing the bags, one at a time, through a window. He was about to pitch the last bag through when he heard a noise, like an animal moving through the brush, coming from the other end of the field. Probably just a deer, coming in to drink out of the cattle pond, he thought, then tossed the bag in and followed it through the window and into the barn.

The reek of burned wood was strong, the wet of the rain intensifying the already unpleasant smell, and Elvie wrinkled his nose against it. Even after all this time, the heavy air carried the additional odor of livestock: urine and cowshit mixed with old straw.

Even with his lighter giving some weak light, he bumped into stalls and tripped over an old pail and other debris on the floor. He hoped the ladder hadn't been at the burned end. He wasn't sure how he'd get the bags up into the loft if the ladder was burned up.

To his relief, about halfway across, he saw the ladder still propped up against the access to the hayloft.

He turned and located the window, a slightly lighter square of black, and made his way back, kicking objects on the floor to the side. When he reached the bags he stopped, listening. There was that noise again, closer now. He darted nervous looks out into the darkness of the pasture. He squinted, trying to bring something out in the field into focus, but it was just too dark.

He was gettin' a little spooked and would be glad when he was done. He shook off the nervous tension and shrugged. Just a critter of some kind, he told himself, if it wasn't a deer, it was raccoon or possum: one of those that liked the night better than the day.

The bags were heavy and Elvie was tired, but it didn't take him long to get the bags over to the ladder. He stopped for a moment and thought about smoking a cigarette, then had visions of a spark igniting the barn and all his pot going up in flames. He decided to wait and started up the ladder with the first bag.

He'd planned on laying the plants out on the floor so they could start drying out a little, but once he got up in the hayloft he didn't feel safe moving away from the ladder. He used his lighter, but still couldn't see where the destruction from the fire ended and the remaining floor began. Even if the floor was still there, were the supports still there? How far could he go out and not risk falling through?

Standing near the top of the ladder, with his torso through the opening, he leaned out and felt the floor, covered with dirt, bits of hay and bug carcasses, then pounded on it with his fist. It felt solid enough right here by the ladder. He'd just get the bags up in the loft and come back tomorrow when he could see better.

Elvie'd never been a fan of hard physical labor, preferring to con other people into doing it instead. The bags were awkward and the plastic stuck to his sweaty legs. He had to hold the bag with one hand while he used the other keep himself on the ladder.

After manhandling the last bag up and through the hole, he sat on the hayloft floor and let his legs dangle over the edge. He leaned back cautiously against the mound of bags and gave an exhausted but satisfied sigh. How many guys could claim to have laid on a bed made of pot? He couldn't wait to brag about it, saw in his mind the reactions of kids at school when he told them.

He was normally a night owl, not wanting to go to bed until the small hours, but it had been a long day, filled with the excitement of harvesting his crop, then the heart-pounding terror of being chased, followed by his fight with John and now the exertion of getting the bags stashed. By now, it was probably getting close to 2:00, maybe even later. He found himself drifting into sleep and decided he was ready for this night to be over. But he had to get the truck back and then ride his bike all the way home, so bed was still at least an hour away.

He roused himself and started the climb back down, not surprised that his legs had gone all rubbery on him after the repeated trips up and down the ladder.

He crossed to the window. It had been easy getting into the barn that way from the bed of the truck, but he was too tired to try and climb out the same way. He stopped to get his bearings and cocked his head, listening intently, trying to catch the same noise he'd heard earlier. There was nothing but the drip of water off the roof and the cry of an owl in the distance. He could see the outline of the door further along the wall and headed that way, pulling his cigarettes and lighter out as he walked.

He waited to light up until he left the barn, and was crossing in front of the truck, head bent to the flame, sucking in a lung full of smoke when he felt the hair on the back of his neck rise. He stopped and started to turn, had an instant to recognize the sensation of displaced air, but no time to understand what it meant.

Elvie hit the ground hard, but he didn't feel it.

CHAPTER TWENTY-TWO

Chastain kept Aronson in sight, but stayed way back, afraid to get too close. When he saw him turn off the highway onto the county road, Chastain figured he was heading for the farm house and let himself fall even further behind, taking the same turn, but dousing his headlights before he left the highway. It was damn dark out on this county road, but once his eyes adjusted, as long as he followed Aronson's tail lights, he could see well enough to keep the truck out of the ditch.

Chastain closed the gap and got to what he felt was a more comfortable distance when Aronson's lights disappeared.

"Shit!" Chastain said, braking hard.

His first thought was that Aronson had identified him somehow and was waiting for him up ahead. In Aronson's world, when a truck with no lights tails you, you assume the worst, and don't concern yourself with whether you're right or wrong.

In this case, add the fact that the truck on your ass looks a lot like the one that blocked the road so some kids you were chasing could get away, it's pretty much a sure thing.

Chastain let his engine idle, peering into the void ahead. He wished he still had the GPS to rely on, but he didn't.

Aronson wasn't that far ahead, but without the taillights, Chastain couldn't tell if he was moving or stopped. He pulled his truck over until it was almost in the ditch and killed the engine, listening for the sound of Aronson's truck.

Ahead of where he'd last seen Aronson's lights and to his right, the dense weeds and brush of a deserted pasture were lit, illuminated by the lights of another vehicle, blocked from Chastain's view by a thick stand of trees. He could just see the headlights in brief, shining glimpses through the trees, traveling perpendicular to the road Chastain was on.

It wasn't Aronson. Couldn't be. It was too far off the county road for it to be him, unless he'd floored it, and why would he? The vehicle certainly wasn't barreling along right now. Besides, Chastain would've seen the taillights make the turn, not just disappear.

The vehicle left the cover of the trees and the deep growl of an engine straining in low gear made its way across the field to him. Definitely not Aronson's truck.

He cracked the door just far enough to get out and crouched next to the front wheel. He had his gun out, but it was pointing up, the butt resting against his shoulder, muzzle next to his right ear. It was cool and heavy, familiar in his hand, giving off the faint smell of the oil he used to clean it. He listened intently for any other sound: a rustle in the grass, the unwary crunch of gravel under a foot, but there was nothing.

He waited two minutes that felt like an hour and raised his head slowly above the hood.

He stayed where he was, motionless, except for the slow turning of his head. While he crouched there, he began identifying noises he hadn't been able to hear earlier over his breathing and the pounding of his heart: nocturnal rustlings in the thick brush of the fence row behind him, the occasional whine of a car or truck out on the highway.

No matter what the directors of the blood and gore slasher movies would like you to believe, it wasn't really possible to creep up on someone in complete silence, not outside, anyway in dense grass or over gravel. Had Aronson been approaching, he would've made noise; slight, nearly indistinguishable from other nighttime sounds, but it would've still been there, and Chastain had heard nothing out of place. He didn't let his guard down, but allowed himself to relax slightly while he thought what to do next.

He needed to find out what Aronson was doing. If he hadn't stopped because of Chastain, then why? Trouble with the truck?

He kept low and went around to the back of the truck, climbing over the gate as quietly as possible. He unlocked the tool box in the bed and removed a pair of night vision goggles. Aronson's truck appeared as a vague outline about fifty feet ahead. A slow scan of the area, turned ghostly in greens and grays, didn't reveal Aronson.

Once he was sure the area was clear, he vaulted over the sagging cattle fence next to the road and began wading, at a crouch, through scraggly weeds and brush until he was about thirty feet into the field. He turned and began moving cautiously, parallel to the road toward Aronson's truck.

The field was mostly mud and before long, Chastain had what felt like ten pounds of it coating his black tennis shoes. Every time he pulled his foot free to take another step, the mud tried to suck his shoe off.

Hell of a way to sneak up on someone he thought, pausing to scrape the mud off before he closed in on Aronson's truck.

It was pulled completely off the road and appeared to be empty. Only normal night sounds reached him where he squatted.

Had to be engine trouble. No other reason to leave the truck there. He kept his distance, passed the truck, and turned to study it from the front. The hood wasn't up and unless he was lying down in the seat, Aronson wasn't in there.

Where the hell was he? He would've had a look under the hood if he was having engine problems, wouldn't he? Otherwise, why had he stopped here? He wasn't out of gas. He'd stopped at a gas station on his way out of Bradley. They weren't close yet to the farm house where Aronson was holed up; it was still a good five or six miles away. He wouldn't just ditch it. He had to have transportation. Aronson had taken the time to swap out the license plates on a truck that probably wouldn't even be reported stolen until daylight, if then. Why would he have done that if he wasn't going to drive it for some period of time?

Chastain hesitated to approach the truck in case Aronson was still inside. Aronson had been stabbed and while he hadn't acted like he was hurt that bad, he could've had internal injuries. But if he'd passed out, he wouldn't have pulled off the road and turned off his headlights.

Aronson could have walked away on some unknown errand. Even now, Chastain could conceivably be between Aronson and the truck.

He moved closer, trying to watch every direction at the same time, but there was no sign of Aronson.

He sighed. He really didn't think Aronson was lying in the truck unconscious. Chastain had two choices: stay or go.

If Chastain left and drove on to the farmhouse, what was the down side? He could miss Aronson doing something out here that Chastain should know about. He could be meeting someone, planting something, ditching something. At least if he waited and Aronson came back, Chastain would see where he'd come from. If he waited and Aronson had just walked on to the farmhouse for some reason, no harm done.

It wouldn't hurt to stay and wait for a while, see if Aronson came back. He heard a screech owl in the distance and then the scream of a rabbit, probably the owl's supper. He slowly shifted his position, kneeling, trying to get a little more comfortable, ignoring the mud soaking into his pants and the sharp whine of a mosquito flying close to his ear. He hunkered down, settling in to wait.

CHAPTER TWENTY-THREE

Elvie woke to a sharp, agonizing pain in his foot. He tried to jerk it back, but it was caught, held somehow.

He opened his eyes and found himself laying on his back, looking up at the sky, the moon just a remote, dim silhouette behind the clouds.

He'd just gotten his bearings and was trying to sit up when the pain came again, so intense it made him cry out through the cloth that had been stuffed into his mouth.

He became aware of another presence and felt a chill of dread.

A low voice said, "I want the names of the other two boys."

Oh God. It was the man with the Blazer. The one who'd taken Jessie. He couldn't see more than a dim shape, not enough to recognize him, not that he'd gotten a good look anyway, but he knew, down in his gut that that's who the man was.

He tried to sit up again and found that his hands were tied to the bumper of the truck. Oh, sweet Jesus! He felt fear he'd never known before. Oh God.

Cold sweat beaded his forehead and then the pain came again. He uttered a sound, half squeal, half sob. He understood now. The man was calmly, deliberately, burning the arch of his foot with a lit cigarette. He could hear the sizzle, smell the burning flesh. His foot throbbed, pain spreading up his leg.

"Don't!" he managed around the gag, his voice cracking, "I'll tell you. I'll tell you." As the words came out of his mouth, his brain was busy, trying, futilely to make a deal with God. Promising to turn his life around, go to church, never steal or lie or disobey his parents. He wished he already had a relationship with the almighty. Now was a hell of a time to try and start one.

"John Kitzinger and Lyle Nelson," he gasped out when the man removed the gag. It never occurred to him not to rat the other two boys out.

"Where do they live?"

When Elvie paused, just a split second too long, searing pain ran from his foot to his groin when the man ground the cigarette into his skin.

"Out in the country, both of 'em." Elvie was crying now. "I ain't never noticed their addresses, I swear." For once in his life he was telling the truth. In a flash of inspiration, he said, "but I can show you."

The man didn't respond. "What'd you tell the cops?"

"Nuthin'!" Elvie said in a rush, "Nuthin'! We didn't even talk to the cops, and we won't say nuthin'. None of us."

There was skepticism in the man's tone when he said, "You didn't say anything to the cops?"

"No! No, I told ya.'"

"You're lying," the man said as he applied the tip of the cigarette once more.

Elvie screeched, "No!" He sobbed, "No, I swear. We didn't tell nobody."

"Why?"

"We was somewhere we wasn't supposed to be." Elvie said evasively. His natural tendency was to lie about what they'd been doing, but then he realized the last thing this man would do was go to the cops. "That field where we was. It was full of pot. We was puttin' it in plastic bags so we could dry it out and sell it. John borrowed his grandpa's truck so we could get it out of there and store it somewhere." He continued quickly, "We can't tell nobody what we saw 'cause we took the truck without askin' and we don't none of us have licenses. Then we'd have to say where we was and why we was there. Even if we didn't say why, cops'd go out there, see a bunch of plants got pulled up. Don't take a genius to figure that one out."

Elvie found himself rattling on, searching for the right combination of words that would make the man believe that none of them were a threat to him. "Me 'n John, we got in trouble for breakin' into the high school this summer. We're both on probation. We get in trouble again, means we violated our probation and we go to juvie."

The man didn't answer, but he put the gag back in Elvie's mouth, got up and moved away.

Aronson took a high intensity pin-light out of the tool kit he'd salvaged from the Blazer and searched the ground where the kid had fallen. It took him a few minutes, but he finally found what he was looking for. He bent and picked up the lighter the kid had dropped. It would look like the boy was carelessly smoking a cigarette in all that old hay and straw, when he accidentally caught it on fire.

Elvie strained his ears, trying to figure out what the man was doing and heard the crackle of fire.

He turned his head and saw that the interior of the barn was lit with a soft, dancing, glow that was getting brighter with every second.

Elvie thought, for just an instant, about the pot in the bags in the hayloft, but then the meaning of the fire struck him. There wasn't no reason, at least none that were good for Elvie, for the man to burn the barn down.

He started squirming, yanking on the ropes that tied him, twisting himself around like a fish on a hook.

Elvie heard the man coming back, then for the first time, with the light of the fire, got a good look at him. He had on a Miami Dolphins baseball cap and Elvie thought that was a strange thing. It didn't seem right, somehow, that this man should do anything so ordinary as to watch football or have a favorite team.

In the midst of the terrified stupor that had taken over his brain, Elvie wondered how he could have such normal thoughts, how any part of his mind could be considering anything but what this man was going to do and whether he'd be alive this time tomorrow.

Aronson picked up Elvie's cigarettes and shoved them and the lighter into the back pocket of the boy's jeans. He released Elvie's feet first, then his hands. For a second, Elvie thought he was going to be let go until the man grabbed the front of Elvie's shirt, pulled him to his feet and wrapped his forearm around his neck. Elvie's vision blurred and narrowed, the dark around the edges closed in, and then there was only black.

The boy was still alive. Aronson had been careful, controlling the amount of force. He wanted to knock the kid out, not kill him. He wanted to make the kid's death look like an accident, so he needed him unconscious, but breathing. Most bodies weren't completely consumed in a fire. Portions of clothing, internal organs, the brain, random, unpredictable parts of bodies, were left nearly unscathed.

If the boy went into the fire already dead, he'd have no smoke in his lungs, or damage from inhaling superheated air.

A good forensic scientist could elicit a surprising amount of information about what had happened to a body before it burned.

He let the boy sag onto the ground and took the gag out of his mouth. He picked him up and flung him over his shoulder, wincing at the pain in his side. The fire was burning hot, so far still contained to the lower floor, but soon it would become a howling, devouring inferno that would take the building completely. With dry straw and old wood, it was only a matter of time.

Aronson got close enough to feel scorched by the intensity of the heat, put his hands on the kid's rib cage and heaved, like he was throwing a sack of grain off his shoulder, and the boy landed in the middle of the fire.

Aronson didn't stay to watch. The boy was unconscious and probably wouldn't feel a thing.

He left the barn, the fact that he hadn't ever even learned the kid's name never crossing his mind.

CHAPTER TWENTY-FOUR

Chastain stayed in position for about half an hour and had just decided to make his way back to his truck when he caught an unmistakable whiff smoke. He turned toward the misshapen old barn to his right and winced when jagged shards of flame bled through the sparse stand of trees. He pushed the goggles up on top of his head and moved cautiously toward the barn, slipping from tree to tree until he reached the perimeter of the barnyard, beyond the increasing glare of the fire.

He stopped and squinted into the light. Next to the barn, an old farm truck sat. The cab was a dusty red, and the truck had a wood stake bed. It was disturbingly similar to one he had seen just that afternoon.

Shit. Had Aronson caught up with the boys after all?

He crouched and looked for a way to get closer, but there was just no cover between the trees and the barn. He'd decided that he was going to have to stay put when he saw Aronson toss something over one shoulder and enter the barn.

Just as Aronson walked through the door, Chastain knew what Aronson carried. It looked like a body. A small body. One of the boys.

It was already too late for the kid and all he could do was watch. Flames were curling up out of the windows and licking the outside walls. The low, loud roar of fire in a feeding frenzy came clearly across the field, and he could see that at one end most of the interior was already being greedily devoured.

Aronson came right back out of the barn without the bundle, moving quickly.

From inside the inferno, a short, harsh, sharp scream pierced the air. Chastain closed his eyes and let his head drop forward. Aronson looked over his shoulder and paused, then kept moving to the front of the truck.

He pulled out a flashlight, searched the ground, bent a few times to pick something up, and tossed whatever he'd found through the window and into the fire.

Aronson backed away from the heat but stood watching the fire for maybe five minutes. Satisfied that there was no way the kid was still alive, he went across the yard to the gate, unlatched it and gave it a shove. He walked the weedy track that led out to the road, only looking back once, when the gas tank of the farm truck exploded with a roar.

Chastain began running back into the trees and through the field toward his truck. He heard Aronson's truck start up after a few minutes. Aronson would get ahead of him some, but Chastain was getting close to his own truck and should be able to keep Aronson's tail lights in sight.

Chastain tailed Aronson back to the dilapidated farmhouse and watched for nearly an hour, then trotted the quarter mile or so back to his truck, keeping off the road.

He no longer had the GPS signal to rely on, so until he could plant another, he'd be stuck in his truck watching the track that led back to the farmhouse.

He didn't bother to report back on his trip into Bradley right away. He'd made the trip into Bradley the last eleven weeks, so it wasn't exactly news, and he'd gotten all the information he was likely to during the first trip.

Several grainy pictures of the older, portly man Aronson met with every week as well as the muscle that accompanied him was all he'd been able to send back to the Department. Although it was as dark as the inside of a shoe at midnight behind the store, the man, Walters, had looked in Chastain's direction long enough to allow him to take several pictures.

Getting a look at the man Aronson was meeting had identified who Aronson was working for, but it hadn't helped them figure out what Aronson's game was.

That was Chastain's job, and so far, he'd come up with a big fat zero.

Chastain stretched out across the seat of his truck and closed his eyes. It had been a long day.

Where the girl was concerned he'd done what he'd been trained to do, what, in the larger scheme of things he knew was the logical, necessary thing to do. It didn't feel good, it never felt good, but he'd done it.

Where the boys were concerned, it was the first time he'd lost the battle between the well-trained, logical operative he'd become and the compassionate human being he'd suppressed for the last thirteen years. He'd risked the operation, his cover, for three boys, and for what? In the end, Aronson had gotten them anyway.

CHAPTER TWENTY-FIVE

Ronnie Chilcoate loved being a volunteer firefighter. He felt like he was doing something positive with his life that had nothing to do with making money and everything to do with danger and excitement. There was something reaffirming about overcoming the raw power of an elemental force. This was his seventeenth year and he never got tired of it.

He watched as Dennis Captra and Jimmy Fullerton continued to soak down the area around the old truck, the only thing still burning.

They'd pretty much let the barn burn itself out. Old wood burned hot and fierce and nothing they could have done would have saved it, or even put it out for that matter. By the time they got there, one whole side of the barn had already collapsed inward and the upper floor had tilted drunkenly down into the first. The other side had gone shortly after, allowing the floor of the hayloft to crash completely down to floor level. Once the walls had collapsed and the upper story caved into the floor, they'd begun spraying it down until all that remained was the one small, stubborn area.

"What do you think, Ron?" asked one of the other firefighters, "think it was a lightning strike?"

"Could be, but it waited a long time to catch if it was. I've seen lightning fires that smoldered, but the storm was over by what, eight, eight thirty?. After that, it was just rain. We got the call at 2:00 am, maybe a little later, so we're lookin' at a fire that smoldered in this old tinderbox for five or six hours?"

He shook his head. "Could be, but I don't think so. Started on the ground floor, too. It was this here wall in front that went first."

"Then what do you think it was?"

"Not sure. Still too dark to really see much. We'll wait 'til daylight, let her cool off some, then we'll take a look."

CHAPTER TWENTY-SIX

Lyle tossed and turned in his bed hoping his brain would turn itself off and quit flashing those pictures of Jessie, hurt and bloody, in his head.

He had to be at work at Melba's at 5:00 a.m., and when he got there, he would know that Jessie wasn't going to show up for her shift at 5:30. He would know that some crazy man with a gun had her, was doing God only knew what to her, and that he could have, might have, been able to help her, but he hadn't. She could be dead by now, and if not, he couldn't even imagine what she might be going through right this very second.

He rolled over again and looked out the window. Thick clouds raced across the moon, hiding it from his view. He wished he could sleep.

≈≈≈

Melba's busy fingers worked a ball of pie dough into the flour that covered the metal table, something she'd been doing every day of her life for the last thirty years, and could do in her sleep. She stared into space, enjoying her own company, the quiet of the kitchen and the solitude of her lonely task. The only sounds were comfortable, familiar ones: the faint hiss of gas feeding the oven burner, the tick of metal as it warmed, the hum of the huge walk-in refrigerator.

Lyle, her nephew and weekend kitchen help, wouldn't be in until 5:00. By then, the pies would be in the oven, she'd be browning sausage for the gravy and keeping an eye on the mounds of sausage links and bacon cooking on the grill. She'd set Lyle to transferring clean glasses from the dishwasher racks to the waitress station out front, filling the ice bins and washing the already growing pile of used bowls, utensils and so on. When it was time for Bud, the grill cook, to come in, he'd finish up the meat and stock his area. Rita, her weekend kitchen helper, would be in soon to get the biscuits ready for the oven and just generally do whatever needed to be done to get ready for the Saturday breakfast rush.

Marybeth and Jess were supposed to be in at 5:30 to set out the butter, cream and syrup, fill pitchers with orange juice, make coffee and get a start on the side salads they would need for lunch, but it would probably be Jess doing all that and Marybeth breezing in at 6:05, as usual.

Melba slid the last pie into the oven and thought about Marybeth; she wasn't sure what to do about her. If she hadn't been the owner of the place and Marybeth her daughter, Marybeth would've been hittin' the streets looking for work a long time ago. She was always late, careless in her work and pushed what she could off on Jess. Fortunately, Jess wasn't one to make a fuss, because truth be told, if Melba'd had to choose between having Jess quit and keeping Marybeth a job, she'd have been hard pressed to let Jess go. Melba had overheard Marybeth make a few comments that sounded like she thought the diner was as good as hers when Melba retired. As she turned on the grill and began lining up the link sausages to cook, she wondered how Marybeth had gotten it into her head that she'd be runnin' the diner after Melba was ready to retire; not that that was going to happen any time soon: she was only sixty-two. Even though Marybeth had worked there for three years, Melba couldn't think of another person who was less qualified to run a business, any business, much less a diner, than Marybeth. Now, Jessie. She'd turn the place over to Jessie in a heartbeat, she thought as she opened the back door for Lyle. If Jessie was interested. Which she wasn't.

Melba was well aware of Marybeth's faults, but when she'd come home three years ago, so hurt after two years of marriage to a man who had cheated on her before the ring was on her finger, she'd welcomed her back into her childhood home and given her a job without a moment's hesitation. There was no denyin' Marybeth, as the youngest of her three daughters, had been spoiled rotten, and she'd only herself to blame for that. There'd been a big gap, twelve years, between Karen, her middle girl, and Marybeth, so she'd almost been like an only child, and so like Hal, her dead husband that she'd fussed over her and given her anything she'd wanted, in the process, alienating her older two girls.

Melba remembered the day Jessie'd first come in, fifteen years old, huge blue eyes in a skinny face, wild black hair tumbling down her back, asking in a halting voice if Melba was hirin'. Melba'd known who she was: the DuBois girl. Town this size, most everybody knew who everybody else was.

She remembered thinkin' that she wasn't sure she wanted any of the DuBois clan workin' there, stealin' her blind and maybe bringin' in that bunch her daddy hung around with, but Melba'd always had a soft spot for a stray and even though she wasn't really hiring, she'd found work for the girl to do a couple of nights a week after school. When one of the busboys quit, she'd let Jess take his job.

Jess'd come in, more than once, with bruises on her. It'd made Melba boil with rage that that worthless bastard, Tommy DuBois, would raise a hand to a frail waif like Jess was back then, but when Melba would ask her about it, she'd always say she'd fallen, or ran into something.

Jessie'd been only seventeen when one of Melba's long-time waitresses had quit unexpectedly so she could go on the road with her new trucker husband. Jessie'd asked Melba to let her try her hand at waitin' tables, said if she wasn't any good at it, she'd understand if Melba had to find someone else, but asked if she could just try, just for a couple of shifts, see if she could do it. Melba hadn't thought she had the personality for it, and she'd been far too young and inexperienced to deal with some of the assholes who plunked their butts down in her seats; but she'd had no one else, and she'd had customers to be waited on, so she'd said yes, and Jess had begun covering the weekend shifts. Melba'd never regretted it.

Once, right after Jessie'd got out of high school, Melba'd asked her if she could do any job in the world, be anything she wanted to be, what would it be? Jessie'd blurted out, "Paint. I'd be a painter."

Surprised, Melba'd said, "What, houses?" which had made Jess give one of her rare laughs and then she'd said with a wistful, faraway look in her eye, "No. Pictures. I'd be an artist." Then she'd grabbed the plates Bud had just put up and slipped out of the kitchen.

Melba'd fretted when Marybeth had come home and the two girls started waiting tables together. Marybeth and her friends had been in and out of the diner constantly when they were in high school. They'd come in after cheerleading practice for a cherry coke and some fries. After football and basketball games on Friday nights, the place swarmed with high school kids: spectators, players, cheerleaders, band members; Melba's was where they'd celebrated victory and commiserated over defeat, gobbling down cheeseburgers and French fries.

They hadn't been subtle when their focus and conversation had locked onto Jessie, talking about her with the brutal unkindness of popular kids everywhere, making a pretense of hiding their comments behind their hands while their eyes and cruel laughter followed Jess around the dining room. Melba had raised two girls before Marybeth and figured it would only make matters worse for Jess if she tried to intercede. The kids' attention always shifted fairly quickly from Jess to other things, so she'd decided to leave well enough alone, settling for a serious talk with Marybeth about the golden rule that went in one ear and out the other.

Maybe Marybeth had learned something about life, or maybe she felt bad about how she and her friends treated Jess in high school. Whatever the reason, there hadn't been any real trouble between the two girls, not that Melba would've expected it from Jessie. Jessie tended to shrug things off mostly.

Melba checked the clock over the door and then looked at her watch. 5:43, and Jess was usually there by 5:20. "Lyle," she called out, "You seen Jessie?"

He jumped, his face flamed, then paled, "Unh uh." He shook his head, and then scuttled into the dining room with a load of glasses.

She looked over at Bud and he shook his head.

"Ain't like Jess to be late," she said, "'specially on a Saturday."

CHAPTER TWENTY-SEVEN

Brewer, while small and rural, wasn't a one-horse town, At least not anymore.

Years ago, the square would've been parked up with pickup trucks and Chevy sedans because back then, when Brewer had been mostly a farming community, that's what most people drove. Nowadays, there might be a BMW, a Hummer, or the occasional Porsche tucked in at the curb in front of the businesses that lined the square.

About thirty years before, the county water commission had determined that Brewer County had a need for a larger source of fresh water. After a bitter court fight, the commission had acquired a little less than twenty thousand acres so that Big Buck River could be damned and the gullies and ravines east of Brewer flooded to create a nine thousand acre reservoir. They'd said the land was 'unimproved,' but most of it was farm land that had been owned by the same families for generations. If the owners didn't want to sell their land, and many of them didn't, it was taken from them anyway, and they were paid what they'd been told was 'fair market value.' Imminent Domain. That was how they'd explained how the rich and powerful could take what belonged to someone else so they could get more rich and powerful.

The members of the commission had claimed that their difficult decision to deprive farmers of their land and homes was done for the greater good, and it was. The greater good of a consortium of fortunate people who happened to be ready and waiting with the cold hard cash needed to buy from the commission the thousands of acres of land that rimmed the reservoir. Once the deal had gone through, the land had been re-sold, for hundreds of dollars a square foot so some developer could plunk down houses worth up to three million dollars, one right after the other.

The land was bare as a newborn baby's butt: no trees, no bushes, just houses, sprouting up like warts where corn and soybeans and alfalfa had grown for more years than anyone living could remember.

Most of the locals didn't see the sense of moving all the way out here, paying at least a half a million to live in a house that sat so close to the one next door you could spit on it. A lot to pay just to see some water, and you couldn't even see the water from some of those houses.

They'd found out fast enough that with all that wonderful tax money also came a whole lot of problems, and the Brewer County Sheriff's Department had doubled, then tripled in just a few years, and had kept on growing.

Drunken brawls, disturbing the peace and domestic disturbances in quiet sounding communities such as "Glen Harbor," "The Cove" or "Deer Run" kept sheriff's deputies busy every weekend. There were plenty of spoiled rich kids with absent parents, looking for something, anything, to break the pall of boredom that afflicted them. A lot of time was spent confiscating alcohol and drugs, arresting vandals and scraping the inexperienced young drivers of BMW and Jaguar convertibles off winding country roads. That's not to say that the bulk of the populace wasn't made up of quiet law abiding citizens, but the amount of craziness per capita didn't seem to decrease as the income increased.

Like thousands of small towns, Brewer had a square in the center of which sat a faded, red, brick courthouse. Being the county seat, the town square was busy during the day. The sheriff's office was just down the street in a building that used to be the First Home Trust Bank.

On the perimeter of the square were storefronts, a few still old and sad, but most housing upscale businesses and with new or restored facades.

Melba's Diner didn't sit right on the square, but was just around the corner on Brewer Street. The good people of Brewer had grown up eating real food: fried potatoes and sausage gravy and pork fritters and corn pudding and big slabs of homemade apple pie. The cucumber and bean sprout sandwiches at the Starbuck's just didn't fill the bill, so most of the locals ate at Melba's if they happened to be in downtown Brewer at lunch time, especially if they were in the course of county business. After all, aside from the

Cornerstone Bar and Grill, there wasn't any place else to get a real meal within walking distance, and any desire by County employees to eat their lunch at the Cornerstone, innocent though it may be, was pretty well eliminated by the ugly mud-slinging election of 2010.

It was a well-known fact that former Sheriff Bobby "Chunk" Winters, lost his bid for re-election that year to George Farber because of his presence in the bar while he was on duty. Chunk's defense, namely that he never drank on duty and only went in for a sandwich and an iced tea, sweetened, was attested to by many of his Deputies. The fact that they were also regulars at the bar somewhat reduced the effectiveness of their testimony.

To be truthful, a beer at lunch by a good old boy like Chunk wasn't seen as a real threat to his job of eighteen years. The real problem was Daisy, Shawna, Tawny and Dawna, who were present at The Cornerstone on a pretty much daily basis, and who were observed on several occasions accompanying the sheriff up the back stairs to the rooms above the bar.

Two weeks before the election, the bar was raided by the Brewer City Police. The women were arrested for prostitution and the owner of the bar was arrested for operating a brothel. Unfortunately for Chunk, he was with two of the two girls upstairs in one of the bedrooms at the time. The bust was headline news and Old Chunk's fate had been sealed. There was only so much looking the other way the women of Brewer County would let their men get away with.

Melba's Diner occupied an old glass fronted building and had the advantage of a fairly large parking lot, an acquisition made by Melba in 1994, when the insurance agency next door burned to the ground. The exterior of the building was cement block, painted a bright buttery yellow with "Melba's" in red script painted both on the side of the building and on the big front windows

Melba had had the same menu for the last thirty years. She served breakfast starting at 6:00 a.m. and had a blue plate special for lunch every day of the week as well as the usual stew, chili, hamburgers and tenderloins. She was only open 'til 2:00 p.m. weekdays, but stayed open 'til 11:00

p.m. Friday and Saturday evenings when she served thick steaks and prime rib for dinner. The food was hot, plentiful and not expensive, but nothing fancy. You weren't likely to find a sprig of parsley decorating any plate that came out of her kitchen. She made fresh lemon meringue, apple and cherry pie every day, and you could get the apple or cherry pie heated up and a scoop of "a la mode" on the top.

The booths that lined the perimeter were covered in dark green vinyl accented here and there with duct tape of a slightly different green, covering the small rips and tears to be expected after more than thirty-five hard years. The center of the room was crammed with 1950's tubular steel tables and chairs. Up front, a counter stretched almost the width of the room, with four swivel-seated bar stools on either side of a lighted glass case where Melba kept pies you could buy and take home.

It was only 7:30 a.m., but the diner was already crowded and Marybeth was frazzled. Jessie hadn't shown up, leaving Marybeth to cover her own section and part of Jessie's until they could get another waitress to come in.

Denton McIntyre sat in his booth and watched her trot from table to table, hot and pissed off, although she tried to hide it. His law practice was just across Brewer Street from Melba's, and every morning he parked in the small lot behind his building and walked across for breakfast. For Denton, Saturday morning was just another workday, but without phone calls, court appearances and appointments: a chance to catch up, uninterrupted, on the mountains of documents generated by his profession. He could get a good breakfast, work 'til noon and have the rest of the weekend to do whatever he wanted with a clear conscience. Otherwise, whatever else he was doing, he'd be thinking about the piles of paperwork he knew were waiting for him.

At Melba's, he always sat in Jessie's section, in this same booth in one of the windows at the front, if he could get it. There was a good view of the street where he could see who was coming and going while he drank his coffee and waited for his breakfast. Jessie was a good waitress; she'd have his coffee sitting on the table before he got settled in the booth most of the time. It didn't hurt that she was easy to look at with long, curly dark hair, dark blue eyes, great legs and every now and then, a killer smile.

Not that Marybeth wasn't one of the prettiest girls in town and downright stacked besides, but she and Denton had grown up next door to each other, and they'd been getting on each other's nerves since they were kids.

While he'd been ahead her in school by three years, because they'd lived next-door, the two families had shared countless cook-outs, pot-luck suppers, birthdays and other events until Denton and Marybeth couldn't stand the sight of each other. Chubby, shy Denton, with his thick glasses, slight stutter and asthma that kept him from playing sports had been sensitive about his rank in the outer circle of high school society. He'd pretended not to care, but the fact that petite, blonde, bubbly Marybeth had been an instant success had rubbed salt into the wound.

The last time they'd said more than a dozen words to each other had been at a birthday party for Denton's mother. Marybeth had called him a fat, loser, four-eyed geek, and he'd retaliated by calling her a lazy, selfish, stupid bi... uh, brat. They hadn't bothered to patch up the quarrel, because neither cared if they ever set eyes on the other again, and shortly after, Denton had left to go to college.

Denton had gotten over it a long time ago. He was happy, healthy and reasonably attractive. He'd worked out like crazy to lose the baby fat and was in better shape than most of his former jock classmates. Thick eyeglasses had been replaced, first by contacts, then laser surgery, revealing hazel eyes that sparkled with wry humor. He'd overcome the stutter, had grown out of his asthma and become a hell of a racquet-ball player. His law practice was growing steadily and he counted as clients some of the same kids who had spurned his friendship as teenagers.

Since Marybeth made a point of pretending he was invisible when he was in the diner, he gave her a shocked look when she actually stopped at his table, notepad in hand, ready to take his order.

"Wow." Denton folded his newspaper and laid it beside him on the seat. "What'd I do to deserve this honor?"

Marybeth narrowed her eyes and glared at him, but didn't respond.

"If I'd known you were working this section this morning, Marybeth, I would've sat somewhere else."

"Denton," Marybeth paused to blow the bangs out of her eyes, "you gonna' order somethin' or you gonna' just sit there takin' up one of my tables?"

"Where's Jess? She sick or something?"

"I don't know where little Miss Perfect is this mornin', Denton. She didn't show up and nobody answered the phone at her house. Momma's fit to be tied 'cause Saturday's our busiest day, next to Sunday after church. Course, she's not mad that she didn't show up and left us short-handed. No-o-o-o-o-o. Momma's worried she's been in a car wreck or caught the epizootic or fell over dead or somethin', cause everybody knows Jessie's never tardy or absent and is destined for sainthood, or would be if she was a catholic."

"Your momma been chewin' on you this morning? I bet that just gripes your ass doesn't it, hon?"

"Oh, shut up, Denton," she said as she slapped her notepad down on the table and put her hands on her hips. "Walk in here three minutes late and you'd think the world was coming to an end. You'd think if your momma owned the place, you'd get cut a little slack, but no-o-o-o-o. I swear, Denton, if Momma tells me one more time she wishes I were more like Jessie, I'm gonna' spit."

She rested the edge of her empty tray on her hip. "Well, I can't yell at momma and I can't get mad at Jessie 'cause she ain't here, so I guess I'm glad you sat in my section. I can yell at you 'cause I don't care if you get pissed off at me or not. It's not like you'd start goin' somewhere else for breakfast since there isn't anywhere else."

The little bell above the door tinkled and Marybeth looked up. "Holy crap."

Denton started to twist around in his seat, but Marybeth put her hand on his shoulder. She leaned down and whispered, "It's Jessie's daddy. Jesus, I think this is the earliest he's been outa' bed in twenty years. He looks like hell, too. He never comes in here unless he's tryin' to get a few bucks outa Jess."

Tommy stopped just inside the door and took a look around the diner, saw Marybeth and made a bee-line for her. "You know where Jess is at, Marybeth?"

Marybeth took a step back from the overpowering smell of alcohol that surrounded him. "No, I don't, Mr. DuBois. She didn't come in and we just thought..."

"Say anything to you about goin' someplace after work?"

She shook her head. "No, yesterday she said she had a headache and just wanted to go home and lay down. She did work a little late, though 'cause Mandy..."

"When she leave, you know?"

"Unh uh. I was already gone."

"Jess didn't come home from work last night. Her momma thought maybe you'd know where she's at."

Marybeth frowned. "She wouldn't just not go home without sayin' somethin' to her momma. Jess just wouldn't do somethin' like that." She looked at Denton as if for confirmation. "You mean she just never showed up after work?"

"That's what I said, ain't it? Jessie was drivin' the Chevy yesterday and Sheriff found it out on Patterson Road with her purse still in it, but there wasn't no sign of Jess. Now the car's gone, but Jess never came home."

"Jess wouldn't leave her purse layin' in the car. She just wouldn't do that. I know she wouldn't. And yesterday was payday."

"Well, tell her she needs to let her momma know she's alright if you hear from her. She been up frettin' all night. Storm last night musta' knocked out the phone. Glenna don't drive my truck, and the car's gone, so she woke me up to come in town and ask about her. I think she's makin' a whole lot of fuss about nothin' and Jess'll turn up when she's damn good and ready, but I gotta' admit it ain't like her to not tell her momma where she's gonna be at."

"Let us know when you hear something, okay?" Marybeth called after him as he left, then watching him through the window as he got into his truck said, "I wonder where she can be. She woulda' told her momma if she was goin' somewhere." She was frowning, a crease cut between her brows. "Somethin's wrong, Dent. Jess isn't like that. She's real careful about her purse, always makes sure it's locked up in the back. Momma says it's 'cause she's had her daddy or her brothers takin' anything she ever had from her for her whole life."

CHAPTER TWENTY-EIGHT

Ronnie copied down the license number of the burned out truck. The paint was gone, but the number stamped into the metal was still visible. Just as a matter of form, they'd run the plate; notify the owner if they could find him. Truck wasn't really all that old for a farm truck and he thought back, trying to remember when Riley'd gone belly up. He was thinking twelve, maybe thirteen years, which would've made this truck about five years old when he'd gone under. Big truck like this, only five years old, would've sold in the bankruptcy proceedings, so, once he'd thought it through, he didn't believe this old truck was one of Riley's. So whose was it and what was it doing out here?

Ronnie was glad it was Saturday and he didn't have to work at his regular job at the water treatment plant. Ronnie didn't see how the fire could've been caused by lightning, and he and Dennis needed to take their time going through the still cooling rubble and ash, to figure out what happened. The Fire Marshall would make the official ruling, but in a lot of cases, since he had the whole county to work, he relied on the findings of the volunteers. They would make a report of the facts they uncovered at the scene and the conclusion they reached based on those facts. More often than not, the overworked Fire Marshall signed off on it and moved on.

They would begin by looking for the origin of the fire. Based on what they'd seen when they reached the scene, it was probably someplace on or near the south wall.

Once they'd determined where it started, they'd move on to how, looking for signs of an accelerant or multiple starting locations which would indicate arson. It was painstaking work and meant sifting carefully through what was left of the building, looking for pieces of the puzzle. In this case, arson for insurance money wasn't a realistic reason, but they had to rule out the fire having been started by a firebug. People who set fires for no reason except to watch something burn didn't do it just once.

Ronnie's partner, Dennis Yates, stood with his hands on his hips and watched as Ronnie made his way across to the remains of the heavy support beams that had held up the hayloft floor. This was nothin' but a friggin' lightning strike to a deserted barn out in the middle of nowhere he thought, and Ronnie, as usual, was treating it like it could be the crime of the century. There wouldn't be any insurance, the reason for 95% of set fires. He liked Ronnie, but sometimes he got on Dennis' nerves.

Ronnie squatted and peered beneath the beams, not wanting to shift them until he'd eliminated the possibility that the fire had started on the upper rather than lower floor. He moved slowly but efficiently and had worked his way back near the end of the barn when he saw what looked like a bony finger, pointing at him. It always amazed him, the forms burned wood could take and he bent closer.

"Jesus!" he shouted, and took a quick step back. "Jesus H. Christ!" He turned, excited but feeling slightly sick. "Dennis, c'mere and look at this." He wanted another pair of eyes to tell him he was imagining things.

Ronnie pointed. "Does that look like a finger to you?"

Dennis squatted and looked closely where Ronnie was pointing, then jumped to his feet. "It doesn't just look like a finger, it *is* a finger."

≈≈≈

Gary Murphy, the Fire Marshall, bent to look beneath the burned rubble. "Son of a bitch," he murmured. Most of the body was visible. It was small: could be a teen-aged boy or a woman. "I'll notify the sheriff, but for now, let's get this whole damned area taped off." There was no way to tell how the victim had died, no way to tell what he or she had been doing there. Until they knew more, it was a crime scene.

His job was to enforce the fire code, prevent fires whenever possible, and once one had occurred, determine the cause. His job did not include excavating a corpse.

≈≈≈

Ronnie and Dennis stood guard over the barn until the Fire Marshall got a deputy dispatched. Part of Ronnie wanted to go back in, get a closer look, but the other part knew better than to contaminate the scene of a possible crime. He'd worked fires where people had died, and he'd seen the corpses, but he'd known what to expect. This body out here in this deserted barn, on this failed farm, with nobody around, had been unexpected and it had spooked him.

CHAPTER TWENTY-NINE

When George Farber woke up the next morning, Jessie was on his mind. He'd been wrestling with the reason she might have left her purse in the car, especially with a week's pay in it, and nothing he thought of made sense.

He didn't really know Jessie that well. He didn't think many people did. The only one of the DuBois family he could say he really knew anymore was Glenna because he saw her a couple of times a week at the nursing home when he visited his mom.

In school, he'd been a year behind Tommy and hadn't run with the same crowd. He knew him to speak to and that was about it. He'd had a crush on Glenna, like all the boys did, but she'd only had eyes for Tommy. Even back then, he was smart enough to know it didn't make any sense to break your heart over something you couldn't have, but he'd spent many sweaty nights thinking about her.

He hadn't known for quite a while that his mother was in the nursing home where Glenna worked because she worked first shift and he'd always visited in the evening or on the weekend. He'd come in earlier, during Glenna's shift, one day and when she'd walked toward him down the hall, he'd felt like he was in high school again.

Thirty-five years had added some grey to her dark hair and fine lines around her intense blue eyes, but otherwise, she'd looked just the same. He'd been surprised and a little dismayed, by the familiar tug in his groin when she'd recognized him and given him a big smile.

George had joined the Marines and been gone while Glenna and Tommy'd had their kids, but the first time he'd seen Jessie at Melba's he'd known she was Glenna's girl. Spitting image of her ma.

She didn't strike him as one of those flighty gals who would just take off and leave her purse behind, even if someone had stopped and they'd gotten into a conversation.

He'd gone by the DuBois place last night to see if Jessie had made it home. Glenna'd told him that they hadn't heard from her, and when they went out to get the car, it was gone. There wasn't any reason Jessie wouldn't have been home by then, and she was worried. George was uneasy because Glenna was uneasy, but he knew from experience that just because he couldn't think of a logical reason for something didn't mean there wasn't one.

He put on jeans and a tee shirt, brushed his teeth and went down the hall to check on his son, Mark. He was still asleep and he'd let him stay that way. He was home on leave and had been out with friends, finally making it home at 2:30 this morning. Mark was a happy kid, always had been, and one of those people everyone was glad to see. Not a kid anymore, George thought, observing the dark stubble on his son's face. He'd be twenty-seven on his next birthday. George softly closed the door and went downstairs to make coffee and a bowl of cereal.

His breakfast was interrupted when the call came about the barn fire. A body had been found. Most of it was still covered by debris, but it could be a woman.

Could be Jessie.

He stopped only to clip his badge and holster to his belt and secure his gun, and he was on his way out the door.

≈≈≈

Jim Thompson had been the Brewer County Coroner for most of twenty years and couldn't remember having had such a terrible couple of days. Most of the time, death in Brewer County was a peaceful affair and required little more than a signature at the bottom of the death certificate.

He was a Funeral Director, for heaven's sake. He owned Thompson's Mortuary, and although he was a duly licensed and qualified mortician, he was feeling more than a little inadequate. He didn't personally conduct the autopsies, thank the Lord; it wasn't part of his job. He, or more usually, a representative of law enforcement, decided if one was needed and then the body went to the morgue in Bloomington where, at least for the last twenty-four hours, the corpses had been stacking up like cordwood.

The law required that the Coroner pronounce the corpse dead before the body could be disturbed, which really made no sense to Jim since he wasn't even a doctor, but that was the law.

He'd taken a look at the small, distorted body, pronounced it dead and got the hell out of there.

While the state crime scene techs had been waiting on the Coroner, the Medical Examiner from Monroe County had arrived. Dr. Melton from the Monroe County Morgue covered Brewer County since they didn't have a Medical Examiner of their own. George stood by and watched as the debris covering the body was cleared and Dr. Melton began his preliminary examination. The body wasn't Jessie's; it was too small. Remnants of clothing: jeans, a tee shirt, a belt, clung to the side of the body lying on the dirt floor and not exposed, directly, to the fire. Tennis shoes had melted to the victim's feet, black lumps not recognizable as any particular brand. The back pockets of the jeans were somewhat intact and netted them a wallet with a partially melted plastic ID card. A panther snarled at the Doctor from the upper left corner of the card. Doctor Melton closed his eyes and shook his head. "It's from the high school." He held the card up to the light. "I can't make out the name. Just a few letters. Looks like E-l-v."

The crime scene unit photographed the body from every angle and took video of the entire operation. The body was bagged, a grisly operation, and put in the ambulance to be taken to the morgue.

George asked the Doctor when he thought they'd have a cause of death, which made him shake his head. "Soon as we can."

CHAPTER THIRTY

Glenna stood in the window and watched while Tommy's old truck came up the road and pulled into the yard to park next to the house.

Her mind was busy, darting from thought to thought, unable to keep from thinking about all the horror she'd ever seen on TV or in some movie or read about that could be happening right now to her baby. Trying to not wonder if, at this very moment, the life that was Jessie was gone, her body left alone and empty somewhere in a barn or a cellar or out in the woods.

Tommy didn't come into the house. He'd been pissed that she'd gotten him up to go into town. She walked into the kitchen to see him going through the door of the shed.

Fear and anguish and anger flashed through her. He couldn't even be bothered to walk into the house to tell her what he'd found out before he went to the bottle he'd left out there. She stalked across the kitchen, slapped open the screen door and went across the yard where she flung open the door of the shed. She stopped just inside and looked at her husband. He was sitting on a cinder block, turned on its end, a bottle halfway to his mouth.

"What? What did they say?" Glenna asked.

His eyes met hers, he shrugged, dropped his head back and tilted the bottle to his lips.

Glenna saw it all like a picture and recorded the instant in her memory, stark in outline and color: the flat bottle half full of amber liquid, her husband's blunt fingers, nails dirty and uneven, knuckles just starting to swell with arthritis, wrapped around the bottle.

Glenna found herself there, in front of him, hand blurring as it arced toward him before she even knew what she intended. The bottle went flying and shattered when it hit the grinding wheel mounted on his workbench.

His mouth went slack and he stared at her like he'd never seen her before. She bent and grabbed fistfuls of his tee shirt in her hands and screamed into his face, "You son of a bitch! Don't you dare crawl in that bottle. Don't you dare! She's your daughter too!"

She was sobbing as she let him go and backed away, hands covering her face.

Stunned, he looked slowly at the broken glass; at the liquid dripping from his work table onto the floor, then turned and looked at his wife.

With a bellow of rage, he stood and knocked her into the wall where her head hit the old wood with a crack. Before she could move, his fist slammed into her face followed by a punch to her ribs.

She ducked and twisted, turning her face to the wall and almost in slow motion watched a fat, red, drop of blood fall from her face onto the top of her foot. He grabbed a fistful of her hair and as he pulled her around and away from the wall, she threw her weight sideways into him. Surprised, he let go, stumbled backward and fell over the cinder block he'd been sitting on.

Glenna saw her chance and ran. She'd reached the house, flung the screen open and was in the kitchen before Tommy made it into the yard.

When he burst through the door she spun around, a small gun clutched tightly in both hands. "I will use this."

"Horseshit," he sneered and took a step toward her.

She fired and a small glass jar on the shelf next to Tommy's head exploded, making him duck. "At this range, I can't hardly miss, but I'll tell you a little secret. While you been out playin' cards and drinkin' and whorin', I've been practicin'. If I can hit a little can at a hundred feet, I can sure as hell hit you."

Tommy doubled his fists, but was just enough afraid that she'd really shoot him to come after her again.

After he slammed out of the house and roared away in his truck, Glenna sagged against the counter and let the gun fall to her side.

CHAPTER THIRTY-ONE

Melba'd fussed and fretted over it when word of Tommy DuBois' visit to the diner made its way back to the kitchen. Bud just shook his head, a frown furrowing his large forehead.

Lyle had been in the dining room when old man DuBois had come in, and he'd known instantly why he was there. He'd felt cold all over and thought for a minute that he was either going to pass out or puke.

Since then, word had spread through the diner like wildfire, and as he'd mechanically dumped empty coffee cups and dirty dishes into the tub he carried, pushed the salt and pepper shakers, the little dishes of individually wrapped butter and half and half back into position, wiped down the tables, he kept seeing in his head the way Jessie had looked yesterday.

Lyle didn't like many adults, but Jess was easy to be around. She was real pretty, too, but not stuck up about it like his cousin, Marybeth. She never lectured or found fault, or teased him about girls. She was just a nice lady.

He heard bits and pieces of the conversations in the dining room: nothing unusual in that. He'd found out that people tended to forget he was there and he'd heard some pretty surprising things in the couple of months he'd been working for his aunt Melba.

Mostly, people had been shocked at the disappearance at first, then had wondered aloud what could have happened to her. He heard a theory that Tommy DuBois had killed her and buried her body out in the woods. He heard that she'd maybe had a boyfriend nobody knew about and had run off with him. He heard that maybe she'd just gone to visit her brother, Junior, over in Illinois.

As the noise and voices swirled around him, he tried to shake off the memory of her face, but the image was burned into his brain. She'd begged him with her eyes for help and he had run away. She had saved his life and he'd turned his back on her.

CHAPTER THIRTY-TWO

"John!" Roy Kitzinger bellowed.

He came through the door into the milking shed where his grandson had just finished mucking out the stalls and was hosing down the concrete floor.

John looked up and saw his grandpa's face, flushed with anger, and felt his stomach turn over. He turned off the hose, tried to look as normal as possible, and said, loud enough for his grandpa to hear, "What? What's the matter?"

"You got any idea where the truck is? The GMC, I mean?"

"Ain't it over next to the bull pen?" John asked, genuinely surprised.

"No, it ain't, and the key's not on the hook in the kitchen."

John stared at the old man for an instant while the happenings of the night before flashed through his mind, and he wondered if he'd only thought he'd returned the truck and the key.

No, he told himself. He knew that the truck had been parked back where it belonged and that the key had been on the hook when he'd gone up to bed.

John shook his head, "That's where it was the last time I saw it," he was able to say with absolute truth.

"Well, then," his Grandpa said, "somebody's stole it." He went on, "Did you lock the screen door when you came up to bed last night?"

John paused for a second, trying to remember, then he shrugged, "I can't remember. I think so."

"It wasn't locked this morning." He threw his work gloves down on the bench by the door, "Somebody must've broke in last night after you went to bed. When was that?"

"Nine thirty, maybe a little later," John responded while a horrible, dreadful, but entirely possible explanation suddenly came to him.

"Whoever it was knows where we keep the key," his grandpa continued. "Somebody that's been in the house." He stared intently at John, then said, "Don't lie to me, boy. If you know anything about this, you better tell me now and not let me find out about it later."

"I swear," John said, "until you came in here just now, I thought the truck was parked next to the bull pen where it always is."

His grandpa looked long and hard into his eyes, then said, "I'm gonna' go in then and call the sheriff." He waited for a reaction and when he didn't get one, turned and started for the house.

John looked after him helplessly and hoped his world wasn't about to come crashing down on his head.

CHAPTER THIRTY-THREE

George angled his cruiser into the space next to the DuBois house and got out. The place was quiet and neither the car nor the truck was there.

He knocked on the front screen hard, what his son called his cop knock. The inside door was open and so were the windows. Pretty normal out in the country. Folks around here never locked up. He didn't hear a sound from inside the house, so he called out, "Tommy! You in there?" He paused a moment, then yelled, "Glenna! It's George Farber!"

"Just a minute," he heard Glenna's voice from someplace in the house, then the sound of feet coming slowly down the stairs.

She stopped in front of the door, but a few feet back in the dim hallway. Her hair, normally in a fat braid down her back, was loose, allowing dark, curly strands to fall forward and cover part of her face. Even the darkness and the shield of her hair didn't hide the raw bruise on her cheek or the swelling around her eye.

"Jess?" she asked almost in a whisper.

He frowned, his eyes narrowed, trying to bring her face into clearer focus through the screen. "She hasn't come home?"

She shook her head, then he saw her registering the tee shirt, blue jeans and tennis shoes he wore instead of his uniform. "I'm off duty, but I was thinkin' about Jess. I came out to see if she made it home last night."

Her shoulders sagged a little and she shook her head. "Not so far."

George reached for the door handle. "Look," he said impatiently, "can I come in so I don't have to talk to you through this damn screen?" She took a step back and turned her head away as he came through the door.

He put a hand on her shoulder and tried to turn her around so he could see her face, but she evaded him and went into the living room.

He stopped and looked slowly around. He'd never been in the house before, and although the furnishings were sparse and worn, it was clean. He thought about what the walls of this room would have seen and what they could've told him about the family who'd lived there for the last twenty or so years. Under the shade of the trees at the front of the house, the room was somewhat dark, but with splashes of bright color here and there, dispelling, a little, the feeling of abject poverty.

His eyes were drawn to a large, roughly textured parchment; ragged edges unframed, with brass-headed upholstery tacks in the corners. The two sides had curled in slightly, but didn't hide the image drawn boldly in ink: flowing strokes, drawn with confidence and strength, they perfectly caught the essence of Glenna in profile. Her head was tilted back a little, hair loose and flowing, eyes half closed, lips curved up slightly, like she was enjoying the feel of a cool breeze on her face.

"Jessie drew that for my birthday a few years ago." She turned and her eyes were full of tears.

George studied her face, the bruising and swelling more visible to him now, and blew out a harsh breath. "Glenna..." he began.

"I got some coffee made. You want a cup?" she interrupted and turned away, moving toward the back of the house.

He shrugged. "Sure."

He followed her into a long, narrow dining room and through an arch into the kitchen. Even though the cabinets and flooring were old and dilapidated, the kitchen was spotless. The only thing on the worn counter was a faded, flowered dishtowel, neatly folded, lying next to the sink.

As she bent slightly to put his cup on the table, she sucked in a breath and pulled her other arm close to her body, nearly spilling the coffee. He started to get up, to help her, but she shook her head. "I'm fine."

"No, you're not."

She placed the cup on the scarred wooden table, filled it, and moving slowly, put the pot back. Instead of sitting across from him at the table, she picked up her own cup and leaned her back against the counter in front of the sink. The light was behind her and her face was now in shadow.

George shrugged and decided to concentrate on Jessie for the moment. He took a notebook out of a back pocket and put it on the table. "When does Jessie usually get home from work?"

"Well, since yesterday was Friday, she would've stopped at the bank to cash her check, so around 3:00."

"Jessie didn't say anything to you about goin' somewhere after work?"

"No, she didn't. Since she doesn't have class on Friday this semester, we usually go to the grocery after supper, and I'm sure she would've said if she wasn't going to be home to go with me."

"She have anyplace she might've wanted to go, stay overnight?"

"No. Jess doesn't have any real close friends, not the kind she'd want to spend the night with, anyway. She kind of keeps to herself."

"How about family? Anybody she'd go visit?"

"Only one lives far enough away would be Junior, everybody else lives close. Well, except for Mason, but he's in the Marines and he's in Afghanistan."

"She wouldn't have gone to see Junior?"

"Not without tellin' me. We go together every now and then. She's never gone by herself."

"Would she go to Junior if she was in some kind of trouble?"

"Jess?" Glenna said, shocked. "Jess isn't the kind that gets into trouble."

"But if she did, who'd she go to, do you think?"

"My brother, Harlan, I guess, after me," she said. "She'd come to me first."

"Last night, you said when you went out to get the car, it was gone. When was that exactly?"

"It hadn't started rainin' yet when we got out there."

"So, about seven?"

"Probably close to it. It was dark and when we got to the bridge, the rain started comin' down hard. I thought maybe we just missed seein' the car. You said it was on our

130

side of Coon Creek Bridge, but we didn't see it. I thought maybe it was off the road farther, so we drove over the bridge and turned around and came back. The only thing we saw was a truck pulled into the woods pretty good, a little ways before the bridge. I wanted to make another pass, but by then Tommy was aggravated and headed for home. Said Jess'd come back with the car when she was ready and he'd have a few things to say to her when she did."

"You ever see the truck before?"

"The truck?" she repeated, not expecting the question. "I don't think so."

"You remember what it looked like? Was it a pickup?"

"Yeah, a pickup, I think. Could have been an SUV. It was backed in and I could only see the front. It was black, I think, or dark blue. I didn't really notice. We were looking for the car."

"You see anybody around?"

"No. I would've noticed if there were, rainin' and hailin' like it was. Would've been odd to see somebody out walkin' in that."

"Anybody in the truck?"

She frowned for a minute, remembering. "No, I'm pretty sure. I don't remember seein' anybody in it. But I wasn't really lookin' at it and it was pretty far back in the trees."

"Jessie ever say anything about anybody bothering her? Anybody that made her nervous?"

"No, not really. There's this guy comes into Melba's all the time gives her the creeps. Keeps tryin' to flirt with her and gives her a hard time 'cause she won't go out with him."

"What's this guy's name, do you know?"

"She said his name was Earl Price."

"He ever approach her outside the diner?"

"Not that I know of. She saw him at the grocery once and went down a different aisle to keep him from seeing her. I asked who he was and she told me it was Earl Price. Said he came into Melba's and never ate anything but pie, and never tipped. Said she thought he just came in to aggravate her."

"When was that?"

"Not long ago. Maybe last weekend or the one before."

"She ever mention him again?"

"No."

"You ever get any hang-ups? Somebody call then hang up the phone when you answer?"

"No."

"She ever complain about anybody else bothering her?

"No."

"Jessie have a boyfriend?"

"No."

"An ex-boyfriend?"

"Not really. Nobody steady. She used to go out with the Durbin boy now and then, but he got married and moved to Spencer, two, maybe three years ago. And then she saw Josh Minton for a while maybe a year ago."

"She goes to school, right?"

"Up at the University. She's been goin' a long time, takes as many classes as she can and still work at the Diner. She'll finally be finished this May."

"She ever mention any other students she might have met?"

"No. She rides back and forth when she can with her cousin Kimmy. Kimmy might know some of them. Jess has study group too sometimes, but she never mentioned any of the other kids in particular."

"You think it's possible Tommy had anything to do with this?"

Surprised, she answered, "Oh, no. He was with my brother, Harlan, until around five when Harlan dropped him off at the house. Then he came in here and talked to me for a few minutes. The truck wasn't runnin', so he went out to tinker with that for a while before he got it started and then went out to run an errand. You were at the house tellin' me about the car before he got back."

"How long was he gone?"

"Half hour, maybe."

"He go anywhere from the time he got back 'til you went to get the car?"

"No, we ate dinner, then went right after, to get the car."

George paused for a moment, took a drink of coffee. "How bad did he hurt you this time?"

She looked down into her cup and replied, "I said I'm fine, Sheriff."

He waited, hoping she'd look up at him. What did he expect? She'd been covering up the abuse for years, never telling anyone, never, as far as he knew, going to the doctor or the ER. Why did he think after all these years, that she'd confide in him if she hadn't anyone else?

He took a breath and decided to push.

He crossed the room, took her chin and tilted it up so she couldn't hide the bruises. "You're not fine. You and I both know it was Tommy did that to you. It's time it stopped."

She pushed his hand away, then surprised him. "In all these years, no one ever asked me. No one ever asked me how I got those bruises. They'd just look and then look away, like I'd done somethin' shameful.

"Even if they asked," she admitted, "I wouldn't have said. I never filed charges before and I'm not gonna' this time either.

She went to the table and sat. "I tried to get away once, when the kids were still little. I took them and moved into a trailer with money I borrowed from Harlan, but he came after us. He said if I ever left again he'd kill my kids. He said he'd kill them all and make me watch and I knew he would if he was drunk and mad enough. Nothin's changed since then to make me think he wouldn't keep his promise. The boys may be gone, but Jess is still here, and now Junior's got kids.

"It didn't happen all the time, and it was mostly me he went after, late at night, when he'd come home drunk and pissed off at the world. I never knew what would set him off and sometimes, months would go by when he wouldn't do any more than holler and then pass out. When the kids got bigger, especially the boys, they'd get between me and Tommy, and then they'd get some of it, but even he wasn't any match for four teenaged boys." She smiled slightly. "So things seemed to calm down and I thought it was over."

"But it wasn't," George said.

"No, it wasn't. Once the boys left home and it was just me and Jess, it started again.

"I never went to the emergency room 'cause I was afraid they'd ask questions or call the police, and then they'd talk to Tommy and he'd think I told them."

She looked up at the wall straight ahead, not focusing on it, but on memories, seeing her past in bits and pieces. She drew in a slow breath. "A couple of years back, Mason, my second boy, was home on leave. We'd stayed up for a while, talkin' and I'd kept Tommy some dinner in the oven, but by eleven we were all tired, and Jess 'n me, we both get up early, so we put everything away and went to bed.

"We'd just gone up when Tommy came in. He started slammin' things around in the kitchen, knocked somethin' over or threw it, I never knew which, but anyway, I ran downstairs and when I came into the kitchen, he went after me.

"Next thing I know, Mason's got him by the back of his shirt and slings him around and out the back door. I could hear them out there on the porch, knockin' stuff over and swearin'. Jess 'n me, we ran out there in time to see Mason hit Tommy so hard he went through the porch rail. He knocked Tommy all over the yard, and I swear, Tommy never landed a punch. Then when Tommy went down and stayed down, Mason got in his face and said somethin' to him I couldn't hear. That was the last time Tommy did more 'n just shove me or Jess around now and again.

"That next day, Mason took me into town and bought me a gun. He showed me 'n Jess how to use it and made us practice. He said if ever Tommy came after one of us again, to use it.

"Except for practicin' with it and cleanin' it, it's been in one of the canisters on top of the refrigerator ever since. "I never really thought I'd be able to get up the nerve to use it. 'Til today."

"'Til today?" George asked, eyebrows raised. "You shoot Tommy, Glenna?"

She smiled a little at that and shook her head. "But he thought I would after I gave him a little warning shot right next to his ear."

"Melba told me a while back that Jessie came to work several times with bruises. You know anything about that?" he asked.

"He'd start in on me and Jess would try to pull him off, but it never did any good, and she'd just get bruised up too."

"But you don't think he did anything to Jess this time?"

"I don't see how he could've, or why he would've either."

"Where is he now?"

"Don't know for sure," she said and smiled a little again, "Made him pretty mad when I took a shot at him, so he didn't say where he was goin', but you might try Tat's. Tat's car's been actin' up and Tommy was s'posed to take a look at it today."

"I'm going to go into town, see if I can track down Dan Carlisle, one of the State detectives, get them involved." He took a second before he said, "You need a ride?"

She looked like she was about to refuse, but he said, "No sense you waiting out here by yourself when I'm going into town anyway."

When she just stood there, he said, "Go on now, get your purse."

He rinsed his coffee cup out and put it in the sink. He wanted to get Glenna out of the house so she wouldn't be here alone when Tommy came home. Give him some time to cool off. Most men would have the sense to be afraid of a woman armed with a loaded gun, but drunk enough, crazy enough, sometimes they just weren't.

CHAPTER THIRTY-FOUR

Dan had only gotten two hours sleep before he got called in for the massacre in Bradley. He'd worked the scene and questioned witnesses until after 3:00 a.m. and then had gone home and fallen into bed for a couple of hours. Back at the State Police Post at 7:00 a.m., he'd learned about the fire in the barn at the Riley place and the latest body, fourteen year old Elvie Morris if the ID found on the body could be trusted.

"Was it an accident?" he asked Rolly Ferguson, the detective who had been assigned to the case.

Rolly shrugged. "Who knows? Nothing obvious on the body. We got the kid's dentist's name so we can get records, but it's almost sure to be Elvie Morris. Nobody seems to know where he is. He wasn't in his bed this morning, which his mother said was unusual. Said most of the time they had to pry the kid out of bed with a crow bar. Once we've got positive ID, we'll talk to his friends. See what we can find out. See if they know why he was out there."

Dan went to the evidence processing unit and tracked down Ben Halsey, the unit supervisor. "What have you got so far?"

"According to the prints in the truck, your shooter's Jonas Aronson. Convicted of rape, attempted murder, criminal confinement about twelve years ago, nothing since. You ever heard of this guy?"

"Don't think so." Dan leaned in to look at the picture on Ben's computer screen. "Should I?"

"He's a person of interest on Homeland Security's list, and the print file has a warning and a notify FBI on it."

Dan frowned. "That's interesting." He looked more closely at the picture, but the man didn't look familiar. "What else you got?"

"We've just got started on the Blazer, but so far, we found some blood on the front and back seats and on the floor, O negative. According to the records, that's this

Aronson's type." Ben got up, went into the workroom, pulled on a pair of gloves and spread a black jacket across a metal table. "Got a black rain jacket, pretty pricey brand with a slice in the back, low on the left side, lots of blood, same type, O negative." He spread the fabric apart showing the cut and picked up a plastic bag with a knife in it. "Blood on the knife at the Ryerson scene is the same type as the blood from the truck and the jacket, and the blade width matches the slice in the jacket

"No bullets yet from the bodies, but we did get the bullet they took out of Neilson during surgery. Haven't run it yet, but should have something in an hour or two." He looked over his glasses at Dan. "He's hanging on by a thread, by the way. Dr. Melton took prints from the four DOA. He's sending those over now. That's it for now."

"How about the keys? They go to the Blazer?"

"Haven't tried them yet. Have to see if we can lift some prints first. I'll let you know."

Dan finished jotting down his notes, pulled the door open and nodded at Ben. "Thanks. Let me know when you get ballistics."

CHAPTER THIRTY-FIVE

Jessie opened her eyes. The lights in the cellar were still on and it was still quiet. She'd been dozing off and on, but hadn't heard any sign of movement. Her head still pounded and when she lifted it, the room tilted and made her stomach churn. She tried to ignore it and turned her head slowly to look at her watch: 8:45.

She listened intently, finally picking up the sound of soft snoring somewhere outside the enclosure. He was asleep, then, she thought as she laid her head back down and studied the underside of the workbench. It was sturdy. Solid. A thick slab of wood sitting on a base of four by four posts with cross members stabilizing it on the back and sides. The cords tying her wrists were looped around the front posts about six inches from the floor, and she saw that even though they were tight around the posts, they were just loose enough that she could work them back and forth. She grimaced with pain as she pulled the loop of cord tight against the raw skin of her wrist, then slid the cord on the post back and forth, working it down until it was close to the floor. She tried to slide it out from under the post, but her knuckles hit the dirt before she got the cord low enough. She tried gouging her knuckles into the dirt, but it was packed hard and by the time she gave up, she'd made a bloody mess of her hands and embedded the cord deeper into the flesh of her wrists.

Frustrated, she let herself go slack, staring up, trying to think of a way she could get the cord down further. Without the use of both hands, she couldn't do more than work it back and forth. The cord was nylon, too strong to break, and the wood of the leg was too smooth to fray it.

She turned her head and stared at the loop of cord, still about two inches from the floor. Staring at it didn't provide her with any inspiration, so she looked up again, studying the bottom of the slab of wood that made up the workbench table.

What if...she thought, as she brought her feet up to the front edge of the workbench. She slowly straightened her knees putting pressure on the workbench from below. She took a deep breath, braced herself and pushed harder, head pounding, legs trembling with the effort, and thought she felt the workbench tilt slightly.

She relaxed for a few seconds, then pushed again and saw a tiny gap between the bottom of the post and the floor. Suddenly, everything---the pain, the nausea, the cold and the damp, faded into the background as she pushed harder.

She heard a sound and realized that the snoring had stopped. She heard him moving around outside the enclosure. She'd figured it out too late, she thought, lowering her feet to the floor and going limp just as he opened the door.

≈≈≈

Aronson woke with his brain clouded by a dream about the girl. He remembered bits and pieces of it, flashes that surfaced, then, when he tried to pull it into focus, disappeared. He rarely dreamed, at least that he remembered, but he could still see black holes where her eyes should have been.

Probably the OxyContin he'd taken before he'd gone to sleep. Good shit for pain, but it messed with your head.

He threw the blanket off, carefully rolled onto his right side, put his weight on his right elbow and pushed himself into a sitting position. A quick check of the bandages showed that he'd bled just enough to soak through the gauze pads, but not much. He knew from experience that the pain would subside some when he got up and started moving around, so he forced himself to stand and stretch. He felt cold. Remnants of shock, he decided, since normally, he didn't notice being hot or cold, unless it was extreme. He pulled on a black tee shirt from the supply neatly folded on a footlocker next to the cot, then draped his blanket over his shoulders.

9:23 a.m., according to his watch. It was quiet in the cellar and he looked at the door to the wooden enclosure at the back, wondering for just a second if she was laying back there dead. When he threw the door open she didn't move, but he could see her breathing. Probably playing possum, he thought. He wasn't in any shape right this minute to fuck the willing much less the girl.

He logged onto the internet using his cell phone's Wi-Fi hot spot. Most people didn't realize that any computer connected to the internet, even if it was turned off, could be invaded. A cyber-invader could not only access your files, plant spyware that could record every keystroke or infect your computer with one of hundreds of viruses, but could activate the computer camera and get a look at your surroundings. Without his cell phone the computer was inaccessible from the outside.

He checked e-mail and the news services. He ate a couple of power bars. Not tasty, but it was nourishment.

Nothing yet on the date and time of the shipment.

Nothing about the girl either, but he hadn't expected anything. Most police jurisdictions wouldn't even consider a person missing for forty-eight hours.

He found a few reports of a multiple homicide in Bradley, but details were sketchy and there were no suspects.

He would check in with Stephanos and make sure all was quiet at the quarry, but if there had been, Stephanos would have let him know. He'd be surprised to have any at this juncture: the men had finished their preparations and now it was just a matter of waiting. It was the hurry up and wait all grunts in the military experienced. And, like in the military, none of the men, except Stephanos, knew what the job actually was. They knew their individual piece, but were never allowed to see the whole picture, and they were paid very, very well not to ask questions.

CHAPTER THIRTY-SIX

Major Adam Marsh sat in a Starbuck's at Indianapolis International Airport, waiting for his flight to Laredo to be called.

He was about to start a new life and at the same time, shitcan Colonel Dipshit Newell's career.

That was how this whole thing had gotten started.

He'd been lied to, embarrassed and humiliated when Newell had been promoted to Lieutenant Colonel and Marsh had been passed over for the third time.

His father was Chairman of the Senate Armed Services Committee for Christ sake. He'd engineered Marsh's promotion from First Lieutenant to Captain, from Captain to Major, and he'd been assured the right palms had been greased and favors called in for promotion to Lt. Colonel.

He knew everyone thought he'd only gotten where he was because of his father's influence. Well fuck 'em. He was who he was. If people didn't like it, tough. If George W. Bush could do it, why couldn't he?

Unfortunately, not even a month before the promotion was to have gone through, his father had been indicted for mail fraud and influence peddling.

When the announcement had been made of Newell's promotion, Marsh had been nearly insane with rage and hatred. The sly smiles and smirks pointed his way had made him sick with fury, and he'd wished that all of them, but especially Newell, would die, killed in a terrible way. He pictured himself, over and over, with a rifle to his shoulder, Newell's head exploding into red mist.

He'd been laughed at and talked about behind his back. He'd been forced to endure that cocky bastard Newell every day, having his nose rubbed in his father's disgrace.

He'd started having panic attacks, had been unable to sleep, unable to eat. Had laid in bed, night after night, filling the lonely darkness with plots for revenge. One night, a little idea formed.

Newell was an internet junkie. He was constantly on-line and talked about the things he bought or sold on eBay, Craig's list and a bunch of other sites no one had ever heard of.

Marsh had waited a couple of weeks, thinking it through before he began.

He'd paid cash for a used laptop and only used it at free Wi-Fi hot spots so the IP address wouldn't lead back to him. Marsh was proficient at buying on the internet, but it wasn't something he talked about since he frequented websites that catered to the darker side of human nature: S&M porn, rape porn, snuff films.

He'd set up accounts at a few chat rooms he knew of where just about anything could be bought or sold. He'd created email accounts in derivatives of Newell's wife's maiden name. He'd used a combination of Newell's birthdate and the high school he'd gone to as passwords. Marsh spent hours in the chat rooms, masquerading as Newell.

To make it believable, he needed to offer to sell something they actually had on site.

A few months ago, a shipment of the nerve agent VX had arrived at the base to be used in testing a new generation of chemical warning systems. When the testing was completed, his area would handle the transport of the remaining chemical to be neutralized. He'd decided "Newell" should try to find a buyer for it.

Marsh had put just enough information out so a knowledgeable person would know what was being offered, and it had worked.

After a fairly short period, cagey, nebulous correspondence had flowed back and forth.

He'd kept his responses vague, implying that he had another buyer, but the unknown, would-be, buyer had cut to the chase and named a price that made him gasp. On that day, Major Marsh had discovered two things. One: he had a price, and two: the unknown buyer was willing to pay it.

So here he was.

He'd been given a new identity as part of the deal. He'd land in Laredo as Adam Marsh, walk across the border into Nuevo Laredo, Mexico and disappear.

As he'd been instructed, he made sure the shipment would travel north, straight up State Road 37. All that was left to do was to send the date and time.

He'd been paid half of the money and the other half would be transferred to an offshore account when he sent the date and time of the shipment.

He'd downloaded a program that would wipe the computer he was using, and just to be sure, he'd take it with him and drop it in the first body of water he came to after he got off the plane.

His sweaty hand hovered over the keyboard. There was no going back. He hit send.

≈≈≈

When the informant's email came, Aronson felt a rush of adrenalin. "VX shipment going today 21:00. Agreed route."

Tonight!?!? Shit! The son of a bitch was supposed to notify them three days ahead of time. Now they only had a little more than eleven hours to get everything in place.

He got Stephanos on his cell. "Tonight. Twenty-one hundred."

Stephanos had the same reaction he'd had. "Tonight?! You gotta' be fuckin' kidding me!"

"I'll be there in half an hour, forty-five minutes at the most."

He glanced at the room where the girl was. He'd expected at least three days before the strike, time he would've spent enjoying the girl's company.

He had to go out, wrap up some loose ends with Stephanos and give the men final instructions, but there was no reason, once everything had been set in motion, for him to wait at the quarry until twenty-one hundred. He could just as easily spend the four or five hours he'd have with the girl. He wouldn't have as much time as he would have liked, but beggars can't be choosers.

CHAPTER THIRTY-SEVEN

Dan listened to the phone ring at the other end of the line. It was only 7:45 a.m. in D.C., but he knew Sammy would've been awake for hours. Sammy'd been a Navy Seal, in the same class as Dan, and they'd served together for nearly all of their eight years in the service.

When he got out, Dan had wanted to go back to his home town, work in law enforcement, get married and have about a half dozen kids. He'd taken a job with the State Police that would let him do all of those things, while Sammy, who had had no ties to anyone and had planned on devoting his life to his career, had joined the FBI.

Strangely enough, Sammy'd ended up with a house in the country, a beautiful wife and four great kids, while Dan's fiancé had broken up with him and married a used car salesman.

Dan asked about Pam and the kids, said for the hundredth time that they needed to get together soon, then asked, "You ever heard of Jonas Aronson?"

There was a pause. "Maybe. Why?"

"He left his prints all over a truck at the scene of a quadruple homicide. When we ran them, we got a hit on IFIS that had red lights flashing all the way to D.C. Who the hell is he?"

"I know the name, but I'll have to do some digging for more than that. Can I call you back?"

"Sure."

"How soon you need it? Marcus has football practice in fifteen minutes and we're already going to be late."

"Get it to me as soon as you can, and tell Pam I said hi."

≈≈≈

Sammy called Dan back less than two hours later.

"Okay. Aronson's ex-army. Captain in Special Ops, ran one of the most ruthless search and destroy teams they've ever had. Skated pretty close to the line, but he got the job done, so the brass just looked the other way and left him and his team pretty much alone.

"There were rumors about some rough stuff with women, and then he got himself in some hot water in Columbia when a woman accused him of raping her. He'd tied her up and beat her pretty bad, but he got out of the country before they could throw his ass in a cell. The girl turned up dead, cut to pieces, about six months later when Aronson was allegedly in Chile.

"Then a woman was raped, stabbed and left for dead in a condo in San Diego. He'd been careful about the security cameras in the common area of the complex: kept his head down, had a hat on, and there wasn't any way to ID him from those tapes, but he hadn't managed to kill the woman, even though he strangled her and stabbed her more than a dozen times. She gave them the make, model and color of the car, and they got the plate number from the security cameras at the complex entrance.

"He served eleven years in the Federal pen. When he got out, he disappeared off everybody's radar. Then about a year ago, we got some intel linking him to The Righteous Voice. Likens, the guy that runs that group is about as big a zealot as you'll find anywhere. He and another man, Walters, have got lots of money, access to more, and a militia with some pretty scary characters.

"There isn't any proof, but we think that Likens and some of his militia members are responsible for the burnings of several abortion clinics, and for the bombing at the gay rights rally last summer.

"Anyway, Aronson made a lot of threats when he was convicted, not only against the woman he'd raped, but against the Army for prosecuting the charges against him, his JAG attorney for not getting him off, you name it. He's pissed off and dangerous. I know a lot of guys make threats and never follow through, but the woman who testified against him was tortured, killed and beheaded about two weeks after he got out of prison. Couple days later, somebody took a knife to the attorney who represented him. Damn near sliced his head off."

"Jesus." Dan shrugged to relieve some of the tension that had gathered in his neck. "Why is he here?"

"We don't know. Explosives are his specialty. If we go by his record, he's planning on blowing something up. Crane's the only thing in the area that might be of interest to someone like him, but they don't have any of the really scary shit like VX or GB there anymore. All that went to Newport and they got rid of it. They've got lots of munitions, but security's so tight, they can detect a mouse fart at 300 yards."

Dan filled him in with what he knew about the killings in Bradley and Sammy asked, "Think the guys who jumped him were targeting him specifically?"

"Possible, I guess, but not likely. The guys he took out were local thugs, not very bright from their rap sheets and what we've learned about them so far. Witness says it looked like an opportunistic robbery."

"Well, Aronson is about the last guy you'd want to back into a corner. Somebody stuck a knife in him though, must be hurt. Anybody see him after?"

"Yeah, one woman saw him, said he didn't move like he was hurt, but there was a lot of blood in the truck and on a jacket."

"Well, that's not surprising, I suppose. Wouldn't act hurt unless it was bad, I mean really bad. Little knife stick, unless it hit a vital organ, wouldn't slow someone like him down,"

"He was on foot and ran between two houses. Nobody saw him after that."

"Probably stole a car."

"Probably. We'll keep on top of stolen vehicle reports, but by now, he's holed up somewhere. We've notified hospitals, clinics in the area, but the last place a guy like him would go is the E.R."

"Listen, Dan," Sammy said after a pause. "You know the drill on something like this."

"If you're saying what I think you're saying, forget it."

"You can't pursue this. You can't pursue him," Sammy responded. "We both know FBI will have agents at your office today, tomorrow at the latest. They'll take possession of your files, your evidence and even your notes, and that'll be it for your involvement. They'll want you to leave him strictly alone while they pursue an investigation into his activities, and you'll do it, or end up in jail." He paused again, waiting for Dan to interrupt.

Dan held kept his mouth shut because he knew to argue was pointless.

Sammy went on, "You're going to have trouble making any serious charges stick anyway when both your witnesses say he got jumped."

"How do we know he's in the area on business?" Dan asked. "Even somebody like Aronson has to live somewhere."

"Just coincidentally within a few miles of Crane? You don't believe that horseshit any more than I do.

≈≈≈

Dan loved Melba's. It was one of the first places he'd gone when he'd been discharged from the Navy.

He and his mom had moved to Indianapolis when he was fifteen, but he'd been born in Brewer, where his Dad had owned the one and only Chevy dealership.

Melba's was a childhood memory that hadn't changed in any way. So many times, places you remembered from when you were young were bigger, smaller, brighter, darker or just different and going back was a disappointment. Not Melba's. It was just the same and for a reason he couldn't name, it was comforting to go there.

Instead of the usual flirtation Dan usually had to endure from Marybeth, she was subdued, with a worried frown creasing her forehead. She looked like she might burst into tears at any second.

"You okay, Marybeth?"

She nodded and sniffed. "It's Jessie. You know, the other waitress? Her daddy came in this morning, said she didn't come home from work last night and Sheriff found her car out on Patterson Road with her purse and all her money and everything still in it."

Dan felt like he was in a bad movie with people dying or disappearing all over the damn place. He thought about the last time he'd seen Jessie, just yesterday, here in the diner. She'd been the same as always, working her section, taking care of him and her other customers.

He'd heard Jessie described as "shy," but he didn't really think she was. She made eye contact, frank and straightforward, not the awkward, ducking glance of a shy person, and now and then, he caught a flash of amusement in her eyes.

It was just her way of keeping people at a distance and he couldn't blame her. She'd gone through school and lived most of her life with people distancing themselves from her; not surprising that as an adult, she would do the same to them.

He couldn't say he knew her well, probably few people did, but he liked coming into the diner and having a snippet of conversation with her. He remembered her from when she was bussing tables: a skinny, skittish kid, slipping from table to table. She'd come a long way and he found her present composure and quiet efficiency endearing.

He had to admit that he also enjoyed watching her because she was an attractive woman. Not that she dressed that way: black shorts, not tight, that ended about four inches above her knees, and a white, cotton, button down shirt. Her hair was always brushed back into a ponytail or a long braid down her back. Even with clothes that could have doubled for a Catholic school uniform, his weren't the only male eyes that followed her around the diner.

CHAPTER THIRTY-EIGHT

Jessie laid still and tried to slow her breathing when the man opened the door to her cell. After several seconds, he slammed it shut without coming in.

She could hear him moving around outside her cell and then typing on the computer. After a while, she heard him say "Son of a bitch." Then a few minutes later she heard him say "Tonight. Twenty-one hundred." He talked some more, typed some more, then she heard the printer going, and a few minutes later, she heard him go up the steps. The lights went off, the door closed, and she heard the upstairs floor creaking as he walked across it. Then it was quiet.

As soon as she heard the door upstairs close, she braced her feet against the underside of the bench, took a deep breath, and pushed. She felt the bench tilt, but couldn't see if the legs were off the floor with the lights out. She relaxed her legs and put her feet back on the floor, then squirmed back toward the bench and to one side until she could feel the end of one leg with her fingertips. She pushed on the underside of the bench and felt the leg move, but only about a quarter of an inch, not enough to allow her to slide the cord down and under. She pushed harder and the bench tilted a little more, but then the back edge hit the cellar wall; there was just no room for the bench to tilt backwards far enough.

She rested for a few minutes, panting with exertion and tried to ignore the pain pounding in her head. Maybe, she thought, if she centered her feet in the middle, she could lift the whole bench far enough to get loose. She scooted forward until she could position her feet directly above her hips, where she could exert the most pressure. She pushed again and felt the bench break loose and begin wobbling when all four legs were off the floor. She straightened her knees, getting the bench as far off the ground as possible, and began working the cords back and forth, but couldn't keep the bench off the floor long enough. When she'd held on as long as she could, she brought her feet forward, stiff legged, hoping the table would tip over away from the wall. It didn't.

She moved so that her fingers touched the bottom of one of the front legs and positioned her feet at the front edge of the bench again as she had to begin with. The bench tilted backward, but instead of stopping, kept going until there was a gap big enough to get the cord under. She realized that while she hadn't been able tip it over she'd managed to move the bench away from the wall.

In just a few seconds, she was free!!

She wanted to run, to dart outside the cubicle and start doing whatever she had to do to get out of there, but sitting up too fast made the room spin and brought on a wave of nausea that caused her stomach to heave.

She wasn't ever going to get away if she couldn't even stand up, she thought, so she stayed where she was until she felt steadier, and moved to her hands and knees. As long as she moved very slowly and held her head still, she could keep the vertigo from getting so bad she'd fall down or throw up.

She got to her knees and then cautiously to her feet, holding onto the wall until the room settled and the worst of the dizziness had passed. She took a shaky breath and began edging along the wall. She felt her way to the door of the cubicle. It wasn't latched and she pushed it open.

Outside the enclosure, four small television screens cast a blue glow over most of the cellar floor, making it easier for her to negotiate her way to the stairs. She stumbled several times and tripped on the bottom steps, but made it to the top where she put her ear to the door and listened. Nothing. She thought about trying the knob, but what if he was still up there? She decided to swallow her impatience and wait, making herself sit through ten minutes of one-one-thousand, two-one thousand, three-one-thousand, all the while listening intently for any movement on the other side of the door.

She put her hand on the knob and twisted gently: it turned but the door didn't open. She turned it again and pushed harder, but the door stayed closed. It was locked with a dead bolt from the outside.

CHAPTER THIRTY-NINE

Dan was nearly finished with his breakfast when George Farber came into the diner with Glenna.

When George and Glenna came through the door, conversation stopped, the noise level muted as though the volume knob had been turned down on a radio.

George murmured something to Glenna, and after looking around uncertainly for just a few seconds she continued through the diner, behind the counter and into the kitchen.

George stopped beside Dan's table. "Hoping I'd find you here. Mind if I sit?"

Dan gestured to the opposite seat with his coffee cup. "Help yourself."

George slid across the seat. "You hear about the Morris kid?"

Dan nodded. "Hell of a thing. No positive I.D. yet, so we're trying to keep it quiet, but you know how it is."

They were both quiet a moment, then Dan leaned in, elbows on the table. "I was about to call you about Jessie DuBois." He took another swallow of tepid coffee. "Hear you found her car and purse out on Patterson road yesterday."

George nodded and Dan gestured toward the waitress talking to a customer at a table across the room. "Marybeth told me. Still no sign of her?"

George shook his head and told Dan everything that had occurred the night before starting with finding the car on Patterson Road. "I ran out to Mrs. DuBois' house this morning, just to check. Never really thought she wouldn't be there, but it was on my mind and I knew it'd bug me if I didn't follow up. Expected to see the Chevy sitting by the house, but it's still missing and Jessie hasn't come home."

Melba came out of the kitchen with Glenna, slapped a pad of paper down on one of the tables near the counter and sat down with her.

Dan's eyes narrowed as he studied Jessie's mother. "Not to change the subject, but what the hell happened to her?"

George frowned, rubbing his forehead. "Tommy DuBois beat the crap out of her. Again. I only heard rumors about it, never saw for myself 'til I went out there this morning."

Dan started to say something, but George interrupted, "No, she won't press charges. I already tried." He shrugged. "He threatened to hurt the kids."

"But they're all grown now, aren't they?"

"Yeah, but Jessie still lives at home and Glenna's got grandkids."

He'd been staring at Glenna while he spoke, but returned his attention to Dan. "I've got a little something in the back of my mind that might get Tommy DuBois some jail time without bringing Glenna or the kids into it."

Dan raised an eyebrow. "Is it legal?"

George gave him a look. "'Course it's legal. Sneaky, but legal."

Dan nodded and returned to their original conversation. "I'll have a talk with the Lieutenant. It'll be his call whether we hand Jessie's disappearance off to Missing Persons or keep it. It would normally go through their department before it would come to us."

George nodded. "The car was just left there with no one around, then later was gone with the driver not showing up where she's supposed to. That's not a good sign, but when you add in the fact that her purse was in the car, with a week's pay in cash, makes it a lot more than that."

Dan agreed. "Even if she took off on her own, which I don't really believe, leaving her purse there like that would mean that she left with no money and no I.D.

"I'll go on over to the post right now, talk to the Lieutenant." Dan counted out bills and laid them on top of the check and both men headed toward the door. "I'll let you know."

CHAPTER FORTY

Chastain parked his truck behind a deserted silo, a two minute jog from the quarry. Aronson was nowhere in sight but the truck he'd stolen was parked inside the fence near the construction trailer. Chastain held another GPS transmitter in his hand, one he'd buried inside a large gum eraser. He gauged the weight of the eraser and the distance to the truck, then lobbed it over hand where it arced over the tall fence and landed with a tiny thunk in the bed of the truck. It would do until he could arrange something more permanent.

On the other side of the quarry, he climbed an outcropping of rock then moved into the same spot from which he'd watched for most of the last five months. He'd permanently embedded a post, about the size of a pencil, in a crack in the stone above the quarry and had attached a small camera, capable of remote positioning up to several hundred feet away. A directional eavesdropping device was on its own stanchion. He monitored the movements inside the quarry on a small screen and had an ear bud which just got him a word here and there over the sound of the equipment and static. He'd thought about planting a few bugs around, but the background noise level inside the quarry was so high that it would be almost pointless, and Aronson or one of his men might find a bug.

From the dirt trapped in a crevice of the stone where he perched, a small tree continued its precarious hold and provided welcome shade and cover. From this vantage point, he could see two thirds of the operation and so far, all he'd seen was what looked like a bunch of men working a quarry: blasting, drilling, heavy equipment trundling back and forth, a crane lifting slabs of limestone, a sound that, until these men came, hadn't been heard in this pit for more than sixty years.

The quarry was known to the locals as Bronson's south pit, still owned by Bronson Stone Co., but closed in the mid-1950's when the accessible stone had been exhausted.

It was here Aronson spent much of his time and from Chastain's examination of the site in the dead of night, after the workers had stopped for the day, they were certainly digging, and appeared to be operating the quarry as a quarry.

Chastain had searched the old rusted construction trailer sitting just inside the fence, but had found nothing more than you'd expect to find: beat up hard hats, thick leather gloves, picks and sledges, rolled up charts, and a large first aid kit; everything covered in a fine layer of dust. A battered computer sitting on a worktable had been innocent of even slightly incriminating data, only containing geological charts and graphs, soil and rock analyses, time-keeping reports and supply requisitions. At the rear of the trailer, a smallish safe was bolted to the floor. Chastain had opened the dial lock easily, but all he'd found inside was dynamite and blasting caps, the quantity and grade what you'd expect to find in the operation of a quarry. No modern day explosives, no weapons, nothing of interest.

The equipment used in the quarry itself was nothing out of the ordinary either: huge cranes, power awls, and earthmovers, not new, but functional. He'd found no munitions of any kind.

So far he'd been unable to figure out what Aronson was up to. The most unusual thing he'd discovered was that the workers, including the foreman, a muscular giant named Stephanos, were housed on site, using a large modified pole barn as their quarters.

An agent posing as a reporter doing an article on the reopening of the pit had questioned Phillip Bronson, the current owner. About six months ago, a corporation named Kreftcon International had leased the site for a year. A derelict church in Philadelphia which had been built using stone from Bronson's south pit, had been purchased by Kreftcon and was scheduled to be renovated. Several damaged exterior stone facings were going to be replaced and Kreftcon had leased the pit so that stone exactly matching the original could be quarried.

Bronson, a crusty, plain-speaking, seventy-two year old, had agreed that technological advances made it possible to extract useable stone from a previously closed pit, but he'd made it clear that he thought the lengths to which the company was willing to go to get stone from the original pit was a ridiculous waste of money. "We got an open quarry 'bout three miles from the south pit that would match what came out of there as close as you could get at this point, at least in color, texture and markings. Only stone's really going to match would have to come from another building in the same environment for the same amount of time," he'd said. "If that stone went up in the 1800's, it's gonna' be discolored. Back then, coal was what was used for heat and electricity and it wasn't "clean" coal, either. That was before the EPA and pollution filters and so on. Air was full of smoke and the smoke was full of acid and you can only do so much with sandblasting. Stone like that, exposed to more than 100 years of pollution and the elements isn't going to look the same as stone fresh out of the ground, even if it did come out of the same hole.

"Lot of foolishness if you ask me, and I'd tell this company that someone's giving them some bad information, but nobody asked me. They want to pay us to lease a pit that hasn't earned the company a dime in sixty years, it's fine with me.

"Now somethin' I wasn't too happy about, and they didn't bother to tell me either, was that this Kreftkon's got some program to rehabilitate ex-cons, so what they've got out at the south pit is a bunch of jailbirds."

The agency had checked and Kreftcon had purchased a church, but no work was being done on it, and how they knew where the stone had come from was a little cloudy.

Kreftcon was buried under so many layers of corporate blinds and shell companies that the real owners hadn't yet been identified, but they were nearly certain the end of the trail would lead them to The Righteous Voice. Chastain expected one of the desk jockeys at the Bureau to unravel the tangle of corporate ownership at any time, but it really wouldn't mean a whole lot to him out here in the field. Knowing where the money was coming from was helpful in figuring out the why, the laying of blame and identification of possible end targets, but it didn't help much with the how.

Chastain focused on one of the backhoes as it growled its way across the quarry floor. It appeared to be business as usual: men shifting tons of dirt and small rock, moving around inside the quarry, tending to the business of digging and excavating the limestone for which the area was famous.

The door of the trailer opened and Aronson and Stephanos came out, walking purposefully to an open area. Chastain was surprised at how easily Aronson moved and studied him carefully for any sign of pain or guarding of his side, but there was none. He'd gotten stabbed last night. Chastain had seen it with his own eyes, but he seemed to be moving without restraint, just as he always did.

Chastain jumped and winced when Stephanos emitted an ear-splitting whistle, amplified and delivered directly into his ear. The whistle was picked up and passed on across the quarry. While the heavy equipment still growled at idle, the three dozen or so workers gathered in a tight knot around Aronson and Stephanos.

CHAPTER FORTY-ONE

The door didn't budge. She'd turned on the lights and saw that there was a deadbolt about two feet above the doorknob, with no way to open it except with a key.

Jessie sat on the top step, so close to freedom, and tried not to scream her rage and frustration.

She'd stood a chance of getting away with him gone, but in the shape she was in, there was no way she could overpower him, or outrun him, probably couldn't have anyway, even without being about to fall down or puke any second.

She couldn't waste any more time with the door. She didn't know when he'd be back. If there was another way out of here, she'd better get off her ass and find it.

She checked for windows, but the few there were had been bricked up. The coal chute door was just as immovable as the upstairs door had been. She was pretty sure there weren't any openings in the cubicle he'd had her in, but she checked anyway, then moved on to the one next to it. It was lined with shelves and on them were several dusty jars of some kind of food someone had canned a long time ago. There had been a window in this cubicle, but it was bricked up like the rest.

She moved on to a door in the wall next to the cubicle. It was new and made of metal like the one at the top of the stairs, but this one wasn't locked. A large generator sat inside. She looked to make sure the room didn't have windows or any other way out and closed the door.

She looked at her watch. Almost eleven. She hadn't checked what time he left, but she thought he'd been gone for about a half hour.

Anxiety overwhelmed her. She should be moving, doing something to get out of here. She needed to go. She needed to be gone. She needed to think, not just stand in the middle of the floor.

What she needed was a gun.

He'd had a gun last night. He'd almost shot Lyle with it. Had he taken it with him? He was obviously a criminal. Maybe he had more than one.

She started searching the long sturdy table set up in the center of the open area. It held a lot of rolled up papers, a map with the shading and measurements she recognized as geological charting taped at one end, and the most beautiful computer she'd ever seen, but no gun.

She moved the computer mouse and the screen lit up, but it was password protected. She could've gotten in, but it would take time, and the most important thing right now was to find a way out of here before he came back; or a way to hurt him bad enough that she could get away.

She moved on to his cot: canvas over a metal frame with no mattress to hide a gun under. She shook out the blanket, neatly folded at the foot, and draped it over her shoulders.

She turned carefully, scanning as she did; there was no gun in plain sight. She went around the room, all the time knowing the clock was ticking, expecting that she'd hear his footsteps over her head any second.

She went over to the shelves against the wall and looked at the four little black and white TV's, two on one shelf, two on the next shelf down, with pictures of the outdoors, sweeping silently to the right, stopping and sweeping back to the left. Like at Wal-Mart, she thought: the screens from the security cameras in the parking lot that nobody ever paid attention to. She stared at the screens, seeing mostly woods and a big barn, the kind you saw all over the place out in the country: the wood grey from years of sun and rain, sunken holes in the roof, any paint that had been applied in years past, long gone. Was that the barn he'd parked in last night? She looked closer. It could be. And if that was the barn, then what she was seeing was the outside of where she was. And if that was so, she'd know when he came back before she heard him upstairs. She'd have some warning.

She went back to searching the cellar, keeping an anxious eye on the monitors. Two stacks of large metal footlockers, four in each stack, sat against the wall opposite the television screens with a few smaller ones stacked on top. She tugged on each padlock in turn, but all were fastened tight.

After a half hour of uneasy searching, she decided there was no gun. She'd been so relieved at the thought of a gun. A gun would've meant she could keep her distance, not have to get near enough for him to overpower her. But she didn't have a gun, so she'd have to make do with what she did have.

She had surprise on her side. That was something. A big something.

With all this stuff down here, surely she could find something to hit him with. She needed something that would hurt him bad enough that when he went down he wouldn't get up again.

Broken down boxes and other junk had been piled in a corner in the front. She tried to pull a metal kitchen chair apart, but there were just enough rusty screws left to hold it together. Next, she focused on a heavy old rocker with the seat gone. Looking at it from the back, Jessie could see that on either side, a single thick piece of wood ran from the top of the chair all the way down to where the rocker had been attached. She grabbed the bottom of the piece and started working it back and forth until the wood pulled away from the seat frame, then the arm, and then the back. She swung it like a baseball bat, imagining how it would feel when it made contact with his head. It felt good and solid in her hands. She liked the length, wanting to put as much distance between him and her as possible, but if she was going to hit him at the door, before he had a chance to defend himself, she'd have to confront him at the top of the steps, which didn't give her much room.

She put her makeshift club on the steps, then moved on to look through the boxes tucked underneath. They were labeled, and Jessie didn't think "curtains" or "books" would help her much, but she pulled out a box and took off the lid. The box was full of old china, fragile and delicate. If a box that said "books" didn't have books in it, she thought, it stood to reason the other boxes mightn't have in them what was written on the outside. She drug them out, one at a time, far enough that she could root through them and still see the monitors, but found nothing more dangerous than a flimsy curtain rod.

She went over to the bottom of the steps and looked up, playing through what would happen when he got back. At the top of the steps, there was a small landing about three feet by three feet, where she could stand, piece of wood over her shoulder like a baseball bat, but she wouldn't be able to swing nearly hard enough to really hurt him.

She could hide under the stairs, she thought, wait for him to get to the bottom, then come out and hit him, but she'd have to move fast, without making any noise, and she just didn't think she could do it and be sure that she wouldn't stumble or lose her balance. Maybe it would be better to wait in the cell where she'd been tied up, stand beside the door, and when he opened it, swing at him. But if she did that, he'd see the boxes pulled out and other stuff she'd moved as soon as he came down the steps and he'd know she was loose somewhere down there. Even if she tried to return everything back to where it had been, he'd probably see something out of place, giving him just a second of warning, and for him that would probably be enough.

She was only going to get one chance and she'd better get it right.

She needed to try it, see if it would work, but hesitated. At the top of the steps, she couldn't see the monitors.

She stood facing the door, one step below the landing and brought the club up over her head so that she could bring it straight down. The club hit the door about four inches down from the top without hitting anything else first.

Okay, then, that's how she'd do it. It wasn't great, but it was all she had. She took a few practice swings, and satisfied with her plan, went back down into the cellar.

The footlocker next to his cot had clean blankets, a few toiletries and some clothes, including black sweat pants and three unopened packages of extra-large, black, long sleeved tee shirts. She kept a close eye on the monitors while she used one package of shirts with a bottle of water to clean herself up some. After that, she pulled on the sweatpants and several of the t-shirts, covering herself from her neck to her feet.

They were just cloth, just cotton fabric, but putting them on made her feel less defenseless, somehow.

She rooted around some more and came up with three pairs of heavy socks that she put on her cold feet, one pair over the other. She was too nauseated to try eating anything, but she took another bottle of water from his supplies and sipped at it carefully.

One side of her face felt stiff where the blood had dried, and her eye was swollen almost shut. She wet another tee shirt with water and used it to soak off as much of the blood as she could. The teeth marks he'd made in her shoulder were an ugly mottled purple, the impressions deep and ugly.

She knew what she'd already experienced was just the beginning and if she didn't get away from him, it was going get a whole lot worse.

A large metal case with a big red cross on the front had gauze and tape and bandages. There was a pair of small scissors in the kit and she used them to cut the cords that were still looped around her wrists, gritting her teeth when she pulled them free where they had embedded themselves in her flesh. Nestled in with the rest was a plastic container with packets of drugs of all kinds, from antacids to cough syrup to aspirin. There were also small bottles of pain pills, including Vicodin and OxyContin. She longed for just an hour, a few minutes even, without the vicious pounding in her head. She snatched one of the bottles out of the box and shook two Vicodin into the palm of her hand, then paused. The drugs would cloud her thinking and probably make her nausea worse. She stared at the pills for a moment longer, then reluctantly put them back in the bottle and the bottle in the pocket of the sweatpants she wore.

She continued her search and found a packet labeled "Phenergan" which said "take one tablet every four hours as needed for nausea." If she could get that under control, she'd be able to move around a lot easier, maybe get some food down, but she didn't know what the side effects were, and didn't want to take something that might knock her out cold.

She tore the packet open, broke one of the two pills inside in half, broke one of the halves in two and downed the quarter pill with a sip of water.

If it helped the sickness and didn't make her loopy, she'd take the other quarter in a little while.

She sat down in front of the computer again. This was something she was good at. Really, really good. The computer was password protected, but she got in without too much trouble.

There was no phone line and no wireless service available. She thought he must use his cell to pull in a signal, so there was no way to send an email.

She didn't know where she was, couldn't have counted on getting help, but she could've at least sent something out that would've gotten back to her momma, let her know she was alive, at least for now. She could've described the man and the truck he drove, where she'd been when he'd taken her, although Lyle should've already told them all that.

The computer might tell her something about the man, she thought. If she got away and he took off, how would they find him? She didn't even know his name. He had to have another home somewhere. This house wasn't his home. Nobody with the kind of money he had tied up in this computer really lived in the cellar of an abandoned farmhouse.

She began looking through his computer files hoping she might find something with his name, maybe his real address. His e-mail in-box was empty and there weren't any letters or papers, aside from charts and graphs, things like that. There were complicated diagrams of valves and cylinders, the pieces blown apart and then labeled with dotted lines showing where each part had come from. There were architectural drawings of three buildings, one with a big oval in the center, cut into four sections, marked "A," "B," "C" and "D." Each of the four quadrants then had its own drawing, sliced into four pieces. Quadrant "A" was divided into sections "A-1," "A-2," "A-3" and so on, and each of those had its own complex blueprint, showing a maze of water piping, sewer lines and gas lines, each one measured and labeled. There was a similar break down for all the sections, down to "D-4," sixteen of them in all.

Aside from knowing that they were drawings and blue prints, studying them didn't tell her much, so she moved on to a folder marked "Walters Meetings," and several digital files, all labeled with a date appeared. She opened one at random and hit "play."

A pool of light appeared with a small table in the center and there was talking in the background. Footsteps came closer, then the sound of a chair scooting back. An older man walked into view and sat down at a chair next to the table. Another figure blocked the camera for just a second or two and sat, back to the camera, taking a seat almost out of the frame to the left.

The hair on the back of her neck stood up and she broke into a cold sweat when she heard the man who'd taken her start talking. For a few seconds, she was frozen, not listening to the words, just the voice, and all she could think about was the man, what he'd done to her, what he might do to her if she didn't get away.

Then she made herself listen. It was hard to follow, like a conversation they'd picked up after being interrupted for a minute or two.

She went cold, then hot all over when the man facing the camera, Walters, she guessed, asked if their source had determined how much they would have. The man had answered that it was plenty to kill the target group and thousands more. By the time anyone knew what had happened, it would be too late.

She was stunned and after the second or two it took her to realize what she'd just heard, she hit rewind and played the section again. She was sure she'd misunderstood and leaned in, but as they talked, there wasn't any doubt: they were talking about killing people.

Near the end of the recording, the older man nodded at someone Jessie couldn't see, then another man came into the picture carrying a large suitcase he put on the table. The suitcase was opened and the man who had taken her, still with his back to the camera, stood up, completely blocking her view. The two men talked a few minutes longer, then both walked out of camera range. The third man picked the suitcase up off the table and walked out of range too. She heard muffled talking and a door close, then footsteps, and the screen went black.

She sat there without moving, staring at the screen, trying to make herself believe what she'd just seen and heard.

She backed the recording up, froze a frame and looked at the older man closely. He didn't look like a monster. Balding and a little on the plump side, he looked like somebody's favorite uncle, or an insurance salesman. Not like a murderer.

The date on the file was about a month ago and they'd mentioned that Phase One would go down in about four weeks. She wondered if it had already happened, then decided that it couldn't have. An attack like they were talking about, she would have heard something about it.

If she had anything to say about it, the bastards wouldn't get away with it. She searched over the table for a USB drive, but couldn't find one. A canister of new CD's sat next to the printer. She put one in the disc drive and began downloading. She'd get the digital recordings first, then every other file on his computer.

Her mouth was a little dry and she was a little drowsy, probably from the medicine she'd taken, but when she stood up, although the room still shifted, the nausea was better. She thought about which problem would cause her the most trouble trying to get away and decided to take the other quarter of the pill. What good was it going to do her to whack him over the head if she was too sick to run?

While she waited for the files to download, she paced, slowly at first, then a little faster, ignoring her aches and pains, the way the room shifted when she turned. She stopped and stretched, forcing herself to pull the kinks and knots out of bruised muscles, getting the blood going. She kept moving but was getting sleepier, and it was getting harder to ignore the pounding in her head.

She wasn't hungry, but pulled two power bars out of one of the boxes and sat down on his cot. When he came back, she'd need all her strength and concentration, so she sipped her bottle of water and in tiny bits, slowly choked the energy bars down.

She resisted the urge to lie down; she couldn't afford to rest and stiffen up, or worse, run the risk of falling asleep.

She shivered and reached down to feel blindly for the blanket she'd dropped. Instead, her hand hit something bulky and hard. She lowered herself to the floor to take a look and slid a black bag out from under the cot.

Whatever was in it was packed tight, straining the zipper, and it was heavy. She grabbed the zipper pull and worked it across the bag, then knelt there, staring at more money than she'd ever seen in her whole life. She got to her feet and struggled to heft the bag up on the table, staring hard at the cash as though she expected it to disappear. She kept an eye on the monitors as she pulled a bound stack of worn one hundred dollar bills out and counted them. There were one hundred of them. Ten thousand dollars in one stack. She began pulling the bound stacks out of the bag, counting as she went, and when they were all lined up on the table, she couldn't take her eyes off them.

One million dollars.

She didn't notice the empty bag sliding off the table, until the hard object still inside landed painfully on her foot. She felt around on the floor for the bag, lifted it back onto the table and opened the zipper to see what was in the side pocket. She broke eye contact with the money on the table long enough to look inside.

It was a gun.

CHAPTER FORTY-TWO

The Lieutenant had given Dan the go ahead on the DuBois missing person case. Crime scene techs had scoured the area where the car had been sitting and had come up with nothing. The heavy rain from the night before had washed away any foot prints or tire treads they might've found, and the creek had risen, overflowing its banks long enough to deposit trash, tree branches and other debris in the vegetation on its banks. A pair of women's underwear had been snagged on a branch downstream. They would show them to Mrs. DuBois, at least see if they were the missing girl's, but any DNA evidence would have been washed away.

A description of the car had been issued to every law enforcement agency in the state, but so far, no one had seen it.

The only prints they'd picked up from Jessie's purse had been on the handle and the wallet. They'd belonged to Mrs. DuBois and George Farber, which they'd expected, and Tommy DuBois, which they hadn't.

There was no money in the wallet and with DuBois' fingerprints on it, it was pretty clear that her father had stolen the girl's money.

The dirty bastard, Dan thought. His daughter's missing, might be dead for all he knew, so he'd gotten in her purse and stolen her money. What a prick.

He hoped whatever plan George Farber had in mind for Tommy DuBois worked and he hoped he was put in a cell with the biggest, meanest son of a bitch in the county.

Dan left Patterson Road and headed to Melba's. The lack of evidence was frustrating and he hoped questioning her co-workers might lead to something.

It was after eleven and Jessie hadn't been seen, as far as he knew, since around five p.m. yesterday. Eighteen hours and no sign of her, no sign of the car. He reminded himself that even though he didn't think so, and no one he'd talked to thought so, there was still a chance she'd just taken off. People had secret lives they successfully concealed from their families and friends; it was a fact. Nothing he'd seen so far suggested Jessie was one of those people, but he had to keep it in mind.

≈≈≈

"That girl didn't just take off without telling nobody," Melba said, hands fisted on wide hips, daring Dan to disagree. "Might as well have been my own daughter, workin' here for more 'n thirteen years, ever since she was fifteen," she continued, "but that girl purely loves her momma and wouldn't do nothin' like this to her: just take off without a word."

Dan began, "Sometimes we don't know people like we think we do..."

"No," Melba said emphatically. "You may not know Jess, but I do, and I know you're wrong. Besides her momma, I'm probably as close to Jess as she lets anybody get. Never knew a child as closed up as she was. She came in here all bruised up and never said a word about it, 'cept to lie about fallin' down or runnin' into somethin', and then, only when I pushed the issue.

"Once, she got a pan full of hot gravy spilled down the front of her and without thinkin' I pulled her shirt off. That pore little thing had bruises all down one side. That was back when Chunk was still sheriff, and I went down there, tried to get him to do somethin', but you know what he was like. Too busy drinkin' and screwin' to do his job, and I knew what he was thinkin': it's just that DuBois girl, one of those troublemakers outside town."

"I used to go pick her up at four in the morning and bring her in with me on Saturdays and Sundays so she could help with the prep work. After a while, with just the two of us here, she began to loosen up a little, talk a little, ask questions and answer some of mine. Nothing like a couple of girls kneadin' pie dough to get the conversation goin',", she said with a tight smile.

Her expression changed and she looked uncertain, then nodded her head like she'd resolved some inner conflict. She turned and walked back to her tiny office, motioning him to follow. She went to a large safe under a shelving unit, worked the dial and pulled out an expandable folder. She nodded for him to sit in the straight-backed wooden chair across from the desk, then closed the door and settled herself in an old swivel chair behind the desk. "I know Jess, and I know she wouldn't just take off, but there's another reason I know she didn't just leave." She turned the folder upside down and a cascade of twenty-five dollar U.S. Savings Bonds, a paper clipped stack of twenty dollar bills and several one-dollar bills fell out. "These savings bonds are hers. More'n two hundred of 'em." She gave him a look over her glasses.

"Jess never had it easy. Not even when she was a kid, what with the kids at school makin' fun of her clothes or where she lives, and all of 'em knowin' her daddy's the town drunk.

"After she started workin' here, I had more than one person tell me, loud enough for Jess to hear, that I'd better check my cash register, make sure somebody wasn't dippin' into the till. Then there were the ones that would never sit in Jess's section and when they were ready to go, they'd bring their waitress' tips up to the front, makin' sure, they said - lookin' at Jess the whole time - somebody with sticky fingers didn't end up with it. Most folks treat Jess fine now, but there are still those who won't give her the money for their check and bring it up to the front instead.

"Not too long after she started waitin' tables, she said she needed to save up money to go to school. She asked if I could hold some of her tips for her, lock 'em up in the safe. I tried to talk her into opening an account at the bank, but she was afraid her daddy'd find out somehow, and I couldn't convince her he wouldn't. I did get her talked into lettin' me buy savings bonds instead of just leavin' the cash layin' in the

168

safe. Jess does real good with her tips. She's been givin' me a few dollars out of 'em every day and I been keepin' 'em for her ever since. Only time she's asked me for some of it was to pay for school."

"Last five or six years, she's been takin' classes at I.U. Now Jess is one smart little gal. Real smart. Genius smart, maybe, and real good with the computers. I got this little one here for inventory and to order supplies and such." She nodded at an older model that sat on the corner of her desk. "It was Jess talked me into havin' it. She set it all up for me and showed me how to use it. I'd a never thought of such a thing if it wasn't for Jess. That's what she's goin' to school for. And to study art. Told her daddy she'd got a scholarship, else he'd be wantin' to know where the money came from. Sad thing is, she coulda' probably got a scholarship if she'd of been able to apply while she was in high school. But she woulda' had to go full time and she needed to work, help her momma with bills. Last year, she got a grant from some foundation or other. It all but paid for her classes last year and this year too, so she didn't have to dip into her money." She nodded at the bonds on the desk, "Won't let me tell her how much she's got. Says she'll find out when she needs it."

She started stacking the savings bonds into a neat pile, "Nobody else knows about these except her momma," she said, looking sternly at Dan, "unless Jess told somebody else, which I doubt. I'd appreciate it if you'd not let anybody else know. The only reason I told you about 'em was because you need to know she's not just one of those girls gets a wild hair and takes off. Way I figure it, you think she might've just took off, you might just stop lookin' after a day or two."

Melba jutted her chin out and said, "Jess is out there and she's in trouble, sure as I'm sittin' here.

"I don't mean to step on any toes," she continued, "but her momma and me, we're gonna' get some people together, organize a search."

She paused as if waiting for him to disagree, "I can't just sit here and wait for somebody else to do it. People didn't treat that girl right when she was comin' up, but like it or not, she's one of us. If I have to shame some of these people into helpin' that's what I'll do, but help they will."

CHAPTER FORTY-THREE

When Dan approached Marybeth and asked to speak to her, she led him to the back without more than a subdued, "OK."

When they reached the break room, she stopped next to a small table and, head down, traced a water stain on the table top with her fingernail.

"I understand you and Jessie had a fight yesterday," he said.

Marybeth wondered who had told him and said defensively, "Wasn't really a fight. Jess don't fight."

"What was it then?" he asked, keeping his tone neutral.

Marybeth tossed her blonde hair back and responded, "Jess ended up havin' to work late and she wanted me to cover for her. I had somethin' to do after work and I couldn't work late and she was upset about it. Said she had a headache."

"What time did she normally leave?" he asked.

"Two o'clock usually, but Mandy, the waitress that comes in at two called in sick and Jess had to stay to cover."

"Jess had to stay?" Dan asked. "Is that a rule or something?"

"Well, she just always does. 'Cause she needs the money and everybody knows she needs the money and so she just always stays when somebody doesn't come in.

"Yesterday wasn't any different, 'cept she said she had a headache and wanted to go home and lay down. I might'a stayed 'cept I had something I had to do." She looked down at her hands. "Jess got kind of upset that I couldn't stay what with the headache and all. She don't get upset like that much."

"So she wasn't acting like usual yesterday?" he asked. When she shook her head, he said, "She seem nervous, on edge?"

"No, I think it was really just it was so hot in here yesterday and she said she had a headache. She was just kind of cranky, but I think everybody was, because of the heat."

"She ever tell you about somebody bothering her? Maybe somebody she was afraid of? " asked Dan.

"Jess didn't never say nothin' like that." Marybeth paused for a few seconds. "Earl Price, maybe. He didn't never really do nothin' but he liked to flirt with her and she didn't like waitin' on him."

"She ever say anything about him approaching her, bothering her, outside of work?"

"No, and I think she would've."

"Have any idea where this Earl Price lives?" he asked Marybeth.

"He's old Alice Price's nephew or great nephew or somethin'. He lives out there." Marybeth said nodding her head in the general direction of the Price farm. Dan remembered Glenna DuBois' description of a truck out on Patterson Road the night before and asked, "You ever see this Earl Price's car?"

"Um, it's a truck. Dark, probably dark blue. I never seen it up close, just through the window. Yeah, I'm pretty sure it's dark blue."

"You know what make it is?"

"I never really paid attention, but it's a big truck, not one of those little ones. You think he maybe did somethin' to Jess?" she asked.

"We're just tracking down every scrap of information we've got," he said, hoping to quell the gossip he knew would travel through the small town like shit through a goose. "We'll be checking out everybody she talked to over the last several weeks and he's no exception, but since he talked to her yesterday, probably close to the time she left, maybe he saw her leave with someone or saw someone come in and talk to her. Might be able to tell us if any other customers came in while he was here."

"Oh." Marybeth's disappointment was clear.

Dan made a note, then handed her his card. He started to turn away when Marybeth put a hand on his arm to stop him. "You think somethin's really happened to her?" Her face reddened and her eyes welled with tears. "She wouldn't of just took off. I know Jess," she continued, pulling a napkin out of a package on a shelf and dabbing at her eyes. "I asked her once why she stayed in that house out there with that mean old son-of-a-bitch when she could've maybe shared an apartment with me or someone else, got out of there. She said she wanted to save up enough money to go to school and she couldn't pay to live on her own and save up any money. Besides, she didn't want to leave her momma out there alone, so she just stayed."

"You think of anything, even if you think it's silly or not important, call me." He tapped the card. "Thanks for your help."

Dan had talked to Bud, the grill cook before he talked to Marybeth and was trying to get a complete sentence out of the pimply-faced Lyle when his cell rang.

The site of the disappearance had been a wash out, almost literally, and now Nicki Bondurant was telling him there'd been no physical evidence at the house either, at least nothing out of the ordinary. She'd processed the meager results from both the sites and found no traces of semen on Jessie's bedclothes, several long, black hairs that appeared to match the hairs on a brush on the dresser, a few pictures of Jessie with what looked like friends or family members, a small address book, some letters from her brother Mason. She'd lifted three sets of fingerprints in her room. Tommy DuBois was one set, mostly on the dresser drawers and some shoeboxes in the closet. The other prints were unidentified, but were probably Jessie's and her mother's since they matched prints found in other rooms of the house.

"Oh, and something else," she continued, "Ben said to tell you the keys go to the Blazer and they didn't get any prints off the ring or any of the keys. Haven't run ballistics, yet, he thought you'd rather have the print stuff first. He also said to tell you that he got a hit on a stray set of prints from two of the Blazer doors. Belong to...um..." she paused as she looked through her notes, "Elvie Morris, arrested for vandalizing the high school over the summer with another kid, John Kitzinger. Morris is fourteen. His dad runs a little livestock farm out near Patterson's place."

"Huh. The kid who was killed in the barn fire last night has been tentatively identified as Elvie Morris. They're comparing dental records to confirm. This case just gets stranger and stranger."

When Dan got Charlie on his cell, he brought him up to date. "I'll let Rolly know about the kid's prints on Aronson's truck. I don't know if it means anything, but he'll check it out.

"You know, it bothers me that what sounds like maybe this Earl Price's truck was parked out on Patterson Road last night around the time the DuBois car disappeared. From what Marybeth, the waitress at Melba's told me, he could have been stalking her. Mrs. DuBois said Jessie didn't like him, avoided him when she saw him at the grocery. We should get the plate number for Price's truck, and I think we need to go out, have a little talk with this guy."

≈≈≈

When they got out to the Price place, no one was around. No sign of the truck Marybeth had described and no one answered the door.

The area in front of the house was dirt, still slightly muddy from yesterday's rain, and Dan looked at the few footprints there were, hoping to see some smaller ones, maybe belonging to Jessie, but they all looked like they'd been made by the same large feet.

The porch was bare. Earl apparently didn't sit out in the evenings like most folks in the country. He tried to look in the window that faced onto the porch, but the shade was pulled all the way down.

"No point hanging around here," Dan said, and after taking another look around, went down the steps and out to the car.

On the way back to the post, Charlie said, "I need to sit down and get everything we've got so far in some kind of order. Need to run Price through the system too. See if he's got any priors."

CHAPTER FORTY-FOUR

Lyle rode away from town on his bike, his brain whirling. He'd told Aunt Melba he was sick and he wasn't really lying. He'd felt sick since yesterday when the man had taken Jessie.

Then this morning her Daddy had come in, and later, even worse, Jessie's Momma. All morning, he'd had to listen to people talking about her. Aunt Melba was organizing a search and people were coming in to help and all he'd heard was Jessie, Jessie, Jessie. Every time someone, especially his Aunt or Mrs. DuBois, looked at him he thought they would see his guilt, would ask him what was wrong.

He turned into the drive at the Kitzinger farm. It was almost noon and John should be about done with his chores by now. He didn't want to be alone to just think. At least with John, he wouldn't have to pretend everything was ok.

He found John and his grandpa almost done replacing a rotted post for the gate into the pasture behind the barn.

"Hey, John. Hey, Mr. Kitzinger."

"John's got chores to do, Lyle." John's Grandpa growled at him.

"That's okay. I can help him."

A grunt was all he got in reply.

When they'd finished putting the hardware on the gate, the old man took the tools they'd used to the barn and left the boys to pick up the old post.

As soon as he was out of range, John turned to Lyle and said, "I think that fucker Elvie stole my grandpa's truck."

While John told Lyle about the truck and they called Elvie every stinking name they could think of, they'd finished up John's chores and got fishing poles out of the barn. They asked John's grandpa if they could go fishing, and after he told them they wouldn't catch anything this time of day, he told them to go ahead. The boys headed toward the pond, but when they were out of sight, they jogged out to the unused barn where they'd left the marijuana the night before.

It was gone. Any doubt John had that Elvie had stolen the truck evaporated.

≈≈≈

Roy Kitzinger was crossing the barnyard, headed for the chicken coop when Rolly Ferguson pulled up in front of the house. The car wasn't marked, but Roy knew a police car when he saw one.

His heart skipped when the man got out of the car. "Help ya?"

"You Roy Kitzinger?"

"Yeah."

"You report a GMC truck stolen this morning?"

"Yeah. You find it?"

"You know a kid named Elvie Morris?"

≈≈≈

The boys sat on the bank under a big walnut tree beside the pond. They didn't fish, didn't talk much, just watched the water until the sun sank low in the sky.

His grandpa would be mad if he was late for supper, but John wasn't really hungry and he just didn't want to go home and try to act normal.

When it was almost dusk, the boys gathered up their unused poles and tackle and headed back. They went through the gate they'd just fixed that afternoon and into the barn.

When they came out into the barnyard, John's grandpa was sitting in the rocker on the porch.

Roy Kitzinger felt old. He was tired. Damn near worn out, and except for his grandson, alone. He'd spent most of his life farming this land like his daddy before him and trying to do right. In return the Lord had tried him with more hardship and heartbreak than any man should have to bear. He'd lost almost all the people he cared about most: his daughter to leukemia when she was seven, his oldest son to Desert Storm, his wife to ovarian cancer, and worst of all, his youngest son, John's father, to drugs.

Rolly Ferguson had told him that the truck he'd reported stolen burned up, along with a teen aged boy, who they believed was Elvie Morris. Roy hadn't flinched at the news, but his mouth had gone dry and dread had washed over him like a bucket of ice water.

He had answered truthfully that yes, John had been in his bed where he was supposed to be at 5:00 that morning, and no, he hadn't noticed any smell of smoke about the boy or his clothes.

He'd told Ferguson that John and Lyle had gone out to do whatever it was teenaged boys did when chores were done. He wasn't really sure where they were.

After Ferguson left, he'd sat down to wait.

He watched the boys cross the yard. John looked up and met Roy's eyes and Roy knew. John was in trouble. Before a word was said or a single question asked, he knew. He'd seen that look on his son's face enough to recognize it on his grandson's.

John's friend, Elvie, was dead, and somehow, John was involved. In the pit of Roy's stomach, a ball of fear was lodged, so big he felt like he could hardly take in a good breath.

"John. Lyle." Roy stood up. "You boys come on in the house and sit. We're gonna' have a talk."

CHAPTER FORTY-FIVE

Melba's had been packed all day, not with customers but with volunteers. Most of the customers who had been there when Glenna came in stayed to help, and then they called friends and neighbors to come in too.

A huge map of the county had been spread out over four tables pushed together, napkin dispensers holding down all four corners. Groups of volunteers had been assigned areas to canvass, knock on doors and pass out flyers. Lakes, ponds, ravines, even sections of Big Buck Reservoir, anywhere the car could have been hidden, had been identified and assigned to volunteers.

Melba'd started out by making copies of flyers on her little copier, but it was too small and too slow to keep up, and Bull Armitage, the owner of the print shop on the square, had offered to print as many as they could use.

National Guard and about fifty civilian volunteers had already begun a grid search of the woods near where Jessie's car had last been seen.

George left Glenna at Melba's and went home to exchange tee shirt and jeans for his uniform. When he got back, he discovered that Glenna and her two boys, Darrel and Duane, had gone out to join the search in the woods.

He drove out to Patterson Road and pulled his car into the grass, joining dozens of other vehicles parked along the road. He hoped he could talk her into going back into town, to stay at Melba's instead of searching for Jessie in the woods.

He hadn't had many situations like this since he'd been sheriff, but those he'd had did not have happy endings. The last one had been two years ago when Mona Spencer's' dad, senile and confused, had wandered away from the house into the woods. They'd spent the better part of three days looking for him before they'd found him face down in a pond.

In Jessie's case, she wasn't senile and he couldn't think of a reason she would have been disoriented. If she was found in there, it wasn't going to turn out well.

≈≈≈

Charlie lowered his bulk into his protesting swivel chair. "An old picture of Aronson is going to run on the evening news tonight. Report'll say he's wanted for questioning about the shootings in Bradley. Made the national news, by the way."

"Big doings in Brewer County," Dan said.

"Yeah, well, the news services are having a great time with what they're callin' Brewer County's crime wave, what with the little Higgins boy, the missing DuBois girl, Elvie Morris and five stiffs gettin' whacked in Bradley."

"Five?" asked Dan.

"Yeah, Nielson didn't make it."

He continued, "The DuBois girl's picture will run with a description of the car and where it was last seen. We're goin' through all the motions, but isn't anything about this whole scenario that says she's gonna' be out there walkin' around so somebody can I.D. her picture. Somebody might see the car maybe, but if she's not with it, we've still got nothin'.."

"Kinda' odd when you think about it," Dan said. "Guy like Aronson shows up in the area and the place just goes to hell with stiffs on every corner."

"Yeah," Charlie nodded, "seems like a big coincidence."

"A very smart man told me a long time ago that in our line of work, coincidences are automatically suspect, and I believe he was probably right."

"You think these cases are connected somehow?"

"Don't see how they could be," Dan said, "but we could be missing something."

"Okay, the DuBois girl gets snatched at what, about 5:00?" Charlie said.

"According to the teller at the bank, she cashed her check at about 4:45 and Sheriff Farber found her car out on Patterson Road at about 5:30."

"If she got in the car at the bank and headed straight home, it'd be, what, seven, eight minutes to get to where the car was?"

"Yeah, so 5:00 sounds pretty close."

"What next?" asked Charlie, "Tommy and Glenna DuBois go out on Patterson to get the car and it's gone?"

"Right, and that was at about 7:00 as close as Mrs. DuBois can remember."

"And that's also when she says she saw a truck that could be Earl Price's parked off the road in the woods, not right at the bridge, but near enough that she noticed it. We'll have to ask her exactly where it was in relation to the bridge, if she can remember."

Dan made a note and then said, "Okay, so nobody knows anything about Jessie after that, right?

"Right," responded Charlie. "I haven't found anybody who does, anyway. Then we have the shootings in Bradley, and the shooter is a pissed off Special Ops guy who might be a gun for hire doing what, exactly, in Bradley, at midnight? Your guy at the bureau give you any idea what this Aronson guy is up to?"

"He doesn't know. At least if he does, he acted like he didn't. He also said, and he's right, that tomorrow at the latest we'll have agents from the FBI or the joint task force breathing down our necks."

"They didn't already know he was here?"

Dan shrugged. "Your guess is as good as mine."

Charlie continued, "Now we have Elvie Morris. Not our case, but I'd like to know how he got his fingerprints on Aronson's truck. Do we know anything about him?"

"From everything Ferguson's heard, he was just a kid. Got into trouble a couple of times. He and another boy were arrested at the beginning of the summer for breaking into the high school. Spraying fire extinguishers around, that kind of thing. Not somebody Aronson would know or have an interest in. He was only fourteen for God's sake. Still, his prints are on Aronson's truck."

"They have a time of death for him?"

"Well, the fire was reported sometime after 2:00, so he was most likely dead before then, but that doesn't tell us anything."

Charlie shook his head. "I don't see any connection."

CHAPTER FORTY-SIX

Aronson ticked items off in his head as he drove, too fast, he realized, checking the speedometer and slowing a little.

He and his men had worked toward this day for months and even with the operation going down in an unexpected rush, they were ready. The quarry floor was more than a hundred feet down and while some of the men had kept up the pretense of cutting limestone slabs from the quarry over the last several months, the rest had drilled and blasted steadily into the west rock face near the quarry floor, creating a long, narrow tunnel that now ended less than a foot from the edge of the highway. From the highway side, it still looked like solid rock, but a small charge would easily blast the last of the rock away when they were ready.

The shipment of VX didn't leave Crane until 21:00 putting it at their site at about 21:45. For the time being, all they could do was wait.

≈≈≈

While she waited for the man to come back, Jessie'd spent some quality time at his keyboard, typing in code that would seriously fuck up his computer.

She'd turned the lights off a long time ago, probably almost an hour, afraid that she wouldn't be able to get down the steps fast in the sudden dark if she waited until he came back. Her eyes had adjusted, and she could see everything she needed to with just the light from the TV monitors.

A truck Jessie didn't recognize approached the house, its path winding around the edge of the field to the barn. Was it him?

She was both relieved and terrified when she recognized the man.

Her hands were wet and shaking. Would she even be able to pull the trigger and if so, would she hit him when she fired? She stood for just a moment, thinking that it might better to stand on the landing and shoot him as he opened the door.

Stop, she told herself. Just stop. You practiced this and this was the best way. She took in a steadying breath, pulled the blanket around her and sat down on the chair she'd dragged to the end of the table, facing the steps. She draped a second blanket over her shoulders from the front to hide the gun. She grasped it firmly in her left hand, her right hand supporting it from underneath.

The floor creaked overhead.

The gun was heavy and she braced her elbows against the back of the chair. This gun was larger and nothing like the one Mason had brought home for her and Momma to use. She'd had time to explore it, to figure out how to remove the clip and check for bullets, then put it back. There was one bullet in the chamber and four in the clip. She was as ready as she was going to be.

She heard the door open and the light came on. The man started down the steps.

He turned onto the landing and stopped when he saw her, sitting in his chair, wrapped in his blanket. Instead of cowering in a corner, she faced him, chin up, meeting his eyes, stare for stare. He cocked his head and gave a little smile. Oh yeah, he thought, this one was going to be fun.

"Well, well, well, look what we have here." He slowly took the last two steps down and started toward her.

She knew she couldn't count on hitting him at any distance, so she let him come, shaking so hard she thought she would drop the gun.

He stopped a dozen feet away, opened his arms, taunting her. "Come to papa, little girl."

She fired from beneath the blanket once, then again. The first shot missed him. The second one didn't.

He stared at her for a stunned instant, then fell. She saw it in slow motion: his head snapping forward when the bullet hit him, then lolling back and tilting to one side. His knees folded under him, and while they went one direction, his hips went the other. He landed on his side, rolled onto his back and stopped moving.

Jessie grabbed the duffel and skirted cautiously around the man, never taking her eyes off him, gun ready to shoot if he moved, even a little. She hadn't been sure where she'd hit him, but saw the gleam of blood on his black shirt, spreading out over his chest.

Aronson wasn't out, not completely, and over the roaring in his ears, he heard the girl going up the steps. God damn it! She'd shot him! Where'd she get a fucking gun?

She'd hit him at least once, in the left chest. He could still breathe, so she hadn't hit a lung.

He couldn't let her escape. She didn't know much, but she knew where he was. Until he could get the explosives and weapons out of here and to the quarry, he couldn't afford to have company.

His wits were returning slowly and he gathered his strength, rolled over onto his side and got his knees under him. He breathed in deeply, held it, then got shakily to his feet, swaying like a drunkard.

He gave himself just a moment or two to get his balance, then lurched up the steps, releasing his gun from the holster at his back. He was surprised when he got to the back door and saw that she'd only made it through the yard to the driveway. He steadied himself by leaning on the doorframe and brought her down with a single shot.

≈≈≈

Chastain was a good five minutes behind Aronson, but since the GPS signal showed he was headed to the old farmhouse, Chastain didn't try to catch him.

As he neared the driveway, he heard gunfire coming from that direction, and not from a rifle or shotgun, something you came to expect out here in the country.

He hesitated for an instant, told himself he was an idiot, then pulled his truck to the side of the road on the left shoulder and got out.

≈≈≈

Aronson' heart was pounding from his run up the steps and across the kitchen, so he hung onto the doorframe waiting for his pulse to settle and the black spots at the edge of his vision to clear. He was about to step out onto the porch when the girl raised her head and fired at him, the shot breaking the window next to his head and showering him with broken glass.

Son of a bitch! He took cover behind the doorframe, and when he poked his head out again, she fired. This shot wasn't as close as the first one, but there was something, apparently, to be said for dumb luck, so he waited a few seconds before looking out the broken window.

She was gone.

He'd hit her, he knew he had. He crouched and made a slow, stumbling run out to the bridge where she'd gone down. Blood. She was hit. Where the hell was she? He staggered down the drive, scanning the woods on either side, looking for a blood trail, but it was as though she'd vanished. He rested one knee on the ground and put his head down, fighting to stay conscious and waited for the feeling to pass.

≈≈≈

Jessie leaned against a tree, saw him kneel and thought about taking another shot at him. He'd keep looking until he found her, she knew that. If she could just count on hitting him again – anywhere - she would, but she wasn't a good shot, and she'd probably miss. Then he'd know where she was.

Her breath was coming hard and she was tiring fast. When she touched the bullet wound at the top of her shoulder, her hand came away covered with blood and she wondered how much longer she could stay upright.

She'd gotten away after he shot her by rolling from the drive into the creek, then scuttling into the culvert beneath. He'd actually run down the drive over her. She'd been tempted to just stay there and let her head clear and her pulse steady, but his back had been to her and she might not get another chance. He hadn't been expecting her to come from behind him, which had given her a chance to get clear. Besides, she'd known that sooner or later, when he was thinking more clearly, he'd look in the culvert and she'd be trapped. The black bag had been too heavy for her to carry any further, so she'd taken the discs out of the side pocket and left the bag hidden in the dense brush at the mouth of the culvert.

Duck-walking, then crawling, she'd followed the creek bed, keeping low, until the creek had narrowed and it had been impossible for her to stay in it and stay hidden. She'd slipped out of the creek and behind a tree while he was looking the other way, and had made it, passing from tree to tree, until she was nearly to the road, could actually see it, maybe twenty feet away through the trees ahead. But then what? It might be an hour before a car came by. Leaving the woods meant going into the open and giving the man a clear target.

She didn't know where she was. With him there, she could only go one direction, but with enough time and some luck, she might make it to another house. She'd just decided to follow the road, keeping to the cover of the woods when she was grabbed from behind, a large hand covered her mouth and the gun was taken out of her hand.

"Don't make a sound," a voice rasped in her ear.

She didn't struggle, it was pointless and she knew it, and she was suddenly just too tired. She hadn't realized there were two of them.

He began to move, but instead of going toward the man, he turned and propelled her toward the road. Jessie heard a shout from behind them, then a shot, and the bark from the tree next to her head exploded.

"Move!" shouted her new captor as he shoved her forward into a truck which was pulled off the road, door open, engine running.

He shoved her across the seat then jumped in, released the brake, pushed in the clutch and put the truck in gear, flooring it before his door was closed.

Another shot shattered the rear window of the cab, hitting them both with tiny chunks of glass, but then they were around a curve and out of the line of fire.

Jessie turned to look at her rescuer. "Earl Price," she said. "Great." Then her eyes rolled back in her head.

CHAPTER FORTY-SEVEN

"Just have to be Sir Galahad, don't you?" Chastain asked himself as he glanced at the DuBois girl bleeding all over the seat of his truck. He didn't know if Aronson had gotten a look at him, but he sure as hell had gotten a look at his truck. It had a different license plate than it had had last night, but there was little else he could do to disguise it. It had been dark last night, visibility had been bad and the county was full of dark colored pick-up trucks. He'd been very careful to stay out of Aronson's way during the surveillance, so even if he'd seen him, he hoped Aronson would think he was nothing more than a guy in the right place at the right time to help a woman in distress. At least that's what he told himself.

As he drove, he realized that now that he'd stuck his nose in and helped the girl, he couldn't let her go. He'd have the sheriff at his door asking questions, and the press would be on him like stink on shit.

What was he going to do with her? She was hurt, he didn't know how badly. He could drop her off somewhere she'd be sure to be found, but she'd seen him and she'd tell everyone he'd gotten her away from Aronson, he could count on it. If some hungry young reporter dug around and discovered that Alice Price never had a nephew, great or otherwise, then his cover was blown and the investigation was screwed.

He was going to have to take her to the farm and figure out something from there. When Fitz found out, he was going to burst a blood vessel.

He turned into the rutted track that led back to the house and the girl slid sideways, landing with her head on his thigh, giving him a good look at the damage Aronson had done.

Poor kid, he thought, pulling a dead leaf out of her hair. She'd had a rough twenty-four hours from the looks of things and now he was going to take her and lock her up again, giving her no explanation because he couldn't.

He carried her in and laid her on the sofa, then sat her up so he could pull her shirt up and see how bad she was hit.

"Christ," he said as he got a look at her shoulder. The gunshot wound was ugly and painful, but not dangerous, going through the top of her shoulder just before it curved up into her neck. What made him cringe were the teeth marks, deep and brutal, the swollen flesh around them a dark, mottled purple.

She wasn't entirely unconscious and began to struggle.

He held onto her, trying to subdue her without hurting her, when she screamed, "No!" and began to fight in earnest, using feet, hands, knees, whatever she could.

"Wait," he said, "...damn it..." and heard an ugly crunch when the back of her head connected with his nose. He saw stars for just an instant, long enough for her to tear out of his grasp and make a run for it. He'd stupidly left the door open when he'd carried her in and she managed to get out of the house, down into the yard and behind his truck before he caught up with her.

Jessie knew she couldn't outrun him. She was weak, her legs barely held her up and the dizziness she'd fought all day was worse than ever, but he wasn't going to take her without a fight. She looked at him over the hood of his truck and spat at him, "You'll have to kill me!"

"I'm not gonna' kill you," he said in as soothing a voice as he could muster. "I'm not gonna' hurt you." She was holding her shoulder and weaving slightly; with any luck, she'd pass out again.

"You're a liar," she raged at him, "You were trying to take my clothes off! You had your hands on me!"

"No. No, listen to me," he said wiping the back of his hand across his nose, smearing it with blood. "I pulled your shirt up so I could see your shoulder. I wanted to see how bad it was." He started edging around to the front of the truck, but she countered, moving around the truck to the door. "I'm not gonna' hurt you, I promise. I was just takin' a look, tryin' to see how bad it was, that's all."

He was losing patience fast and wanted to just grab her and shake the living shit out of her. The damn girl had probably broken his nose and now he was playing ring around the rosie with her.

"Why'd you bring me here, then?" she challenged. "You think I'm stupid, Earl? I know what you want."

"Goddamn it," he ground out, then tried to gentle his tone. "I just need to talk to you."

"Yeah, right," she raised her chin and looked him in the eye, opening the truck door as she did.

"Where the hell you think you're going?" he asked. "I've got the keys in my pocket."

She reached into the truck and stood up, holding the gun he'd taken from her earlier.

"Well, hell," he said.

≈≈≈

"Throw the keys on the seat," Jessie said, holding the gun on him with shaking hands.

"Listen..." he began.

"I said, throw the keys on the seat. You don't have anything to say I want to hear," she said. "Throw the keys on the seat, then back away from the truck."

When he hesitated, she said, "I already shot one guy today, Earl, I can make it two."

He shrugged and threw the keys on the seat as she'd asked and backed away.

She slid across the seat, keeping the gun on Chastain the whole time, put the key in the ignition, and turned it. The truck lurched forward and Chastain winced. "It's a stick."

"I can see that," she said, frustrated. She had never driven a stick. Her daddy's truck was a stick but she'd never hardly even rode in it, much less driven it. She knew you had to shift, but that was about it. She turned the key again with the same result. She kept the gun on him while she considered what to do.

"Okay," she said sliding over and getting out of the truck on the other side, keeping it between her and Earl. She held onto the door to stay upright. "I'll just go inside the house and use the phone."

"No phone in the house. Just this," he said as he reached in his pocket and pulled out his cell.

"Put it on the hood and back away," she said.

The way the gun was wobbling and sagging in her hand, she'd be lucky to hit anything but dirt, but he approached the truck and put the phone down, then started to back away.

When she reached for it, he leapt across the half dozen steps to the truck, launched himself forward and slid across the hood, his momentum carrying him off the other side where he took her down with him.

He tried to break their fall as much as possible, but still landed sprawled on top of her.

While she was pinned underneath him, he jerked the gun out of her hand, but she wasn't fighting him now: she was out cold.

He rolled off her and sat on the ground next to her, propped his arms on his bent knees with the gun hanging from his hand between them.

The girl was going to be nothing but trouble, he could just tell.

CHAPTER FORTY-EIGHT

Aronson ran out into the road and brought the gun up to take another shot, but the truck was rounding the curve and then was out of the line of fire. The sound of the engine disappeared into the distance.

God damn it!! The girl had gotten away. He couldn't fucking believe it. Once she talked to the cops, they'd be crawling all over the place. He had his cell in his hand before he'd even turned, then he was talking to Stephanos as he forced himself into a trot back to the farmhouse.

He would pull some of the men off their assignments long enough to get them over there and get the containers out. It was something they were going to do anyway, he'd just move it up to the top of the list.

Stephanos wasn't happy about the change in plan. Well, tough shit. He wasn't in charge of this operation, Aronson was.

Aronson was figuring quickly in his head, fifteen minutes for the guys to get here, but only five for them to get everything out and loaded into the van, ten at the most.

His breathing was ragged and the searing pain in his chest was hard to ignore, but he had no choice. His mind was racing, part of it dealing with packing up the essentials he would need later, part of it thinking ahead to the strike, and part of it wondering how the girl had gotten free.

He opened a large nylon satchel and put it on the table, then clumsily began loading it with papers, using only his right arm. The rolled charts didn't quite fit, but he stuffed them in anyway, leaving the ends sticking out the top. How could the damn girl have gotten loose? He resisted the impulse to go and examine the cell in the back where she'd been tied.

Where had she gotten the gun? All the storage containers were still locked and he had had the Glock with him. The AK was in the truck, under the seat.

Then he remembered.

He'd shoved his extra Glock into the side pocket of the bag last night when he'd left the Blazer.

The bag. He strode quickly to the cot and looked underneath.

It was gone.

≈≈≈

Why not, Aronson thought. Why wouldn't the God damn little nobody steal the money? Probably more money than she'd earn if she lived to be a hundred. Which she wouldn't, not once he caught up with her. She only thought she'd had it rough the short time she'd been with him. She had no idea.

He gave himself just a moment to reign in the fury that boiled through him, when a picture popped into his head. He saw her clearly in his mind, running for the truck, the man behind her. She hadn't been carrying the bag and neither had he. He was sure of it. She would hardly have left it down here, would she? Not once she found out what was in it. But it had been heavy, bulky, awkward to move. On the other hand, she'd expected him to go down and stay down, not come after her.

She'd hardly want to be carrying it once she got out to the road where she could flag down a car either. She'd want to keep it secret. That much money could turn a good Samaritan into a thief and murderer in no time.

It wasn't between the house and the driveway, he would've seen it. If she'd dropped it out there in the woods, it would be just lying there. He looked at his watch.

He wasn't sure he had enough time to get everything they needed out of here, much less go out and search for the bag. That made it worse somehow, knowing it was probably close: upstairs, out in the woods, or near the house and all he had to do was walk out there and get it.

There was no time, none, to search for it. He was going to have to drive away and leave it here because the stupid bitch would have the sheriff down on him in no time.

He opened one of the smaller containers and began stacking blocks of C-4 on the table. He'd never planned on cleaning the place out once they were ready to move. Blowing the house would serve two purposes: it would get rid of any evidence he may have left behind, and it would create quite a diversion, drawing every cop in the county.

All of the data on the computer was backed up on a personal cloud storage account, so he inserted a disk that would wipe the hard drive. There should be nothing left after the C-4 did its job, but he'd stayed alive because he made a habit of being sure. He used duct tape to fasten one block of explosive to the CPU, wrapping it around several times so it was snug against the housing.

He would place one block in each of the four corners of the cellar and attach the detonators he'd already wired into place. Another block would be placed at the only working door into the house.

One monitor alerted him to a dark brown cargo truck coming toward the house. The men had arrived. He'd have to hurry.

Aronson ignored a wave of nausea and lightheadedness, forced his left arm into the sleeve of a black jacket, pulled it on the rest of the way and zipped it up as he heard the back door open and footsteps cross the floor over his head. He didn't want the men seeing blood on him.

Except for a few stealthy looks his way, they didn't show any curiosity about the change in plan, but Stephanos was clearly pissed. Too fucking bad, he'd just have to get over it.

He stared down Stephanos and told him curtly to see to the transfer of the storage containers while he rigged the explosives to blow.

Stephanos wasn't one to keep silent when he had something to say, but he was smart enough to know when he could push Aronson and when he couldn't. He waited a moment before he broke eye contact, and then snapped an order at the men, and they lifted the first container and began lugging it out of the house and into the truck.

Twenty-three minutes after Aronson had placed the call to Stephanos, everything was loaded and Aronson was setting the trip wire at the back door. He couldn't resist taking a last, quick look at the woods then chastised himself for being stupid. The bag wouldn't be just sitting there in plain sight.

If anybody tried to go back into the house now, he'd know about it. The noise it would make when it went up would rattle windows for miles.

CHAPTER FORTY-NINE

Chastain dabbed at his nose with a towel while he rummaged in an old chest and pulled out two moth eaten blankets.

Damn girl, he thought, looking at the blood on the towel.

He put the blankets over her and checked her pulse. It was too fast and she felt warm to the touch, warmer than she should have. He put the first aid kit on a kitchen chair he'd drug over to the sofa. He'd have to get some acetaminophen or ibuprofen down her if he could.

He'd forwarded everything he'd gotten from the quarry that day so the lab could start working on it, then bit the bullet and shot Fitz a quick text message about the girl. He'd be pissed: civilians just got in the way and generally fucked things up, but she was here and had to be dealt with. Maybe she knew something, had heard something useful while she was with Aronson.

He found a big metal bowl in the kitchen, rinsed it with alcohol, filled it with warm, almost hot, water and carried it into the living room.

The girl didn't do more than moan when he sat her up so that he could look at the bullet wound. The tee-shirt she wore was so big he could pull the collar down off her shoulder to get to the bullet wound. He used a large gauze pad to wash the blood from her shoulder and an antiseptic wipe to clean around the small holes where the bullet had passed through. He folded two more pads in half, placed several gauze squares over them and taped them down firmly, hoping the pressure would slow the bleeding. He couldn't do more than that for now and laid her back down.

He tore open another gauze pad and washed the blood and grime from her forehead. The gash at her hairline was nasty: down to the bone, it was swollen and red, and looked like it might be getting infected. She was coming to, whimpering a little and trying to knock his hand away as he used several of the antiseptic wipes to clean the wound.

He threw the pads he'd been using on the floor and tore open several more as he wiped blood and dirt away from the other abrasions and cuts on her face.

Jessie frowned and shifted as the cold antiseptic made contact with raw skin and opened her eyes.

She squinted a little, like she was trying to bring his face into better focus.

"I'm not going to hurt you. You're safe here." He repeated, "Nobody's going to hurt you. I promise."

He tore open a small packet from the first aid kit and gave her a bottle of water. "Ibuprofen," he said. "You're a little feverish."

She was wary, like a starving cat, wanting to trust, but expecting a kick.

He held up the packet for her to read. "Should help with the pain too."

After she'd downed the pills, she closed her eyes while he put antibiotic ointment on the cuts he'd cleaned. "I'm not going to put anything on this cut on your forehead," he said, "Looks like you're going to need some stitches."

He got a worn pillow from the opposite end of the sofa and put it behind her head.

"You call the sheriff?" she mumbled. "Tell him what happened?"

Chastain didn't answer right away. "Not yet."

"Why?" She opened her eyes.

Chastain tried to stall. "I will, but I wanted to ask you about that guy. The one you were running from. Who is he?"

"I don't know. I don't know who he is. I never saw him before. I had a flat tire and he grabbed me. Earl, you gotta' call the sheriff."

He stood up. "How long since you ate?" he asked, as if she hadn't spoken.

"What? I don't know. I'm not hungry."

"That's not what I asked you." When she didn't answer, he said, "You'll feel better if you eat. How about I heat up some chicken noodle soup?"

After a long pause, "You're not going to call anyone about me, are you, Earl?" For the first time, he heard her voice wobble a little.

"Not right now. I've got my reasons, and it's not what you think."

After a second, her voice more steady, she said, "Why'd you help me get away from that man?"

"Good question," he muttered.

"You don't have to call anybody. You don't have to take me anywhere," she said desperately, "Just let me go. Please."

"I won't hurt you. I know you don't believe it. I probably wouldn't either in your shoes, but you're just gonna' to have to take my word for it." He looked at her, his brown eyes cool. "Now let it go."

He was almost to the door of the kitchen when she said, "He's gonna' kill a bunch of people."

He stopped and looked at her over his shoulder. "What did you just say?"

"I said, the man I was tryin' to get away from: he's going to kill a bunch of people. That's why you have to let me go. I've got to tell the sheriff or somebody ... whoever will listen to me."

"How do you know that? What did he say?"

"Nothing. I mean he didn't tell me anything. I saw a digital file of him and another guy named Walters. He had bunch of meetings with this Walters guy stored on his computer."

"How'd you get in his computer?" He came back into the room and stood in front of the sofa. "This guy just leave it up for you to rummage through?"

"Well, he didn't exactly plan on me gettin' loose," she said, "and he didn't leave it up. I hacked in."

Chastain sat in the chair in front of the sofa and studied her in silence. Aronson was good with a computer, better than most, according to his dossier.

"I watched one of them. One of his meetings, I mean." She paused for a second, looking inward, seeing the image again, hearing the men's voices, calm and matter of fact.

"There were a bunch of charts and drawings in his files too, and a lot of diagrams. I wasn't sure anybody'd believe me, so I downloaded everything to disk."

"You downloaded everything?" he asked.

"Well, I couldn't just let him get away with it," she said. "But I dropped them when you shoved me in the truck. They just slid out of my hand."

He waited a few seconds. "Do you think Aronson might've found the disks, where you dropped them?"

"Is that his name? Aronson?"

"Jonas Aronson, yeah. Do you think he might've found them?"

Jessie swallowed then asked slowly, "How do you know his name, Earl? A minute ago you didn't know who he was." She got very still. "Are you in this thing with him? Is that why you won't call the sheriff?" Suddenly she was moving again, lashing out with her feet trying to kick him and get up all at the same time.

"No! No, God damn it!" He grabbed at her feet. "Use your head for Christ sakes. If I was in this with him, I would have just given you back to him. And if you kick me again, I'm going to deck you." He rubbed his chest where one of her heels had connected.

He ran one hand through his hair and stared at the water stained ceiling. Then he looked at her, studied her for several long seconds. "I work for the Department of Defense. Aronson is my assignment. I've had him under surveillance for months."

"So you're not really Earl Price?"

"As far as you're concerned, I am." He picked up where they'd left off. "Do you think he might find the disks?"

"He will if he goes all the way out to the road."

"So that's where the disks are now?"

"Unless he found them."

He looked outside. They still had several hours of daylight. "Do you think he's going to know you were in his computer if he doesn't find the disks?"

"If he tries to use it, he will. He can log on, but that's all."

Great. Even if Aronson didn't find the disks, he'd find out Jessie'd been in his computer. If he thought the girl had accessed his files, he might abort whatever his operation was and run.

Or, more likely, he'd come after the girl. Or he'd do both. "Just out of curiosity, why?"

She looked Earl right in the eye, "I did it to piss him off, okay?"

He had to let himself smile a little at that. No sense dwelling on it, it couldn't be helped.

He looked at the GPS tracker. The truck hadn't moved. He couldn't go after the disks with Aronson still there, so he would do the next best thing.

She had her eyes closed again. "I wish the room would stop spinnin'."

She heard him rooting through the first aid kit. "Here." He handed her another pill. "This one is for vertigo." When she hesitated, he said, "Meclizine. Same stuff you'd take for motion sickness. You can get it at any drug store."

He pulled his cell phone out of his pocket and walked toward the kitchen. "While you wait for that to kick in, try putting one foot on the floor."

"Do what?" she asked.

"Go ahead. Just put one foot flat on the floor."

She tried it, and after a few seconds, thought the room steadied a little.

"It help?" he asked.

"Yeah. It did, a little."

"Trick I learned a long time ago."

"Well, thanks for the tip," she responded. "You sure as hell never left me any at the diner."

The remark startled a chuckle out of him.

This wasn't the Earl Price Jessie knew from Melba's. He still looked like Earl Price, he still sounded like Earl Price but this man was nothing like Earl Price. She heard him talking on the phone in the kitchen. His voice was low and she couldn't hear what he was saying. After a short conversation, he came back into the room and sat in the chair next to the sofa.

"Listen, all this time I've been on Aronson's tail and haven't gotten jack shit. Until I can get out there and look for the disks, I need you to tell me what you remember. Tell me everything: anything you saw on his computer, any papers you saw, anything he said, even if it seems stupid or trivial. Can you do that?"

Jessie hurt everywhere and she was tired down to the bone. She wanted, needed, to weep, to howl her rage and sorrow and shame until the pain was gone, but she did what she'd done her whole life: she took a deep breath and tucked it away, pushed it down, and just kept going. "I can try."

"I'm going to put you on speaker phone," he said. "I need someone else to hear this."

She had a good memory, and she tried to tell him everything she'd seen.

She talked and he asked questions, and while she told him what she knew, he fixed her a bowl of soup. Although she said she didn't want it, she sipped at some of the broth.

"Do you remember anything about the diagrams you saw, any markings that would tell you what they were?" he asked.

"I remember some of the details about the buildings, but there wasn't anything to say where they were. There weren't any names or anything like that. And the other drawings were just pipes and valves, I think"

"And at the meetings, they never gave any dates or times?"

"I didn't watch all the meetings. I didn't know how much time I had. I watched the two latest ones, and all they said was it was going to be soon. The guy said they'd move when their source gave them the date and time and that it would be soon."

"He didn't mention any dates at all?"

"No! I already told you," she snapped, and put a hand to her head.

He saw the gesture, but ignored it. "Did you see anything in his e-mail?"

"There was nothing in his inbox, but I didn't read his deleted e-mails," she said, eyes closed. "I didn't want to take the time. I didn't know when he'd be coming back and I didn't know what was going to be important," she continued wearily.

He knew she was exhausted and in pain. She was doing her best to tell him everything she remembered, and through it all, hadn't broken down, hadn't had hysterics, hadn't whined or cried or complained.

He picked up the phone and walked back into the kitchen with it. He came back, still listening, clearly frustrated. "I can't answer that until I go out and look," he said to the person at the other end. "GPS shows his truck at the quarry, so I'll go now." He paused, listening. "Yeah. I'll let you know either way."

He disconnected the call. "It looks like Aronson has left the farmhouse, so I'm going to go out there, see if I can find the disks. It sounds like with what you downloaded, we might be able to prove who he's working with and put them away. Without evidence, until he does something illegal, and we can prove it, we can't touch him."

She stiffened, her face drawn and pinched. "What he did to me," she said in a tight voice. "You don't think that counts?" She tried to get up, and shoved at him when he pushed her back down. "Get your hands off me."

"I didn't mean ..." he was holding her down, his hand on her uninjured shoulder. She took a swing at him and would have connected if he hadn't thrown a forearm up to block it.

He grabbed her arm before she could try again and squeezed hard enough to make her gasp, then regretted it when his gaze actually focused on the wrist he held. It was a bloody, swollen mess: lacerations from a rope or cord worn deep into her flesh. The skin on her hand wasn't any better, raw and torn, the knuckles skinned bare, dark with and dried blood. The too-long sleeves of her tee shirt had hidden them before.

She must have put up a hell of a fight, he thought as he gentled his grip. That she'd escaped from Aronson was astonishing, and he'd been so focused on his own agenda that he hadn't even asked her how she'd done it. She'd shot him, but how she'd managed it, he didn't know and didn't have time, right now, to find out.

"Listen," he said, regretting the way he'd phrased what he'd said. "What he did to you is awful, horrible, a crime. But for that he gets ten years and is out in five. With treason, he gets the needle."

She didn't respond and he let go of the wrist he held.

"I can't feel what you're feeling. I didn't experience the things you have." His voice hardened. "I can't allow you the time you need to work through whatever emotional turmoil you're going through, and I'm sorry about that. I don't have the luxury of unlimited time to baby you and pick and choose my words for fear of hurting your feelings."

As he spoke, she'd gone completely still. "You got everything from me there is to get. I want to go home."

"I wish I could let you. But I can't. Not yet. We need to wait 'til I figure out what's going on."

She took a breath to argue, but he didn't let her. "Look, one in a million, ten million women could've done what you did. You got a hit on the head that would keep most people down for a month, but you got loose, hacked into his computer, recognized what you saw for what it was and then managed to get away."

"Me bein' found don't have to have anything to do with you," she argued stubbornly. "I can walk 'til I get to another house or flag down a car. I won't say anything about you. I promise."

When he shook his head, she asked "Can I at least call my momma, let her know I'm okay?"

"No!" he snapped. "Now stop asking."

She clamped her lips shut and turned her head away.

Shit! He hated dealing with civilians in the field.

He squatted down, so that his face was even with hers, "You really think you can just go home and not say a word about what happened? You think the cops are just going to let you say you'd rather not talk about it? Even if there was no missing person report made, a lot of people will know you're missing. Your family, everybody you work with, your regular customers: all of those people will talk to other people. If I let you go, as soon as the word gets out, everybody will know where you are, including Aronson.

"If he tries to use his computer, he'll know you've been in there and he won't leave you alive to tell what you know.

"Even if he never realizes you've been in his computer, you're still a threat. As long as you're alive, you can put him in prison.

"If he knows where you are, he will kill you." He stood. "Now, let it go."

CHAPTER FIFTY

As he got out of his truck at the quarry, Aronson looked down at a piece of white paper lying on the ground, and saw a picture of the girl looking back up at him.

The picture was torn and covered with dusty boot prints, but he could still see her face. Above the girl's picture was one word: "MISSING." Below the picture was her name, a description of her and the Chevy, and a number to call if she was seen.

He turned to Benson and said, "Where the hell did this come from?"

Benson shrugged, but Donaldson responded, "A couple of people in a truck left it." He nodded toward the picture. "Said she was missing."

Aronson ground the paper into the gravel with his boot. When he caught up with her, she'd be more than just missing.

≈≈≈

Aronson went directly to the trailer while Stephanos put the men to work.

"What the hell happened?" asked Stephanos as he came through the door into the trailer.

Aronson didn't want Stephanos, or anyone, knowing about the girl. "I was on my way back from checking the ridge. Surprised some kids in a field near where I parked my truck. One of the little bastards shot me."

"Shot you!?" Stephanos responded. "Why the hell would he do that?"

"They were harvesting a field full of marijuana. It was on the other side of the creek from where I parked."

"Did they get a good look at you? Could they identify you?"

"No. I had my cap on and they weren't all that close. Looked like they were nearly done; had a big old farm truck loaded up with a pile of plastic bags full of the stuff. They took off when they saw me, but one of them turned and fired a shot in my general direction. I think he was just trying to scare me, but the son of a bitch hit me."

While Aronson talked, Stephanos helped him take his jacket off and pulled up his tee shirt.

"Bullet's still in there," Aronson said. "Must've hit bone but not the lung. I can breathe fine, but my chest hurts like hell."

Blood still oozed from the hole and the tissues surrounding it were a dark purple, almost black, and swollen. It was on the left side, but appeared to be too far over to have hit anything important.

Stephanos didn't like it. Didn't like that Aronson was injured. Especially didn't like that he'd let a "kid" as Aronson had described him, get the jump on him.

Aronson must have read what Stephanos was thinking, because he grabbed his arm, narrowed his eyes and said, "Just numb it with the stuff in the kit and get the bleeding stopped. You've got your job to do and I've got mine." He released Stephanos and leaned back. "I'll do mine. You can count on it." He nodded toward the kit. "Now get on with it."

CHAPTER FIFTY-ONE

Chastain went to the staircase and pushed the bottom of one of the risers. Jessie was dozing when she heard a muffled click and opened her eyes. A section of what appeared to be wood paneled, solid wall under the steps swung free of the decorative molding that framed it and became a door.

"It's a little cramped, but you'll have a cot, blankets, some water, and no one will ever find you in here."

He went across to her and held out his hand to help her up, "I shouldn't be long," he said, "just long enough to go out and get the disks."

"Can't I just stay here?"

"No," he said, and reached for her hand.

"Can I get out of there, if I need to?"

"You won't need to."

He reached for her again and when she pulled her hand back, he said, "Don't make this difficult. We are not negotiating here, and if I have to handcuff you and carry you in there, I will. We've already talked about why you can't leave here and why you can't talk to anyone. You, of all people, should understand what Aronson would do if he found you."

It wasn't a large space and it was crammed with a computer, other electronic gear and several storage bins, like the ones Aronson had, only smaller. There was just enough room for him to unfold a cot, and once she'd settled on it, he covered her with the blankets from the sofa.

He unplugged a cell phone from its charger and punched in some numbers. "My cell is speed dial #1. It's the only number you can call."

He put the phone on the shelf next to her head and looked down at her. She was a mess: blood matted her hair above the livid, jagged wound on her forehead, cuts and bruises stood out starkly on her pale face and one of her eyes was grotesquely swollen.

"If it'll make you feel any better, you can have your gun back." He had stuffed it into his waistband and when she nodded, he pulled it out. He started to hand it to her, but paused. "I'm trusting you not to do anything stupid."

"Like what?"

"Like shoot me."

She gave him a half-hearted smile and he handed her the gun. "You'll be fine in here until I get back."

After he left, the quiet settled down around her. The Meclizine, he'd given her had helped the dizziness and calmed her stomach, but it had made her groggy. She still had the pain pills she'd put in her pocket in the cellar, but didn't want to take it on top of the other and the Ibuprofen. Cold and achy, she curled herself into a ball and burrowed down into the blankets, the musty smell not even registering. She put her hand on the gun and closed her eyes.

≈≈≈

Chastain drove as fast as the roads would let him. He knew the way to Aronson's blindfolded. If he could get his hands on the disks, the analysts back at the lab would be able to do a thorough search of the files, pick up what Jessie hadn't. She hadn't looked at all of them and when she'd been looking through the files, she had to have been distracted, wondering when Aronson would come back.

For the first time, he was accomplishing something with this surveillance, but he wished he had more information. He felt like he was flying blind, about to run into a tree, or a tall building.

He wondered for the thousandth time what Aronson's game was. They'd thought in the beginning that it had something to do with Crane Naval Base to the south. He was just too damn close to the base for it to be anything else, but they'd been assured that anything stored there, chemical weapons, warheads, guidance systems, anything someone like Aronson would be interested in were so secure no one could possibly get to them.

Aronson's truck was at the quarry. He had to assume Aronson was there with it. Jessie had shot him, she said. Could be he was in no shape to go anywhere. But somebody drove his truck out of there. If it was one of the men from the quarry they wouldn't have just left him there. Unless he was dead.

The farmhouse looked deserted, but he couldn't think of a time when it had looked occupied. Jessie'd said the surveillance cameras were focused on the area immediately around the house and that she could only see about a quarter of the woods on the monitors.

He parked where he could be certain his truck couldn't be seen from the house and got out, walking along the tree line until he got to the skid marks his truck had left earlier. "Damn it!" he said when he saw the plastic splinters that were all that remained of the disks.

He was going to have to get into the farmhouse and get the computer. If it was still there. And if Aronson wasn't.

If he were Aronson and a girl he'd kidnapped got loose and could lead the cops straight back to him, he wouldn't stick around. Odds were definitely in Chastain's favor that Aronson had cleared out. Aronson's truck was gone and hadn't been at the farmhouse for more than a half hour after Jessie'd gotten loose, so he'd been in a hurry. How much would he have had to leave behind?

He took Jessie's route through the woods, ducking into the creek bed until he reached the driveway.

He stayed in the creek until he located the camera that faced the woods. He timed the sweep, just in case there was someone still watching, and when it reached the far end of its arc, made a run for the house.

He had his gun in his hand and flattened himself against the wall of the house out of camera range. He stepped up onto the back porch and looked in through the open door, listening for any sound that might indicate a human presence, letting a full minute pass while he stood absolutely still.

Everything looked clear but until he got inside, he couldn't know for sure. He started through the door.

CHAPTER FIFTY-TWO

Jessie'd been cold for so long, she'd forgotten what being really warm felt like. She pulled the blankets more closely around her and let her thoughts wander.

She thought about Earl and wondered who he really was. Wondered what it was like, pretending to be someone else. He'd been so loud and obnoxious in the diner. She thought undercover agents snuck around and tried to be invisible. The Earl she knew had disappeared and this new Earl was hard to pin down. Detached. Impersonal. She wondered whether this new version was the real Earl or just another disguise he slipped into.

Earl had been watching Aronson for weeks. He'd said so. He'd been going where Aronson went, watching what Aronson did. If that was true, and she had no reason to think it wasn't, then he had to have known Aronson had taken her.

He had to have known that she was a prisoner in that house and he'd done nothing to help her. He hadn't called the cops, he hadn't tried to get her out when Aronson was gone. He'd left her there for Aronson to do with as he pleased.

The job came first. She needed to remember that. Earl might keep her out of harm's way and he might not. She couldn't count on it.

Didn't matter, she thought as she felt for the gun next to her. If Aronson came after her again, she'd blow his balls off. At first, she hadn't been able to believe she'd really shot him. She'd been so afraid that when faced with the man, a live human being, that she wouldn't be able to pull the trigger. But she had. She did what she had to and she could do it again.

It was reassuring, knowing that about herself, something most people never had to find out.

≈≈≈

Chastain paused, about to go through the door, and thought, this is too easy.

He pulled his foot back and examined the doorway. At ankle height, a thin length of nearly invisible nylon line was suspended above the floor.

He looked through the crack in the door and discovered that the line led to a small black box with a blinking red light.

He stepped over the line into the house and carefully crossed the floor to the cellar door. It was standing open.

In the cellar he found five blocks of explosive: one attached to the floor joists at each corner, and the fifth attached to the Computer. Aronson apparently didn't want to take any chances the computer might survive the explosion.

Under ideal circumstances, if there were such things when it came to explosives, even an expert deactivating a bomb was a nerve-wracking, time-consuming ordeal.

These were not ideal circumstances and he was not an expert.

He was knowledgeable, but unlike Aronson, he hadn't spent ten years of his military career working with explosives.

He stood there staring at the PC, wishing there was a way he could disconnect it, take it with him back to the Price place and hook it up to the monitor there, but he couldn't without risking the computer and himself.

He left the farmhouse and went through the woods to his truck. Jessie wasn't going to like what he was going to ask her to do.

"I'm on my way back," he said when she answered. "The disks were destroyed...looks like I ran over them.

"You said you messed with his computer so that he wouldn't be able to get into his files. Can you still get to them? Is what you did reversible?"

There was a pause before she said, "I can get to them."

"I'm going to have to ask you to restore the files and download them again. I've got to send them to my contact so he can get some people on them; see if they can figure out what Aronson is going to do."

He heard her sigh, not with irritation but exhaustion before she said, "It might take me a little while."

"What's a little while?"

She'd already been in the computer once, so that would go a lot faster, but now she had to undo what she'd done to the hard drive. She thought for a few seconds. "Maybe an hour."

"Faster would be better."

"I figured."

"There's a little hitch." Before she had a chance to say anything, he continued, "He's got the computer wired with explosives. It can't be moved out of the cellar."

She was silent, knew what was coming, but wanted, for some perverse reason, to make him say it.

"You're going to have to come here."

She didn't respond. She wanted to scream **NO**. She wanted to hang up. Cry. But she didn't.

People would die.

Chastain said, "Jessie?"

"I heard you."

"I'll be there in about five minutes."

≈≈≈

Jessie stared straight ahead through the windshield, not speaking, swaying with the movement of the truck, but otherwise, not moving. She appeared calm on the surface, but was wound so tight, she was about to break.

Chastain glanced at her as he drove.

She hadn't fussed. She hadn't tried to talk him out of taking her back to Aronson's. Her lips were clamped tightly together, but she kept her chin up. He had to admire her grit.

There wasn't a damn thing he could do about the situation and he was surprised that she seemed to understand that. There was no way he could make this any easier for her. He'd told her he was certain Aronson wasn't coming back and that was about all he could do.

He glanced at her again as he neared Aronson's house. She was as silent as a stone and just about as easy to read. She gave him absolutely no indication what she was thinking.

Chastain pulled off the road and when the house came into view, Jessie thought she might just fly into a million tiny pieces.

CHAPTER FIFTY-THREE

Chastain killed the engine, giving Jessie a few seconds before he got out of the truck.

She opened her door and got out slowly.

"Look..." he began but she interrupted him.

"Don't." Her voice was raspy, her throat and mouth dry. "Just... don't."

He nodded and helped her out, then followed her as she moved from tree to tree, using them to keep her balance, keeping them between herself and the house. She followed the path she'd taken not long before, using the cover of the creek. She stopped, breathing hard, and he leaned in to speak softly into her ear. "You wait here. I'm going to go back in, make sure the place is still clear."

He was gone for what seemed a long time to Jessie, but was probably only four or five minutes.

He jogged back out to the creek, gave her a hand up the bank and pulled her along behind him until they reached the porch.

Because her balance was unreliable, he took her hand to steady her as she crossed the wire in the doorway. Her hand was trembling in his grasp, giving him the first real indication of the emotional turmoil she was suffering, something he couldn't help and wouldn't dwell on.

He stepped over the wire, went down the first few steps into the cellar, and turned to give her his hand.

Jessie stopped at the doorway.

He's gone, she said to herself as she made herself step down onto the first step. You can do this. Earl is right here. Aronson is gone. This is just a place. Just an empty cellar. She kept up her internal dialogue as she went down the steps.

Halfway down, without warning, she froze, unable to force herself down another step.

She sat down hard, shaking so much her legs wouldn't hold her. She was tingling all over and her lips and fingers had gone numb.

Chastain turned to look up into her face. "Hang on a minute," he said, then ran down the rest of the steps into the cellar.

She heard him below her moving around; by the time his feet came pounding back up the steps, she was nearly unconscious, her fingers cramping, she could feel them bending themselves into strange contorted shapes.

She tried to brush away the plastic bag he was holding against her mouth, but her movements were weak and jerky, and he easily resisted her efforts. "You're hyperventilating." When she jerked her head away, he repeated, "Jessie, you're hyperventilating. You're getting too much oxygen. Try to slow your breathing down."

Jessie heard him, but thought he must be insane. She couldn't suck *enough* air into her lungs.

He was holding her in place, keeping the bag to her mouth until her senses began to return.

"Oh, God," she gasped confused and tearful. She leaned weakly against him and started to cry.

Chastain had nothing to say. He just sat there, holding her and allowing her a few precious minutes.

Abruptly, she pushed him away and sat up, sniffing and wiping at her cheeks.

She took a shaky breath and said, "I'm okay now."

After a second or two, she stood up, holding onto the wall for support and made her way the rest of the way down into the cellar.

The place was a mess and the containers were gone, but oddly, the chair she'd sat in to shoot him was still there at the end of the table, right where she'd put it. Her eye traveled to the spot where he'd fallen and she saw a dark stain ... blood. His blood. She'd made him bleed and she was glad.

"Whatever you do, don't touch these." Chastain pointed to the wires attached to a block of what looked like clay taped with duct tape to the side of the CPU.

He moved the chair from the end of the table to the computer. "As long as you don't touch anything but the keyboard, we should be fine."

She gingerly took her seat and re-booted the computer, waiting for an explosion.

She wondered what being blown into mist would feel like or if it would be so fast that it wouldn't feel like anything at all.

Once she started typing in commands, Jessie tried to focus completely on the screen in front of her. It wouldn't help to think about being blown up or let her attention wander to the cell in the back.

The faster she got to Aronson's files, the faster she'd get out of here.

Getting rid of the virus she'd planted was going to be more time consuming than she liked. She regretted doing it until she discovered that he'd tried to wipe his hard drive. The virus would have shut the program down before it could run, so at least by planting the virus, his files were still intact.

Chastain began looking through the items Aronson had left behind, hoping for a clue to what he'd been doing. There wasn't much and what there was didn't tell him a damn thing.

Every few minutes, he'd return to the table, standing behind Jessie, silent, motionless, willing her to hurry, feeling the minutes flying by. Finally, she stopped typing, turned in her seat and just looked at him.

"Sorry," he said and moved away from her, toward the back of the cellar.

He entered one of the small cubicles, searched it thoroughly, then moved to the other and did the same thing. Opened the door hiding the generator and made his way back to the table, searching, examining, wasting time, covering ground he'd already covered just to give himself something to do.

He moved back to the table and went through the sparse documents Aronson had left behind again, finding nothing more sinister than a few maps of the county, some satellite pictures of the same with nothing marked on either, and blank paper.

The GPS signal on Chastain's phone beeped. Aronson's truck was moving.

He watched while it paused before turning onto Ice House Road, west. He wasn't coming to the farmhouse.

Chastain was going to have to follow him.

"How soon 'til you're done?" he asked.

She didn't look up. "An hour maybe," she answered, still typing, "and that's just getting into the computer. Then I've got to transfer the data to your flash drive."

"Aronson's truck is moving."

Jessie did stop typing then, to look at him.

"I can't see what he's doing if I'm not there."

She didn't say anything, but her face had gone paler still.

"Well, do you have a better suggestion?" he asked, harsher than he'd meant to. "You have the cell phone. Call me when you're done."

He softened his tone and said, "He can't come back here without me knowing about it."

"If he's in the truck," she said.

"If he's in the truck," he agreed, brusque again. He looked at his watch. "You've got your gun. I'll be back as soon as I can."

He felt her eyes on him all the way up the steps.

≈≈≈

Chastain was a little more than fifteen minutes behind Aronson. He pulled onto the road, his foot hard on the gas. As long as Aronson was still moving, he had a chance to catch up before he reached his destination.

From behind him he heard a siren, one short whoop. Chastain braked and pulled part of the way off the road to give the deputy room to go around, but the deputy didn't pass him. He stopped behind him about twenty feet back.

"Hands where I can see them," the deputy blared over the loud speaker.

Chastain knew he'd been going pretty fast, but there weren't any speed limits posted on these little county roads. He didn't have time for this shit. The truck looked beat up on the outside, but it could outrun the cruiser.

But if he ran, he'd have every cop in the county on his ass. He thought a five minute delay while some deputy wrote him a ticket was preferable to being the object of a police chase. He looked in the side mirror, watching the deputy approach with his hand on the butt of his gun. The deputy stopped several feet behind the truck. "Get out of the truck! Open the door, put your hands on your head and get out of the truck!"

What the hell?! Okay, Chastain thought, this is not a routine traffic stop.

The deputy paused, then shouted, "I said get out of the truck. NOW!"

Chastain hit the gas and sprayed gravel, the rear of the truck fishtailing as he pulled back onto the road.

The deputy yelled "Stop," as Chastain pulled away, and ran back to his cruiser.

Chastain thought he had a good chance of getting away, the gap between the truck and the cruiser was widening, then he saw the flashing blue and red lights coming from the other direction.

The oncoming cruiser slid sideways across the road and stopped. Chastain slammed on his brakes, spun the truck around and headed right at the deputy coming up behind. The deputy didn't have enough time to pull his cruiser across the road and Chastain managed to blow by him, but the other deputy was now on his ass.

He heard more sirens in the distance and when he saw more flashing lights coming at him, he knew they'd have him boxed in. He stopped the truck and considered making a run for the woods, but that would leave him with no vehicle, he'd lose most of his equipment and he'd have half the county looking for him. It was a no-win situation.

His cell phone had gone flying when he'd spun the truck around and he was blindly searching the passenger floor board when the barrel of a rifle came through the passenger window. "Get your hands up in the air. I'd hate to have to blow your head off."

They drug him out of the truck and into the road, face down in the gravel. The knee in his back while they cuffed him carried a lot of unnecessary weight, and when he tried to raise his head to speak, his face was smashed back down into the rocks. "Shut up. We want you to talk, we'll tell you," snarled the deputy who'd cuffed him.

Less than a minute later, the same deputy was back. "You wanna' tell me what all that blood's doing in your truck?" He grabbed Chastain's hair and jerked his head back. "When we test that blood, we gonna' find out it's the missing girl's? Jessie DuBois'?" he asked.

≈≈≈

I didn't take that girl!" Chastain shouted.

"Didn't I tell you to shut up?" the surly deputy responded, prodding Chastain, not gently, in the ribs with the toe of his county issue, steel-toed boot. "You just shut your mouth and save it for the detectives."

"Listen," Chastain began, then grunted as the toe made contact again, this time, more in the nature of a kick than a prod, with enough force behind it to crack a rib.

"You gonna keep talkin'?" asked the burly deputy who bent over until his face was inches from Chastain's.

Another voice, younger and deeper, snapped, "Knock it off, Frank. You want to bust up somebody, you do it when my career's not on the line."

"Pussy," Frank muttered under his breath and yanked on the cuffs, hauling Chastain to his feet, nearly pulling his arms out of their sockets.

The deputy grabbed Chastain's collar and his belt and gave him the bum's rush toward one of the cruisers. He gave him a shove in the middle of the back that nearly sent him sprawling.

He'd gotten a look at the deputy when he'd pulled Chastain to his feet: a stocky man, about fifty pounds overweight, still a deputy at the age of forty-five or so. If he had to guess, he'd say Frank was one of those cops who'd lost all interest in the job, except for the power it gave him, and was just marking time until he could start collecting his pension. Frank had heard it all a million times and wasn't interested in talking to Chastain. That was someone else's job. Nonetheless, Chastain decided to try again. "I need to make a call. You let me do that, I'll shut up."

"You'll shut up anyway," the deputy said as he tossed him in the back of the cruiser, shut the door and sauntered away.

Chastain had two options. He could let the arrest run its course or try to escape.

Even if he told them the absolute truth and even if they believed him, which they wouldn't...none of the troopers milling around his truck would let him go, they didn't have the authority.

He could send them out to Aronson's, but it would be a while before they'd be able to go near the place. They'd set up a perimeter and wait for the bomb squad. Once the bomb squad got there, they'd want to get Jessie out as quickly as possible, but they wouldn't want to take any chances with her or their men, and it would be a slow process. That's what kept them alive.

What if Aronson had backed the trip wires up with a timer Chastain hadn't seen? A man as thorough as Aronson would have a backup. The minutes would be ticking away while he sat in a cell or an interrogation room. How long before the house blew up? An hour? A half hour? Ten minutes? Five? If the house went up, Jessie would go up with it, along with the information on Aronson's computer. And they had to have it. Had to.

Once he was loose, he could get to a phone and have Fitz call the hunt off. His cover would be blown, but the information on Aronson's computer would be secure.

Chastain pulled his cuffed hands down under his butt, down the backs of his thighs until he could draw his feet up and pass the cuffs under. A quick, painful jerk that popped both shoulders allowed him to bring his hands in front of him. He knew without looking, that the back of the cruiser would be escape proof, but he tried the doors just the same. He could pick the handcuff lock if he could find something to do it with and he began a methodical search of the car. Nothing useful on the floor. What he really needed, he thought, was a bobby pin. He felt under the seat and came up empty, then shoved his hand down into the crack between the seat and the back. He came up with a gum wrapper, a condom, still in the package, a penny and a cheap barrette.

The barrette had a metal clasp, hot damn.

Using his teeth, he worked the clasp loose from the plastic, then flattened out the loop of metal until it was reasonably straight. He was out of practice and it took him a several minutes, but finally, the cuffs were off.

He began kicking the inside of the door, quick hard thumps that rattled the windows and even with its heavy-duty suspension, rocked the car.

He heard a shout from outside, then voices coming closer, "God damn it, Frank," said the young voice that had kept Frank from kicking the shit out of him. "Why'd you have to put him in my unit?"

"It was closer. He don't calm down, we're gonna' have to Taser him," Frank said, then raised his voice. "You hear that, Price? You stop kickin' this car or we'll Taser your ass!" He reached inside the front door and released the trunk lid, then went around behind the cruiser, presumably, to get the Taser.

If anything, Chastain put more vigor into the kicks, hoping the young one would at least try to talk to him first before they hit him with 50,000 volts of electricity.

The other deputy, Brad Ford, according to his nametag, approached the door. He was huge, a hulking bear of a man, and he was pissed.

The bear/man wrenched the door open. "What the hell's the matter with you?!"

Chastain had stopped kicking and was on his knees, hands behind his back as though he was still cuffed, facing Deputy Ford, when he shouted, "I said I want to make a phone call!" When the deputy said, "Oh, brother," looked down and shook his head, Chastain launched himself, shoulder first into his stomach.

While Deputy Ford lay on the ground trying to suck in a breath, Chastain relieved him of his side arm.

Frank came around the car and Chastain said softly, "Don't be a hero, Frank," but with the gun under Deputy Ford's chin, there wasn't a lot Frank could do. "You make a sound and Deputy Ford here is gonna' lose part of his head. You understand, Frank?" Chastain said, "Get up," and Deputy Ford got slowly to his feet.

The other men, down the road only fifty feet or so away, hadn't yet realized what was happening and Chastain kept his voice low, keeping the big deputy in front of him. He detached the cuffs from Deputy Ford's belt and instructed him to put them on, which he did, slowly. Once the big deputy was cuffed, he said to Frank, "Your gun," and nodded at his side arm. "Drop it and kick it over." When Frank just stood there, indecision playing across his face, Chastain said, "Of all the deputies here to choose from, if I was gonna' shoot somebody, it'd be you. But I'd still rather not. Your gun."

Frank slowly pulled his weapon from its holster, then nervously licked his lips, eyes darting, looking for an opportunity. Chastain knew how risky this situation was and how disastrously ugly it could turn in a heartbeat. Although the men didn't know it, he was on their side, and he didn't, even accidentally, want to shoot one of them, even Frank.

Unexpectedly, Deputy Ford spoke, "Frank, don't be an ass hole. You can't put a bullet in him without going through me first. Just give him the God damned gun."

Frank threw the gun down and kicked it hard in Chastain's direction where it slid under the cruiser. "Now your cell and your shoulder mic."

Chastain backed away from the open door, pulling the deputy with him. "Frank, your cuffs are on there on the floor." He nodded toward the back of the cruiser. "Climb in and put them on."

Frank reached in, putting a knee on the seat and Chastain murmured to the big deputy, "Why don't you help him in?"

Deputy Ford hesitated, then put a foot on Frank's big backside and shoved. Chastain slammed the door and felt a whole lot safer. Frank was the kind of loose cannon that got innocent people killed.

Now all Chastain had to do was to relieve five other deputies of their weapons and their cell phones and their radios and herd them and Deputy Ford into the backs of the cruisers where they would be locked in.

"Hey!!" came a shout from across the road as one of the deputies started to run toward them, reaching for his gun. He stopped when Chastain turned the big deputy slightly, making sure he could see the gun he now held to his head.

"Hands up!" Chastain shouted and four pairs of hands reluctantly reached for the sky. There should have been five pair and Chastain had just realized there were only four when a solid hunk of wood crashed into the back of his skull dropping him like a rock.

CHAPTER FIFTY-FOUR

George hadn't gotten Glenna to agree to leave the search party and go back to Melba's, but he hadn't really expected her to, so he'd joined in the search until he got the call about Earl Price.

When he got to where his deputies had cornered Price, Price was handcuffed, sitting on the ground, having his head bandaged by a paramedic. Bruises had started to darken around the cuts and gouges on his face.

"All that happen when Dearing clobbered him?" His gaze zeroed in on Frank.

"Yeah." Frank hitched his pants up over his belly and stuck his chin out. The other deputies had been giving him non-stop shit about being handcuffed and locked in Ford's unit by their prisoner. It didn't help that Frank had no sense of humor and the incident had, if anything, been more Ford's fault than his.

"You hit him more than once?" George addressed the question to Dearing.

Dearing flicked his eyes over to Frank then shrugged.

"Landed on his face." Frank offered.

George looked Frank up and down. "What are we going to see when we review the dash cam?" George asked.

"Ain't workin'" Frank said.

"Convenient," George replied.

He turned his attention back to Dearing. "Glad you had the good sense to knock him in the head instead of shooting him. He's the only one who can tell us where the DuBois girl is."

Dearing accepted the praise without revealing that he hadn't shot at Price because he wasn't sure he would've actually hit Price and not deputy Ford.

"Anybody ask him where the DuBois girl is?"

"He ain't talkin'," Frank answered. "Except to say he wants to make a call."

George took a good look inside the Price truck before the tow truck pulled it away. Blood. A lot of it. Not completely dry, but clotted and crusty around the edges. They didn't know the blood was Jessie's and if it was, they didn't know she was dead. But if it was her blood, and if she was dead, and if she'd been in this truck recently, they weren't likely to find her body out on Patterson Road where Glenna and others had been searching for a couple of hours. Small blessings.

He would have liked to keep Price's capture quiet until they'd confirmed whose blood was in the truck, but DNA would take weeks. Already, he'd bet the details were whipping through the county like newly laundered sheets hung out to dry in a high wind.

Once Price had been patched up he was transported to the State Police Post with George following behind. He had no authority, no standing in the investigation. This was the State's case, but he wanted to be there when Price was questioned.

CHAPTER FIFTY-FIVE

Dan had barely gotten to sleep when the phone rang. "They got Price," said Charlie, his voice rough with fatigue, "There's blood all over the inside of his truck. Girl could be at his place," he continued.

Dan had crawled out of bed and grabbed his clothes as soon as he heard Charlie's voice. "You request a warrant?" he asked.

"You think we need one?" Charlie asked, surprised. "We've got probable cause."

"You think so, I think so, but we can't be sure what some judge is going to think a year or two from now when this comes up for trial. I don't think we should take any chances," Dan replied.

≈≈≈

There were three state cruisers and Charlie's car at the Price place when Dan got there. They had the battering ram out and were standing on the porch, waiting for the go ahead.

Dan held the warrant up as he got out of his car and the men began breaking down the door.

Dan stepped up onto the porch. "Anybody inside?"

One of the troopers shook his head, "If there is, they aren't comin' to the door. I hollered and I knocked, but nobody answered."

"Got the back of the house covered?"

"Yeah," the trooper answered.

"Man," said the trooper wielding the ram. "What's this damn door made of, anyway?"

It took several hits, but the door finally gave and the men crowded into the house, guns drawn.

Charlie shouted, "Police! Police! Drop your weapon."

"Blood!" Dan nodded at the sofa. "We've got blood here, lots of bloody bandages too."

The troopers pounded up the stairs, while Dan and Charlie cleared the rest of the downstairs. They got to the kitchen and Dan tried the cellar door while Charlie opened the back door and looked out.

The cellar door was locked and Dan put his shoulder to it, but it didn't budge. There wasn't enough room between the door and the wall to use the battering ram, so he backed up, braced himself against the wall behind him, kicked until the bottom panel came loose, then reached in and unlocked the door.

Dan flipped the light switch, but nothing happened and one of the troopers said, "Here," and handed him a flashlight from his belt. He went just a few steps down and ducked his head below the floor joists so he could see. "Jessie! State Police!"

He went on down into the cellar but aside from an ancient furnace and water heater, some boxes piled haphazardly in one corner and a couple of stacks of newspapers tied into bundles, it was completely bare. The walls were block, undisturbed, as far as he could tell, since the day they'd been laid. There was certainly no sign that they'd been moved recently. The floor was the same with no indication that a grave had been dug.

He moved the boxes aside, looked behind them and had just concluded that there was no place Price could have stashed the girl down here when one of the troopers came back to the cellar door and called down, "Anything?"

"Nope. Nothing upstairs?"

"Nothing."

"You check the attic?"

"It's clear."

"How about the barn?"

"Nothing there either."

"Son of a bitch! She's not here."

The blood in Price's truck wasn't even completely dry. If the blood belonged to Jessie, she'd been in his truck only hours before he was pulled over. She'd disappeared last night, more than twenty-four hours ago. Dan could think of only one reason Price would risk moving her: to dispose of the body. But why in daylight? Why not wait until dark?

It just didn't make sense, unless Price was just as stupid as he looked.

He went out through the back door and walked toward the barn, looking past it to the woods beyond. It was six o'clock, still light, but not for long. "Get forensics out here," Dan ordered, "and get on the phone to the National Guard post. Get some people out here to search the woods while they can still see. She could be out there."

They would search the property, but it would take a lot of manpower and time and they didn't have enough of either. The sooner they found Jessie, the better the odds she'd be alive.

"Let's go talk to Earl Price," said Charlie.

CHAPTER FIFTY-SIX

It took longer getting back into Aronson's computer than Jessie thought it would. Her eyes were tired and she struggled to keep the screen in focus.

Being back down here made all the images get scrambled up in her head, a confused cascade of sensation and sound. When she'd been at Earl's she'd been able to tuck it all away, lock it in its own little box and shove it into a dark corner. But now, alone, surrounded by the dank smell of musty earth, the hum of the monitors, the constant drip over in the corner, the cold and damp, she couldn't keep the thoughts away.

She eyed the blanket on the floor. It was right where she'd dropped it when she'd gotten up to run after shooting Aronson. It was a little damp, but she put it around her and sat back down. Her fingers started moving again over the keys. Earl would be back soon, she told herself, and when he got there, she wanted to be ready.

The pills she'd taken had made her feel better for a while, but she was starting to ache all over and the chill had settled back in.

Jessie shivered, even with the blanket wrapped around her. Every joint in her body hurt. Even her teeth hurt. Even her hair hurt.

While Aronson's files downloaded, she opened his deleted emails folder and started reading the only information on his computer she hadn't already seen. She opened the first one. It was dated today.

'VX ships tonight. 21:00.'

"Oh my God," she said. "Oh my God!"

She'd heard him on the phone, telling someone, "Tonight. Twenty-one hundred." She'd thought he was giving someone an amount, like twenty one hundred dollars. But it wasn't an amount. It was a time. Military time.

CHAPTER FIFTY-SEVEN

Earl Price looked sullen and stupid under the glare of the unforgiving fluorescents. He was escorted down the hall and into an interrogation room. A bloody gauze pad was stuck to the back of his head and his face was pale, cuts and bruises standing out.

Once he'd been shackled to the chair, he was left alone. Charlie, Dan and George studied him on the monitor that showed everything that happened in the dingy little room.

Aside from his driver's license he was an unknown. They hadn't gotten a hit on his finger prints, so he'd never been in any trouble and he hadn't been in the military.

Normally, they'd let him sit and stew for a couple of hours, but they needed him to tell them where Jessie was. The blood in his truck had looked like a lot, but it wasn't as much as they'd first thought. She could still be alive.

He'd almost gotten away. Would have if Deputy Dearing hadn't gone up into the woods to take a leak about the time Price tackled Deputy Ford. On his way back, he'd seen Price holding the gun on Ford and had made a long wide arc, coming up behind the man, taking him down with a tree limb.

They'd just begun to process the truck, and so far, the contents of the storage bin in the bed had yielded a number of illegal weapons, bugging and tracking devices, high powered binoculars and night vision goggles.

The phone on Dan's desk rang. He answered, and then said, "Be right down." He looked up at Charlie. "There's an old guy downstairs with a couple of kids. They say they saw Jessie DuBois get kidnapped. I'll bring them up. See what they have to say."

George stood leaning against a file cabinet, looking at Price on the monitor, hands in his pockets, making like what he was, just an observer. "Looks like things are starting to come together."

"Yeah, another nail in this guy's coffin."

"Why don't you see if you can get anything out of Price while I talk to the kids," Dan suggested.

"Sounds good to me." Charlie stopped at the door to the interview room and took a deep breath.

≈≈≈

Jessie sat in front of the computer, huddled under the blanket, but couldn't get warm. The Vicodin she'd found in her pocket wasn't helping and she hurt all over. She'd texted Earl the e-mail she'd found, but he hadn't responded, and she'd called his cell over and over.

The data from Aronson's computer was still downloading, but was almost complete.

She could hardly think anymore. She was desperate for sleep, if only for a few minutes.

She put her head in her hands and did her best to keep her eyes open.

≈≈≈

Aronson looked at his watch and reflexively, Stephanos looked at his. "Be time to blow the house soon."

Aronson nodded. "Give it another half hour or so."

CHAPTER FIFTY-EIGHT

Dan opened the door to a small waiting area and was surprised to see Lyle sitting there with another kid.

A man who looked to be well into his seventies was on his feet, leaning against one wall, his arms folded across his chest. He wore the farmer's uniform: well-worn bib overalls sagging on his spare frame, a John Deere cap covering his head. Years of sun and wind had left their mark, but couldn't hide the anger tinged with sorrow that Dan saw on the man's face. The man straightened. "This here's my grandson, John, and his friend, Lyle. They got somethin' to say."

"Your name is?" Dan took out a notebook.

"Kitzinger, Roy Kitzinger."

"John, what's your last name?"

Roy answered for him. "Kitzinger, same as me." He spared his grandson a quick look. "John lives with me. He's my son's boy."

The kids looked terrified and Dan thought Lyle might pass out any second, so he got right to the point. "I already talked to you once today, Lyle and you didn't know anything about anything. Now you say you saw somebody take Jessie Dubois?"

Lyle swallowed, then nodded.

"Who?"

"I don't know, some guy, I never seen before," Lyle answered.

"Why'd you lie?"

Lyle started to speak, but nothing came out. He cleared his throat and tried again. "We was where we wasn't supposed to be."

"Who is "we"?"

"Me and John here, and another guy."

"And what is this other guy's name?"

"Elvie." He stopped and swallowed again. "Elvie Morris. He...he's dead. He got killed in a barn fire last night."

"How'd you hear about that?"

"I told 'em," Roy answered. "My truck was in the barn where he died. They came out to ask me about it, told me what'd happened to the boy. Looks like he stole my truck and drove it out there." Roy tipped his hat back with his thumb, pulled a crumpled red bandana from a back pocket and wiped it across his forehead. "I didn't like that boy. Got John in trouble more 'n once. He's in trouble now 'cause of him, but wouldn't have wished dyin' like that on anybody." He trained a look on John that wasn't hard to read. He waited a second, but John didn't look up at him, looking instead at his hands where they were clasped tightly together in his lap.

There was a moment of silence, then Dan said, "Okay. Why don't you tell me what you saw, Lyle, and we'll let why you were where you weren't supposed to be, go for now."

"Well, we were out in old man Patterson's back pasture, the one where he keeps the bulls when he's breedin' and we saw this truck parked on the other side of the creek, pulled way up into the trees. We thought it was a funny place to park, so Elvie went to look inside, see if anybody was in there, but there wasn't, so we kind of forgot about it."

"And then what?"

"Well, we'd been out there in the sun for a while and it was hot, so I went down by the creek, in the shade, to cool off. I was closest. John and Elvie didn't really see nothin' 'cause they were up by the gate." He paused and licked his lips, his eyes moving from object to object in the room, never staying in one spot for long. "I was pretty close to the creek when I saw this guy come up the bank on the other side and go over to the Blazer, and he had Jessie with him."

"Blazer? You're sure it was a Blazer, not a pickup?"
Lyle nodded.

"Now you say Jessie was with this guy. How do you know she wasn't just with him, I mean voluntarily?" Dan asked.

"She was tied. Her hands were tied and she was hurt, too. She had blood all over her face. She looked right at me." Lyle talked faster, blurting it out, getting it off his chest. His voice cracked, the voice of a child becoming a man. "The man, he had a gun and he pointed it right at me. He was going to shoot me, and he would have, but Jessie ran into him and knocked him down, and then I ran." He was crying now, and sobbed out, "I ran, and I didn't try to help her. I let Elvie talk me into keepin' quiet and if she dies, it'll be all my fault!"

In the seat next to Lyle, John stared down at his worn tennis shoes. A tear plopped on the back of his hand, but he didn't seem to notice.

"You said you hadn't seen this guy before. The guy who had Jessie?"

Lyle wiped his nose on the tail of his tee shirt. "Unh uh." He shook his head.

"Lyle, you know Earl Price?"

Lyle sniffled. "Yeah. Well, I don't know him exactly, but I know who he is."

"And the man you saw, the man who had Jessie, that wasn't Earl Price?"

"Unh uh. He didn't look nothin' like Earl Price. You mean the guy comes into Melba's? Likes to flirt with Jessie?" he clarified.

"Yeah, that Earl Price."

"No, it wasn't him."

"Lyle, you already lied about this once," said Dan. "How do I know you're telling the truth now?"

"'Cause when I saw them, the man and Jessie, I was somewhere I wasn't supposed to be, and I'm gonna' be in a world of shit, uh," he threw a sideways look at Roy, "I mean, I'm gonna' be in a lot of trouble when my dad finds out."

Dan wearily rubbed his eyes. "Okay, this guy you saw, you never saw him around?"

"No."

"Can you describe him?"

"I guess," Lyle answered. "He was tall, a lot taller than Jessie. Had on a black tee shirt and jeans, I think. He had a hat on, but I didn't see no hair stickin' out or nothin'."

"You get a look at the license plate?" he asked, without much hope.

"Part of it. I noticed 'cause it wasn't a Brewer County tag. The first two numbers were 99 and then a D, but I didn't notice the rest."

Dan remembered seeing, just last night, a Blazer with a 99D plate. "This Blazer wouldn't happen to be black, would it?"

"Uh huh." Lyle nodded.

"Did Elvie try to open any of the doors when he took a look inside?"

"Yeah. Yeah he did. I forgot that."

The question of how Elvie's fingerprints had ended up on Aronson's Blazer had just been answered.

CHAPTER FIFTY-NINE

Charlie entered the interview room and as he turned to close the door said, "I'm Charlie Mayhew, Earl. Detective with the homicide division, State Police."

He leaned on the door and forced himself to relax, staring at Earl without speaking. It was a simple technique, designed to help the interrogator take control of the interview. The longer the silence stretched on, the more control was at stake.

Earl either didn't recognize the power struggle or didn't care, because after only a second or two, he said, "I want my phone call."

Charlie remained at the door, crossed his arms. Casual. "You're not under arrest, Earl. You don't get a call. You don't get squat."

"Horseshit. I want my call."

Charlie stared at Earl. "We found Jessie DuBois' blood in your truck. We found Jessie DuBois' blood in your house. You want to tell me how it got there?" They couldn't be sure the blood was the DuBois girl's until they got the DNA results back, but Earl didn't know that.

He went on, his disgust plain. "Nothing as sick and pitiful as a man who has to force himself on a woman."

Earl responded. "I didn't kidnap her, but I know where she is. Let me have my phone call, I'll take you to her."

"So you can try to escape again?" Charlie responded. He put his hands on the table and leaned in, a subtle threatening gesture. "Where is she? Just tell us where she is and we'll go get her."

"No. I take you or no deal."

"You aren't goin' anywhere Earl."

"I didn't hurt that girl. God damn it! We're wasting time."

"Not us, Earl. You're the one wasting time. Tell us where she is."

"I have to make a phone call. Just let me make my phone call."

"If you didn't take her, then how'd her blood get in your truck?"

"The guy who kidnapped her shot her when she was trying to get away," Earl said. "I heard the shots and pulled over, stopped my truck. She came running out of the woods and I picked her up, put her in my truck and took off. He took a shot at us, took the back window out of my truck."

Charlie had seen the truck. The back window was blown out and they'd found pieces of glass inside the cab. Still, it didn't mean his explanation was true. Charlie had run across some champion liars in his time. "Now that's a real good story Earl, but it doesn't explain how come you didn't take her to the hospital, or maybe the sheriff. She's been shot, you said so yourself, and instead of taking her to the hospital, you take her, bleeding all over the place, first to your house and then to some undisclosed location. You leave her there while you go out running around the county." He paused for a long moment. "Now, does that make any sense to you?"

It was clear that this rube wasn't going to give Chastain his phone call, and he wasn't going to convince him he hadn't kidnapped Jessie when her blood was all over his truck unless she told them herself. But how could he send them out to Aronson's and still keep a lid on the surveillance?

He couldn't.

The clock was ticking. He had to get out of here and get Jessie out of that house. He had to get the data downloaded to Fitz. That was the bottom line. He had to do whatever it took to accomplish that.

Chastain straightened in his seat. "I'll talk to you, but not if somebody else is listening in. No microphone, no recorder."

Charlie cocked his head to one side, appearing to consider the offer. Then he said, "Let's get one thing straight, Earl. You don't call the shots. Besides, we're just having a friendly little chat. No harm in that."

Mayhew was bluffing. He wanted to get it on tape, sure, but he'd cave. Like most of the detectives on the planet, he had an overwhelming desire to know. That's how detectives ended up being detectives. "Take it or leave it."

Well crap, Charlie thought as he studied Earl intently, trying to see beyond the poker face Earl was giving him. The problem was that the guy had nothing to lose by clamming up. It always amazed Charlie how difficult it was for most felons to just shut-up. Didn't look like Earl was one of those.

"Work with me here, Earl," Charlie began when Earl interrupted him.

"Take it or leave it."

"Listen, Earl," Charlie said, "That's how these things work. You help me, I help you, we help each other. I can put in a good word with the prosecutor. Guy who cooperates, the prosecutor's going to appreciate that."

"Take it or leave it."

Charlie frowned at Earl, irritated that he was going to have to play the game Earl's way, but he turned toward the camera in the corner near the ceiling, and with the edge of his hand made a slashing motion across his throat, "No video," he said at the same time.

"No audio," Chastain said.

"No audio," Charlie repeated to the camera.

Chastain nodded toward the chair across the table and lowered his voice, "This goes no further."

Charlie glanced at the chair but remained standing. "You got something to say, say it."

"You're about to fuck up a Department of Defense operation."

Charlie stared at Earl. "Well, that's a new one. Very inventive." He let some of his pent up anger loose. "What kind of bullshit you trying to hand me? Huh, Earl? You're some kind of spy? Is that it? Well, what I think is you're just yankin' my chain here, Earl and you're really startin' to piss me off. I don't care if you're the reincarnation of J. Edgar Hoover. We found Jessie DuBois' blood in your truck and in your house. If she's just fine and dandy like you say, why won't you tell us where she is?"

Chastain leaned forward in his seat, head low, voice intense. "I've had a man under surveillance for months. He's the man who took the DuBois girl. We've gained access to this man's computer files. The computer is at a farmhouse loaded with explosives, rigged to go up at any time. That's where the DuBois girl is: hacking into the man's computer, waiting for me to come back. I don't know when the house is going to go up. There are trip wires, but there could also be a transmitter or a timer. The house goes up, we lose the girl, we lose the computer with everything that's on it."

Charlie studied Price for a moment, uncertain for the first time. "What's this guy's name?"

Chastain hesitated only a second. "Aronson. Jonas Aronson."

When Charlie didn't respond, he went on, "You can verify with the Department of Defense. 912-555-5769. Tell them it's a code call and ask for John Fitzgerald."

"I'll be back," Charlie said.

This goes no further," Chastain said as Charlie reached for the door handle.

"I heard you the first time." He stopped just outside the room and let the door close behind him. "Shit."

George stepped out into the hall. "What did he say?"

Ignoring his promise to keep his mouth shut, Charlie looked around to make sure they were alone and said, "You know about the killings in Bradley?" When George nodded, he went on. "We have a suspect. A guy named Jonas Aronson. Price claims he's with the Department of Defense and he's had this guy Aronson under surveillance for months. He says this Aronson guy took Jessie DuBois."

Dan joined them outside the interrogation room. "Kids say a guy with a black Blazer took Jessie. Definitely not Price, but it sounds like it could've been Aronson."

"We might have a problem," Charlie responded. "A big one. A gigantic one."

"You mean besides the fact that we've been holding the wrong guy and we still don't have any idea where the DuBois girl is?" asked Dan.

"No. Like we've been fuckin' up a DOD undercover operation because we've been holdin' the wrong guy." Charlie told Dan what Earl had said.

"Problem is," continued Charlie, "This guy has an arsenal in his truck. He may not have anything to do with kidnapping the DuBois girl, but we gonna' just turn him loose because we call some number he gives us and we talk to some guy we never heard of? And what about the farmhouse? What if all this stuff about explosives is the truth and the girl gets blown to hell while we're dickin' around?"

"I can make a call," Dan said. "The guy I know isn't with the DOD, but he can find out pretty fast who this Fitzgerald guy is."

≈≈≈

"What do you want us to do?" asked Dan while he unlocked Earl's handcuffs.

"Call off the dogs."

"Done," George and Charlie said together as they trotted down the hall with Earl.

"I don't suppose you can get my gear," he said brusquely, then, "I need my truck. And my cell. What the hell time is it, anyway?"

"A little after 8:00," Charlie responded. "The lab's getting your gear together and they'll meet us in the garage."

The four men were walking quickly, nearing the elevator when they heard a blast that rattled the windows and shook the floor beneath their feet.

After just an instant of motionless shock, Dan said, "In here."

They followed him into an empty conference room with a window.

An orange glow of fire against the darkening sky pinpointed the location of the explosion. Chastain said quietly, "The farmhouse."

≈≈≈

The techs had barely started their inspection of Chastain's truck. They'd replaced the items they'd removed from the locked metal box in the bed before Chastain and the other men arrived. Chastain felt around on the floor until he found his cell phone where it had slid under the seat. There had been several calls and texts. His shoulders sagged. They were all from Jessie. He opened the last text she'd sent. "Oh, sweet Jesus."

He hit speed dial on his cell. They might have just enough time to avert disaster.

CHAPTER SIXTY

To successfully steal the VX, Aronson not only had to be able to get his hands on it, but he also had to have time to escape the intense manhunt that would follow.

During the months they'd been at Bronson's South Pit, while most of the men had quarried stone as cover, one smaller team had been dedicated to boring a tunnel eighteen inches wide that ran from the west edge of the quarry through almost a mile of limestone to State Road 37.

Another team had spent nights drilling shafts 100 feet down into the west face of Midnight Ridge and loading them with explosives. A cluster of shafts were 500 feet north of the tunnel, the rest, more densely spaced, were above and on either side of the tunnel.

The north cluster would blow when the transport was 250 feet south of the tunnel.

The transport would be in radio contact with the base within seconds of the slide.

Before taking any additional action, Aronson would allow two minutes to pass so the base could be alerted to a landslide blocking the transport's way. The base had to be made to believe the transport had been stopped by the landslide, not a hostile force. They'd send support, but not as fast and not as deadly as they would if they thought the shipment was compromised.

Aronson would then jam the radio signal, so no report of an attack could get through. Stephanos and his men would use the thick dust generated by the slide to mask their movements and take out the soldiers guarding the shipment.

The VX canisters, each not much bigger than a thermos, would be removed from the transport and placed on a skid which would be pulled through the tunnel, and in just minutes, there would be 5,000 feet of limestone between the transport and the VX. Stephanos and his men would then move away from the quarry, across the highway, to disappear into the cornfield on the other side of the road. If something went wrong and the pursuit started immediately, any witnesses would send the chase west, away from Aronson and in the direction of Stephanos and his men.

Once Stephanos was clear, the explosives planted in the honeycombed rock would be detonated, bringing the entire ridge down into the road. The transport, the tunnel and any other evidence of the theft would be buried under tons of rock before personnel from the base arrived.

It would take days to excavate the transport and discover that the VX was gone. All Aronson needed was a few hours to get the VX away. He would have the VX loaded and gone in under ten minutes. He'd given himself plenty of time.

CHAPTER SIXTY-ONE

Staff Sergeant Bridgewater drove the hazardous materials transport away from the dock and pulled onto the road that would eventually lead out of the base. Crane was a huge facility, stretching over more than 100 square miles, and he would not actually leave the base for a little over six miles. He'd made these runs several times and knowing he hauled cargo that could kill him and the entire population in a fifty mile radius no longer made him nervous. Hyper-alert, but not nervous.

He'd gone about two miles, hadn't yet left the secure, restricted personnel area, when a camo Humvee pulled onto the road ahead of him. Another pulled in behind. The front Humvee angled across the road and stopped as did the Humvee behind the transport.

"What the hell?" Sergeant Tyson, sitting in the passenger seat, activated his mic to report back to base. Over his headset, he heard: "Stand down Sergeant. Surrender yourself to the security team surrounding your vehicle. Your shipment has been compromised."

A dozen soldiers, dressed head to toe in black, poured out of the two Humvees and formed a ring around the truck. They stood with their weapons ready, but didn't fire and didn't speak.

≈≈≈

Aronson listened to his men reporting in. The transport was late. It should have reached the first checkpoint more than twenty minutes ago. Aronson had just started to consider if he'd been double crossed by Marsh when the first team reported a visual of the target.

State Road 37, even at night was a busy highway. He didn't want to have to deal with a bunch of civilians coming up the highway after the operation had started. People were unpredictable. They had cell phones. Some of them had weapons.

Southbound traffic had been pretty easy to get rid of. A mile north of the quarry, Aronson had set off a rock slide that would block the southbound lanes and take quite a while to clean up.

Coming up with a plan to separate the target from northbound vehicles had been more difficult, but not impossible. It was vital that the driver remain unaware that his vehicle was being isolated, so the first step, to get rid of traffic behind, had been set up so it wouldn't be obvious to anyone, much less the driver.

About ten miles south of Bronson's South Pit, three of Aronson's men pulled out behind the transport from an abandoned vegetable stand. One was in a pickup, one in an SUV and one in a mini-van. The mini-van pulled ahead of the other two and kept pace behind the transport. The pickup went into the left lane and the SUV went into the right lane, side by side, gradually slowing until their speed was slightly slower than the transport.

With the pickup and SUV blocking both lanes, northbound vehicles behind them began to stack up. A minute or two later, the pickup turned on its right signal and sped up slightly, as if it was going to get over and let the frustrated drivers behind it go by. When changing lanes, the rear corner of the truck struck the front corner of the SUV causing the two vehicles to spin across the road. The vehicles behind were too close to stop, causing a chain reaction accident that would close northbound SR37 for the foreseeable future. Aronson's drivers stayed to join in the uproar caused by the accident, but faded quietly away into the darkness when an opportunity presented itself.

Since military vehicles are speed restricted on public roads, even the slowest northbound vehicles ahead of the transport were quickly out of sight. The driver of the minivan stayed several hundred feet behind the transport, his headlights giving the transport driver the illusion that there were other vehicles on the road behind him.

CHAPTER SIXTY-TWO

In place of the original transport, a decoy was already nearing the gate that would exit the base.

Bridgewater, Tyson and the crew were relieved of their fire arms and placed under guard. The source of the information leak was in a very small, select group, which included members of the squad transporting the VX. Until the leak was identified, the men would be secured.

Aronson could have eyes anywhere, including unsecured or public areas inside the base boundaries. The informant could very well be someone at the dock. Aside from the security team and the men occupying the decoy, no one knew that the transport leaving Crane wasn't the one that had left the dock.

They took a chance and delayed departure twenty minutes past the time the transport had been scheduled to leave so Special Ops squads had time to get into place on the ground near the quarry.

≈≈≈

Based on information supplied by Chastain, forces were deployed and dropped two miles north, two miles east and two miles southwest of the quarry, each approaching on foot. The squad deployed to the east met up with Chastain at his observation post. The squad leader, Lieutenant Perry, made it clear that he would be expected to stay out of the way when Aronson set the operation in motion.

"These men don't know you and you don't know them. We've worked together a long time and I don't have time to explain who does what to you or to them. Besides, I'd hate to have to explain to the DOD how you got your ass shot off if you end up at the wrong place at the wrong time."

He motioned to one of the other men, tapped his ear and said, "Newsom there will get you a helmet and get you wired so you know what's going on." To another solder he said, "Get him some body armor." To Chastain he said, "They'll get you fixed up. I've ordered the men to transmit only if absolutely necessary. Don't want anybody picking up any chatter.

"My squad is concentrated here, near the quarry, since that's where Aronson's been spending most of his time, and as far as we know, where he is now. Another squad is across 37 to the west, and the third is on the highway about an eighth of a mile north of here. My orders are to capture, not to kill, and since we're not sure what Aronson's plan is, for now, we'll just stay close.

"The real transport would have been here," Perry checked his watch, "about twenty minutes ago, give or take. The decoy should be here any time."

A shadow slid into the area, seeming to materialize from nowhere, and trotted toward them.

"Sir. No guards posted. Nobody moving around that we could pick up, but we couldn't get a good view down inside. My men would be exposed approaching the rim, and the walls are too steep to..."

He stopped talking when the ground shook, followed by a rumble and the tumbling crash of rock plummeting to the highway below.

"Here we go." Perry opened his mic and said softly, "Whaley. Report."

Perry bent his head, listening, then said, "Rock slide to the north ahead of the transport."

"Stay put," Perry said to Chastain. He gave a hand signal and men moved out of the shadows and joined him. He left enough men behind to guard the quarry gates and started down the steep decline of Ice House Road with the rest.

≈≈≈

Lieutenant Berringer felt the landslide before he heard it. A deafening crash was followed by a mass of dirt and rock thundering down, and small stones peppered the roof of the truck. Huge slabs of stone bounced across the road ahead.

He braked and checked his side mirror in one motion. Alvarez in the seat beside him had ridden from base with his MP7 in the up and ready position. He lowered the muzzle and steadied it, ready to fire.

CHAPTER SIXTY-THREE

The landslide was triggered. The two minutes passed. The radio signal was blocked. Through his earbud, Aronson heard Stephanos give the signal to go. There would be no gun shots to arouse suspicion. Stephanos and his men were experts at killing silently.

Aronson waited for Stephanos to give the signal that the VX had been loaded on the sled and was ready to be pulled through the tunnel.

Three minutes passed, then one more.

"Stephanos! Status!" he whispered into his mic. There was no response and he turned to look at Riley. "You get that?" he asked him tapping his earpiece. Riley nodded.

"Stephanos!" he whispered again. His watch counted off the seconds of another minute, then two.

He scanned the rim of the pit above his head for movement.

Riley had his weapon up, darting looks around the pit. "Somethin's wrong."

The quarry lights were off, so the pit and the area around it were dark. Aronson stood against the huge crane used to lift limestone slabs from the bottom of the pit, slowly scanned the area through his night vision goggles and waited. Had the operation simply gone wrong, somehow? If so, what could have happened that would prevent Stephanos or someone else from contacting him? If the transport squad had managed to put up some resistance, he would have heard something: gunfire, or shouting, or something, and Stephanos would have warned him.

Had they been made? If so, was the quarry being watched or just the road and the transport? If they had the quarry under surveillance, Aronson wouldn't be able to get out any of the gates.

Riley, without knowing it, was going to get him some answers.

He'd told him go ahead and get clear, and Riley had gone, gladly. The plan had called for Riley to exit through a back gate using a motorcycle he'd left there earlier for that purpose.

Riley mounted the bike and as soon as he put his hand out to start it, two men approached him.

Aronson had his answer.

CHAPTER SIXTY-FOUR

One of the helicopters swept its searchlight over the quarry, while others lit the roadway and surrounding areas. Aronson's truck was where he'd parked it next to the trailer, but that didn't mean Aronson was still there.

The helicopter pilot was reporting no visual from inside the pit but they had picked up a single thermal image moving toward the main gate.

The six men they'd captured weren't talking, except the big one, Stephanos, and only to keep from being buried alive under another rockslide. The men had barely cleared the road with their captives when the entire west face of the ridge collapsed. Dirt, sand, and rock particles, thick and gritty, boiled up, making it impossible to see more than a foot in any direction, forcing the helicopters to fly clear of the airborne debris.

Aronson's move toward the main gate had been a feint, intended to lure the search away from his actual destination on the other side of the quarry. Wearing goggles and a respirator, Aronson used the noise and dust from the last explosion to cover his movements until he reached the edge of the cliff. His escape was going to be difficult, more difficult because of the bullet wound, but he never doubted his ability to do it. Besides, he really had no choice.

One of the first things he'd done when he'd finalized the contract for the use of the quarry had been to provide himself with an alternate escape route. He'd spent several days, waiting until dusk, working his way up the sheer cliff outside the quarry, marking footholds, setting pitons, creating a route he, but no one else, could easily use to get back down. If everything had gone according to plan, he would have had no need for it. But everything hadn't gone according to plan.

He tightened the harness across his chest and forced himself to ignore the pain throbbing through his shoulder and down his arm. The carabiner snapped into the first piton with a tiny reassuring click. It would take him about ten minutes to reach the ground below, and his descent would be masked by the trees growing at the foot of the ravine. He'd have to walk the dirt bike he'd hidden at the base of the cliff for some distance or they might hear him. After he left the woods, he'd be traveling on open ground for some of the ride, and if they heard him, the helicopters would be all over him.

He turned and let his legs slide over the edge, giving the rope some slack, groping for the first foothold with the toe of his boot. He found it easily enough and began the long trek down.

CHAPTER SIXTY-FIVE

"What have you got?" Fitz asked.

"Nothing," Chastain responded. "Zip, nada, a big fat zero." He was pissed, really pissed, and not just about losing Aronson. He was pissed about the kids that had gotten away, only to have Aronson catch up with them again. He was pissed about the girl. Especially the girl. He was pissed that he'd had to let Aronson take the girl to begin with, but to make it worse, she'd managed to get away from the bastard, had been safe, and Chastain had put her right back in harm's way. She'd trusted him and he had gotten her killed.

The kids and the girl had gotten to him and he was pissed about that too.

Aronson hadn't gotten the VX and that was some consolation, but he wasn't in custody. They would continue their search: more troops poured into the area every second and the net they spread would widen, but Aronson was gone.

Chastain rubbed his eyes and sighed, the anger dissipating, leaving him feeling drained. Defeated. "We still don't know how he got away. We'll figure it out tomorrow when we have daylight to work by."

"Well, the area is secure. The seven men who were captured are in the stockade at Crane and the base is on lockdown. They don't know yet who at Crane set this up, but it had to have been someone inside, and there are only a few who had the authority to make it happen." There was a pause and to Chastain's surprise, Fitz said, "It's 2:00 A.M. Go home. Take some ibuprofen. Get some sleep."

"I can't..." Chastain began.

"Check in tomorrow," Fitz interrupted him abruptly. "You're no good to me like this. You're so exhausted you can't think straight. Now get some rest and get back with me in the morning."

Chastain ended the call and looked around him. Once they'd determined that Aronson was gone, urgency had been replaced by calm efficiency. A tent, portable lights and tables had been set up near the trailer to create a command post of sorts.

There were still several men setting up equipment, moving lights around or standing guard. Sergeant Davis, head bent, studying a computer screen, was having a quiet word with Lieutenant Perry and another man, a Captain Chastain hadn't seen before.

Chastain removed the helmet and body armor and was looking for a place to put them when Lieutenant Perry left Davis and approached him. "Put those down anywhere," he said. "One of Davis' men will stow them."

"If you don't mind my saying, you look like hell." Perry cocked his head as he took a good look at him. "First time I've seen you in the light. You want a medic to take a look?"

Chastain shook his head, "Looks worse than it is, but I am going to call it a night. I could do with a few hours sleep. Been a long day."

≈≈≈

In the darkness, some of the scattered debris left when the farmhouse had blown was visible, but not much else. Not even a burned out shell remained. Yellow crime scene tape was strung from tree to tree and a deputy was parked in the drive, making it impossible to take a closer look.

He sped up and went on past the house before the Deputy could tell him to move along. The hunt for "Earl Price" should have been called off, but he didn't want to take a chance that this was the one deputy who hadn't gotten the memo.

During the short drive to the Price place, he tried to empty his mind. 'What ifs' were not helpful and changed nothing.

From the road, the moon lit the old brick of the Price place with a mellow, kindly light. It wasn't a bad place to spend a surveillance and he'd appreciated the calm quiet of the solid old house, if not the inadequate plumbing. He'd been in a lot worse.

In another day or two, he'd be gone and he'd move on to the next terrorist, the next arms dealer, the next whatever. It was a pattern that had been his life for almost fourteen years; it was what he did and who he was.

He'd always wanted to be a cop, but during his Junior year in college he'd been recruited by the DOD, and about the same time he'd met Jill.

He hadn't planned on meeting her and falling in love, but it had happened and the summer he graduated, they'd gotten married.

When his daughter, Cassie, had been born, he'd thought he had the world by the tail.

He'd been so lucky to end up with Jill. He'd believed what he was doing was important. She'd accepted that fact when they married and bless her, hadn't tried to change him or his dedication to the job. She'd been the most serene woman he'd ever known, solidly grounded in her belief in herself and her place in his world. She hadn't liked the urgent phone calls in the middle of the night, the missed birthdays and anniversaries. But for the most part, she had understood. Until the last time.

They'd been going on vacation. He had two weeks leave and a promise from Fitz that he wouldn't be called in, come hell or high water. The night before, he'd turned off his cell, then he'd winked at Jill and made a show of unplugging the house phone, just, he'd said, laughing, pulling her close, in case. The next morning, the bags had been packed and loaded into the van. They'd just finished an early breakfast and were about to leave for the cottage at the beach, just a twelve hour drive away, when Fitz' government-issue black Ford had pulled in at the curb.

Face pinched and angry, Jill had unbuckled the car seat and carried Cassie back in the house without a word. Chastain had walked down to the car and let Fitz convince him that another Oklahoma City was about to unfold in St Louis. Every agent was being called in.

Fitz had been apologetic but insistent and while he waited in the car, Chastain had gone back inside to talk to Jill.

He remembered everything about the last time he saw her and Cassie with such clarity. The flowered top she'd had on, the little dangly earrings he'd bought her for her last birthday, the way the sun shone on Cassie's short brown curls. Jill had stood at the kitchen sink, her back to him. Cassie had drifted back to sleep, her head resting on Jill's shoulder, too young at two and a half to understand the tension between the two most important people in her tiny world.

Jill had been angry and had had every right to be. He'd been angry too. Angry at Fitz and at his situation. Angry that Fitz could say, and mean it, that his country needed him more than his family did. Angry that his burden was so heavy and so important and so impossible to ignore.

Without turning around, in a tight little voice, she'd told him to go. Just go. She'd drive down to the shore with Cassie and he could join them in a day or two or whenever Fitz thought the country could get along without him.

And so he'd gone. He'd put his arms around her and Cassie, kissed them both and left them standing at the sink, thinking he'd make it up to them later.

He never got the chance.

Just a few hours later, a sleepy trucker had crossed the median and hit them head-on, killing Jill instantly. Cassie had died three days later.

He'd managed to survive the loss. He'd learned to cope with black despair when every thought was a reminder, every day was a struggle, a fight, just to get out of bed, to shower and shave and brush his teeth.

As bad as the days had been, the nights had been worse. Every night, he'd fallen into bed exhausted, asleep before his head hit the pillow, knowing that in the dead of night, his mind would jerk him awake, his thoughts chasing each other in endless circles until dawn.

He'd requested field duty a few months later: undercover ops. The training, the brain wracking lies and subterfuge, the adrenalin rush that was the essence of the work required absolute terrifying concentration and commitment. The endless hours and days following had shoved everything, every personal consideration into the background and had forced him past his grief, past his sorrow. It had saved him.

He turned on the kitchen light and groped around in the back of the cabinet over the refrigerator until he found the bottle Old Man Price, or hell, maybe old Alice Price had left behind.

The whiskey burned its way down, spreading heat when it hit bottom. After a second swallow, then a third, without thinking, he refilled his glass.

He'd never allowed himself to feel disappointed or elated based on the outcome of a mission. It was what it was and then it was time to move on.

This one left him feeling empty.

The fluorescent light over the bathroom mirror accentuated the several bruises and cuts on his face, most of them compliments of Frank's rough handling.

He rubbed a finger across the small cut and swollen bruise on the bridge of his nose where the girl's head had connected and took another swallow of whiskey, wishing he'd thought to bring the bottle upstairs with him.

He frowned at himself in the mirror and watched himself take another drink.

"This is really not a good idea," he said to his reflection.

The phone in his pocket vibrated.

It would be Fitz.

It was always Fitz.

How pathetic is it, he thought, that the only person who ever calls you is your boss?

"Yeah?" he growled.

There was an uncertain pause, and then a voice he'd never expected to hear again whispered, "Earl?"

CHAPTER SIXTY-SIX

She'd managed to make it through the woods from Aronson's to the barn at the Price place, where Chastain found her, curled into a ball under a mound of dirty straw and empty feed bags. When he knelt beside her, she looked up at him and opened the fist she had tightly clenched to her chest. The flash drive fell out.

He picked it up and shoved it in his pocket, then pushed the feed bags and straw to one side. "Here," he said and put his hand out to help her up. "Jessie?"

There was no response.

≈≈≈

He should really call Dan Carlisle or Charlie Mayhew, he thought as he bent to pick her up. Have one of them take her in to the hospital and preserve what was left of his anonymity.

That's what he should do, he thought as he laid her down on the seat of the truck.

He should be in the house right now, downloading the flash drive, he thought as he settled her head on his thigh. The truck spit gravel turning around in the drive.

He should really slow down, he thought. He'd been drinking. He touched her face with the back of his hand. She was hot, burning up.

The trees flashed by in a blur.

≈≈≈

Chastain sat in a hard plastic seat in the tiny waiting room, drinking a cup of really bad coffee.

He'd barely gotten through the door when Jessie'd been put on a gurney and pushed through double doors at a run. It was after three in the morning, but the treatment area, which had seemed deserted when he'd arrived less than ten minutes ago, was now busy with scrub-clad personnel. A portable x-ray machine rumbled down the hall. A small Asian woman carrying a basket rattling with glass vials trotted away.

He told himself he'd done all he could do for her. Whether he was here or somewhere else would have no effect on what happened to her now.

He took another drink of coffee.

With all the people milling around, shouting orders, he still felt like if he left, she'd be alone. Not that she would know. Or care.

He hadn't called Fitz.

He'd called Dan Carlisle.

Chastain had told the triage nurse that he'd found Jessie hiding in his barn, but he could see trouble in the furtive looks she was throwing his way.

Carlisle walked through the sliding doors, looking rumpled and sleepy.

"How is she?" he asked as he sat next to Chastain.

"Not sure," Chastain responded, then, "Bad." He shrugged, "No one's telling me anything."

"You look like hell."

"Yeah."

"Any sign of Aronson?"

Chastain shook his head.

"She tell you anything? How she got to your place?" Dan asked.

He shook his head again. "She wasn't in any shape to talk."

CHAPTER SIXTY-SEVEN

When Glenna got home, it was almost ten. It had been a bewildering, disappointing day. Late in the afternoon at the search site, George had gotten a call on his cell and had to leave. Then, just as the light was going and they had called a halt for the night, a farmhouse west of the woods where they were searching had exploded. She sat on the steps and put her head down on her knees. Darrell had dropped her off and promised to be there to pick her up at first light in the morning, but she wasn't sleepy and didn't want to go inside.

Tommy wasn't home. Nothing unusual. Tommy was seein' somebody in town, had been for years. It wasn't that she even really cared what he did. Even if he'd found somebody else, he'd never let her go. Because that's not what men did. Men who were married and foolin' around wanted to stay married. They didn't want another wife, they wanted a girlfriend.

A mosquito buzzed around her face and another landed on her arm. She waved them away and stood up. It was time to go in.

She couldn't stand the thought of going to bed upstairs and sleeping next to Tommy when he finally stumbled in, so she wandered into Jessie's room. Exhausted, she curled up on the bed, clutched Jessie's pillow to her chest and tried not to think. She was more successful than she thought she would be and woke up when she heard the crunch of tires in the gravel next to the house.

Tommy. She didn't want to talk to him, didn't want to see him, but she got up and went into the living room. When she looked out the window, she saw George getting out of his cruiser.

She ran out onto the porch to meet him, breathless, her heart pounding.

"She's alive, Glenna," he said, and had to catch her when her knees gave out.

≈≈≈

George had insisted on driving Glenna to the trauma center in Indianapolis where Jessie'd been air lifted. He'd convinced her that if she rode with the boys or her brother, she'd be held up for hours because of the roadblocks set up by Homeland Security. With George's lights and siren going, they'd gotten through the bottlenecks fairly quickly, only having to stop long enough to have grim faced soldiers inspect the trunk and back seat of the cruiser. After that, they'd gone straight up 37, and Glenna couldn't see the speedometer, but she imagined their speed hovered around the one hundred mile an hour mark. George got them to Indianapolis in a third of the time it would normally have taken.

She'd scribbled a note for Tommy and left it taped to the bathroom mirror. She called her brother, her sons and Melba on George's cell on the way in and they all said they'd be there as soon as they could. Mason was in Afghanistan, but she'd been promised that word would be gotten to him as soon as possible.

She made herself stop thinking about what Jessie might have been through, what might have been done to her. She was alive, and for now that was enough.

CHAPTER SIXTY-EIGHT

"Coming up next, new information on the weekend's failed terrorist attack in Brewer County, Indiana."

"What the hell?" Chastain muttered and waited for the series of commercials to end.

"The Washington Post this morning revealed that information provided by a Brewer County woman gave authorities time to prevent the theft of the deadly nerve agent, VX, from a military transport."

A picture of Jessie, younger, in a posed school picture, appeared on the screen, followed by video of a crane lifting a large slab of rock out of the road, an aerial shot of the quarry, and then Aronson's mug shot.

"An unidentified source reports that Jessica Marie DuBois, who had been abducted by alleged domestic terrorist, Jonas Aronson, managed to free herself when she was left alone. While held captive by Aronson, she discovered that he and another man were planning a terrorist attack. That belief prompted her to search Aronson's computer files for information about the plot. DuBois escaped from the building where she had been held, subsequently alerting authorities to the planned attack."

Jessie's picture appeared again.

"Ms. DuBois, was critically injured while a captive of Aronson and remains in a coma at Methodist Trauma Center in Indianapolis."

Chastain tossed the towel he'd been using to dry his hair on the end of the bed. "God damn you, Fitz."

There were only two people who knew for sure that the information about the VX shipment had come from Jessie.

"How could you think staking that girl out as bait for Aronson is a good idea?" Chastain asked as soon as Fitz answered the phone."

"It's necessary," Fitz said. "And you'll be there to protect her."

"Me?!" Chastain responded. "He's already seen me."

"You said he didn't see your face, just the truck and you'll be in a different vehicle.

"Listen," Fitz went on, "We've got seven of Aronson's men. They don't know squat. They have no idea who Aronson was working for. They can give us Aronson and Aronson can give us The Righteous Voice, but no one knows where he is. We've still got Fielding feeding us intel from The Righteous Voice and no one there knows where he is either."

"Maybe he's dead," Chastain said.

"He's not dead." Fitz answered. "No one at TRV has seen him, but the rumor is that he's talked to Likens."

He continued, "We've got Aronson's videos and it's clear that they're talking about killing people, but a smart lawyer could twist it, give it a different meaning. Aronson was careful not to expose himself to the camera and juries don't generally like voice frequency analysis for identification. If we can't prove it's Aronson on the video, we can't link Aronson to Walters or Likens."

"Why don't you send somebody else down here to baby sit?" Chastain asked.

"Because you're already there. You'd be more likely to see something or someone out of place than anyone else we could send."

"If something goes wrong, if he gets to her, you know what will happen."

"Nothing will go wrong. We've got you and we're sending Malcom, Dunlop and Hershey."

"You know he tortured and slaughtered the woman who put him in prison. They never found her head."

"I've read his file. He'll come after her all right. You just make sure he doesn't get to her."

CHAPTER SIXTY-NINE

For two weeks, Glenna spent most of her time in the intensive care waiting room, dozing between times she was allowed to see Jessie. By the time George got her to the trauma center, Jessie had been in surgery. They had successfully relieved the pressure on her brain, and although Jessie's skull fracture and cerebral hemorrhage were still both extremely serious they didn't believe the injuries would prove fatal. What threatened her life was the infection that raged through her bloodstream.

Glenna had stood by her bed, talking to her, gently rubbing the inside of one arm, above the cruel and horrifying cuts on her wrist, telling her she loved her. Each time she was sure there'd be something, some flicker of the eyelids or a twitch of the hand, telling Glenna that Jessie knew she was there. But there'd been nothing, just the steady beeping of the machines, the whisper of the ventilator that breathed for her.

The man who had found Jessie hiding in his barn, Earl Price, came every day and sat by himself in the waiting room. Glenna wasn't sure she wanted him there, even though he never asked to see Jessie. Jessie'd said she didn't like him and Glenna knew that he'd harassed her at work. But he'd most likely saved her life, finding her and then getting her to the hospital. At first, there'd been talk that he was the one who had kidnapped Jessie to begin with. He'd even been taken in and his truck impounded, but George had told her that the State cops in charge of the investigation had completely ruled him out.

When Glenna had looked up once and found Earl studying her, he'd given her a little smile. "She looks just like you."

Glenna hadn't been sure what to make of that.

≈≈≈

Elevator doors opened and closed. Voices murmured in the hallway. The breakfast cart rolled past her door. Jessie couldn't decide if the smell of toast and eggs and coffee made her hungry or nauseated.

She opened her eyes in the still, dark room and stared at the ceiling.

She remembered.

Not everything, but some.

Yesterday, she'd only known that there was a blank where there should have been memories. It wasn't like she hadn't known she didn't remember.

She'd gone to sleep last night, not knowing something and woke up knowing it. It was a strange feeling.

There was still a big chunk gone. She had some cloudy images: pictures, sounds, too quickly gone to get ahold of that were probably parts of the missing time. She didn't really remember how she'd ended up with Earl Price, or how she'd gotten shot, or really, anything after she'd left the bank that afternoon after work until she woke up on the sofa at Earl's.

The doctor said it was normal, having these scattered pieces of her past she was trying to pull together.

It didn't feel normal.

She didn't feel normal.

Yesterday, after they'd moved her out of intensive care, she'd gotten a look at herself for the first time. Parts of her head had been shaved. Although the stitches were out and the doctor said she was healing just fine, the jagged scar at her hairline and the other one, long and curved, on the side of her head were red and swollen. The skinny pale person in the mirror didn't look like her, and coupled with the fact that there were parts of her life she couldn't remember, it made her feel like she wasn't her any more.

≈≈≈

Jessie looked fragile, almost skeletal, with the light from the window casting the side of her face into shadow. The hospital was quiet, hushed, in the nighttime lull before the bustle began.

Chastain had had several days to decide how he was going to handle this. While Jessie had still been in a coma, it had been easier. He and one of the other agents just had to be there, watching, making sure she was safe.

Then yesterday afternoon, Jessie woke up and her mother, who had held herself tightly together while her daughter was in a coma, had completely fallen apart. He'd heard her telling Darrell that Jessie had woken from her coma not knowing anything that had happened after she left the diner that day. That meant she had no memory of him, except as Earl from the diner, so this morning, she could wake up, see him, and start screaming.

Early morning sunlight fell directly on her face and she frowned. He got up and closed the blinds.

How hard could he push her?

He'd have to tell her the truth. For her own safety, and to some extent, his, she was going to have to remember, or at least know about Aronson, and she was going to have to know why he was there. Fitz hadn't wanted him to tell the girl the truth. He'd wanted him to tell her some horseshit story about him falling in love with her. They might be able to stuff that crap down everyone else's throat, but Fitz had never met Jessie. She'd never fall for something like that and she really didn't like Earl all that much anyway.

≈≈≈

When Jessie woke up again, the blinds had been closed against the sun and Earl Price was sitting in the chair beside the bed.

Jessie blinked, but he was still there. His hair was shorter and he looked, not cleaner, although he was, but, she struggled to think of the word. Normal was the best she could do.

"Did you get my texts?" she asked.

He nodded.

"Good," she said, and went back to sleep.

≈≈≈

Glenna stopped in the doorway and watched Earl working on his laptop in the chair next to the bed while Jessie dozed.

She'd been puzzled by Jessie's reaction when Earl came to visit at first. While Jess hadn't been exactly thrilled to see him, she hadn't seemed to mind either.

Glenna had been as sure as anything that Jessie couldn't stand him. Hadn't she watched Jessie in the grocery store, just three or four weeks before, doing her best to avoid him?

Now, though, she saw that there was somethin' there when there sure hadn't been a few weeks ago. Not that she'd really even seen any, what she'd call fondness, between the two of them. Sometimes, they didn't even seem like they liked each other.

Jess was quiet, always had been. Not that she didn't have her opinions, she just kept them to herself, mostly, especially with strangers, but with Earl, she sure said what was on her mind. It didn't seem to faze him at all. When she said she wasn't hungry, he'd nag her until she at least took a few bites. This afternoon, she'd told him she wasn't sleepy when he suggested that she take a nap, so he'd turned out the light and told her to "just lay there and be quiet then."

≈≈≈

It was late. Visiting hours had been over for a long time, but Jessie was restless, couldn't fall asleep. She stood in the dark and looked out the window. From here, on the third floor, she had a good view of the flat roof over the first floor reception area and a section of parking lot.

She hadn't been able to shut her brain off all day, and now that it was time for sleep, she still couldn't stop the thoughts whirling around in her head.

She'd recalled a little more every day, things that had been cloudy and indistinct had become clearer, but her brain stubbornly refused to fill in the missing piece after she left the bank that afternoon, before she woke up at Earl's.

She'd be going home tomorrow, and she'd had to convince her momma not to come to pick her up. Momma'd said that Melba had been letting her drive her car when she needed to, and George Farber had volunteered to drive up with her to get her.

But Earl had told Jessie that it was too far and it would be too difficult to protect her in somebody else's vehicle.

Earl said they had a team of agents trading off shifts, making sure she was safe. It didn't make her feel much better.

She didn't like being used as bait. The fact that the decision had been made when she'd been lying unconscious in a hospital bed had pissed her off. The fact that Earl's boss wanted her to act all mushy about him had set her on fire.

"You want me to act like I got some sort of...of...thing for you?!?!?" she'd asked when he'd told her what Fitz had come up with as a reason for him to stay close to her. "A guy who wears a belt buckle that says "RIDE IT HARD?"

"I'm not exactly thrilled either," he'd responded, "but unless you can think of something better, that's what we're going with. And get used to the belt buckle, it stays."

≈≈≈

Chastain pulled his SUV out of the hospital parking lot onto the street and headed for the ramp to I65. A dark green van that had been parked on the street let a few cars pass, then pulled in behind.

"Are you sure you don't want to lay down on the back seat?" he asked.

"I'm sure. I been doin' nothin' but lay down for a month."

She'd been up most of the morning. She'd had her clothes on and her things in a small bag when he'd arrived and had refused to wait for the doctor in bed.

The doctor had come in around nine, but then they'd had to wait for him to write up the paperwork, and then they'd had to wait for the wheelchair that would carry her to the door.

She laid back against the head rest and closed her eyes. A week ago, she'd had her momma bring in the electric shears she'd used to cut the boys' hair when they were little and had had her shave off the rest of her long curly hair.

"What am I supposed to do with hair on one side of my head?" she'd asked, and Chastain admitted she'd had a point. It had already started to grow back in, but short black stubble was all that covered her head under the hood of her sweatshirt.

Traffic was light, it was early afternoon, and most people were at work. He merged easily into traffic on I65 and headed south. In a few miles, he would take the ramp onto I465 West, curving around the south side of Indianapolis until it met up with SR 37.

Although they knew it was probably too soon, they'd hoped Aronson would make a move on her while she was still in the hospital, but he hadn't, and now Jessie was on her way home.

Having Jessie stay at the Price place would have been better: it was far better equipped, far better protected than the DuBois house, but he'd had to admit that Earl and Jessie living together, might raise some eyebrows, and they wanted everything to appear as normal as possible.

Besides, Jessie had refused.

He looked over at her and found her watching him. "I thought you were asleep."

"Can I ask you a question?"

"Depends."

"You know what happened," she said. "After I left the bank, I mean."

There was a pause before he said, "Not a lot, but some of it."

"The doctor told me that that part might never come back. He said it like it's a good thing, but I want to remember. People say I should put it behind me and move on, but how can I when I don't even know what it is?"

"What made you think I'd know?"

"I don't know, I just did."

When he hesitated, she said, "Just tell me."

CHAPTER SEVENTY

For the fifth night in a row, George Farber sat in his pick-up truck outside Tat's and waited. It was late, almost two o'clock and he was tired, but the outcome would be worth it.

Tommy DuBois could be found just about every night at Tat's. When he left the bar, usually after closing, he'd walk to his truck and drive away. He didn't stagger; he didn't weave. He'd been a drunk way to long for that.

Every night so far, DuBois' girlfriend, Anita, had been with him when he left the bar, and they'd gone to her place.

George had discovered, when he'd pulled up DuBois' record, that he'd been arrested for fighting multiple times and had been charged twice for assault, but the charges were later dropped. More useful was the fact that he'd been arrested and convicted three times for drunken driving. The first time, he'd been given probation and had to attend some classes. The second time, he'd done some token time in jail and had been back out on the street in just a few days. That had been before the laws had been toughened and the sentences beefed up. The third time, he'd been sentenced to thirty days in jail and had his license suspended for five years. The last arrest had been a little more than three years ago, so he was driving on a suspended license.

DuBois hadn't been arrested for a few years, not because he'd given up drinking and driving. He just hadn't gotten caught.

DuBois stayed strictly on the side streets and back roads where at two or three in the morning, he wouldn't encounter any traffic at all, much less a cop. It was less direct and took longer, but for someone with three alcohol convictions, it was a good choice.

DuBois came out with Anita, they climbed in his truck and pulled out of the parking lot. George, instead of following this time, stayed right where he was.

DuBois slowed for the first stop sign, but didn't stop. He'd done the same thing every night. He knew there was never anything coming.

Unfortunately, when DuBois ran the stop sign, he didn't see the city police car sitting on the side street.

Before he'd been elected Sheriff, George had been on the Brewer City Police force. He'd made, and kept, a lot of friends in the department during those years.

All he'd had to do was make a phone call.

When DuBois was cuffed and put in the back of the police car, George started his truck and headed for home.

CHAPTER SEVENTY-ONE

Jessie woke up from her nap, threw the covers off and stood up slowly. If she got up too suddenly, or moved her head too fast, it made the room spin some, but it lasted only a second or two as long as she took the medication the doctor had prescribed. She still had some vicious headaches, but the doctor had said that those and the dizziness would go away after a while.

She went into the living room, and pulled one of her big sketch pads out from under the sofa, sat with it in her lap, but didn't open it.

It was one of the few times since she'd been home that Earl wasn't there with her. It was reassuring, knowing he was close by, but sometimes, she just wanted to be alone.

As alone as she could be, anyway, as long as there were agents out there somewhere in a van or a truck.

She'd never actually seen them, but Earl had told her they were there, monitoring cameras, microphones and an alarm system installed while she'd been in the hospital.

"There is no way," he'd said, "Aronson is going to get close without us knowing about it."

"But," he'd handed her a small box, "if something happens - it won't - but if," he'd said, "this is your failsafe." In the box had been a necklace that looked like an old fashioned silver locket, but it transmitted a GPS signal. It had a small button inside she could push if she thought she was in danger or needed help.

"You mean like the 'I've fallen and I can't get up' lady?"

"Same principal, it's based on the same technology."

He'd put it around her neck and said, "Don't take it off. Ever. Not even in the shower."

George Farber, the sheriff, had come by yesterday. Asked how she was feeling. Asked did she remember any more than she had before. He was clearly fine with Earl hanging around, which made her Momma feel better about it.

She leaned back and closed her eyes.

Jessie'd thought, once Earl told her what he knew about what had happened that day, it would all come back to her.

It hadn't. After two weeks, it still remained a frustrating blank, and in some ways, it was like what Earl told her had happened to her, had really happened to someone else. She'd shot a man. Earl had said so. She had no memory of it aside from a splintered glimpse here and there, too short to understand or get ahold of, before it was gone.

She'd seen pictures of Aronson, but otherwise didn't remember what he looked like. What would she do if she was ever confronted by him? Would she fight? She thought she would. Earl said she would, said she had.

Until she could remember everything, know everything that she'd done, everything that had happened to her, how could she know what to expect? It was like she knew something was coming at her in the dark: she knew it was there, knew it was bad, but she couldn't stop it because she didn't know what it was.

CHAPTER SEVENTY-TWO

Aronson had been furious when he'd found out the bitch had gotten in his computer. If he could have, he would have gone after her right then and strangled the life out of her. But when the news report aired, he was in a private room, in a private clinic, healing.

For the right amount of money, Dr. Neff knew how to keep his mouth shut, and he provided the seclusion some of his more notorious patients needed.

The stab wound had turned out to be worse than the bullet wound, because by the time he got to the doctor, it had gotten infected. The doctor had removed the bullet from his shoulder and had opened the stab wound so it could be properly cleaned and debrided. He'd put drains in both sites and Aronson had spent ten days receiving IV antibiotics and thinking.

Once he'd made himself take a step back and look at it calmly, the news release shouted 'TRAP'.

They must think I'm an idiot, he'd thought.

He'd watch and he'd wait. There was a way to get to the girl no matter what they did. There was always a way. He just had to find it.

≈≈≈

Aronson got a room in a cheap motel in Bedford where they didn't care what you did as long as you paid the rent.

Even if the DuBois girl saw him, she wouldn't recognize him. His hair and his beard had grown and instead of being blond were dark brown. A set of crooked, discolored, fake teeth covered his real ones, his slightly yellow tinted glasses were about five years out of style. L O V E was inked on the knuckles of one hand, D A W N on the knuckles of the other, and padding around his middle gave him a rather large pot belly.

He was good at disguises, but the feds would know that, so they'd be looking for anyone who was new or out of place.

He'd lived in the Brewer area, had gone into town a few times, and it had given him the advantage of knowing something about the place. The girl worked at Melba's, but she wouldn't be going back to work for a while. The feds weren't likely to be keeping Melba's under close surveillance if the girl wasn't there, so he waited and he watched.

It didn't take him long to figure it out.

A box truck from Sunblest Produce Supply delivered to Melba's twice a week. An accident engineered by Aronson created an opening at Sunblest for a new driver, and he made sure he was the one who filled it.

By the time the girl came back to work, his would be a familiar face at the diner with a legitimate reason to be there, especially once he got in the habit of sitting at the counter to take his morning break. He never asked questions about the girl or showed any curiosity about her, but she would be coming back to work at the diner once the doctor released her.

An opportunity would present itself, or he'd create one. Either way, she was dead.

CHAPTER SEVENTY-THREE

The judge set Tommy's bail at a hundred grand. A hundred grand for a fuckin' DUI!! Said it was because he was a habitual offender with multiple charges pending, including assault on a police officer.

Assault. All he'd done was shove the pussy cop a little with his shoulder. His hands had even been cuffed behind his back at the time.

His public defender, a sly weasel named Neal Allen told him they would have to cop a plea to get his sentence reduced, but he was going to do some time.

Tommy'd decided to hell with that. He wouldn't do time if they couldn't find him. But first he had to get out of here.

It'd take ten percent, ten thousand dollars, to buy a bail bond. Most people he knew didn't have that kind of money just layin' around. He'd used up some of his limited phone calls trying to get his sons to boost a couple of high-end cars and sell them to Ryan Escobar to dismantle in his chop shop. He knew they could do it 'cause he'd taught them how just about as soon as they could drive. He had to be careful what he said on the phone, couldn't come right out and say it, and they'd acted like they didn't understand what he was talkin' about. Now, Darrel and Duane, and Junior even, weren't answering when he called. The sons of bitches would pay for that when he got out.

Tat, a man he'd called friend since grade school had turned his back on him. He'd laughed. *Laughed,* when he'd told him to come down and bail him out.

And Glenna. As soon as he was arrested, she should've been down at the courthouse, money in hand. Her brother Harlan was smart about money. He could sure as hell raise ten thousand if he wanted to. Instead, Glenna hadn't been around at all. Hadn't been to see him, hadn't answered the phone at home, spending all her time at the hospital with Jessie was what Duane had told him.

Tommy'd been in the county jail before, but never as long as this, and he hadn't even gone to trial yet. He'd been in stir now, one way or another, for more than two months, and he was about to lose it. The only time he'd been outside was to go to court and to the hospital for three days when he'd gotten the D.T.s. From there, he'd been transferred from a holding cell to the resident inmate section of the jail.

Every day, his rage burned a little hotter. He needed a drink and he needed to punch something. Or someone.

The faggot they'd put in the cell with him seemed like a perfect candidate. Fuckin' queer. Had "Virgil" and a heart tattooed on his arm. Spent his days sittin' on his cot, stroking the tattoo and starin' at nothin'.

Tommy wasn't a big man, but he was tough and wiry. His cellmate probably outweighed him by forty pounds and had three inches on him, but Tommy'd kicked the asses of a lot of guys bigger and stronger because Tommy was just flat out mean. And what was the cocksucker gonna' do anyway?

Tommy found out too late that the fuckin' queer was even meaner than he was.

≈≈≈

"I loved him, you know. For a long time, even after he...even after the trouble started." Glenna stared at the casket. The plastic grass carpet didn't really hide the metal frame that would, soon, lower her husband into the ground.

"I know, Glenna. You don't have to tell me that. I was around, remember?" George kept his distance: didn't reach for her, didn't touch her. Now was not the time.

There hadn't been many people at the funeral, mostly family. They'd already gone, all except Harlan and his wife, standing next to their car, waiting for Glenna. Earl and Jessie had come together and left together. He hadn't seen anyone shed a tear.

Tommy had gotten into a fight with his cellmate. No surprise there. When the cellmate punched Tommy and knocked him backwards, he hit his head, the back of his neck really, just at the bottom of his skull, on the sturdy steel sink bolted to the wall of his cell. He'd lived for a few hours after, long enough for Glenna to get there to see him take his last breath. He hadn't regained consciousness.

Tommy DuBois was dead because of events George had set in motion, but he didn't feel any guilt. George hadn't been driving drunk, hadn't been beating his wife and kids for twenty years, hadn't picked a fight with a man just because he felt like it. People who invited violence, instigated it, rarely died peacefully in their sleep. They died violently, unexpectedly, as Tommy had.

George had wanted Glenna. Had wanted to take her away from Tommy since he was sixteen. George would give Glenna space and time, but he would not feel sorry that Tommy was dead.

CHAPTER SEVENTY-FOUR

Jessie had finally stopped jumping out of her skin at every sound, but part of that, she realized was because her daddy wasn't there and wasn't going to be. Not ever again. It was hard to take in.

The house felt different to her now. She'd always thought before, when he'd been out of the house, that she and her momma had been able to relax, that things had been normal.

She'd been wrong about that. What they'd been doing was holding their breaths without knowing it.

It was different, knowing that he wasn't gonna' just walk through the door any minute. He was really and truly gone since he'd rolled through a stop sign and got pulled over. He'd been drunk and flunked the field sobriety test, and then the cop had found an open bottle of whiskey on the seat and a gun on the floor under the seat. The gun was loaded, it wasn't registered, and he didn't have a permit. Then he'd gotten into a shoving match with the cop and got charged with assault.

He'd ended up with half a dozen charges, and nobody was willing to bail him out. This had all happened when she was still in a coma, so she hadn't known about it when it happened. Darrel had told her Daddy'd been madder than spit and he hoped he got twenty years so he'd be too old to want to fight about it by the time he got out.

In the end Darrell didn't have to worry.

She'd never thought about her daddy dyin', had never imagined a time when he wouldn't come through the door again.

After the funeral, her momma had talked a lot about how it had been, how different Daddy had been when he'd been young.

Momma had told her about when she was younger than Jessie was now and the dreams she'd had. She'd looked around her when she was in high school and saw girls her age getting married just to get out of where they were, or getting pregnant and having to get married and sometimes, getting pregnant trying to force a reluctant boy and ending up raising a kid alone, tied more tightly than ever to the life they were trying to escape. Momma said she'd known that you had to have a plan. You couldn't let life trap you into where you didn't want to be.

Momma had decided that that wasn't going to happen to her. She said she'd seen everything about her life and future with a clarity she was certain none of those others girls did. And back then, when Daddy's eyes had been bright and clear, when he'd seemed to love her so much, had shared so many of her plans, she'd believed in him. So she'd put all her young energy and hope with a wild boy who already had a reputation with alcohol and a temper.

Her mistake, she'd told Jessie, was counting on another human being to want something as bad as she did.

≈≈≈

It was going to be a beautiful day, Chastain thought as he parked his truck at the DuBois place. The grey drizzle hanging over them for most of the past week had cleared, and suddenly, it felt almost like summer again.

Jessie had been getting increasingly restless, cooped up at home most of the time. She had a makeshift summer studio out in the barn in the loft and she'd been able to spend a couple of days out there before it turned cold and rainy again.

Not many people knew she was an artist. It was something she just never talked about. The drawing over the sofa was the only piece she'd ever done that she'd let more than just a handful of people see.

She'd reluctantly told him when he'd read the signature at the bottom aloud and commented on the drawing that the only reason it was up there was because Mason had tacked it up there after she'd given it to her momma for her birthday and hadn't let her take it down. It'd been there ever since.

Once, when Earl had pissed her off, which seemed all too easy to do, he'd seen her glance at the edge of the sketchbook sticking out from under the sofa.

He'd pulled it out and handed it to her. "Go ahead. Draw me with horns, if it makes you feel better."

He hadn't told her that he'd been out to the studio in the barn, or that he'd seen her work, because he didn't want her to feel like he'd invaded her privacy. He hadn't been snooping. He'd been doing his job. Before she came home, while surveillance equipment was being installed, he'd gone through the house, the attic, the cellar, the barn, the shed, the whole place, so he would know all the weaknesses and vulnerabilities of the place in which he would be protecting her.

He had to admit, though, that it probably hadn't been necessary for him to look at every painting and several of the drawings and sketchbooks, but he had. It had been a complete surprise to him at the time, a side of her he'd never imagined.

Being able to go out to the loft and paint had helped with the fidgets, but she'd been home from the hospital for more than a month, and before long, she was going to want to get out of the house. She was going to want to go back to work at Melba's, and the more active she became, the more exposed she would be to Aronson.

≈≈≈

Earl went inside the house and the first thing he saw was a small pistol on the coffee table. He nodded at the gun. "Problem?"

"No. I was thinkin' about what you said about Aronson chasin' me after I shot him. If he could do that, then still try to steal the VX and then get away, I must not've hit him any place important."

Earl picked the gun up, glad to see the safety was on. "It's probably a good idea to practice, if that's what you're getting at, but I got a good look at him after he came down the driveway. You hurt him. You definitely hurt him."

"I don't want to just hurt him, Earl," she said calmly.

≈≈≈

They started with just target practice out behind the barn at the DuBois place, but it gradually became more than that. She decided she wasn't content with just the ability to shoot Aronson dead, she wanted to be able to beat the crap out of him first.

"I think it would be good for you to do some training, get you stronger, build up your stamina, but Aronson has had years of practice. So have I, and I'm not sure *I* could kick his ass."

They'd agreed to concede that Jessie wasn't going to become a match for Aronson in whatever time they had. She was a beginner and would also have to compensate for the fact that at 5' 5", she was smaller, lighter, had a shorter reach, and in other words, was female. But it would be good for her, hell it would be good for him, and it would give her something to work toward.

He agreed to train her, but insisted that if she was going to learn from him, they were going to do it right. He made her clear it with Dr. Hill and while she'd half expected him to say no, he'd approved it with the caveat that she must protect her head.

Another of Earl's requirements was that she also do strength and flexibility workouts, in addition to self-defense training. Most of what he planned to teach her used leverage, the element of surprise and a basic knowledge of human anatomy, but the stronger she was the more effective she would be, and the more flexible she was, the less likely she'd get hurt while he was teaching her.

It had gotten too cold to work outside and there was no room at the DuBois' house, so they worked out at the Price

Place. It got her out of the house, she was secure there and they had plenty of room.

He'd moved what little furniture there'd been in the dining room into the living room and put a large thick mat down. He already had free weights, and a bench and a heavy bag, but the weights were too heavy for her to use, so he'd made a trip to Walmart for some inexpensive, lighter ones, and in a few hours, their makeshift gym was ready.

The first few days, he hadn't gone easy on her exactly, but he'd held back, not sure how much she could handle. Now that he had a better idea of her limitations, he pushed her until he thought she'd had enough, then pushed her just a little more.

When he began teaching her some simple defensive moves, they'd hit a snag. Close personal contact made her uneasy. She tensed up at anything but the most casual contact and actually flinched when he came from behind her. He was impersonal in his touch, made a point to be, but every time he grabbed her firmly, or stood up against her to position her or correct her footwork, she tightened up and pulled away.

"Relax," he said over and over, "You have to be fluid, loosen up." He found himself becoming more careful, even tentative about contact during their workouts. She was uncomfortable, he was uncomfortable, and they were getting nowhere.

"Listen," he said finally, "Do you want to do this or not? We're just getting started and I'm going to be touching you a whole lot more as we go on." She didn't move, so he turned her around and pulled up her chin so she had to look at him. "I'm not touching you to feel you up or get a thrill. This is a contact sport. That means I will touch you, with my hands, my feet and my body. It isn't sexual."

"I know it's not sexual! You think I'm doin' it on purpose?" she asked. "I can't help it."

"Yes you can help it. It's a matter of concentration."

He decided to stop ignoring the elephant in the room. "What happened to you didn't have anything to do with sex either. He hates women. He wants to control them. And he still controls you."

He put his hand on her shoulder to keep her from turning away. "You might not be able to consciously remember what he did to you, but somewhere inside your head, you know. We can't tiptoe around it and expect it to get any better."

"We? There is no 'we', Earl. It didn't happen to you."

"Right. It happened to you and you can't ignore it, you can't bury it, and you can't pretend it didn't happen."

"Let go of me." She tried to shove him away.

"No." He grabbed her hands. "You're going to stay right here and listen. You fought Aronson. You got away from him. You came home and you're going back to school in a couple of months. You're going to be able to go back to work again next week. And you know what? Aronson still has control over you."

He let her go. "You aren't thinking about what you're doing, you're thinking about me touching you, and as long as you're reacting to what happened in the past and not what's happening right now, you aren't in control. He is."

He grabbed her hand and put it on his chest, held it there. "This is me. I'm not Aronson."

She turned to walk away from him. "Just take me home."

He grabbed the back of her tee shirt and stopped her, then pulled gently, forcing her backward. "You're not a quitter, Jess."

He softened his tone. "Your mother said Dr. Hill gave you the name of a therapist, but you said you didn't need one. I'm not saying you have to talk to me. I *am* saying maybe you need to talk to someone."

"But I don't remember!" she said.

"I know you don't. But you feel."

She looked at his face, his eyes, trying to work past the reticence she'd always had about sharing her feelings.

From the very beginning, she'd been able to speak her mind with him. Maybe it was because she knew with him it wasn't personal. She was a job. He didn't care what she thought about him and had always been brutally frank with her. When this was over he'd go, and they'd never see each other again, and that was all right with both of them.

But this was different. Being blunt was one thing. This was something else. This was crossing a self-imposed line that would leave her feeling exposed.

"What do you want to do?" he asked. "You want me to take you home, I'll take you home. If not, you're going to have to help me understand."

"I don't remember," she said almost defiantly. In a small voice, she said, "but I dream.

"I'm always runnin' in the dream, but I can't go fast enough. I never see him, but I know he's behind me. I know any second, I'm going to feel his hands on me."

"And that's what it feels like when I'm behind you," he stated.

She nodded, "I don't know how to not feel it."

"You replace that memory, that feeling with another one."

He turned her around. "I may have started this out all wrong. Maybe it will help if we deal with some trust issues."

He took two steps back and put his hands on her shoulders. When she started to lean away, he said, "No, don't move. Just stand there and relax." He shook her gently with both hands still on her shoulders. "You're not relaxing. Let your arms hang loose."

He took his hands away and said, "Okay, now, just let yourself fall backward. You have to trust me not to let you fall. That's the point. Don't think about falling, think about me catching you."

It hadn't happened overnight, but gradually she stopped concentrating on him and started concentrating on what she was doing. Once they got past the specter of Aronson breathing down her neck, they made good progress.

She wouldn't be able to outmaneuver someone of Aronson's caliber, but if Chastain did his job, she wouldn't have to.

CHAPTER SEVENTY-FIVE

Lyle dropped a rack of silverware with a crash, barely missing Melba's foot. "Sorry," he mumbled.

"Lyle, what in the wide world is the matter with you?"

He ducked his head, attempted a casual shrug. "Nuthin'."

"You haven't done anythin' this morning but drop things and every time I say somethin' you jump like a scalded cat."

He shrugged again.

"What in heaven's name's got you so jumpy this mornin' of all mornin's when we got all of this stuff to do because Jessie's comin' back and..."

Lyle's face flushed beet red, then paled. He tried to turn away from her but she grabbed his tee shirt and wouldn't let go.

"She don't remember, Lyle. She still don't. Probably never will."

"I know she don't." He managed to pull away from her. "But I do."

≈≈≈

Jessie went back to work at Melba's the middle of November, just two days a week to start.

She only knew what her momma had told her about what everyone had done to try and find her: the search parties, the flyers, the radio station announcements, the volunteers who had gone door to door and searched the woods, but she really hadn't been able to imagine it. She thought Momma had been exaggerating until the day she went back to work and found a diner packed to the rafters, even at six o'clock in the morning, and a banner strung across with "Welcome back Jessie" on it, signed by just about everyone in the town.

It took her by surprise. She knew she'd changed a lot, learned a lot in the years since high school. What she hadn't realized was that the same people who'd only thought of her as that DuBois girl all those years ago had learned a lot too. They'd all learned that she was one of them.

CHAPTER SEVENTY-SIX

The e-mail appeared in Chastain's in-box at eight o'clock on the dot.

He was being reassigned, recalled to D.C. So were the other three agents. They were to take only enough time to pack up and be there by Thursday, day after tomorrow.

The operation was over. Just like that.

Chastain understood the need for certain agents to be sent certain places: ethnic background, the ability to speak a language fluently, contacts from previous operations. Those were important considerations in deciding who would be most effective in any operation.

If he had to go somewhere else, that was fine. But to pull the entire team and leave Jessie down here to be taken by Aronson whenever he got damn good and ready wasn't, at least shouldn't be, an option.

He called Malcom, "I need to get on a plane," he said, struggling to remain calm. "They can't just stake her to a tree and walk away."

To tell the truth, Malcom didn't think Aronson was likely to come after the girl at this point either, but it was a pretty raw deal for the girl if they were wrong. Would he want to take that risk if it was someone he cared about?

No he wouldn't.

Malcom said, "Go on. We'll be here."

≈≈≈

Earl had been driving Jessie to work in the morning at five thirty, and coming back at around 1:30 to have a piece of pie and wait for her shift to end so he could drive her home.

It was only the tail end of the breakfast rush when he came in, caught her eye and slid into one of the empty booths in her section.

She finished what she'd been doing, grabbed an empty cup and the coffee pot and headed for his table, curious but not worried about his unexpected early arrival.

She put the cup on the table but before she began to fill it he said, "Can you sit down for a minute?"

"I'm working" she said, but he pulled her down into the seat next to him.

Perturbed, she tried to pull away from him and glanced over her shoulder, "What are you doing?"

"I have to go to D.C.," he said abruptly. "Malcom will pick you up at two, keep an eye on you 'til I get back."

"Why? What happened?"

"I'm being reassigned and I have to go in, check out some details. I'll be back tonight, take care of wrapping some things up."

She went still, "You're leaving?"

"I'll be back tonight."

"No, I mean, after you 'take care of wrapping some things up,'" she said.

He nodded.

"Pretty short notice."

"Almost always is."

She stood up and nodded at the pot, "You have time for a cup?"

He shook his head and she said, "I have to get back to work."

CHAPTER SEVENTY-SEVEN

"It's been three, almost four months." Fitz said, "He's not going to show."

"He is going to show: just on his timetable, not yours," Chastain responded.

"The girl will be given an agent contact in Indianapolis, that's the closest office. If she sees Aronson, if she feels like she's being watched, if she feels threatened, she can call twenty-four/seven. The locals will be brought up to speed."

"You put her in harm's way. You made Aronson look like a fool, a bumbling idiot, defeated by a woman. You wanted to make sure he'd come after her."

"Nothing is ever sure. We took our best shot and it didn't work out. We're cutting our losses and moving on. It happens. Sometimes the innocent get in the way and sometimes they suffer for it. It's a calculated risk. Collateral damage is unavoidable. We can't let it get in the way."

He went on, "Malcom, Hershey and Dunlop have been reassigned." Fitz picked up three fat file folders, nodded at them then put them in his 'out' tray.

"You have been reassigned." he said as he picked a fourth folder and dropped it into the tray.

He sat at his desk, opened another file and began reading. After a few seconds, he looked up and said, "We're done here."

Chastain unclipped his holster and put it, gun still inside on Fitz' desk, then followed it with his I.D. folder, "You're right. We're done here."

≈≈≈

It was after eight that night when Chastain landed in Indianapolis. He checked in with Malcom, confirmed that everything was quiet and headed for Brewer. He hadn't had time to really talk to Jessie before he left, and he'd asked Malcom to delay removing the surveillance equipment until he got back. He'd hoped he could talk Fitz into continuing full surveillance at least for a while. He hadn't really thought through what he was going to do when Fitz refused, even though he'd known that's what would happen.

In the truck, he called Jessie, told her he was back, that he'd be there to pick her up at nine to go target shooting as usual the next day.

"I thought you were leaving," she said.

"Change of plans," he told her briefly, "I'm staying."

≈≈≈

Jessie lay awake that night and stared at the ceiling.

She didn't want to feel this way and until this morning, when he told her he was leaving she hadn't even known it had happened. He'd sat there at Melba's and said it like it was no big deal, and to him, it wasn't. It was part of the job, to drift into a life, shake it to bits and then leave.

She wanted to feel like he did: detached, reserved, uninvolved. She didn't want him or anyone to have the power to hurt her.

He was working. She was his job. When the job was done, he would leave and go on to the next. He'd been about to do that very thing this morning.

She'd made her plans and he wasn't in them. She'd decided what she was going to do with her life and it didn't include anybody else. Her momma had learned the hard way that you can't trust anybody else to feel the same way you did. Everyone saw the world their own way, had their own way of deciding what was important.

He'd crept up on her somehow and she hadn't seen it coming. She'd learned something today and it was something she needed to make sure she took to heart.

≈≈≈

Chastain picked her up the next day like he always did and they went to the shooting range, just like yesterday had never happened, which was fine with her.

She was a little distracted, but thought she'd been hiding it pretty well until he said, "Jessie, what's wrong with you this morning? You have to concentrate. Empty the clip as fast as you can, but hold your hand still. You're letting the muzzle wobble and drift up. Tighten up the cluster."

"I have to slow down to cluster the shots like I'm supposed to."

"You don't want to give whoever you're shooting at enough time to get to you. While you're aiming, he's going be on you, take the gun away and use it to shoot you."

"I know. You told me that already."

"But it isn't going to do any good if you empty the clip and don't hit whoever it is you're shooting at."

"I said I know, Earl. Just because I can't do it doesn't mean I don't know I'm supposed to."

He looked at her for a minute, then said, very patiently, "Okay. We can try this again and you can think about what you're doing, or, we can quit for today and come back when you're in a better mood."

"Nothin' wrong with my mood," she said as she re-loaded the clip. "Can we stop talkin? Our hour is almost up."

CHAPTER SEVENTY-EIGHT

Thermal imaging cameras "saw" anything that radiated heat. The woods were full of critters from rabbits to deer, and if they were in view of the camera, they showed up as fuzzy red-orange images on one of the screens Chastain watched. It was a sophisticated system that could distinguish the temperature signature of a human from that of a dog or a deer. A small series of beeps would let him know if a human approached and although he told himself he should sleep until or unless the alarm went off, he never managed to fall into a deep sleep.

He was working a tough schedule: getting at most, three or four hours of fitful sleep at night, up all day with Jessie. When she was at work was the only time he could really sleep. He was uneasy, having to leave Jessie at the diner without protection, but he couldn't function with just the occasional cat nap during the day while Jessie worked on a website or sketched or took a nap.

Jessie was smart. She knew to tell him if someone she didn't know started hanging around the diner, staying too long, paying too much attention to her. She knew to tell him if she was uneasy or if something seemed strange or out of place. She knew to push the panic button if there was the slightest indication of trouble.

The fact that a lot of cops: city, county and state, were in and out of the diner made him feel a little easier. Aronson could never know who would be in there at any given time, which made it unlikely that Aronson would want to plan something centered around Melba's.

There wasn't any danger of Aronson picking her off with a rifle while she was in the diner. None of the buildings he could have shot from were short enough to get a view down inside, and there was no place for him to hide at ground level.

Still, she wasn't as secure as she had been with him or one of the other agents staying close, watching the diner, monitoring who came in and who went out, but it was the best he could do.

He'd had to tell her that the other agents had been reassigned and it hadn't been easy. At first, he hadn't understood why telling her was so difficult. Then he'd realized it was because he didn't want to admit to her that she was unimportant. She was expendable.

During his career with the Department, he'd always felt that no matter how ugly or seemingly heartless both his and the Department's decisions had been, they had been right.

He wasn't sure that was true anymore.

Resigning had been a knee jerk reaction and Fitz had recognized it as that.

"Are you involved with this girl?" Fitz had asked.

"You know me better than that."

"Then what's the problem?"

"The problem is that she's done nothing but help us and for that, we're about to throw her to the wolves.

"She got the information off Aronson's computer for us, she went back in that place where he held her and did God only knows what to her, because I told her we needed her to. When she got away from him, I should have taken her to a hospital. Instead, I ignored what she needed and concentrated on what she could do for us. Because it was my job. I looked at the big picture and damn near killed her doing it.

"We turned her into bait for Aronson. We did that. He will come for her. When he does, we should be there.

"If the Department won't take care of the mess they've gotten her into, I will."

Fitz had leaned back in his chair, took his glasses off and rubbed his eyes. "Aronson went after the woman who got him put away within two weeks of getting out of prison. That's why we were sure he'd go after her. It's been three months. Aronson has moved on. He's not going after the girl."

He'd turned to leave and Fitz said, "Goddammit, wait a minute." He stared at Chastain for a few minutes, then said, "Four more weeks."

Chastain had shaken his head, "Until we know for sure where Aronson is."

"Look, money's an issue, it always is. Committing four agents to a dead operation simply can't be justified."

"Not my problem," Chastain had said and shrugged.

"Eight weeks, no back up."

"You're kidding. How am I supposed to give her effective coverage by myself?"

"Take it or leave it."

After a few seconds, Chastain had given a short nod. "All right."

That he would be willing to resign to make sure Jessie was protected, hadn't been a surprise, not really. She hadn't asked for any of the things that had happened to her. He hadn't had anything to do with Aronson taking her the first time, but he'd known about it, and he hadn't helped her. It was his job and it was no more than she deserved to make sure he didn't get her again.

Chances were good, better than good that Jessie would be just fine and Aronson had moved on as Fitz believed. But chances had also been good that fourteen years ago his wife and daughter would have made the trip to the cottage safely.

Without him knowing it, without him meaning for it to happen, Jessie had become important. He couldn't, wouldn't just walk away, leaving her for Aronson to take whenever he was ready.

He obviously couldn't give Jessie the same level of protection four agents could, but it would be a hell of a lot better than none.

≈≈≈

Aronson watched the girl every time he was in the diner without really looking at her, trying to get a sense of her schedule: what she did and when.

It had been almost four months. People only stayed vigilant, really razor sharp, for a short period, even professionals. When each day passed, the same as the last, and nothing ever happened, they stopped paying attention. That was what he was counting on.

CHAPTER SEVENTY-NINE

Christmas was in just a few days and Jessie wasn't quite finished with the sweater she was making for Earl, so she sat on the sofa and knitted while he sat in the easy chair in the corner and dozed. She hadn't been sure about whether to give him anything. They were supposed to be 'seeing each other,' and her family would expect that she'd give him something. She'd decided that she should, but hadn't been sure what to give him. She didn't know anything about his likes or dislikes, not really, which kind of irked her, since he seemed to know just about everything there was to know about her.

There wasn't anything more impersonal than a sweater, unless it was a scarf. She'd decided on a sweater and picked out a bland oatmeal color. She was looking forward to him opening it Christmas and realizing she'd knitted the whole thing practically under his nose.

While her hands were busy with the sweater, she thought about how he'd changed since he came back from D.C. She guessed it was because he was by himself watching her now, but he'd gotten a lot more protective, reminding her not to leave the building while she was at work, asking if she'd seen any strangers, telling her to let him know if she got any hang ups when he wasn't at her house, and on and on.

Every time they'd gone anywhere, he'd asked if she had the locket on. The fourth or fifth time he'd pulled the collar of her coat open and asked the same question, she'd smacked his hand away and said, "You told me not to take it off. Why would I take it off when you told me not to?" They'd been standing outside, in front of Melba's about to go in, so she'd lowered her voice, "I know it has a GPS transmitter in it. I know it has a panic button. You're treating me like I'm eight years old!"

He hadn't backed off, "I'm just making sure. That's what I do."

"You're drivin' me crazy, Earl." She'd been about to open the door when he'd put his hand against it and said, "I just want to be sure you're safe, Jess, that's all.

She'd stopped knitting and was sitting there just staring at him. He was staring right back and she felt like a rabbit being watched by a Cobra.

She got up. "I'm gonna' make a cup of tea. You want anything while I'm up?"

He shook his head and closed his eyes. "No thanks."

She put the water on to boil and got some homemade sugar cookies out to take in to Earl while she waited. While her tea steeped, she carried the cookies into the living room, put them down in front of Earl and went back to the kitchen for her tea.

The first fat flakes of snow fluttering against the kitchen window distracted her for a moment. The first snow was always so pretty. Maybe they'd have a white Christmas.

She carried her tea into the living room and as she sat down, reached for a cookie and hit the bottom of the cup on the edge of the coffee table. When scalding tea splashed across her hand, she dropped the cup, splattering one leg of her jeans and her shoes.

Earl was up and over to her in an instant, but she pushed him away and said, "I'm alright, Earl." She didn't think the tea had been hot enough to blister, but it still stung.

"I'll get some ice," he said and headed for the kitchen.

"Bring a towel, too," she called after him.

He returned with a bag he'd filled with ice and water, sat on the sofa next to her and put it on the back of her hand. "Hold that there," he said and started mopping up tea.

"What the hell am I sitting on?" he asked as he leaned in to her and reached underneath him.

He pulled out the mass of oatmeal yarn she'd been working on.

"Oh," he said, holding it up, "my sweater."

CHAPTER EIGHTY

Chastain wiped his face with a towel and took a drink, dumped a little of the water over his head then ran the towel over it. He and Jessie had both worked hard today. She'd never gotten the better of him before, but this afternoon, she'd come close. She was a hell of a lot stronger than she'd been eight weeks ago.

She looked good too. She looked healthy. Toned. And she had a nice shape. Very nice.

He sat on the mat, leaned back on his elbows and dropped his head back. Four of the weeks Fitz had given him were over, and he was tired. She'd almost kicked his butt today. He had to get some sleep.

She left the mat and walked away from him toward the door. He sat up, took another drink and said, "Don't forget to stretch."

"I won't," she said over her shoulder and held up her empty bottle. "I'm just gonna' get more water first. You want some?"

"No, I'm good." He examined her butt as she walked away from him. Even in sweats, it was a very nice butt.

He shook his head and rubbed his eyes. He had to make his mind stop going in that direction.

She came back, bent over and put her water bottle on the floor, then began stretching.

She was completely unaware of him, just going through her routine as usual.

He found himself staring at her butt again.

He really needed to get some rest.

She sat down on the mat next to him to do some floor stretches and when he didn't move over, she nudged him with her shoulder. "You gonna' take your half out of the middle, Earl?"

Instead of moving over, he turned his head and looked at her. Short, crisply curling, black hair, damp from their workout, touched her forehead. Her smooth skin still glistened with sweat.

She cocked her head at him and gave him a little smile. "Earl?"

He put one hand on the back of her head, leaned in slowly and covered her mouth with his.

He hadn't thought out what he intended. He hadn't thought at all, and when instead of resisting, she bunched the front of his tee shirt in her fists and pulled him closer, he let her weight pull them both down onto the mat.

He was lost in the kiss, one hand buried in her hair, the other resting lightly on her ribs, just touching the curve of her breast. As the kiss deepened, he put his hand under her shirt and slid it up under her sports bra until warm, silky skin filled his hand.

He made himself pull back. He studied her face, rubbed his thumb across her cheekbone. "You can say no."

She stroked his face with the back of her hand, breathing fast, eyes on his. She was being foolish, letting this happen, but it was what she wanted, all she wanted, right here and right now. She'd just have to let later take care of itself.

She lifted her head until her mouth was on his, touched her tongue to his and ran her hands up his back under his tee shirt. His skin was smooth, slightly damp and warm. When she pushed his shirt all the way up, he lifted his arms and she pulled it off over his head.

Without breaking the kiss, he got to his knees, pulling her up with him and lifted her until she could wrap her legs around his waist. He stood up with her and made it up the stairs to his bedroom where he laid her on the bed and settled on top of her.

They lay there, feeling, exploring, touching, until they were skin to skin.

Jessie had wondered what it would be like with Earl. Of course she had. Just because she didn't want to want him didn't mean she'd stopped thinking about it. She'd been a little afraid that he'd do something, say something or that the feel of his body on hers would make her remember Aronson.

But there was nothing but Earl: the way his hands touched her, the way his mouth traveled across her skin.

He moved then so that his erection was cradled between her thighs and pushed her legs apart with his knee. He made himself take his time, easing himself in, savoring every sensation, ready to explode. She rocked a little, making him groan, and they began to move together.

CHAPTER EIGHTY-ONE

It was dark outside when Jessie woke up, and muted light from the hallway shone vaguely into the bedroom. Earl was asleep, his arm across her hip, softly snoring. He must have pulled the blankets up over them because she didn't remember doing it.

She wanted to stay right here, tucked up against him, away from the world, away from the future she was sure would break her heart.

Sometime during that first frenzied kiss, she'd decided to take what he had to give and hope it was enough when she was left with only memories.

She listened to him sleep, the slow rhythm of his breathing, his heart gently beating against her back.

She'd almost dozed off again when she remembered that her momma would be worried because she hadn't heard from her. She needed to at least call her, let her know she was okay.

She slipped out from under his arm, moving slowly to keep from waking him up. She was sitting on the side of the bed, looking on the floor for her discarded tee shirt, when she felt his hand slide down her back.

"Where you going?" His voice was gravelly with sleep, eyes still closed.

"I gotta call momma. She's probably worried sick by now."

"I called her when I got up to make sure the security system was set to night monitoring," he said, then yawned. "C'mon back in here where it's warm."

"You called momma?"

"Yeah," he said, and stretched. "You were asleep."

"What'd you tell her?"

"That we were going to have wild monkey sex all night, and then I'd bring you home."

She raised her eyebrows at him, and he said, "I told her you were with me and not to worry. What did you think I told her?"

"Didn't she want to know why you were callin' and not me?"

"She didn't ask and I didn't offer." He hooked his arm around her waist and pulled her up against him, letting her feel him growing hard against her leg. He rolled so that she was beneath him, "I told her not to hold dinner for you."

≈≈≈

Chastain lay on his back with Jessie sprawled across him and made lazy circles on her back with his fingers. She was almost asleep, he could feel her relaxing, sinking into him. It was after ten and she had to get up at four thirty to go to work.

The fact that she'd gone through what she had, whether she could remember it or not, and not show any wariness, any reserve in her response to him was a gift.

Most people went through their entire life and never felt the way he'd felt about Jill. It wasn't the same with Jessie, couldn't be, she was a much different person than Jill had been, but the feeling was just as strong, the need was just as great.

Now he was faced with a dilemma. He'd done something that was completely against the rules, his and the department's. He'd gotten involved with someone while he was in the middle of an operation.

There were reasons it was a bad idea for agents to get involved with people under their protection. It made it difficult to focus. Not just because of the sex, although that was a large part of it, but you became hyper-aware of the person you were with instead of what was around you.

You had to do things they didn't like and make them do things they didn't like. It was a lot easier when you could give a shit about whether they were mad at you or not.

He rubbed her back gently and pulled the covers up over her shoulders. She turned her head and sighed, and he laid his cheek against her hair. These moments they had had together were going to have to last them for a while: to do his job, to do it like it should be done, he was going to have to distance himself from her. He was going to have to push her away, and it wasn't going to be easy.

CHAPTER EIGHTY-TWO

When Jessie and Earl left for Melba's the next morning, Earl was all business.

He'd explained to her why it had to be that way. He couldn't let her distract him and to do that, he had to keep his distance and his mind on the job. What had happened between them once had to stay that...just once. He apologized, said it was his mistake, he knew better and that it wouldn't happen again.

She'd just nodded and said she understood. What was she supposed to say? That he'd just ripped her heart out? She wasn't going to give him or anyone that kind of power over her.

She'd known better. She'd told herself how it would be. She'd known he would break her heart, she just hadn't expected it to be this soon.

The ride to Melba's that morning reminded him of the ride from the Price place to the cellar when he'd taken her back there to hack into Aronson's computer. It had been difficult then when he hadn't known her, when she was just a woman who could help him do his job.

He parked in front of the diner, pulled the collar of her coat open and checked her locket. She didn't comment or stop him. Her face was a blank, her emotions hidden, her defenses were in place.

He'd hurt her and it felt worse, far worse than he'd thought it would feel. He told himself that it was what he had to do, that it was for her own good, that it was only for a little while, until Aronson was caught, but none of those things made him feel any better. "Jess," he turned her head so she had to look at him, "Don't make this harder than it has to be."

She pushed his hand away, "You made the rules. I'm just following them."

He tried again, "Jess..."

"Don't. Just don't," she said and opened her door.

If he'd had any doubt about whether he'd be able to keep his hands off of her, he didn't any more. Jessie had created all the distance between them he'd need, all by herself.

CHAPTER EIGHTY-THREE

Chastain parked his truck across the street from Melba's at 10:00.

His stomach growled and he thought about going in, ordering some food, but then remembered how Jessie had looked when she got out of the car earlier and decided he'd better just leave her alone.

Nothing eventful happened to interrupt his working the crossword puzzle in the newspaper. People had gone in and out, most of them not alone, and the ones that had gone in alone had been women, older men or people he'd recognized. Nothing to worry about.

He'd just finished the last word in the puzzle, when an explosion from behind him lifted his truck into the air and slammed it, upside down, into the SUV parked in front of him.

≈≈≈

Aronson got to Melba's at ten like he always did, pulled around to the back and began unloading produce from the truck. The old woman was out front talking to a customer; Bud was at the grill, scraping the sticky residue from the breakfast meat into the grease trough. The girl and the other waitress were out front bussing tables and waiting on the few that were still occupied.

After the breakfast rush, usually about ten thirty, the girl went to the back, into the storeroom for more placemats, straws and napkins to stock up before the lunch crowd started to come in.

He looked at his watch. Ten thirty-three. Just like clockwork, the girl headed to the back and went into the storeroom. He gave it thirty seconds, then pressed the button on the transmitter he had in his pocket.

The bomb in the car he'd parked across the street exploded, and the blast made everyone, even the old lady, run to the front to look outside. Everyone but the girl.

≈≈≈

Chastain woke up on the pavement, with a woman bending over him.

She was talking to him, but she sounded far away, and when he tried to sit up, she put her hand on his chest to hold him still.

After a minute or two, her face came into focus, and he began to pull his thoughts together.

He looked toward Melba's, expecting to see it in flames, but it looked unharmed. Then he remembered that the blast had come from behind, not in front of him. Maybe this didn't have anything to do with Jessie, he thought as he pushed the woman away and sat up, working his cell phone out of his pocket.

He brought the GPS screen up and focused on the display. There was no blinking dot on the screen. He made sure he had the right screen up and looked again, then checked to make sure the phone hadn't been damaged. It was working, but there was no signal. Jessie's GPS wasn't transmitting.

≈≈≈

Jessie had her arms full and when she heard the explosion. She came out of the storeroom and turned to look at the door where Aronson was standing.

She hurried toward him. "What was that? What happened?"

He wanted to smash her face in, but held himself back, and only hit her hard enough to knock her out.

She wasn't going to die that easy. She was going to tell him where his money was and then she was going to die. Slow.

"Hey!" It was the red-headed kid, Lyle, coming out of the walk-in refrigerator. "Hey, put her down." Aronson had forgotten about the Christmas holiday and that the kid was working.

Unexpectedly, the kid charged him. Aronson didn't expect the little prick to jump him, but he did.

Aronson hadn't wanted to kill the girl, but the kid was another story. He dropped Jessie and shoved the kid into a wall. He grabbed the kid's arm, twisted it behind him and pulled it up his back until he heard the joint pop and the kid scream. He turned the kid around and with all his strength, punched him in the face.

Lyle reeled back, fell across a small table and slid, boneless, to the floor.

≈≈≈

Chastain staggered to his feet and jogged unsteadily toward the diner. Melba put her hand on his arm and tried to say something, but he brushed past her and went inside.

"Jess?" he yelled as he went toward the back. "Jess?"

The back door was standing open, napkins and placemats were scattered on the floor nearby. Lyle lay in a heap near the back door, his face a bloody mess.

Jessie was gone.

CHAPTER EIGHTY FOUR

"Where is it, bitch?" He shook the girl again, hard, and she tried to pull away from him.

She raised her head and looked at him, trying to focus in the dim light of the single small window at one end of the truck.

"Didn't think you'd ever see me again, did you, whore?" he said.

When she didn't answer, he squatted down, grabbed a handful of hair, pulled her head up and thrust his face close to hers. "C'mon, little girl. You remember me, don't you?"

She shook her head.

"Oh, I forgot," he said, "I've changed a little since then."

He took off the glasses, pulled the prosthetic teeth off and threw them in a corner. "How about now? Anything coming back to you?"

She shook her head again, "I don't remember..."

Sure you do," he said, and backhanded her. "Don't try that shit with me. Where's the money?"

"What money?" she asked.

"What did I just say?" he asked and got right down in her face, "That black bag of money you took from me."

"Black bag...?" she said, still groggy.

"Don't play dumb, bitch. The money in that big black bag," he slapped her again. "The bag you took from me."

Out of the fog of splintered memory, some of the pieces came together and she thought she remembered having a black bag. It had been night. She'd been in pain and so tired..."In the woods," she said without thinking.

"Where?"

"In the woods. I hid it."

"Nice try," he said.

"No! It's in the woods. I hid it that night. They've been watching me ever since, waiting for you to show up. I had to leave it there."

"Horseshit," he said and grabbed her hair again. "You had it. I saw you. Then you got in a truck with a guy, but you didn't have the bag any more. You hid it. Where?"

"No! I didn't know he was there that day. He's an agent," she said, talking fast. "He was watching you and he saw me come running out. He thought I could give him information."

"And you did, too, didn't you, bitch," he said and hit her twice.

"No!" she shook her head. Blood from her nose was running down the back of her throat and she tried not to choke, "I didn't tell him anything," she lied. "They planted that story. To make you come after me.

"He took me to this farmhouse and after I told the guy I didn't' know anything, he got a phone call. He got all excited and left me there. He told me not to leave, but I left anyway and went back and got the money. I couldn't carry it any farther than about half way and I had to hide it."

"I swear," she said as he drew his hand back, "it's the truth."

≈≈≈

Jessie managed to convince Aronson that in order to find the money, she had to start at the ruins of the farmhouse where he'd kept her a prisoner and work her way towards the Price place. She was hoping it would take some time to get there, time she might be able to think of something to get away, time for Earl to find her. She felt for the locket. It was still there.

He drug her out of the truck, cut the bindings on her feet and when she looked around, saw that he'd parked the produce truck in a barn.

"Your lucky day," he said, and when pushed her out the door, she saw the rubble of the farmhouse.

As he dragged her into the woods, he said, "You better not be lying to me."

She wasn't lying, but she didn't know if she could find the black bag again. It was a vague, fragmented memory: dragging the bag through the woods, hiding it under a log. Until he mentioned the money, she hadn't remembered what was in it, just that she'd had it.

If she couldn't find the bag she was dead.

She was dead anyway.

CHAPTER EIGHTY FIVE

Jessie was gone and so was the produce truck.

Lyle, the only person who could have told them what happened hadn't regained consciousness. His cheek and the bone under his eye appeared to be shattered and his shoulder was dislocated. EMTs had stabilized him and transported him to the nearby high school parking lot to be picked up by helicopter and flown to the trauma center in Indy.

A state-wide alert had been issued and a full scale manhunt was under way. Roads were being closed, roadblocks were being set up.

Chastain's truck was smashed so he was riding with Dan Carlisle, racing down tiny gravel roads, looking for the produce truck. It was pointless and they both knew it. Aronson would have found a place to hide the truck before taking Jessie. But it was better than sitting at Melba's.

"Why don't we take a pass out by the quarry?" Chastain suggested. "Aronson might want to stick to a place he knows."

Carlisle nodded, "Good idea."

The cargo box on the produce truck Aronson was driving was metal. Chastain hoped that the metal was interfering with the signal, and that the transmitter hadn't been destroyed. He kept his cell phone in his hand, the GPS display up, hoping to see that little blinking dot that would lead him to Jessie.

They stopped at the gate. It was chained shut. "Let's just check," Chastain said and they both got out of the car.

The padlock on the gate didn't look like it had been disturbed in a long time. They looked for signs that a vehicle had been through there recently, but the snow in the drive had no tire marks at all, old or new. They looked through the fence, but there was no movement, the snow looked completely undisturbed and everything was quiet.

They got back in the car and Carlisle said, "Now where?"

Chastain checked the GPS tracker again. "Shit," he said. "He took her back to the farmhouse."

"The one he blew up?" asked Carlisle as he made a U-turn to go back the other direction. "Why would he take her there? There's nothing left."

"The barn," Chastain answered, "The barn's still there. That's where he's hiding the truck."

Carlisle drove like a maniac, rear end sliding, almost in the ditch a couple of times, but it still took ten minutes to get there.

"They're on foot," Chastain said, eyes glued to the screen. "Where the hell are they going?"

Carlisle had called for backup, but Chastain jumped out of the car before it stopped moving.

≈≈≈

Aronson had had to cut the plastic tie that bound her feet when he pulled her out of the truck, but her hands were still bound. She couldn't hope to get in a physical struggle with him and expect to win, but with her hands behind her back, she had no chance at all. She let herself trip and because her hands were tied, he had to help her up. After the third time, he yanked her to her feet and cut the plastic strip holding her wrists together.

"Go," he said, and shoved her ahead of him. She walked in what she thought was a straight line toward the Price place, like she'd done that night, but it had been dark, and she'd been confused, and had thought, several times, that she was lost and walking in circles. She remembered hearing the explosion, and being relieved it was behind her, because that meant she was going the right way. She'd been leaning against a big tree with light colored bark, and she'd been able to see the fire from where she was.

She was walking slowly, checking now and then over her shoulder to make sure she could still see the barn, hoping it would help her figure out where she'd been when she hid the bag. She paused, pretending to look under just about any log that could have hidden the bag, trying to buy time.

Finally he stopped and grabbed her by the hair, "You think you're going to pull something, think again. Get moving. I'm not going to tell you again."

It was only a minute or two later that she thought she saw the tree where she'd stopped to rest, surprised that she'd been able to carry the bag this far. It should be hidden close by.

"I remember that tree. The bag should be a little bit further, under a log."

She took a quick look around. There was still no sign of Earl and her time was running out.

≈≈≈

Chastain ran as quietly as he could, but with no foliage on the trees, no ground cover and wearing a dark jacket, he'd be an easy target. He hoped like hell he saw Aronson before Aronson saw him.

He slowed. The signal showed he was close, too close to risk making any noise.

He stopped and tried to quiet his breathing so he could listen, but his ears were still ringing from the blast earlier.

He had just decided to move away from the tree when he heard a gunshot, ahead and to his right.

He started running.

CHAPTER EIGHTY-SIX

Aronson stood behind Jessie as she knelt on the ground and reached under the log. She'd been trying to waste time, but Aronson was getting inpatient, and he'd warned her that the next time she stopped was going to be the last time.

The bag was pushed up underneath, wedged in tight, so she grabbed the flap on the side and pulled. The flap opened. There was a gun inside.

She put her hand on it just as Aronson knocked her to one side and bent over to pull on the piece of strap just visible under the edge of the log.

She rolled and got to one knee. Aronson turned to look at her, saw the muzzle of the gun coming up, but before he could knock it away, she fired.

The bullet hit him in the side. She fired three times more, but the gun only clicked. It was empty.

Aronson was still bent over, but was already reaching for the gun in the holster at his back. She took a step back, kicked him under the chin with every ounce of strength she had, and ran.

Chastain saw Aronson fall and saw Jessie take off. Aronson rolled and slowly got to his knees his gun coming up, aimed at Jessie. Chastain yelled, "Jessie! Get down!!"

Jessie dived face down in the snow and Aronson turned the gun toward Chastain.

"Drop it, Aronson," Chastain shouted, but Aronson continued to turn and leveled the muzzle at Chastain.

Chastain fired twice and Aronson fell backwards. He heard a shout from behind him, and yelled, "Carlisle! We're here!"

He kicked Aronson's gun away and bent to one knee to check for a pulse. It was there. Weak and slow, but the man was alive. Fitz would be pleased.

He picked up Aronson's gun and trotted back to where Jessie was just sitting up and knelt beside her. She was beat to hell, both eyes swollen, a gash on one cheek and her nose looked like it was broken. She was almost blue with cold. "Here," he said, as he shrugged out of his coat, "put this on. You shot anywhere? Stabbed?"

She shook her head and he knelt on the ground behind her, eased her back against him, put his arms around her and stayed with her while the EMTs stabilized Aronson and took him away at a run.

A second ambulance crew arrived and after giving her a cursory exam, strapped Jess to a stretcher and carried her out to the road where an ambulance waited.

Chastain stayed by her side until they were ready to load her into the ambulance. He kissed her on the forehead and told her he had to stay, take care of business, but she would see him later.

They closed the doors and she wondered if that would be her last sight of Earl Price: his back to her, walking away.

CHAPTER EIGHTY-SEVEN

Jessie was only in the hospital for two days, just long enough for them to repair her broken nose and make sure the rest of her injuries were limited to cracked ribs, cuts and bruises.

Aronson was gone, taken away in a helicopter to God knew where. Dan Carlisle promised her that he had been taken to a secure facility and would spend the rest of his days in a federal penitentiary, or more likely, die by lethal injection.

The relief she'd expected to feel didn't come. The fear of him still lingered, hard to dispel, she'd been living with it for so long.

In the hospital, she'd seen Earl twice: once when she was groggy with pre-op medication and again when she got back to her room after the surgery and could barely keep her eyes open. She didn't remember that he'd said anything, he'd just kind of hovered over her and then he was gone.

She'd been home for a week and he hadn't come by, hadn't called, hadn't tried to contact her. She didn't even know if he was still at the Price place or if he'd already left.

Didn't matter. Wherever he was, he wasn't with her.

She'd visited Lyle in the hospital, his head swathed in enormous bandages, only one eye visible. His recovery was going to be lengthy. He'd require another surgery, possibly two, to repair the broken bones in his face, but the doctors said he'd eventually be fine.

She went back to work two weeks after Aronson kidnapped her. She started classes a week late, but not so far behind the rest of the class that she couldn't catch up.

Life began to settle back into a routine, the routine she'd had before Aronson. Before Earl. She worked. She went to school.

She moved on.

CHAPTER EIGHTY-EIGHT

The e-mail in Jessie's in-box was signed Stan Chastain, but the subject line said "Earl Price."

Was that his real name? Stan?

It must be, Jessie thought.

The message was brief: He said he'd been out of the country. Said he had a few days, he needed to talk to her, and he'd be down on Friday.

Just like she should drop everything because he had a few minutes to spare.

She'd had a month to stop beating herself up about him, and she wasn't going to start over. She'd been doing just fine without him. She'd decided she was better off without him around, pulling her focus away from school, taking up her time.

So why did she feel like she just got kicked in the head?

Damn Earl Price, or Stan Chastain, or whatever the hell his name was anyway.

She'd answered his message with two words: "Don't bother."

Nothing had changed. There was still no room in her life for anyone, especially someone like him. Someone who could sleep with her one day and leave the next.

CHAPTER EIGHTY-NINE

Based on Jessie's response to his email, Stan didn't think she was going to be happy to see him.

He couldn't exactly blame her. The night Aronson was captured, Fitz had ordered him back to D.C. for an immediate debriefing, and he'd gone. He'd stayed with Jessie until she came out of surgery to repair her broken nose, and while she was still groggy from the anesthetic, he'd gone back to the Price place, packed his gear and headed for D.C.

After the debriefing, he'd been due some time off to decompress, but when Fitz had mentioned a fairly simple situation in Rome that needed immediate handling, Stan had jumped on it.

He'd admitted to himself, when he was already on the plane and committed, that taking the assignment had been nothing but a delaying tactic, something that would occupy his mind so he didn't have to think.

The Aronson assignment had changed him, or maybe he'd begun to change before that and hadn't realized it. It wasn't Jessie, at least not entirely. When he'd blocked Aronson with his truck to keep him from catching the three boys, it had had nothing to do with her, and no personal feeling for Jessie herself had made him risk the surveillance by getting her away from Aronson.

What he had to accept was that he'd lost the emotional disconnect he needed to do his job, and he knew there was no going back.

In all the years since Jill and Cassie were killed, he'd never considered, or wanted, a life other than the one he'd made for himself, with no ties to anyone who could make him feel...anything.

He hadn't given up his career with the Department for Jill and Cassie, but that was when he'd believed he had all the time in the world to make it up to them at some nebulous date in the future. That had been the biggest mistake of his life, and he wasn't going to repeat it.

He needed to talk to Jessie. He needed to apologize for deserting her, for leaving without at least saying goodbye, for not being open with her and with himself about his life and how he wanted to live it. He had to talk to her face to face, whether she wanted to or not, if he was going to have any chance of making her understand.

She'd been characteristically blunt in her response to his e-mail: she'd made no excuses, just "don't bother."

So why had he spent ten hours flying from Rome to D.C., two hours flying from D.C. to Indianapolis, and another hour and a half driving to Brewer?

"Because you're an idiot," he said to himself as he turned onto Patterson Road.

He still had the keys to the Price place and stopped on his way to Melba's to start the generator and turn on the furnace. He planned on spending the night there. No matter what happened with Jess, he wasn't getting on another plane until he got some sleep.

He parked in front of Melba's, but didn't go in. Jessie was inside, moving around. At a little after two, she went to the back and he knew she was getting her coat, getting ready to leave.

He got out of the car and stood next to it.

She came out of the door, saw him and stopped dead. Her heart gave a little jolt.

"Why'd you even bother to email me if you were just gonna' show up anyway, Earl?"

He stepped up on the curb. "Because I hoped you'd want to hear what I have to say."

"Well, I don't," she said and started to turn away from him.

He put his hand on her arm, his tone less conciliatory, "You may not want to talk to me, but I have some things I need to say to you, and you'll listen, either right here on the sidewalk or someplace else. Your choice."

She pulled her arm free then turned to face him, "I don't have to listen to you, Earl. I'm not your job anymore, remember? I can do what I want and that doesn't include talking to you."

He shrugged. "Okay. Out here on the sidewalk then."

They stood there and glared at each other, but after a few seconds, he went from looking like he'd like to break her in half to looking tired and frustrated and not very happy. "Jess, just get in the car. Please. I don't want to fight with you."

She discovered that she really didn't want to fight with him either. He had a few things he wanted to say to her? Well she had some things to say to him too.

CHAPTER NINETY

He drove to the farm and while he hung up their coats, Jessie walked over to the window in the living room and looked out at the trees beyond the pasture. Someplace out in those woods was where she'd shot Aronson. It didn't seem real, any of it.

He came up behind her and put his hands on her shoulders, but kept his distance.

"I hurt you, Jess, and I'm sorry for that. I never wanted that to happen."

She shook her head but didn't say anything.

He could take a step closer, he thought. He could put his arms around her and pull her back against him. He wanted to touch her, have her, without words, without explanation.

But that's not how this worked. Taking her upstairs and throwing her down on the bed wasn't going to fix this.

Earl's hands were warm through her shirt and she wanted to just lean back into him, let him hold her, feel his solid warmth. Instead, she said, "You gave me a chance to say no the last time we were here, but I didn't take it. I should have, but I didn't. It was a mistake. You said so yourself."

He started to say something, but she turned her head and looked at him, cut him off. "No, Earl. I need to say this. Just let me say it.

"I knew once the operation was over you'd leave and move on to the next one. I can't fault you for doing what I already knew you were going to do.

"In your e-mail, you said you have a few days," she turned and faced him. "And then what? Then you leave and go on to the next job and I stay here, wondering if after the next job you might have another few days? Or maybe you spend a few days with me and then go on and live your life somewhere else 'til you find someone else to spend your few days with?"

She shook her head, her eyes never leaving his, "I didn't want you to be important to me. I still don't. I don't want you to be with me only when you don't have something more important to do."

He was shaking his head, "No. That's not what I want."

"Then what do you want, Earl?"

He took a step away from her and ran his hands through his hair. He didn't say anything for a few seconds, then, "I haven't needed or wanted to share anything – my thoughts, my feelings, my past - with anyone for a long time. Goes with the territory. But I need you to understand why I came back, why I needed to see you, to talk to you."

He paused again, studying her face. "Fourteen years ago, my wife Jill, my daughter, Cassie and I were going on vacation. At the last minute, something important at the DOD came up and I let myself get talked into letting Jill and Cassie drive to the coast alone. I was going to go down in a few days, once the big crisis was over.

"They were two hours from home when they were hit by a semi."

He gave a tiny smile that didn't reach his eyes, "I was so damned important. Everything was an emergency. The Department couldn't do without me."

He shook his head, "But you know what? The crisis that couldn't be resolved without me got resolved somehow. I never really knew what happened, didn't care. I was busy sitting in intensive care watching my daughter die."

He saw the sheen of tears in her eyes and said, "Don't feel sorry for me, Jess. I made choices and I've learned to live with them. There's nothing to say that my being in the van would have even changed anything.

"What hurt the most, and what damn near killed me, was that I wasn't there. I was never there. I missed Cassie's first steps and her first words and her first birthday.

"I loved my wife. I loved my daughter. But not enough to put them first.

"After they died, I had to find something that would help me get past it, something that would keep me from thinking or feeling. So I went into deep cover work, the more dangerous the assignment, the better. I *needed* that to cope after they died, and after a while I told myself that that's what I *wanted*. I lived in a shell no one could break into, and that's the way I wanted it.

"After I left here a month ago, I did a lot of thinking, and I realized that even before I came down here for this assignment, something had changed. I had started doing things, making decisions in the field based on emotion instead of logic. And then I came down here, and logic got completely shot to hell. I don't know why it happened, but I know I'm different now than I was a year ago, six months ago, even. There's no going back, and that's okay. Better than okay, and the Department will have to figure out how to get along in the field without me."

He reached for Jessie's hand and pulled her close. "I never thought I'd find what I lost when Jill and Cassie died. I was wrong. I've got a shot at a second chance, Jess, if you'll let me take it." He put his arms around her. "I want to come home every night and sleep with you next to me. I want to make a family with you, to be there when our kids are born, and for every step, every word, every birthday and every anniversary." He put a cheek against her hair. "Whatever it takes, Jess, whatever I have to do to make that happen."

When she didn't respond, he said, "Jess?"

"You're making this hard." Jessie stepped away from him and turned back to the window.

"My momma grew up poor, just like me, but she told me about when she was young, about the dreams she had. She said she didn't think she'd end up like the other girls she knew in high school. Every one of them wanted something more than what they had. Most of them ended up like her: married, with more kids than they could feed, no money and no way to get any. All they'd done, those girls, was to rely on somebody else to get what they wanted.

"Momma had a plan, but it meant someone else had to want the same thing she did, as bad as she did. She said what she learned was that you can't depend on anybody but yourself to make your dreams come true."

She turned to him and crammed her hands into the pockets of her jeans. "I did a lot of thinking too, while you were gone. I decided I was better off without you. I had a plan before you came, just like Momma had. I know where Momma went wrong and that's not going to happen to me. My plan doesn't include anybody else. Nothing that happened has changed that. I have to get where I want to be on my own. *I* have to make it happen. Me. Just me.

"I don't know you. I think I know Earl, as much as you let me know him, but you're not Earl. You're Stan. And I don't know who that is."

"Then give me a chance to show you, Jess." He took her hands. "He's really not so different from Earl. He thinks you are the bravest, smartest, most amazing woman he's ever known. He has no doubt you'll follow your plan until it takes you where you want to go, all the way to the end, and he knows you don't need him or anyone else to do it."

He rested his wrist on her shoulder, played with the curls at the nape of her neck. "Your plan does have an end, doesn't it?"

She let him pull her closer, close enough to place her palms on his chest and feel his heart thundering. "There's something I'd like to know about this Stan guy,"

"Okay." He pushed a stray curl off her forehead.

"Would he be caught dead wearing a belt buckle that says RIDE IT HARD?"

THE END

A note from the author:

I fulfilled a lifelong dream when this book was published, and there's a part of me that still can't believe I did it.

I can't thank you enough for reading *Suffer the Innocent,* and I hope you will look for the next book in the Innocent series, *Blood of an Innocent,* which should be out in early 2018.

If you enjoyed *Suffer the Innocent,* please take a moment to put a review on its Amazon book page at Amazon.com.

Made in the USA
Monee, IL
28 September 2020